OMNIA

A Silver Ships Novel

S. H. JUCHA

This book is a work of fiction. Names, characters, places, and incidents either are products of the author's imagination or are used fictitiously. Any resemblance to actual events or locales or persons, living or dead, is entirely coincidental.

Published by Hannon Books, Inc.
www.scottjucha.com

ISBN: 978-0-9975904-6-3 (e-book)
ISBN: 978-0-9975904-7-0 (softcover)

First Edition: June 2017

Cover Design: Damon Za
3D image of Nanna-Sin Ziggurat by PirateMaster11

Acknowledgments

Omnia is the ninth book in *The Silver Ships* series. I wish to extend a special thanks to my independent editor, Joni Wilson, whose efforts enabled the finished product. To my proofreaders, Abiola Streete, Dr. Jan Hamilton, David Melvin, Ron Critchfield, Pat Bailey, and Mykola Dolgalov, I offer my sincere thanks for their support.

My thanks to the many readers, who commented on subjects of interest to them throughout the series and challenged me with their ideas. Many will find snippets in my novels reflecting their valuable input!

Despite the assistance I've received from others, all errors are mine.

Glossary

A glossary is located at the end of the book.

CONTENTS

-1-
Daelon

"This is Captain Cordelia of the *Freedom*, calling the orbital platform above the Daelon moon," the SADE, a self-aware digital entity, sent via the ship's comm. Her voice was relayed through the speakers of the city-ship's massive bridge for her fellow Harakens, who were arrayed around the bridge and anxiously awaited the reply to Cordelia's hail.

"This is the Daelon orbital station, Captain Cordelia," a voice was heard over the *Freedom*'s speakers. "Your ship isn't in the Confederation's database. Please state your ship's origin and the nature of your emergency."

"We've no emergency, Ser," Cordelia replied.

"Then state your intentions, Captain."

"We're volunteering no information, Ser," Cordelia replied. "We're informing you that within a day and a half we'll be in a stationary position relative to your moon. We've business to conduct with those individuals below and would appreciate no interference from you."

"Captain Cordelia," the voice replied, "we're duty bound to inform you that this is Confederation space, and the people on Daelon are Méridien citizens. You've no authority here, and we require you depart this system immediately."

"You've a most interesting manner of treating your citizens, Ser … incarcerating them on a dead moon in a dead system. But you've touched on the reason we're here. We wish to ask your Independents whether they want to remain Méridien citizens."

Cordelia waited patiently for a response, as the silence dragged on. The SADE could imagine the intense discussion taking place on the platform's bridge. It was unnecessary for Cordelia to check whether the connection was still active. An app in her crystal kernel, which monitored the ship's comms system, would inform her immediately if the link was dropped.

When no reply seemed forthcoming from the platform, Cordelia glanced to her left at Alex Racine, wondering what the architect of this jaunt into Confederation space was thinking. Alex leaned against an unattended bridge panel, arms folded, and his eyes staring into space, while he waited for the conversation to continue.

"Captain Cordelia, this is Maynard Scullers. I'm the manager of this orbital platform, and I respectfully request you include my staff and me in your discussions with those below. You see, we're all Independents here."

Maynard heard the delightful tinkling of silver bells, musical and soothing, over the platform bridge speakers. He glanced left and right at his operation's personnel, who wore myriad expressions ranging from smiles to confusion.

"Captain, am I speaking to a SADE?" Maynard asked cautiously.

"Yes, Ser Scullers."

"A SADE who's the captain of a Libran city-ship … is Alex Racine aboard?" Maynard asked, hoping with all his might that liberation was sailing toward him.

Cordelia glanced at Alex, who shrugged his shoulders, which she took to mean that it was her decision as to how she should choose to answer.

Tatia Tachenko, Haraken's ex-admiral, smiled and gently shook her head. Everyone who worked in Alex's immediate sphere was forced, at one time or another, to apply their own interpretations to his favorite enigmatic gesture.

"He might be," Cordelia replied, drawing out her words, as she often heard Alex do. From the *Freedom*'s bridge speakers burst the sound of laughter, cheers, and clapping, originating from what was obviously a room full of people aboard the orbital platform.

Maynard regained some control, hushing his people, and leaned into the comm pickup to ensure he was heard. "Well, Captain Cordelia, I can't speak for anyone else aboard this platform or below, but you can sign me up."

"Sign you up to what, Ser?" Cordelia asked.

"I don't care, Captain. If Alex Racine is involved, I want to be aboard!"

The twins, Étienne and Alain de Long, exchanged glances.

<Well, we've definitive confirmation,> Alain sent to his crèche-mate via implant, the tiny comms units in Haraken cerebrums. <The madman's mental condition is indeed infectious.>

<Because we've been in close proximity to Ser for two decades, that would imply we must have caught the malady,> Étienne sent in reply.

<Happily so,> Alain replied, adding a wink for his twin.

"How do you transport the Independents below, Ser Scullers?" Cordelia asked.

"We've only two shuttles, Captain, but they're both travelers."

"And how many Independents are incarcerated on Daelon?"

Laughter and whistles again broke through the *Freedom*'s speakers. Those on the bridge could hear Maynard quieting his people. "You'll have to forgive us, Captain. We're the only ones to have ever used that word ... incarceration. Counting the moon base and the platform, we have 18,289 people."

Cordelia glanced at Alex, who was frowning. Julien, her partner, sent a private query to Cordelia, which she relayed. "We expected many more, Ser Scullers."

"Understandable, Captain. For a few years after Libre's evacuation, which was with Ser Racine's assistance, the annual number arriving here was fairly constant. But when Gino Diamanté replaced Mahima Ganesh as Council Leader, the count of individuals transported here slowed dramatically. In the first half of this year, we received one-eighth of the people who were shipped here in the same time period during Daelon's first year.

"You seem well-informed of the historical numbers, Ser Scullers," Alex said, activating the bridge's vid side of the comm signal and stepping into view. "How long have you been on Daelon?"

Maynard glanced around the platform's control room. His people stared at their monitors, taking in the view of Alex Racine. There was no mistaking the wide build of the famous, or infamous, depending on your viewpoint, New Terran, who sported a heavy-worlder body, which was in considerable contrast to the slender physiques of the Méridiens, who inhabited the Confederation. Maynard's people nodded their heads enthusiastically to him, responding to his unspoken query, their eyes gleaming in anticipation.

"Ser Racine," Maynard replied, tears forming in his eyes, and his throat threatening to close, "I had the dubious honor of disembarking from a Confederation ship twenty years ago along with others and becoming the first inhabitants of this fine establishment. Before that, I was the director of a premier orbital station, responsible for starship construction, until I made the mistake of openly criticizing Ganesh."

"Good to hear, Ser," Alex replied.

A scowl formed on Maynard's face. For a moment, he thought he had misinterpreted why Alex Racine had come to Daelon.

"I meant the part of being a director responsible for starship construction," Alex added. "I can't offer much in the way of compensation, at first, but if you're interested, I have a job for you."

The tears that had swum in Maynard's eyes spilled down his face, and he fought to control his emotions, managing to croak out, "Does room and board come with the job, Ser?"

"It does, but, I warn you, Ser, it'll be a demanding job," Alex replied.

"Sign me up, Ser," Maynard replied, and those on the *Freedom*'s bridge watched Maynard drop below his vid's view, but they could hear his sobs and hiccups.

"We'll see you soon, Ser Scullers," Alex said. "Send no comms below of our expected arrival, if you please. It'll be our job to communicate why we're here."

A young woman, tears streaking her face, stepped into the vid's pickup. "We understand, Ser Racine," she said, glancing down, presumably at Maynard. "And might I add from all of us here on the platform … welcome to Daelon, Ser."

"Thank you," Alex replied and cut the comm.

Alex looked to the side, where his love and partner, Renée de Guirnon, leaned against another deactivated bridge station.

Tears floated in Renée's eyes, but anger twisted the planes of her exquisite face. "When will the Confederation stop imprisoning innocent citizens?" she asked hotly. Her fists were balled in frustration at her home world's attitude toward anyone who violated the Confederation's strict rules of behavior. She felt Alex's heavily muscled arms sweep her into his embrace, but in an uncharacteristic display for her, she shoved back and sent Alex an emphatic, <No.>

If it wasn't for Renée's comm, Alex might not have released her. Her outburst took him by surprise, and he watched her exit the bridge in haste.

<I believe Ser has reached her tolerance limit for Méridien society,> Alain sent to his twin.

<A patient woman,> Étienne sent in reply. <When the Confederation failed to conduct an extensive search for our passenger ship to rescue us, ninety years ago, I was done with them.>

Comms flew between those on the bridge, expressing concern for Renée, but, as expected, no one vocalized their thoughts. In the midst of so many extraordinary experiences, throughout the past two decades, Renée had been the center of calm and reason, and Alex's emotional anchor. Now, the Harakens regarded Alex with concern, if not worry, on their faces.

"It appears we might need to walk softly around my partner, for a while," Alex said to the group. "Back to your duties, people; we've some time yet before we reach Daelon." Alex exited the bridge with Julien, Tatia, and the twins in tow.

Renée stalked back to her suite, remonstrating herself for her behavior on the bridge. She managed to send a quick apology and a love missive to Alex. In reply, Renée received a full image of Alex. His face became gooey, smitten by her attentions, and then his entire body melted into a puddle. *Goof,* she thought, and a burble of laughter escaped her lips, as she gained the cabin's door.

For much of her life, Renée believed deeply in the values of Méridien's culture and societal norms, but during the past twenty years, since her awakening from stasis, her eyes had been opened to many of its flaws. The incarceration of good people, judged and labeled as Independents for violating the Confederation's arcane rules, had become too much.

Renée's anger at her society resolved to a single thought, which was directed at the Confederation's Council of Leaders. *If Alex has his way, there will be 18,289 fewer Independents buried on your moon. Then maybe you'll learn.*

* * *

Tatia decided to break the awkward silence, while Alex, Julien, the twins, and she walked the huge ship's wide corridor. "So, Daelon has eighteen-thousand Independents. It's a good start, but you look severely disappointed, Alex."

"A little," Alex replied absentmindedly, his mind absorbed with thoughts of Renée.

"How many were you expecting?" Tatia asked.

"Somewhere between 50K and 100K people."

"Big difference," Tatia acknowledged.

"Huge difference. Might have to go with plan B," Alex replied

"Good to hear you're still thinking ahead, Alex. What's plan B?"

"Recruit the Dischnya," Alex replied.

Tatia was stunned and kept her mouth from hanging open. She dearly hoped Alex was joking.

In contrast, Julien and Cordelia briefly shared thoughts on the concept, and the two SADEs simply reorganized their hierarchical algorithms, postulated potential obstacles, and determined the probabilities of future outcomes.

<I'm getting the madman a slug-proof helmet,> Alain sent to his crèche-mate, referencing the near-fatal attempt of a Dischnya queen and her commander on Celus-5 to assassinate Alex.

<I think we would do better to have Z build Alex a durable avatar that he can wear,> Étienne replied.

<At all times,> Alain added.

<Ser de Guirnon might have something to say about that,> Étienne sent and grinned at his twin. He added an image of Alex housed in a suit of metal-alloy standing in a refresher, with moisture pouring down the avatar, and Renée beside him, wearing a frustrated expression.

Tatia reined in her imagination. "Alex, you're not seriously considering letting those dog warriors you encountered on Celus-5 ... the same ones who tried to kill you … board our ships and act as crew!"

"It was only two of the Dischnya who tried to kill me," Alex replied, trying to minimize the impact of his remark.

"It only takes one dog warrior, if he's a good shot," Tatia riposted.

"Okay, Tatia," Alex said, assuming a command voice and intending to focus her. "Let's start with you learning to say Dischnya. No time like the present to practice."

"But how is it possible to have the warriors aboard our ships, if they can't be separated from their queen?" Tatia asked, her strategic planning skills dominating her thoughts.

"They can, but only for a short length of time," Alex replied. "That's probably the number-one challenge for plan B."

Tatia's steps slowed, and then she stopped in the corridor, as she considered the implications of Alex's plan B, while he walked on.

Julien passed her, and he politely tipped his virtual fedora, which he projected from his synth-skin.

<Charming, Julien,> Tatia sent, tongue-in-cheek. <You're being cute, but you should take note that we're both again following Alex headlong into uncharted territory.>

<But that's what keeps life interesting, Tatia,> Julien sent in reply, as he walked on.

* * *

Fifteen days ago, Alex ordered the city-ship *Freedom* launched from Haraken's orbit. It carried a small collection of humans and SADEs on a ship that easily accommodated a quarter million individuals. The ship hadn't been updated with Haraken technology in more than two decades, and a refit was initiated by Alex after taking possession of the ship but wasn't completed before launch. Much of the equipment to complete the ship's refit sat piled in several cavernous bays.

While still on Haraken, Julien and Cordelia affirmed to Alex that the refit supply orders were fulfilled and delivered. They acknowledged the work could continue aboard ship without issue. That was when Alex approached Cordelia with a job offer. "I need a captain," Alex had told her. "The salary won't be anything like your income as a Central Exchange director, I'm afraid."

"I've come to appreciate the value of commerce, Alex," Cordelia replied, "and the freedom a generous income gives me to pursue my desires. However, in this case, I'm sorely tempted to pay you for the privilege of becoming the first SADE to captain a starship. So, I offer a compromise."

"I'm listening," Alex replied.

"I believe you paid the enormous sum of one credit for this ship?"

"I did," Alex replied.

It didn't surprise Alex that Cordelia knew the details of the Assembly's transaction. When Tomas Monti, Haraken's president, said the sale amount would remain undisclosed, he was referring to isolating the information from the human population. The secrecy was meant to prevent disclosure to the Confederation Leaders that the Haraken Assembly was supporting Alex's intentions. Alex himself was keeping his future actions secret from the Assembly, and he'd warned the august body that they should keep any association with him at arm's length.

Naturally, the city-ship's transaction was shared among the SADEs, who perceived data as critical details to collect. If the data came with stipulations to compartmentalize it, then it would remain so until directives were issued contravening the original requirements. To a SADE, there was no such thing as a secret, just data containing communication restrictions.

"Then I propose that I receive the same payment for the position, kind Ser," Cordelia said, giving Alex a leader's acknowledgment of right hand to left side of chest and a bowed head. This was a traditional Méridien sign of respect with the hand placed over the heart. Despite the SADEs not possessing the beating organ, they'd copied the gesture to express the emotion.

After Alex hired his captain, he turned to completing his next order of business. Signaling Tatia, Alex asked her to meet him aboard the *Freedom*.

Tatia had resigned her commission with the Haraken fleet and told Alex that Alain and she would be joining his expedition, and Alex had replied, "You'll still be an admiral, Tatia."

"An admiral of four travelers," Tatia said, laughing. In contrast, Tatia intended to bring nearly twenty-five times the number of pilots as Alex possessed of fighters aboard.

When Tatia exited her traveler aboard the *Freedom*, Alex led her around the ship's ring to another bay, where Mickey Brandon, Alex's principal engineer, had set up shop.

The huge city-ship was shaped like a giant saucer, with its massive engines interrupting the circle. Landing bays dotted the mid-level of the entire circumference and were enormous spaces capable of holding ore-excavating and processing machines, giant cargo shuttles, and an incredible amount of raw manufacturing materials. The Librans, who were evacuating their planet in advance of the deadly Nua'll sphere, planned to live on their city-ships for decades, while they searched for a new home. The ship's layout meant that walking between bays was exercise in itself.

Tatia and Alex passed through another airlock into Mickey's bay. While the engineering lab would eventually occupy the entire bay, at this moment, the equipment, much of it still in crates, took up less than one-twentieth of the space.

Alex led Tatia to a small setup surrounded by the usual individuals and stepped back, while Mickey, Emile, and Edmas demonstrated their world-shattering invention.

Tatia's performance during the presentation was as bad as Alex's had been when he first watched the demonstration, anxious to interrupt with questions before its completion. When a substrate layer of nanites fell from the newly sprayed shell, Tatia, who was speechless, alternately stared at Alex and the piece of shell.

"Impressive, isn't it?" Alex commented. He played it low-key, but the engineering team looked as if they were ready to jump out of their skins. It was a rare opportunity to celebrate the secret with a new confidant.

"Somehow, uttering black space doesn't seem to cover this," Tatia finally said, which released the engineering team to cheer and clap. They gathered around her, slapping her back in sympathy with the momentous knowledge she now shared.

"What … I mean … wait. Let me think," Tatia said when the cheering died down. "Okay, so you people have invented this capability of creating a Swei Swee shell without the Swei Swee. What do you intend to do with it?"

Demonstrating a pantomime that the engineers and techs had hurriedly practiced, having been forewarned that Tatia was coming to meet with them, they shrugged their shoulders as one and lifted right hands toward Alex.

"Cute," Tatia said, smirking. "Wait … they gave it to you?" she asked, turning around to face Alex. "And don't shrug," she warned him, pointing a finger at his face.

"Yes, they did, unfortunately," Alex replied, admitting the nature of the immense responsibility he shouldered once more.

"Again," Tatia whispered, shaking her head.

"Again," Alex agreed.

"Well, on the plus side, this means we can make warships anywhere," said Tatia, shouting and pumping a fist in the air. It galvanized the engineering team, who broke into another round of cheering and applause.

"Quite true, *Admiral*," Alex said, underlining Tatia's proffered title. His words had the effect he sought. Tatia's eyes narrowed, while she considered future possibilities in light of the engineers' new capability. "Tell them what you need, Admiral. They're all ears and implants," Alex said, gesturing toward the team and walking out of the bay.

"But what are the operational demands?" Tatia shouted at Alex's retreating back.

"How would I know?" Alex said over his shoulder, as he made the airlock hatch.

Tatia glanced at Emile, whose face expressed sympathy for her, but Mickey was grinning. "And why are you so happy?" she demanded of Mickey.

"It's just like the old days, Tatia. The man brings a whole new meaning to the expression of sailing into the deep dark," Mickey replied, chuckling.

"Okay, people," said Tatia, shaking her head, as if the motion would help settle the admiral's stars she would wear again on her shoulders, "Let's see what inventive ideas you have that might help us take on an alien sphere, which, more than likely, will be carrying some sort of miraculous, world-destroying weaponry."

* * *

Before the *Freedom* broke Haraken's orbit, seven traveler flights landed aboard. The first flight caught Alex by surprise. He halted in the corridor to query the ship's controller and received a list of the passengers' bio IDs, which contained their names and occupations. The number of people who were disembarking was also unexpected, and Alex checked the controller to see who authorized them joining the expedition. While he hadn't necessarily stated to the few he expected to accompany him who was and wasn't authorized to approve people joining the expedition, it was Alex's expectation that he would be the final arbiter — apparently, that wasn't so.

In addition to ninety-eight pilots, Alex discovered engineers, techs, medical specialists, flight chiefs and crew, assorted support personnel, and even some entertainers. Alex's intention to limit the number of humans accompanying him to fewer than a hundred had suddenly become moot.

<Hello, my love,> Alex sent. <Your guests are arriving.>

<So Cordelia informed me,> Renée sent back.

<Could I ask why I wasn't consulted?>

<This wasn't a matter that required your input, my love. Your associates, Tatia, Julien, Cordelia, Mickey, Claude, and Pia, requested these people be given permission to join us.>

<Requested it of you?>

<Of course they did, Alex. Why should they ask permission of you when they knew you would say no?> Renée replied. Her thoughts carried an element of dismissal, as if Alex was silly for not recognizing this.

<But this does create confusion about who's in charge of this expedition,> Alex retorted.

<No one questions who's in charge of where we're going. That's you, my love. But your subordinates and I are taking a firmer hand about the conditions surrounding how we go there.> Renée waited for a reply, but Alex closed the comm. *Like it or not, Alex, we're going to do our best to protect you from yourself,* Renée thought, heading to the landing bay with some crew to orient the new people, only a few of whom had been aboard a city-ship before.

One of the few points that Alex and Renée did agree on was that they would take the *Rêveur* with them. If a traveler was too small to accommodate the movement of people during the expedition, then they'd rely on the passenger liner as their primary transport. The city-ship was too massive to move around like some sort of shuttle and would remain in orbit around any planet that became their temporary or final destination. Besides, Francis Lumley, the *Rêveur*'s captain, was determined not to be left behind. The captain had said goodbye to his Sol companions, having a tearful parting with his best friend, Olawale Wombo.

"Come visit me, my friend," Francis said to Olawale. "You won't be able to miss me. More than likely, I'll be parked next to Alex's monstrous city-ship."

-2-
Moon Landing

Alex invited Winston to his home the morning the *Freedom* was due to launch. Winston once served the Confederation as the Council of Leaders' SADE before he was freed. The two stood beside Alex's gazebo, gazing out to sea.

"I need a piece of information, Winston," Alex said.

"I'm at your service, Alex."

"What's the Confederation's new location for the Independents?"

Winston hesitated for a couple of ticks, deciding how to reply. "I promised Mahima Ganesh that I would never speak of this to anyone, especially you. The woman was never fond of you."

Alex laughed at Winston's understatement.

Meanwhile, Winston drew a series of numbers and declinations in the sandy soil with his boot, and Alex recorded the information in his implant before Winston erased the message.

"It's important to keep one's promises, Alex. So, I will continue to never speak a word of the Independent's location," Winston said, smiling at Alex.

"I'll see you again someday, Winston," said Alex, clapping the SADE on the shoulder and hurrying to his house.

Go, Alex; free more of the imprisoned, and may the stars protect you, Winston thought, enjoying the view and the smell of the ocean. With Alex's help, the SADE had gained his freedom from his metal-alloy box after nearly a century and a half of service to the Confederation Council.

* * *

Cordelia had launched the *Freedom* out of Haraken's orbit on Alex's order. She stood on the bridge, wearing a uniform of Haraken dark blue without military insignias. Instead, Cordelia's uniform was adorned with a captain's gold studs and the *Freedom*'s new emblem.

"A destination would be nice, Alex," Cordelia said, as the city-ship broke orbit, a smile tweaking the side of her face.

In reply, Alex sent the information to Cordelia and Julien that Winston provided, leaving it in its original state.

"We're back to drawing in the dirt, Alex?" Julien asked, as Cordelia and he cross-referenced the information to determine the destination.

"The individual, who provided this data, said he promised to never speak of it," Alex replied. "I'm honoring his words."

"These coordinates point to a gas giant in a dead system of the Confederation, Alex," Cordelia said.

"Imagine that," Alex replied, "but, more than likely, we'll be interested in a moon orbiting the planet." He left the bridge, headed for a conference with Mickey's engineering team, who were building a test bed to layup a traveler, one-tenth size, utilizing Emile's faux Swei Swee spit, which Mickey had taken to calling the spraying process.

Cordelia stared at Julien, wondering why the secrecy. When Julien shrugged his shoulders, she said, "And you think that gesture somehow adds something useful to our conversation?"

"Cordelia," Julien said gently. "Alex made you captain because he has confidence in you, but that doesn't mean he'll share everything with you. Recall our early days with him when he led and we followed."

* * *

Cordelia decelerated the *Freedom* until the city-ship took up station 50 kilometers from Daelon's orbital platform. She'd received several inquiries from Maynard Scullers for more information, but she kept her replies to the manager short and uninformative.

Alex boarded a traveler with Renée, Julien, Tatia, Mickey, the twins, and several of the new Confederation SADEs.

<Why the Confederation SADEs?> Tatia sent to Alex. She was seated across from him when she noticed them boarding.

<For color,> Alex sent in reply.

<Please,> Tatia sent, a derisive tone to her thought, although the patterned and colorful skins of the Confederation SADEs did make his point.

<Well, you'll find out sooner or later, Tatia. This began on the first trip to Celus-5. The SIF directors followed me around and broadcast my every movement, outside my cabin, to the entire group of Confederation SADEs. They said they were observing me and insisted they should be present during any of my discussions.>

<Is that why some of them are always present on the *Freedom*'s bridge, standing in the corners?> Tatia asked.

<Yes,> Alex admitted.

<Okay … and why are they observing you?>

<They're learning to emulate a human.>

<And they chose you … oh, please, no,> Tatia sent and burst out laughing. Everyone aboard the traveler heard her say out loud, "May the stars protect us." For Tatia's part, she was pleased to see a flush of embarrassment creep up Alex's neck.

Svetlana, who had been appointed Alex's primary traveler pilot, launched the ship from the *Freedom*'s bay. It was a short flight to the moon below. Telemetry indicated the moon's rock had been excavated to create a flattened base, which led toward an immense overhang. A pair of bay doors was embedded in the rock's face, and Svetlana chose to hover the traveler in front of them.

"Pilot, has the platform received a new traveler?" asked the voice on Svetlana's comm. "Hope that doesn't mean we're going to receive a mass of new tourists for our wonderful vacation spot." The bay control manager tried to sound jovial, but it came out a bit strained.

Alex, who was linked with Svetlana, sent, <This is Alex Racine. I wonder if we might land and chat with you?>

In the control room, Glenn, the manager, glanced around him, double-checking that others had heard what he thought he heard. He went so far as to replay his implant recording. "Get OP up here now," he hissed to his comms operator.

Because it was early in the morning, Daelon time, Ophelia and Perrin, partners and co-Leaders of the Independents, were fast asleep and entwined in each other's arms when their comm buzzed.

Perrin activated the comm above the bed and said in a rough voice, "Better be good."

"Sorry, OP," the operator said. He pronounced the letters individually, which is how the Independents referred to their co-Leaders. "Man at the door wants to land."

"What man?"

"Calls himself Alex Racine," the operator replied. The co-Leaders were linked through the bay control room's speakers, and the personnel were forced to contain themselves, while they waited with bated breath for the reply.

"This early in the morning, Jensen, your humor is unappreciated."

"So, you want me to tell him to go away, or do you want to do it?"

"Let's see how far you're willing to carry on with this farce, Jensen," Perrin growled, sitting up in bed. By now, he had Ophelia's interest, and she sat up too. "Connect me to this individual."

"This is co-Leader Keller," Perrin said, when Jensen told him he was online. "To whom am I speaking?"

<I would have thought your people had already informed you, Ser Keller. The name's Alex Racine.>

"Ser, whoever you are, know that life on this dead rock gets dull, abysmally dull, and people here do whatever they can to amuse one another. I'm about to put Jensen and you on report. Now, properly identify yourself."

<Julien, I don't have time for this. Get me a connection to him,> Alex sent privately.

In turn, Julien linked into the comms operator system, followed the connection to the co-Leader's comms unit, and identified the man's bio ID, which he passed to Alex.

During those ticks of time, Alex pulled up a collection of images from the past twenty years. He linked with Julien, who linked him to Perrin. Alex swept aside the co-Leader's implant security apps and streamed the vid he'd prepared.

Ophelia watched her partner freeze and pale. As quickly as Perrin appeared to be overtaken, he relaxed.

"Quick, get dressed," Perrin ordered Ophelia, leaping out of bed. "It's the world shaker himself, Alex Racine, at the bay doors. Jensen, tell Glenn to let the man land."

In the control room, personnel twittered and chuckled. They had played jokes on one another for years in an effort to relieve the boredom and keep peoples' spirits up. This time, the greatest prank they could have imagined was, in reality, not a joke at all.

When the bay doors slid open, Svetlana glided the traveler into the interim lock, edging the ship's bow near the second set of doors, while the first set closed behind them. She eyed the traveler's sensor in her helmet, which indicated air pressure. To her, the wait seemed interminable.

<Air must be precious here, Ser,> Svetlana sent to Alex. <They probably have to be careful to recirculate it, and their pumps are not up to the demand.>

<They probably don't experience many flights, Commander,> Alex sent in reply, <and people who can't go anywhere won't tend to do anything in a hurry.>

When the second set of doors opened, Svetlana guided the ship into the bay, set it down, double-checked the pressure, and signaled Alex that he had a welcoming committee.

Alex led his small entourage off the traveler and onto the bay's deck. Arrayed in front of him were about twenty people, and Alex was struck by their youthfulness, as opposed to his landing on Libre decades ago. There were no elders here on Daelon. The oldest looked to be about forty to forty-five, which meant about sixty to seventy years for Méridiens.

<I expected the man to be older,> Ophelia sent to Perrin, as she regarded Alex.

<And I thought he would be smaller,> Perrin replied, as they quickly crossed the deck to greet Alex. The hand Perrin extended to Alex was a gesture every Méridien knew was typical New Terran, and Perrin enthusiastically pumped Alex's hand with both of his.

It was the release of tension the assembled Independents were waiting for, and the group of them rushed forward to touch, pat, and hug every Haraken.

Alex was pleased to see the Independents unhesitatingly touch and embrace the SADEs. He'd deliberately chosen some of those with the most audacious avatar colorings. He watched the SADEs taking part in the affectionate greetings and enjoyed seeing the smiles spread across their faces.

<You were testing the Independents,> Tatia sent to Alex.

<Perhaps,> Alex sent back.

<When did you become the devious one?> Tatia asked, referring to the nickname that Alex and Julien had bestowed on her for her tactician's cunning.

<The student becomes the teacher,> Alex replied, giving her a grin.

"Ser, it's early morning by our time," Ophelia said. "I imagine you wish to speak to the entire population. If you'll give us a quarter hour, we can assemble everyone here in the bay. Not everyone will be near a comms station, and our implants don't carry far through the moon's rock." She looked hopefully at Alex.

"That would be fine, Ser Sooth," Alex replied.

Ophelia clapped her hands in delight, and Perrin and she raced for the control room to call the population to an emergency meeting. Their message was terse and simple. "Assemble in the bay immediately. Tell everyone you see. If you're late to this one, you might be left behind."

Within a short time, people came streaming through the general airlock, ten or twelve at a time, to hurry to join the crowd. Most of them stopped in their tracks when they got a look at the New Terrans and SADEs. Word had reached Daelon of the SADEs emancipation by virtue of the Independents, who had arrived during the past couple of years, but none of them had witnessed their choice of avatars.

"Look, darling, painted men," a mother said to her daughter, urging the child to open her eyes. During their few years of confinement, Vivian had begun closing her eyes, more and more often, to keep the crushing mental pressure of Daelon's tunnels at bay.

Vivian snuck a peek through one eye and spied the colorful pattern of a SADE. Both eyes opened wide and her little heart thumped. Vivian pulled her hand free of her mother's and hurried to the SADE whose face was patterned in plaid. The child held up her hands to the SADE, who responded to the little human's desire, lifting her up and holding her aloft.

"Pretty," the child said, touching the SADE's face.

Julien sent an image to the SADE to indicate how to hold the child, and the SADE transferred the girl onto his lower arm. Immediately, the child threw an arm around the SADE's neck and called out, "See, Mommy, it's a plaid man."

The SADEs accompanying Alex were exploiting the entire bandwidth of the traveler's controller to send their experiences back to those SADEs aboard the *Freedom*. Only others of their kind could translate the flow of code that passed for visual, aural, olfactory, and tactile pressure sensory information. Embedded in the data stream were their kernels' cascading algorithms, which shifted hierarchy, as each SADE reacted to his or her welcome. For those SADEs aboard the *Freedom*, it was as if they were standing in the bay, experiencing the greetings themselves.

<Enjoy,> Alex sent to the Confederate SADEs surrounding him, and, as one, they turned and smiled ... great big, generous smiles.

<I believe my brothers and sisters are sensing what it's like to be truly appreciated,> Julien sent to Alex.

<And it's been too long in coming for them,> Alex sent in reply.

Humans aboard the *Freedom* were not to be excluded from enjoying the moment. Cordelia separated the SADEs' data streams, sending vids to every monitor aboard the *Freedom* and the *Rêveur*.

Captain Lumley sat in his command chair surrounded by his ship's bare-bones crew, sipping hot thé and enjoying the images playing across the *Rêveur*'s bridge monitors.

"Everyone is present, Ser," Perrin said, addressing Alex. The entire population of Daelon was assembled well before the quarter hour ended.

Alex received an image from the Confederation SADEs. It suggested they could hold him aloft, either on their shoulders or standing on a small platform, so that he would be seen by the entire assembly.

<Absolutely not,> Alex sent back. <Your offer is appreciated, but you aren't tools. Witness and participate in this event for your own edification and enjoyment.>

Alex climbed several steps of the traveler's hatch. He was conflicted by what he saw — grateful that the number of incarcerated was small and disappointed in the relatively few crew members he might gain for his expedition. But then Alex had a habit of underestimating what the opportunity for freedom, adventure, and, sometimes, just a change in lifestyles meant to people.

"Can you hear me?" Alex asked, his heavy-worlder voice booming across the bay, which was cut from the moon's rock and sealed with Méridien technology. The crowd smiled and chuckled. Someone from the back of the group yelled out, "We're not deaf, you know," which broke out hearty laughter.

Alex smiled and raised a hand to acknowledge the tease. "I have good news and not-so-good news for you." His opening words silenced the crowd, and the tension in the bay elevated. "I'm no longer a Haraken citizen and have renounced all claims on Haraken possessions."

"But, Ser Racine, when I was in the control room, I heard from Maynard Scullers that you arrived aboard a Libran city-ship," Ophelia called out loudly.

"Yes, that's true," Alex said, creating a buzz among the people. He could imagine their single thought. The largest Méridien passenger liner might pack in 400-plus passengers, but a city-ship could carry away every person incarcerated on Daelon. "This is slightly embarrassing to say, but the ship is mine … I own it."

The crowd tittered at Alex's comment, but nerves were on edge, waiting for him to drop the bad news.

"If you won't reside on Haraken, Ser Racine, where will you live?" Perrin called out.

"Aboard the *Freedom*, the city-ship," Alex replied.

"And where are you going?" a voice in the crowd yelled.

"First stop is Celus-5, a planet we've recently visited. It has two intelligent alien species and possibly a third. I've got several commitments to fulfill on that planet before I move on."

"Move on to where and for what purpose?" Ophelia asked.

"Three dark travelers were found buried in the sands along the shore," Alex replied. "One of the Celus-5 resident species is Swei Swee."

A hush fell over the crowd. Dark travelers and Swei Swee meant the dreaded Nua'll once visited the planet.

"You're here for a reason, Ser Racine," Perrin announced firmly. "What are you offering us?"

"I'm willing to free everyone from this prison, but the problem is that the future, yours and mine, is unsettled. I can't transport you to Haraken, and our people have yet to be invited to settle Celus-5, which is quite habitable for humans. It could be that you spend years aboard the *Freedom* before I find you a planet of your own."

Alex stood quietly, waiting for the response.

<Patience, Dassata, the Independents are seeking consensus,> Julien sent, using Alex's Dischnya title. The alien queen, Nyslara, discovering Alex held no title, had named him Dassata, the Dischnya word for peacemaker.

The Méridien process of communicating via implant to reach a community vote could take place in a relatively brief space of time. Once it concluded, an individual called out, "Ser Racine, when do you give us the bad news?" The man's question elicited applause and laughter.

Ophelia smiled at Alex. "Ser, I believe you know us well enough to know that consensus has been reached. Everyone on this forsaken rock is aching to leave with you, whenever you're ready to depart and wherever you're going."

<Consensus,> Renée sent to Alex. <There are some aspects of Méridien society that I do miss, but none of it enough to ever go back.>

Ophelia watched Renée de Guirnon turn toward her partner and wink. It caused Ser Racine to beam back at her. *A private signal between lovers,* she thought.

"What are your orders, Ser Racine?" Perrin asked.

"Two orders of business, Sers," Alex announced. "First, let me introduce Mickey Brandon, my senior engineer, and Tatia Tachenko, my admiral. They need to go through this place with your senior people. Mickey."

Mickey announced in a loud voice, "Admiral Tachenko and I need your help. We're going to load aboard the *Freedom*, our city-ship above, any travelers, equipment, supplies, and raw materials that could be of value."

"Your pardon, Sers," a woman said, "but much of our equipment is more than twenty years old, and it was never the best that Méridien could produce."

"You'd be surprised what we're looking for, Sers," Tatia replied. "Much of it can be repurposed."

"Please, senior engineers and department heads over here," Mickey called out, and Tatia and he headed for a corner of the bay. Mickey was thinking that it was a good thing he swapped one of the *Rêveur*'s passenger travelers for a transport model with its rear-loading ramp.

"Sers Keller and Sooth," Alex said.

"Please, Ser Racine, we're OP," Ophelia said, pronouncing the two letters, each after the other. "Ophelia and Perrin," she added pointing to each of them.

"Okay, OP," Alex continued, "we'll be landing three more travelers. Start organizing your people, I want a traveler to land and lift full of Independents in the amount of time it takes to board."

"We have people who can assist with your reclamation efforts, Ser," Perrin offered.

"I'm landing nearly a hundred and fifty SADEs with these three flights. They can do the jobs quicker and more efficiently. Most important, what they'll be doing, ripping out equipment and cabling, might be dangerous, which the SADEs are more suitable to managing. Times a wasting, and we have 18,289 people to transport. However, one more note before you get started."

<Assemble on me,> Alex sent to the new SADEs, who stood beside Alex and faced the assembled Independents. The SADE called Killian was still cradling the little girl, who was happy to be in the company of her plaid man.

Alex addressed the Independents, saying "You might be thinking these are liberated Confederation SADEs. In that you'd be wrong. These individuals are fellow expeditionary members, who report to the *Freedom*'s captain. They're here to assist your evacuation from this dark pit and nothing more. Am I clear?"

The audience nodded their understanding, wondering why Ser Racine thought it important to clarify that.

<One wonders who you were addressing just then, oh-sly-one, the Independents or the SADEs,> Julien sent to Alex.

<Both,> Alex replied, <I'm trying to launch this expedition on the right note. I never want to see a Sadesville again.> Alex was referring to the persona-less, warren-like structure the Confederation SADEs built when they felt isolated from mainstream Haraken society.

<And you won't, even if you return to Haraken. The Central Exchange owns the property, which was leased to the SIF and allowed the SADEs to build there. On mutual agreement, the lease was terminated, and the structures are slated for demolition. The Exchange directors have chosen to build an open-air park for music and entertainment performances.>

<Well done,> Alex sent, adding a short vid of Julien in an open-air, grav car, riding through a huge throng of citizens, who were all wildly applauding him.

Julien returned the vid. He stood up in the car, excited by the adoring crowd and waving enthusiastically. Suddenly, his eyes rolled wildly, as he lost his balance, and he pitched out of the car.

Alex laughed and slapped Julien on the shoulder.

"Okay, OP, get your people moving," Alex said, and the co-Leaders issued orders, urging the crowd into an orderly exit through the bay's airlock. Bay operations overrode the safety protocols and opened both interior hatches to enable everyone to clear the bay quickly, as they had done to allow the people to assemble to hear Alex speak.

<Bring the travelers down, Captain,> Alex sent.

On Cordelia's orders, the SADEs clambered aboard the three remaining travelers, packing themselves in, and the pilots launched for the moon base.

<Didn't think you were going to get all the Independents to join you, did you?> Tatia sent to Alex, as Mickey and she followed Daelon's engineers and department heads out of the bay.

<You never know,> Alex replied.

<How can you beat us so badly at poker and not know how to anticipate a crowd's reaction to your requests?> Tatia fired back.

<Why do you think I only play poker with my friends?> Alex admitted.

-3-
Evacuation

The travelers bearing the Confederation SADEs descended on the moon base, and they exited their ships with determination. These SADEs, who'd occupied Haraken's minimalist compound of Sadesville, had participated in the *Freedom*'s refit and joined the expedition with this sort of opportunity in mind — worlds changed wherever Alex Racine went. They'd decided that if they were to be part of the future, not shunted aside by humankind, then the best way to achieve that was to stay close to Ser.

For much the same reasons, the Independents were thinking that thought too. The Confederation had deemed them unfit to remain in its society for their aberrant lifestyle choices. In contrast, there was one human, Alex Racine, who appreciated their independent style.

Mickey and Tatia separated, striding through every level of the moon base in the company of senior personnel and engineers. They visually identified every item to extract, loading the images and locations into the *Freedom*'s databases. Then they stood back and let the SADEs go to work.

Miriam, a SADE who developed engineering programs, became the process lead. She coordinated with Ophelia and Perrin, identifying to the SADEs which areas were cleared of Independents and could be reclaimed. For their part, OP ordered the evacuation schedule to accommodate Miriam's request to clear the lowest levels first. This allowed the SADEs to work from the bottom of the moon base toward the upper levels and not to disturb the residents, who were busy packing their personnel items and rushing back to the landing bay. As the levels were evacuated, the SADEs began ripping out communications, lighting, and power systems.

The SADEs stripped out kilometers of power and control cabling, conduit, power crystals, generators, systems control devices, tools, and anything and everything that Mickey and Tatia had identified. Then they added a few items of their own to the admiral and engineer's list. Most of it was raw materials that was thought too difficult to recover. However, when no humans, who could be harmed by their actions, were present, the SADEs ripped metal-alloy sheeting and attachments out of the moon's bedrock and carried them to a central transfer location.

When working on the more arduous tasks, the SADEs were required to work secretly, as Alex and Julien cautioned them. They were told not to display their avatars' full power when humans were in sight of their activities. To accommodate Alex and Julien's request, they carried extremely heavy loads of materials up to the level just below where humans were present. Then they deposited their loads on grav pallets and delivered them to the humans above, who maneuvered them to the waiting transports, where other SADEs stood by to load the transport shuttle.

When the traveler pilot sealed the hatch with the first passengers aboard, the crew exiting the bay for safety's sake, and the transport's ramp closed on the first equipment load, Mickey smiled to himself. He'd never enjoyed himself so much as when he worked closely with Alex. The man required him to apply his entire engineering acuity to anticipating and solving problems. *Long life, Alex,* Mickey thought, *I need you to keep my world challenging.*

Knowing SADEs would be required to be aboard the *Freedom,* to unload the heavy materials carried by the transport shuttle, a bunch of them climbed aboard, lying on top of the fully packed ship. The Independents, who observed them from the control room, were a little surprised by their cavalier action, but the SADEs couldn't have been happier. They were busy postulating new futures based on the actions taking place at Daelon.

The 18,289 Independents were transported primarily to the *Freedom* aboard the Haraken's three passenger travelers and the orbital platform's two travelers. Renée directed OP to send the families with children under five to the *Rêveur.* The city-ship was still under refit conditions and would operate as a manufacturing site until the operations could be shifted elsewhere, and Renée was concerned for the young ones' safety.

Captain Lumley and the small crew were delighted to have the company, especially that of the children. Eventually, the young ones would adopt the captain as a second father, spending hours in his company on the bridge each day, while he taught them a wide range of subjects, including navigating starships, caring for the liner, histories of Sol, Haraken, and New Terra, freeing the SADEs, and, of course, stories of Alex Racine, which the children loved.

Alex was tickled when Tatia contacted him after the first day's efforts on Daelon, sending, <These are mine, correct?> He halted his conversation to focus on the image he'd received. <I see two travelers, Tatia. I'm presuming these are the ones that belong to Daelon. As I said before, take anything you want.>

<Yes! My fleet has grown by 50 percent,> Tatia sent with enthusiasm. <Where else can we visit?> She heard Alex chuckle as he closed the comm.

* * *

Cordelia calculated that the passenger travelers could transport the Independents to the ships above in about ten days. That was until she received the images of the baggage the people hauled to the bay. Some of the large items required they be added to the transport's load.

Fourteen days after the first passenger traveler lifted, the last load of Independents left Daelon's bay for the *Freedom*.

Mickey dearly wanted to strip the control room and bay of its equipment, cabling, and power crystals. It was the moon's premier site of advanced technological equipment, but it would require working in vacuum with the bay doors open. For that, Mickey needed specially trained personnel. He sent a query to Cordelia.

Mickey was standing with Glenn in the bay's control room when the transport traveler came to collect them. They were to be the last two humans on Daelon. As the shuttle entered the bay and the inner doors sealed, Mickey received a comm from the traveler's pilot, and he halted

Glenn from initiating the controller's final sequence, which would allow the remote operation of the bay doors once they exited.

Glenn glanced at Mickey, who wore a huge grin. A tentative smile crossed Glenn's face, although he hadn't a clue why it should. Possibly, it was a reaction to the last fourteen whirlwind days. A prisoner for sixteen years, Glenn had finally accepted that he would never leave Daelon and thought he should search out a partner and have a family, anything to relieve the tedium, but it felt unfair to inflict his dark feelings on others, much less a child. Now, it was supposed to be his turn to leave — except for Mickey's grin.

"Are you space trained, Glenn?" Mickey asked.

"Yes, I led a team constructing starship hulls," Glenn replied.

"My friend, you now work for me," Mickey replied, throwing a meaty arm around the slender Méridien.

"I'm pleased to contribute in any manner I can, Mickey. What will we be doing?"

"The details are a secret for now, but suffice to say, you'll be assisting me building starships of all sorts."

This time Glenn matched Mickey's grin.

The two men watched the transport traveler empty of individuals ensconced in Haraken environment suits, the Méridien's technologically advanced equivalent of New Terran extravehicular activity (EVA) suits.

Via his implant, Glenn identified it was SADEs who wore the suits. "Looks like we're stripping this place," he said to Mickey.

"Yep," Mickey replied.

The two men donned the environment suits the SADEs brought, and, when everyone was ready, Glenn opened the bay to vacuum and powered down the control room. With hours of air available to them from their tanks, the two humans and the SADEs cleared the bay of every valuable component they could load. There was still a great deal of raw materials left in the bay when Mickey called a halt to the process and ordered everyone aboard.

When the ship sealed and air returned to the main cabin, Glenn, seated on a pile of equipment, turned toward a bulkhead and opened his faceplate. He wasn't ashamed of the tears streaming down his face, but he didn't want to talk about what he felt.

* * *

Alex and Renée stood on the *Freedom*'s bridge beside Cordelia. They were holding hands and watching a holo-vid, which displayed an image of the transport shuttle, the last ship to leave Daelon, exiting the landing bay. The bay doors remained open behind them.

"Who knew that our SADEs were space trained?" Alex quipped to Cordelia.

"Apologies, Ser," Cordelia said. "We ensured that their information was quite detailed, and, as you know, we're excellent at following instructions. Mickey considered the bay's equipment extremely valuable and requested the possibility of using SADEs to remove it, while operating in vacuum. The risk probabilities were calculated as minimal."

"But then disaster strikes, and it's experience that means the difference between life and death, Captain," Alex replied, challenging Cordelia's analysis.

"There's that," Cordelia admitted. Deep in her kernel, she was pleased to hear Alex's concern for her peers — not that she expected anything different from the man. But, she'd observed humans change over time, and some of them in disastrous ways. It was her fervent hope that Alex would never be one of those.

<It's been nothing like Libre, has it?> Renée sent to Alex.

<No, not this time,> Alex admitted. <No aliens coming at us from the deep dark.>

<Speaking of risks. I believe I've taken advantage of my partner's patience with my behavior lately,> Renée sent.

<Never,> Alex replied, kissing Renée on the forehead.

"Captain, I'm going to take a traveler to the orbital platform," Alex said. "Send Mickey to that bay when he lands. We need to collect the remaining personnel and deliver our parting gift."

* * *

Maynard Scullers and his people, who worked and lived aboard the orbital platform, were signaled when the final passenger and transport travelers lifted from the moon base.

"That's it," Maynard announced to his people. "It's our turn next." The platform's three working shifts were crowded into the control room. No one had been capable of sleeping during the last turn of the chronometer.

Maynard's people were holding hands or hugging one another. The last waiting hours seemed interminable to them. Then, over the control room's speakers, they heard, "Daelon orbital platform, this is Commander Svetlana Valenko. We're inbound for your location. Please have all personnel ready for evac."

"Commander," Maynard replied, "we've been more anxious to get off this platform for the last fourteen days than you can imagine. I highly suggest you don't stand in the doorway when you drop the hatch."

"Understood, Ser," Svetlana replied, chuckling at the image of politely mannered Méridiens knocking down crew to board. "Apologies for a slight delay, Ser Scullers, but Ser Racine has a parting gift to post."

Svetlana eased her traveler into the platform's tiny bay. Obviously, it was built to accommodate one and only one type of shuttle, a traveler. When the bay pressurized, Svetlana signaled the hatch open, and crew disembarked to help the passengers load, as they came through the airlock. But the first group of platform personnel to reach the ship stood aside as Alex, OP, and others descended from the shuttle.

"Ser Racine," Maynard said, "I'm ready to set the shutdown sequence when you give the order."

"Not on the platform, Ser Scullers," Alex replied. "Walk with us. I want you to see this."

While the personnel climbed aboard the shuttle, Mickey and some techs went to work on the airlock's housing, tapping into its power conduits and rigging up their equipment. When the last group of platform crew exited the airlock and boarded the shuttle, Mickey nodded to Alex.

Alex requested everyone back up, and Mickey signaled the bay lights out and activated the equipment.

"Perrin, Ophelia, and Maynard, if you would be so good as to step forward two paces," Alex requested.

When the three did so, two bright lights suddenly illuminated a small area on the airlock's front wall. A monitor scrolled a text message across its face. It read, "We've grown tired of this moon and have decided to find a new vacation spot." It was signed, "The Independents."

The text message repeated, and Alex's voice issued from the monitor's speaker, saying, "Greetings to the Council of Leaders. I grow tired of rescuing those you deem unworthy of your society. It means I have to start another new world … one that will probably hold your vaunted Confederation in disfavor for years, if not decades. Please allow the next batch of Independents to live in a comfortable establishment, and I'll be happy to pick them up on a semiannual basis. May the stars protect you."

Maynard couldn't resist taking out a marker and signing his name at the edge of the monitor. Perrin and Ophelia crowded in to take their turns in leaving the Confederation a final message.

"You ready to say goodbye to your humble abode, Sers?" Alex asked.

The three Independents smiled, and, before they hurried to board, the two men touched Alex on the shoulder as they passed. Ophelia stopped to give him a hug, whispering, "From all of us, thank you. We're your people, as long as you need us."

Mickey looked at Alex's face after Ophelia hugged him. Sadness was written there, as if what she'd said made his heart heavy.

"Freeing them doesn't make you responsible for them," Mickey said to Alex, clasping his friend's shoulder. "In the future, we'll help many more people, aliens, and who knows what with their problems. After that, they'll have to take what we've given them and make their own way in this universe."

Alex nodded his agreement, and Mickey and the techs joined the Independents scrambling aboard the ship. Alex's mind agreed with Mickey's logic, but his heart couldn't shake the impression that he was responsible for those he helped. He sighed and strode toward the traveler.

A quarter annual later, a Confederation liner would dock at Daelon's orbital platform. A traveler full of newly denounced Independents would be transported to its bay. The doors would open on the pilot's signal, close behind him, and the bay would pressurize, although the lights would remain inexplicably dimmed.

At the age of 186, the pilot, who would soon be seeking retirement, kept his passengers seated while he exited the ship and sought the bay personnel. The message left by Alex lit at his approach, and it scrolled many times before he commed his captain and shared his view of the display. The delay was necessary because the aging pilot was laughing so hard that he needed time to compose himself. His captain was a strict observer of decorum.

The passenger liner returned to Méridien with the Independents still aboard, and the captain was galled to be the one to stand in front of the Council of Leaders and report he'd failed to complete his duties. "The Independents were gone," he said, gritting his teeth. "Alex Racine took them again."

Council Leader Gino Diamanté found himself in the same predicament as the aging pilot. He was forced to cover his mouth to keep from laughing out loud, but there was no mistaking his reaction. While a minority of Leaders expressed outrage, the majority were secretly relieved that Alex had rescued their citizens.

-4-
Experiments

As the passenger travelers unloaded the Independents aboard the *Freedom*, they were met by Renée and a few crew she tasked to assist her. She instituted the old identification and interview process used twenty years ago on Libre. Bio IDs were recorded; interviews were conducted searching for skills and experiences; and then the newly liberated were taken on a tour of the city-ship.

The *Freedom*'s spaciousness overpowered the Independents, who marveled at the wide corridors, the enormous meal rooms, the size and conveniences of their cabins, and, most of all, the grand parks with the potential entertainment centers. The refit crews had been careful to ensure the parks with their water filtration systems were in top working order.

Within days of the city-ship's refit start, Cordelia confirmed the operational capability of her holo-vid center. Then she transferred her Haraken company's entire database of shows and upgraded the equipment from her own credit reserves. She installed a menu monitor inside the door. A sensor would detect the bio ID of an adult or a child's motion, as they entered the room. The monitor would activate, welcome the guest, and offer a list of shows with brief descriptions. Cordelia deliberately made no announcement about the holo-vid suite. She waited and watched to see who would be the first to discover her gift to the Independents. Her credits rested on an exploring teenager or child.

Renée stored the interviews of engineers, techs, construction specialists, medical personnel, and other highly qualified individuals on the ship's controller. Cordelia, Mickey, Emile, Claude, and Pia would scroll through their specific batch of names when they had time and contact the individuals. But there were many people whose skills weren't immediately relevant and Renée took them under her wing, seeking to acquaint them with the opportunities aboard a city-ship. And not to let the young remain idle, Renée drafted them to help prepare cabins and manage meal service.

Some of the Daelon Independents didn't have the specialized skills they sought. Those people Renée turned over to Alex, who walked them through the enormous amounts of materials and equipment stripped from Daelon. Because the materials had accumulated during a period of two decades, as the levels in the moon were expanded, it wasn't readily apparent to the Independents the immense quantity the SADEs transported to the *Freedom.*

"Sers, this is Edmas, an engineer who works with Mickey Brandon, and he's the adopted son of Captain Cordelia and Julien," Alex said, standing next to a 13-meter-high pile of recovered supplies.

"An orphan never had better parents," Edmas added.

"This is a story I want to hear one day," said a middle-aged woman, which made Edmas smile.

"And this is Jodlyne," Alex continued, "also an adopted orphan from Sol and an engineering student. This pair will direct your efforts. The goal is to break down much of this equipment to board or component level, open conduit to get at cable, et cetera. We'll reprocess every kilo for our purposes."

"What will be the purpose of our efforts, Ser?" a young man asked.

"Ships, Ser. We're going to be building ships," Alex replied. "Edmas, Jodlyne, they're all yours."

* * *

"And where to now, Dassata? Celus-5?" Cordelia asked, when her crew and Captain Lumley reported the ships were ready to sail.

"Exactly, Captain," Alex replied. His app chimed, reminding him of an appointment, and he left the bridge headed for his suite.

Julien and Cordelia took it upon themselves to prepare a generous stateroom for Alex and Renée during the refit. They merged three adjacent cabins, creating a work space for Alex with desk and conference table, an entertaining area for the couple and their guests, and sleeping quarters with an expanded refresher.

Renée shipped their personal items, which were collected throughout the years, to the *Freedom.* They were now displayed in cabinets, on the walls, on tables, or stood in corners. So many were unusual, one-of-a-kind pieces, and most of them were gifts.

The twins arrived precisely on time, and Alex signaled the cabin door aside for them. He met them in the suite's comfortable salon, offering them seats on a couch, and Renée served everyone thé before she slipped out.

<Nice amenities,> Alain sent to Étienne. <You don't think he intends to fire us, do you? After all, we're volunteers.>

<Good question,> Étienne sent back.

"I've been meaning to discuss something with the two of you," Alex began. "I want to talk about what happened on Celus-5 … with the shooting, I mean. I was wondering if you have any ... any concerns."

"In what way, Ser?" Alain asked.

"Well, you might be thinking that you could have changed the outcome."

"Would you have allowed us to search the Dischnya prior to the start of the Fissla?" Étienne asked.

"No," Alex replied.

"Would you have allowed us to stand forward of you when you spoke to the queens?" Alain asked.

"No."

"Would you have heeded a suggestion to wear protective material?" Étienne asked.

"Definitely not."

The twins regarded each other for an instant, their implants at work.

"There you have it, Ser. We arrived at the only outcome available to us. Therefore, we have no concerns for *our* actions," Alain stated firmly.

"Alain, you say that as if there was something else on your minds."

"Well, if Ser were open to suggestions from us, as they pertain to his safety, we'd be pleased to advise him," Étienne replied.

Alex regarded the twins' faces. What bothered him was that their pleasant smiles displayed a touch of Tatia's wolfish grin. "Thank you for your time, Sers," Alex replied, refusing to take the bait the twins were offering. If they had their way, he'd probably never leave the ship, except to transfer to another one. "It appears the three of us are satisfied with our actions that day."

Étienne and Alain extended a nod and a quick leader's salute before exiting the cabin.

"I thought that went rather well," Étienne said, while the two of them walked the city-ship's corridor.

"But nothing's changed," Alain objected. "The madman will continue to risk his safety, and we'll continue to prevent his early demise against ever-increasing odds."

"As I said, it went well. Actually, better than expected," Étienne replied.

In one of the rare instances, one twin had failed to understand his crèche-mate. Alain sought to do his duty, as he saw it — preventing Alex from stepping into dangerous situations.

As far as Étienne was concerned, he wouldn't change a thing about Alex. He wanted the madman shaking up the universe, and he intended to stand beside Alex and prevent the worlds' entities from stopping him from doing so.

* * *

It was Tatia's turn to enjoy introducing others to Emile's incredible invention. Only, by now, the engineering team had made significant advances.

Alex led Tatia and her senior people into the engineering lab, which had grown to occupy more of the monstrous bay. During the refit, Alex had thought Tatia and Svetlana were the only other military persons joining his expedition. Meanwhile, Renée had been busy accepting the offers of many more of Haraken's military — four commanders: Ellie

Thompson, Deirdre Canaan, Lucia Bellardo, and Darius Gaumata; and a small host of captains and lieutenants.

Once Alex, Tatia, and the five commanders were arranged in front of Mickey, the engineer rubbed his hands in anticipation of the presentation.

"What we'll be showing you are a series of potential shell-type warships. I have to say, we've made incredible progress in shell designs with the SADEs aboard. It's like we possess the most dynamic and powerful processing power in the universe when they link together to solve design problems."

"How can the SADEs anticipate how the shells will react to gravitational waves?" Deirdre asked.

"They have access to the data collected on the travelers and the variety of sting ship models we tested," Edmas replied. "It allowed them to extrapolate what hull shapes will maintain the harmonics."

"Behold," Mickey said, flourishing his arm. He activated six holo-vids, and twenty-one shell ship designs popped into the air.

"Wow," Tatia said. It came out like the sound of a soft expulsion of air.

Meanwhile, Svetlana prowled the displays like a carnivore hunting her prey.

The models ran the gamut from carriers to sting ship variations. A large, multi-hulled model caught Svetlana's attention.

"Are these to scale? "Svetlana asked.

"Absolutely," Mickey replied.

"I like this one," Svetlana cooed, eyeing the large, three-hulled model.

"A woman after my own heart," Deirdre chuckled.

"What's the advantage of this design, Mickey?" Alex asked.

"It's the SADEs' idea," Mickey replied. "The center hull is a little larger than a sting ship's and would carry both engine types, gravity and interstellar. It would house every operation, including crew and travelers, that a sting ship's hull contains, except for the primary weapon. The two, oversized, outrigger hulls are 50 percent longer than the central unit and possess several times more volume. These two hulls would house enormous beams."

Tatia and the commanders exchanged lupine grins.

Edmas' eyes widened, when he witnessed the expressions, and he glanced toward Mickey, but the engineer was grinning. Mickey was thrilled that the design pleased the expedition's most experienced commanders.

"Will all three hulls contribute to charging the power cells?" Alex asked.

"The hulls' interconnectors will downgrade the design's optimal collection efficiency, but the SADEs assure us that the huge surface area of all three units will supply full power to the ship and the beams for several hours," Mickey replied.

"Only several hours?" Lucia asked, confused as to the limitation.

"The SADEs tell us," Edmas added, "that the ship can operate in system with gravity engines indefinitely. Mickey was referring to the ship maneuvering under gravity power and simultaneously using its dual beams … as if —"

"As if we were in the fight of our lives," Darius declared, completing Edmas' thought. "I believe, Admiral, that a warship like this would best be served by an individual who had considerable experience commanding a squadron of travelers."

"Why thank you for the recommendation, Darius," Svetlana said sweetly. "I appreciate your generosity in placing my name at the top of the list."

"Stand down, commanders," Tatia ordered, "we're only in the design phase at this time."

Svetlana nodded and signaled the holo-vid to cancel the other designs beside the multi-hulled ship so she could concentrate on it. She enlarged the image and slowly rotated it. "Have you named these designs, Mickey?"

"No, not yet," Mickey replied.

"Then this is your Trident class, Mickey," Svetlana whispered, bending to peer closely at the model.

<Love at first sight,> Tatia sent to Alex.

"Isn't everyone forgetting something?" Ellie asked. "These ships are years away from delivery. I mean: How long would it take the Swei Swee to lay up hulls of these sizes?"

"That's the real surprise, Commanders," Alex said, and Mickey and Edmas couldn't control their chuckles. "We won't be using Swei Swee.

Our brilliant team, led by Emile, has invented a means of spraying a shell in such a manner so it retains the harmonics necessary to capture gravitational waves. In essence, we'll be building ships in the traditional manner at an orbital station."

The commanders stared open-mouthed at Emile, and the unassuming biochemist merely smiled in the face of their astonishment.

"Credit needs to be offered to Edmas," Emile said. "It was his idea to see if we could duplicate the Swei Swee spit."

When all eyes turned to Edmas, the young man blushed. Jodlyne watched the female commanders appraise the tall, youthful engineer in a new light, and she took Edmas' arm possessively and declared, "Mine," which broke the group into laughter.

"So, we're not talking a decade to see these ships. We're talking what, Mickey?" Ellie asked.

Mickey nodded toward Alex, who said, "We have a city-ship full of equipment, 18,000-plus Independents, 300-plus SADEs, and a great group of engineers … a lot is possible."

"It's a good start," Tatia agreed.

"And who knows, I might be able to recruit a couple of thousand Dischnya," Alex added, and left the group to consider the new designs. But what everyone was thinking about was how they would work with the Dischnya's fierce warriors.

* * *

Renée and Ophelia, who became fast friends, organized the fête. The occasion took place in the city-ship's grand park, located in the heart of the vessel. Subtle lighting accented the tall trees, blossoming shrubs, winding pathways, and gentle waterways.

On Daelon, the only place the Independents could gather was the landing bay, and it hardly presented a festive atmosphere — not that the confined Méridiens had much to celebrate.

Cordelia played music over the park's hidden speakers. At first, she kept the selections soft to allow people to mingle, chat, and laugh. The Independents had much to celebrate and were making the most of the occasion. Gay, festive clothing was unpacked, and Méridien fashions were displayed everywhere.

Alex was reminded of an occasion, twenty years ago, aboard this same ship and in the same location. Except that time, they were paying homage to those they lost while escaping Libre and the Nua'll.

Alex signaled Perrin and Ophelia to join him. He almost failed to recognize Ophelia. Gone were the heavy jacket, work trousers, and thick boots worn against the chill of the dead moon. She wore a diaphanous wrap that displayed her attractive figure. Perrin held Ophelia's hand, and he beamed with pride.

"Greetings, Ser Racine," Perrin said, and Ophelia smiled, touching Alex's arm. "We never dreamed of enjoying a fête again and in such wonderful surroundings."

"The park is extraordinary, Ser," Ophelia added, gazing overhead at the drape of tree limbs.

"The Librans intended to live on this ship for up to sixty years, while they searched out a new home outside Confederation space," Alex replied. "They wanted the interior environment to be as hospitable as possible."

"And, today, the Librans are Harakens," Perrin said.

"What will we be tomorrow, Ser?" Ophelia asked.

"Whatever you'll call yourselves," Alex replied, "you'll be free."

Perrin and Ophelia nodded their heads in acceptance of Alex's point. For now, it was more than enough for them.

"On another subject, do either of you play an instrument?" Alex asked.

"Perrin does," Ophelia exclaimed, grasping her partner's arm with both hands and shaking it gently. "He's a virtuoso of many instruments and quite the singer."

"Is that so?" Alex commented, a gleam in his eye, which made Perrin nervous. "Then I have just the job for you, Ser. I need you to organize the ship's venues … restaurants, entertainment, fêtes, and anything else that you can think of to support the mental health of this ship's passengers.

"I don't believe I have the qualifications for the job, Ser," Perrin replied with trepidation.

"That's what I keep saying about my responsibilities," Alex replied with a chuckle. Then he slapped Perrin on the arm and said, "But you'll learn. Good leaders often do."

Perrin and Ophelia watched Alex walk away. "Nothing you hear about the man prepares you for meeting him in person," Perrin said, shaking his head in amazement.

"Reminds me of an ocean swell," Ophelia commented. "The foolish swim against it; the smart swim with it."

Alex wandered the park and watched the people before he contacted his next individual. The Independents were celebrating, and the Harakens were joining in the fun. He spotted Alain and Tatia, who appeared relaxed and happy. Their casual clothes were such a dramatic change from their usual manner of ship dress.

Guilt niggled at Alex. His thoughts were dark, wondering which of his people he might lose in the future.

<You're brooding, my love,> Renée sent. <This is a fête, not star services.>

Alex's app focused on Renée's implant, and he swiveled to locate her. She was chatting with a family of Independents and had a view of him over the woman's shoulder. He planted a fake smile on his face for her and signaled Maynard Scullers, who navigated through the grand park to come to Alex's side.

"Greetings, Ser Scullers, have you met with Mickey and Tatia yet?" Alex asked.

"Yes, Ser Racine, I've been told I'll be assisting them in the construction of ships."

"Excellent, but let me make you aware that you'll have three people to please. Mickey and Tatia are only two of them."

"I believe Mickey and I will get along exceedingly well … two engineers, you know. However, the admiral is a formidable woman."

"Look over there, Ser Scullers," Alex directed.

Maynard focused on whom Alex had indicated and saw the admiral dressed for the evening in a red gown. Her blonde, curly hair was piled high on her head. She was relaxing on the arm of one of Alex's formidable escorts.

"Keep that image in your mind, Ser Scullers, when you speak to her. It will help."

Maynard savored the view and stored a few images. He was certain he would need them in the future. "You spoke of three people who I would serve, Ser Racine. Who's the third?"

"Me," Alex said, with a quick grin.

"Is it too late to go back to Daelon?" Maynard replied, half joking and half serious.

"It's actually quite simple. Mickey drives the engineering, and Tatia gets her mix of ships."

"It's the admiral who will choose which ships we build?" Maynard asked.

"Yes, Ser Scullers. We'll be building warships, but that's not approved for dissemination yet."

"And what will be your part in this, Ser?"

"That's where it's simple, Ser Scullers. You keep the two of them happy, and I'll have no part."

"Ah, understood, Ser. Content subordinates make a happy leader."

"Just so, Ser Scullers."

"It appears that I'm to be part of your inner circle, Ser. If so, then I'd like to be addressed as Maynard."

"Then I'm Alex."

"That you might be, Ser, but never to me." Maynard extended his hand in the New Terran tradition, and the slender Méridien did his best to pump Alex's hand in appreciation.

Maynard excused himself and walked away with a newly found, confident stride, which gave Alex a moment of pleasure before other thoughts intruded.

Alex turned to look for Renée, who was saying goodbye to the family she'd been entertaining.

When Renée saw Alex alone, she glided sinuously toward him, a playful smile on her face. Her wrap was in the true Méridien style — a meld of subtle colors, nearly sheer, and extremely short.

<Ah … that's a look that's been absent recently from my lover's face,> Renée sent to Alex.

<Perhaps from my face, my love, but never from my heart,> Alex sent in reply.

Renée languidly wrapped her arms around Alex's neck and kissed him warmly.

"Is it too early to retire?" Alex whispered into Renée's ear, which made her laugh.

"Yes, my love, especially when you've been in the park for less than a half hour. The Independents want to see you, Alex, to celebrate with you. You mustn't disappoint them. Wait until Cordelia changes the music. In the meantime, we'll circulate, and I'll entertain you with thoughts of what I'll do to you this evening." When Alex grinned at her, she took his arm and guided him down a pathway, leading him toward a group of hopeful faces.

* * *

Before the event was handed over to the young, Vivian sought out Cordelia and was able to locate her because the SADE was dressed in her captain's uniform and stood out among the fête's participants.

"Captain," the little girl said in a worried voice, "I can't find my plaid man. Is he in the park?"

The Confederation SADEs did attend the event and were scattered around the grounds. Most stood fixed in place and monitored the humans, fascinated by the free-minded Independents.

Cordelia located Killian across the park. "Come with me, young Ser," Cordelia said, and sent a quick message to Vivian's parents to let them know of their daughter's request.

When Vivian saw Killian, she released Cordelia's hand and ran to him, crying out, "Plaid man!"

Killian caught Vivian when she jumped at him. Repeating what he'd learned, he positioned her on his arm, and Vivian threw an arm around the SADE's neck.

"Dance with me," Vivian pleaded.

Killian implored Cordelia for assistance, and the captain responded with a vid of two people dancing to ancient music performed on stringed instruments. Killian studied the motions, programmed the steps into his kernel, and noted that his movements must coincide with the music presently playing.

"I would be honored to dance with you, little Ser," Killian replied gallantly. He switched Vivian to his right arm, settled her firmly, and took her right hand in his left hand. Then he initiated the newly created application to guide his steps, coordinating his movements with the abstract layout of the park.

The dance program quickly became routine, and Killian found he enjoyed the movements. He augmented them, adding a twirl or a quick leap over an obstacle. The more he danced, the more Vivian laughed.

At one point, the pair swirled past Vivian's parents, and she yelled out, "Look, Mommy, Daddy, we're dancing."

The images of the dancing pair quickly circulated through the park. The fun the two were enjoying was infectious. SADEs linked to Killian to study the program, intrigued by his ad hoc interpretations. And more than one SADE was invited to dance by an Independent.

Glenn, the bay control manager, who was known to be a loner, despite his Méridien culture, saw Miriam swaying gently to the music, the SADE absorbed in the entrancing stringed instruments. Gathering his courage, he approached Miriam, saying, "Excuse me, Ser, I haven't any idea how to dance in this manner, but I would love to learn."

"And I would love a partner to teach," Miriam replied, smiling graciously.

Glenn proved to be an atrocious student, but there could be no more patient instructor than a SADE. At one point, Glenn, frustrated with his lack of progress, was close to calling a halt to his embarrassing performance.

"Ser, your efforts are focused on your feet," Miriam said. "Perhaps, if you let me lead, while you relax and enjoy the music, you'll be pleased with the result."

Glenn nodded, settled his mind, and concentrated on the music. He felt the power of Miriam's avatar, as she moved him in gentle steps around the deck. Soon, Glenn was lost in the music and following Miriam's lead. It had been a long time since the fears that governed much of his life had taken a back seat to the pleasure of the moment.

Miriam had observed Glenn's furtive eyes when he first spoke to her. The human exhibited none of the confidence of most of the Independents, and she wondered why he was exiled on Daelon. That he wanted to learn to dance and had asked a SADE rather than a woman spoke volumes to her, but she was unprepared to extrapolate on what that meant.

In addition, that Glenn had struggled to overcome his concerns about how dismally he acquired the steps made Miriam wonder even more about the human's unsettled mind. Miriam recalled something Alex Racine once said, and it seemed most applicable here. He had spoken of SADEs wishing to join a world of independent-minded humans, but noted that, like the SADEs who had endured incarceration, not all humans were prepared to face the world head-on. The thought made Miriam more determined to help Glenn succeed, and when Glenn chose to stop struggling and gave in to her lead, she witnessed his success. There came a moment when Glenn closed his eyes, as they whirled around the floor, and Miriam smiled. *We have more to give humans than technological prowess,* she thought.

Renée glanced at Alex, as he watched humans and SADEs engage in what they knew was one of Mutter's ancient waltzes. He wore one of the most contented expressions she'd seen in a while. *A child's innocence contains such great power,* Renée thought.

An hour later, Cordelia signaled the controller to shift the music, increasing the tempo and the volume. Parents and children retired for the evening, and the youthful sought partners or groups to dance to songs supplied by Christie Racine, Alex's younger sister.

<Now?> Alex sent to Renée.

<Now,> Renée affirmed, and the couple exited the grand park with many others.

The following morning, it was noticeable that nearly everyone was humming the waltz that had accompanied Killian and Vivian's dance.

-5-
Z

Soon after Alex left Celus-5 aboard the *Rêveur* to return to Haraken and procure the needed resources for the planet, the SADEs, Z, Miranda, and Rosette, who stayed behind, held a virtual conference.

<While the peace planetside is maintained and the survey mission continues, we must consider Alex Racine's priorities,> Rosette sent.

<Our first priority is obvious, dear,> Miranda replied. <It's the green.>

<Yes,> Z agreed. <Ser must know whether the Dischnya and Swei Swee offers to us to live on Celus-5 are legitimate. They would be, if there weren't sentients in the forest.>

<Then we're in agreement,> Rosette sent. <How will the investigation be achieved?>

<It will have to be Cedric,> Z sent, referring to his massive New Terran-styled avatar, engineered with heavy metal-alloy plating and an assortment of weapons hidden around the avatar's cavities. <Whatever lives in the forests has successfully prevented groups of Dischnya hunters and the enormous Swei Swee from returning to their peoples. We can only surmise that they're incredibly deadly. The Cedric Broussard avatar should be able to withstand any assault.>

* * *

Two days later, Z and Miranda stood at the edge of the forest, north of the Tawas Soma nest, which was ruled by the Dischnya queen, Nyslara. They held hands and regarded the dark interior of the thick forest. The dry plains where the Dischnya dug their tunnels gave way over the course of several hundred meters to ever-taller grasses and shrubs until small trees were more common. Beyond that, huge trees of red, browns, and greens towered high into the sky.

The belts of dry plains that ran around the planet's center were an oddity, and the Harakens had yet to spend enough time on the planet to discover why the equatorial area was so dry, compared to the northern and southern regions of verdant forests.

"I expect you back, dear," Miranda said casually.

Z attempted to release Miranda's hand and turn to her, but her hand held his tightly.

"I expect you back," Miranda repeated, more forcefully before she let go of Z's hand.

"I would never wish to disappoint such a formidable woman," Z said with aplomb.

"If you need assistance, Z, you must request it. A traveler can hover, and I can drop to your position. You can be recovered extremely quickly."

Z linked with Miranda and flooded her with intense emotions, generated by his kernel's algorithms. Miranda savored the rush, even while Z waded through the brush, headed toward the forest.

You better return, dear one, Miranda thought, as she watched Z disappear into the undergrowth. *I'm only learning to live with the new me, and I need you.* Miranda was referring to the fact that not more than a few years ago, she was only a persona, an invention of Z. However, under extraordinary circumstances, a young SADE, Allora, who had been sentenced to live in isolation by the Confederation Council, chose instead to give her kernel, her essence, to Miranda, so that she could have a complete existence.

* * *

When Z reached the tall trees, he slowly penetrated the forest. The flora showed unusual protective mechanisms. Thick tree trunks displayed incredibly long, sharp thorns. Several beautiful flower blooms were carnivorous, closing on unsuspecting insects and dissolving their flesh. Insects, not wanting to be left out of the aggressive hierarchy, sported heavy mandibles, poisonous fangs, or stingers.

Hours into his search, Z was already attacked by a host of dangerous insects and reptiles. His trousers dripped with a collection of poisons, which worked on breaking down the clothing's fibers.

Throughout the day, Z recorded an amazing ecology of flora and small animals, which were cleverly adapted to living in the competitive environment. He observed a small, rodent-like animal chew a carnivorous flower off at the stem. Then the creature dragged it backwards, spilling its acidic contents. The little animal hauled the flower up a spiked tree, pinned the flower upside down to continue the draining process, and stopped to chew on a wilted flower of the same species.

Dusk came early to the forest, due to the heavy canopy, and Z chose to lock his avatar, wait, and watch. Soon after night descended, the forest came alive with more fauna species, every one of them carnivores. A large, cat-like species with dangerous fangs slunk past him, stopped to sniff at his poison-covered pants, growled softly, and urinated on a pants leg before silently padding on.

The cat's actions would have caused Z to smile, but he refrained, so as not to give away his position. For the same reason, Z kept his eyes forward, never turning them.

Throughout the night, Z used his thermal imaging to watch other species come out to hunt. The majority hunted individually or, at best, as a pair. But in Z's estimate, none of carnivores seemed capable of taking down a group of Dischnya warriors, as had been reported, much less a massive Celus-5 Swei Swee.

The first day's accumulation of poison on his trousers plus the cat's urine did have one beneficial effect for Z. The next day's insects and reptiles avoided him after sensing the potent compounds.

Z moved silently through the forest each day, cataloging species of plants and animals, but never spotting the dangerous adversary he sought. He'd halt in the evening and watch from a vantage spot to continue his observations. Apps cataloged and cross-referenced the habits of the ecology's residents.

On the sixth evening, an app chimed a warning, and Z focused on the data it offered. The app had accumulated a series of unexplained phenomena — unidentified sounds at low threshold levels, which repeated nightly, and subtle shifts in the moons' light that didn't correlate to the visible flora or fauna.

Z analyzed the data and carefully monitored the app as it assimilated more anomalous points. He swung his eyes to the latest visual data location and waited. An unnatural and subtle shift in the light moved slowly along a branch, high overhead. Z locked in on the anomaly's pattern and ran a search. Nearly thirty other locations matched the pattern, and they surrounded him high in the trees.

Several times, during the night, Z caught glimpses of the creatures. Their skin was covered in fine beads, which reflected their surroundings. Large eyes allowed them to collect the details of their surroundings. Prehensile tails and small, sharp claws clung to the branches. As interesting a species as they were, Z still didn't consider them to be his targets, but he decided to observe them for a while longer.

During the next day, Z built a hide and stayed inside it for the remainder of the day, waiting for the creatures, which he named Nascosto, hidden ones, to reappear. When night fell, a tribe of the Nascosto populated the branches around him. On thermal imaging, he observed a rodent crawling along a branch straight toward one of the creatures, which remained absolutely still.

The rodent paused several times to sniff the air. It twitched its head left and right, trying to spot the potential adversary. But, after every pause, it continued on its way. By the time it sensed the body heat from the Nascosto, it was too late. The hidden one struck extremely quickly. The rodent squeaked, fell to the forest floor, kicked several times in a death throe, and lay quiet. Another of the Nascosto scurried to the ground, snatched the fallen animal, and hurried up the tree to resume its place of safety.

Z enlarged images from the vid recording of the creature's strike on the rodent. Under extreme magnification, the Nascosto's jaws opened to reveal two long fangs. After the strike, drops of liquid glistened at the end of the fangs. *Venom*, Z thought. It explained the rodent's rapid death. Suddenly, a band of camouflaging, poisonous tree dwellers seemed to be exactly the adversaries that Z sought.

Selecting a dart in one of the avatar's fingers, Z fired the tiny missile at a nearby Nascosto and embedded a tiny tracker in the creature's haunch. The animal leapt up but managed to hang on to the branch with his tail. It snatched the offending item from its skin, leaving the tracking head lodged under a bead, and righted itself. Then the creature deserted its hiding place and followed the troop of Nascosto to a new location.

Z tracked his quarry through the forest during the following day, coming upon a rudimentary collection of domiciles laid into the forks of huge trees. The simple enclosures were made of twigs and leaves, woven tightly, to offer shelter from the rains and cool night air.

There was time before nightfall, which Z made use of by investigating a wide circle around the Nascosto's home site. He discovered the proof he was searching for on the far side of their nests. A deep rift had opened in the forest floor, possibly created by a sinkhole, the ground drilled away by an underground river. Peering over the edge, Z examined the bones of an assortment of forest animals.

Utilizing his visual magnification, Z searched the pile of remains for evidence of the Dischnya and Swei Swee, before he realized the error of his intent. The skeletons and carapaces of those species would be buried deep under a century's worth of the graveyard's new additions.

What was obvious to Z was that he'd found the terror of the plains and ocean species, who made their final mistakes when they entered the green and encountered the Nascosto.

Z created another hide to observe the creatures after they returned from a night's hunt, but, before the troop left in the evening, a male discovered him. Screeching its outrage, the animal dropped down from the branches above and attempted to drive his fangs into Z's neck. The single creature's scream summoned the tribe to join in the attack.

While the Nascosto swarmed over Z, biting and scratching, he covered his face to protect his eyes, nose, and mouth. His synth-skin registered an enormous amount of poison, and Z shut off many sensors to isolate himself from the alarms.

As suddenly as the attack began, it ceased. The Nascosto jumped free of Z and formed a rough circle 3 meters away. They chittered and displayed their fangs. Their camouflage was off, and their beaded skin glinted in rainbow colors by the moons' light.

To Z, it was obvious the Nascosto were waiting for him to fall over dead from their venom. He watched as portions of synth-skin, surrounding the bite wounds, turned green, then black, and some patches surrounding his fingers sloughed off. *The Cedric avatar will need an entirely new covering,* Z thought with lament.

Rather than let the stalemate continue, Z swept his hide aside and stepped toward the Nascosto, who shrieked and ran for the trees. He walked around their small enclave and stared up at them. They continued to scream their anger. The more Z observed the species, the more it became clear that the Nascosto were not a sentient species that could offer or refuse the Harakens a place on Celus-5.

Completing his observations of the Nascosto, Z made his way out of the forest. Before he'd gone too far, his comm registered a nearby traveler's controller and Miranda aboard the ship. She'd taken up an overwatch position in a traveler soon after he'd left her, although she was careful to stay at a distance so as not to frighten animals away from him. When he'd turned to leave, Miranda calculated that his efforts in the green were complete.

Z took a direct line from the Nascosto's enclave to the edge of the forest. He was followed by the primitive creatures, which were strangely silent and foregoing camouflage. The females and young that clung to them stayed in the trees, while the males scampered at a distance from him.

Crossing a small glade, a cat broke from cover, and the troop scattered for the trees. A young male, which the cat had targeted, clambered up the only tree in reach, Z. The male Nascosto quickly attained Z's shoulders, ducked behind the massive knob that was a New Terran head, and screamed his defiance at the predator.

The cat made the easy leap for his prey, but was brushed aside. Twisting in air to land upright, the cat snarled and launched itself again, hoping to gain the tasty kill that was trapped on the stunted tree. But when it was mysteriously repulsed again, it snarled in anger and raced off into the heavy brush.

After the attack, the young male animal realized its precarious position and abandoned its perch. Z continued, but, after the cat's attack, the Nascosto stayed behind, safe in their trees.

Z sent Miranda a comm and watched the traveler race skyward. By the time he'd traversed most of the distance to the forest's edge, he saw the traveler overhead again.

<I'm ready, dear one> Miranda sent. <There's only the pilot, Orly Saadner, me, and your new suit aboard.>

Z smiled at the thought that Miranda called his Exchange director's avatar a new suit. The synth-skin and clothes of his Cedric avatar were torn, blackened, dripping with poison, and altogether missing in some places. In addition to the dangerous compounds, the missing synth-skin exposed his metal-alloy avatar, and Z wished to conceal that aspect of a SADE from human eyes.

At the traveler, Miranda waited for him with an extra-large containment suit, which would prevent the various poisons on him from contaminating the interior of the traveler.

"You've seen better days, dear," Miranda said, by way of greeting. "I take it that a walk in these woods isn't recommended for human or SADE."

Z grinned at her, while he climbed into the suit. "Everything in the green fights to live … flora and fauna. I've never conceived of such a hostile place, and, having experienced it once, I'd prefer new adventures of any sort rather than revisiting that dark place."

Once in the containment suit, Z clambered aboard, and Miranda presided over the transfer of Z from his Cedric avatar to his director's.

Then Z closed up the suit entirely, concealing the distressed Cedric avatar from prying eyes.

Orly, who was told to stay in his pilot's seat and had his controller's interior sensors shut off after landing, received Miranda's order to launch. *What's with all the secrecy?* Orly thought. He was dying to know what Z found in the forest.

-6-
Willem

Willem, a SADE and the mission's original co-commander, postulated various futures based on Alex's return with the resources necessary to placate the Dischnya and bring peace to Celus-5. While the survey team proceeded with their analysis of the plains and oceans, careful to stay clear of the forests, Willem determined his priority was to understand exactly what constituted an above-ground structure for the Dischnya.

Every furred, snouted, long-tongued, hock-legged Dischnya had lived their entire lives underground in a labyrinth of tunnels and rooms with only rudimentary services. In addition, they were omnivorous, feeding on the small animals, tubers, and wild grains of the plains.

As the SADE of a highly advanced civilization and who once had flown a starship, Willem had no idea how to begin to elevate the aliens from primitive conditions to modern ones, but he did know who to ask.

"What would be your advice, Ginny?" Willem asked, when he met with the junior crew member.

"Willem, I grew up with the Swei Swee, but I just met these aliens. How would I know how to help them?" Ginny objected.

"As a child of Sol, Ginny, you encountered many drastic changes when you immigrated to Haraken, first aboard our ships and then later on our planet."

"But I was young then."

"Precisely, Ginny," Willem replied. "As a child, your challenges would be similar to those the Dischnya will face when they move into the structures we build for them."

Ginny thought back to those early days when, as an orphan stranded on a huge orbital station, she had been adopted by Julien and Cordelia. Everything aboard the Haraken ships was different but relatable. She, in concert with the entire fleet, had witnessed the vids of Queen Nyslara's visit to the *Sojourn*, the survey mission ship.

"I don't have any specific ideas, Willem, about the structures you should build. My advice is to let the Dischnya choose, but they can only make those choices once you've demonstrated their options."

It took Willem only a few ticks of time to map out a strategy based on Ginny's advice. "An excellent thought, Ginny. You're relieved of long-range telemetry duty. You're now my assistant for this project. We'll travel planetside to request assistance from Nyslara."

Willem swiveled around and marched off, seemingly pleased with their prospects, but Ginny scratched her head, bouncing her blonde curls. Part of her was energized about the idea of helping Willem, but another part was lost as to how she would add value to the project.

* * *

The next morning, a traveler landed on the plains of Celus-5 near Nyslara's nest. The passengers waited out the customary time, while the lookouts, hidden under their tunnel entrances, sent word to their wasat, Pussiro, the warrior commander, who notified the queen of visitors.

Lookouts bounded out of the nest's disguised tunnel hatch and Nyslara and Pussiro quickly followed and loped toward the ship. It was the cue for Willem, Ginny, and Corporal Keira Daubner, their security escort, to exit the ship. There existed a close familiarity among these individuals. The Harakens were three of the five who were first captured by Pussiro's warriors. Teague, Alex Racine's son, and Captain Xavier Escobar were the other two.

The Harakens had made the most of their incarceration time by learning the Dischnya language and customs. The process was encouraged by Nyslara once she'd observed the Harakens' vastly superior technology. She wished to create a bond between her soma and the aliens, in hopes of preventing the decimation of her nest.

"Fellum, Zhinni, Hira," Nyslara greeted the Harakens, her pronunciation of the alien names impeded by a muzzle full of viciously sharp teeth and a long tongue.

"Greetings, Nyslara," Willem said. "We wish to work with a male and a female of your soma, whom you will appoint, to help us design the facilities you'll require in the Dischnya's new structures."

"How would my soma know what you offer?" Nyslara asked.

Ginny chuckled and slapped a hand over her mouth. It was bad manners among the Dischnya to point a finger, lift a hand high, or bare your teeth. All were signs of aggression, and the Dischnya needed no encouragement in that department.

"I know this expression," Nyslara commented, baring her teeth in reply. It was something she'd learned while in the company of Alex Racine, Dassata to the Dischnya.

"I said the same thing to Willem," Ginny replied. Known as Little Singer to the Swei Swee, Ginny was adept at languages and had studied the Dischnya tongue extensively in her spare time, quickly becoming proficient.

Nyslara chuffed in humor. "Females think of these things," the queen replied, and both Ginny and Keira were forced to cover their mouths to hide their grins.

"We could show your soma the facilities on our ship, some of which you've seen, Nyslara," Keira volunteered, and Willem translated her comment.

"But your ships aren't the same as the structures we will inhabit," Pussiro replied.

"The facilities your soma will see aboard the ship will give them an understanding of those things that can be created in your buildings," Willem replied. "We can design the final structure in a holo-vid ... the imaging device on the bridge which Nyslara observed."

"Yes," Nyslara hissed, "a marvelous tool. When do you want your male and female?"

"We can start at any time. Today would be preferable," Willem replied.

Nyslara barked a command at the lookouts, who nodded their understanding and dashed back into the tunnels. "We're ready, Fellum. Pussiro and I will learn the choices. Come, Commander," Nyslara said and marched toward the traveler.

Pussiro exchanged a surprised expression with the Harakens and then hurried after his queen.

Aboard the traveler, Nyslara advanced to the front of the main cabin. To her, it was the rightful place for a queen to ride. Unfortunately, she was forced to stand in the aisle for the flight. Female Dischnya kept their long, scaled tails throughout their lives as opposed to males whose tails were truncated when they were young. The appendages didn't serve any useful purpose for the nest's hunters and warriors.

Unable to sit, while the queen stood, Pussiro took a position beside her, and the Harakens, not wanting to be rude, declined to sit too.

When the traveler landed aboard the *Sojourn*, Nyslara took a small measure of pleasure at Pussiro's discomfort. He had yet to experience much of the Harakens' technology. When the traveler's lights brightened, Nyslara knew it was time to disembark and she had to shoo Pussiro down the aisle with a wave of her fingers.

Having felt no motion aboard the shuttle, Pussiro assumed there was a failure of some sort, but as he exited the shuttle, he stepped on to the hard metal deck of the *Sojourn*'s bay, and his legs momentarily faltered.

"This is my indomitable warrior commander?" Nyslara teased, but she felt sympathy for Pussiro. It occurred to her that before the aliens arrived, she probably wouldn't have extended the courtesy to her wasat. "Much of what we see will be strange, Pussiro. Don't try to comprehend. Simply observe. The Harakens are willing to educate us, and we'll avail ourselves of their knowledge."

Their movements through the survey ship became educations for Pussiro and the crew, most of whom hadn't been planetside. Pussiro was fascinated by the ship, and the humans were entranced by him, especially the heavy scars on his muzzle and areas of exposed torso. The claw rakes on Pussiro's body were testimony to the brutality of the nests' combats against one another, and the click-clacks of the Dischnya's great claws on the metal deck were a reminder of the killing capabilities of those feet.

In a cabin set aside for Willem's demonstration, Ginny ran water in the sink, washed her hands, and took a sip from a cupped hand. Nyslara indicated her wasat should imitate Ginny. Pussiro found the hand washing easy enough, but had difficulty using his long slender tongue to drink from a cupped hand. His poor attempt at lapping up the water sent most of it splashing back into the sink.

Keira held up a portable holo-vid and activated it, which brought a chuff of pleasure from Nyslara. She'd been instrumental in laying out the nest locations for Dassata, as she understood them, using the bridge holo-vid. Keira displayed a Haraken sink, and Nyslara reached a hard-nailed finger into the image and drew a horizontal circle in the air over the sink.

Willem turned the circle into a saucer-like bowl and connected it to the sink's faucet within the holo-vid display. Ginny added a simple valve that could be used to direct the water into the sink or into the bowl, and Keira demonstrated how the bowl could be swiveled aside.

Nyslara glanced at Pussiro, and the wasat grunted his approval. The group continued to move around the washroom's facilities. Changes were made at every point to accommodate the Dischnya physiology, especially the generous female tail.

When Ginny indicated the refresher with a wave of her hand, Nyslara hissed her displeasure, and Pussiro growled, stepping protectively in front of her.

<It's their water phobia,> Ginny commented privately to the Harakens.

<Let's see how far it extends,> Keira sent in reply. The corporal handed the holo-vid to Ginny, stripped out of her uniform, and stepped into the refresher. She activated the mist and proceeded to leisurely clean herself.

Pussiro stepped up to the open door of the enclosure. He sniffed the air and extended a hand into the mist. When he brought it close to his muzzle, Willem told him not to drink it. Pussiro glanced at his queen, who was studying Keira.

"We must test this," Nyslara said to Pussiro.

"We or me, my queen?" Pussiro asked.

"Would you choose to risk your queen with alien technology, Commander?" Nyslara challenged, a bit of her former imperial temperament resurrecting.

Pussiro eyed the floor of the enclosure. He wanted to ensure that the liquid was draining away and that he was in no danger of drowning, a horrendous fate in the eyes of the Dischnya. Pussiro blew out a breath in resignation and stripped out of his commander's bandolier and waist sheath. He hesitated at the doorway, and Keira beckoned him inside. *If Hira is in no danger, I should be safe*, he thought.

When the mist struck his fur, Pussiro would have jumped clear, but Keira held onto an arm. He kept his eyes closed, trying to manage the odd sensations. He felt Keira's hands massaging his upper arm. It was a pleasant experience. Her hands moved from his arm to his shoulders. For a slender alien, her strength was surprising.

Pussiro relaxed under Keira's machinations. When she tapped his chest, he opened his eyes. She pantomimed closing her mouth and her eyes, and then she ducked her head under the sprayer and washed her hair. Pussiro glanced at Nyslara anxiously, and the queen flicked her muzzle toward the nozzle.

Gathering his courage, Pussiro closed his eyes and held his breath, ducking his head in and out of the spray. The mist barely penetrated his thick fur, and he shook his head to clear the wetness.

Keira burst out laughing, as the spray from Pussiro's actions slapped her in the face.

When Pussiro realized what he'd done and that he was unharmed by the mist, he barked in humor. Emboldened, he ducked his head back into the spray and shook it again, managing to make Keira squeal. Pussiro continued to play in the mist, and, at one point, stopped and eyed his queen.

<Time to exit,> Keira sent to the Harakens, recognizing the intent in Pussiro's eye contact with Nyslara. She quickly stepped from the refresher and demonstrated toweling off, even as she made for the washroom's exit, dripping wet.

Ginny grabbed Keira's clothes and Willem and she followed, not stopping until they gained the ship's corridor, where Keira finished drying off and then dressed.

"How long do we give them?" Ginny asked.

"I believe they'll be doing more than trying out the refresher," Keira replied.

"Oh … oh!" Ginny stuttered. "I wondered why we left in such a hurry."

The threesome waited in the corridor, the two women willing to be guided by Willem, as to when they should return. For his part, Willem wasn't prepared to depend on fortunate timing. He'd placed tiny vid cams in the cabin's main room and the washroom, which beamed images and audio to him. If Dassata was to be successful in his endeavors on Celus-5, Willem considered he would require as much detailed information about the Dischnya as he could get.

* * *

When the Harakens left the cabin, Pussiro beckoned Nyslara into the refresher with the same hand gesture as Keira, and Nyslara chuffed in amusement. That her commander seemed to enjoy the strange mist, which hadn't accumulated in the bottom, mollified her. But it was the look in Pussiro's eyes that beckoned her, despite her fear.

Nyslara had yet to mate and give birth to an heir, a queen's critical duty. It was her scent that bound the soma into a unified nest. Her absence from the nest could only be tolerated in a measure of days. Afterwards, the soma's psychological health would suffer. Of all the males in the nest, Nyslara had considered mating with only one, and he was urging her to join him in the alien's water device.

Pussiro reached out a hand, and Nyslara took it. When the mist struck, she sought to yank it back, but Pussiro held on. As a queen, she should have been aggravated, but her mating instincts drove her, and she succumbed to Pussiro's entreaties.

The mist was warm, as opposed to the coolness of the great waters, and its subtle pulsing massaged her — altogether unlike the disturbing crashing of waters against the sands at the shoreline.

Knowing that, at any moment, Nyslara might retreat from her tentative consent, Pussiro treated her with the greatest care. He worked the mist into her fur from the queen's shoulders to her feet. The heat burned inside him for her.

Pussiro had never courted his two mates. They were given to him by the previous wasat when their warriors were lost, and he accepted the duty of protector. The females had been grateful, and he had been an attentive mate. Throughout his life, he'd eyed the previous queen's heir, Nyslara, and thought many times of being the one she'd choose to mate with to birth her heir. The great privilege aside, he wanted to be the one by her side when she walked the corridors.

The Tawas Soma warriors openly admired their wasat's fierce courage, but Pussiro had chuffed in humor, in private, of course, when he thought of his warriors' praise. It wasn't courage that kept him in the forefront of every attack. He fought for recognition — first from his sub-commander, then his wasat, and then his queen.

Nyslara couldn't recall ever enjoying attentions such as applied by Pussiro and the mist. *My soma must have these devices,* she thought, *but I'll keep Pussiro for myself.* Her lips wrinkled in mirth at the thought, and she turned to embrace Pussiro. "You're mine, my wasat," Nyslara said in a husky voice, as her long tongue licked his muzzle.

* * *

"I believe we can return," Willem said to Ginny and Keira, when he witnessed an end to the Dischnya's coupling.

Ginny and Keira stepped into the cabin and proceeded to the washroom, to find the queen and the commander looking like two wet, bedraggled creatures, but both of them bared their teeth in imitation of human smiles.

"Some of my turns in the refresher have gone equally well," Keira quipped.

Ginny ducked into the main salon, opened a storage cabinet, and grabbed more towels. She attempted to help Nyslara dry off, but Pussiro's low-pitched growl halted her, and she handed a long towel to him.

<A little possessive, aren't we?> Keira sent over the comm.

<I believe that this was an important, if not critical, mating of the queen,> Willem commented.

<Ah, yes, for an heir,> Ginny said.

While Pussiro attended to his new mate, Willem instructed Keira to hold up the holo-vid. He projected a refresher and added an image of a wet Pussiro. The lips of the Dischnya muzzles rippled, as they stared at the wasat's image. Willem created a downdraft over Pussiro, showing the fur rippling as it dried. He included a sound effect from the holo-vid to indicate what was happening.

Both Dischnya whipped their heads toward the washroom's refresher, expecting to see the device installed there. Nyslara twigged to it first. "Yes, Fellum, the soma will need your whirlwind when they finish enjoying the wetting." She barked harshly. When the Harakens looked at her with quizzical expressions, she added, "It will be the cause of much amusement when we introduce our soma to these devices."

When the Dischnya finished drying, Willem started to explain about another facility choice, but Nyslara held a palm toward him. "Wait, Fellum, I would witness my wasat experience the room's pallet."

Pussiro wasn't sure he was altogether pleased with the expression on his mate's face, but he dutifully followed her into the main room.

"Lie there, my wasat," Nyslara said, pointing at the cabin's bed.

Not wanting to show any sign of trepidation, Pussiro lay on the bed, but when it moved under him, he launched upright, landing on the floor, uttering a surprised yip.

Nyslara barked and yipped in delight.

Pussiro regarded his queen and the Harakens, who were covering their mouths, and he growled softly.

Nyslara strode over to him and licked his muzzle. Then she reclined on the bed, wrapping her great tail over her legs, sighing with pleasure, as the nanites accommodated her body.

Pussiro ventured as far as placing a hand firmly on the bed, feeling it respond, but he refused to go further.

* * *

Midday meal was another adventure for the Dischnya. Food was delivered to the table for Willem, Ginny, Keira, Nyslara, and Pussiro. Pussiro sniffed at the plates, and saliva dripped from his muzzle, as he smacked his jaw.

<Dining with aliens,> Keira remarked privately to Ginny.

Before Ginny could reply, Nyslara picked up a piece of food from her plate and tossed it high toward Pussiro, who tilted his head back, opened his jaw wide, and let it fall down his throat. Both Nyslara and Pussiro chuffed in pleasure.

<And it gets better and better,> Ginny sent to Keira.

After the meal, the Harakens continued the tour of possible amenities for the Dischnya. One ticklish moment occurred when Pussiro pointed at Keira's stun gun, and asked, "For warriors?"

"That's not for us to decide," Willem replied, diplomatically.

"Who decides?" Nyslara asked.

"Dassata," Willem replied, which effectively ended that conversation.

When the tour was complete, the group assembled around the large holo-vid on the *Sojourn*'s bridge. Willem created a rudimentary structure, which had Nyslara and Pussiro shaking their head in denial. Willem nodded toward the holo-vid, and Nyslara, who had some experience with the device, began touching the image. Her actions were tentative, but Willem intuited what the queen was attempting to do and manipulated the screen for her. Pussiro caught onto the idea and joined in the process.

Together, Dischnya, humans, and SADE created a new, above-ground domicile for a nest's soma, and Nyslara couldn't have been more pleased.

She could envision the Dischnya freed from their tunnels and impoverished existence. That had become her goal from the moment she realized the aliens preferred communication over domination.

-7-
Dassata

Aboard the Haraken survey ship, *Sojourn*, Ginny was reassigned to telemetry duty, scanning the Celus system for anomalies. She froze when her board displayed a huge ship's entrance millions of kilometers outside the system. The extreme distance limited the object's visual clarity, but its similarity to the Nua'll sphere kicked her heart racing.

"Be at ease, Ginny," Rosette said. She was the mission's SADE, who supported Captain Asu Azasdau. She stood behind the journey crew member and had picked up on the teenager's elevated biorhythms via her implant. "I've run algorithms to clarify the image. It's disc-shaped, not spherical. Considering the vector from here to the ship's transition point, I would judge it, despite the improbability, to be a Haraken city-ship.

Ginny regarded Rosette, her eyes wide at the SADE's supposition.

Alerted by Rosette, Captain Azasdau strode onto the bridge. "What's your assessment, Rosette?" he asked.

"Based on the visuals and entry direction, Captain, I would have assigned it a 73.4 percent probability that it's Haraken. However, considering it was Alex Racine, who went for support, I would revise that estimate to a near 100 percent that he's returning with a city-ship, and I would surmise it's the *Freedom*. He has a personal preference for that vessel over the *Our People*."

Asu commed Reiko Shimada, the captain of the sting ship, *Tanaka*, which protected the *Sojourn*. The sting ship supplied the travelers that were on station keeping the peace.

"A city-ship," Reiko echoed after hearing Asu's report. "You send Alex Racine for resources and he returns with an enormous city-ship. You sure he's not hauling Haraken behind that vessel?"

Asu smiled at the image. *If it was possible, I wouldn't put it past Alex to try,* the captain thought.

Word of the city-ship's entry into the Celus system circulated swiftly throughout the fleet's ships and planetside. The pilots and crew aboard the travelers, which guarded the coastline for the Celus-5 Swei Swee, were thrilled that their boring duty would soon be over, as were the SADEs monitoring the Dischnya nests to ensure the peace.

Only a few troubling incidents had occurred for the SADEs, and those took place at the easternmost nests. In the early days, Dischnya warriors from those nests made nightly forays to attack the SADEs on duty, but none of them came to fruition. With their thermal vision, the SADEs tracked the warriors, as they exited their lookout posts, and stunned them before the warriors knew what happened. In the morning, their soma recovered the bodies, surprised to discover that their warriors later revived without wounds. After the attempts failed several times, they ceased.

What the lookouts at every nest noticed was that, at one point, the Haraken sentries, who stood their watches with virtually no movement, day after day, through all sorts of weather, momentarily bared their teeth. Had the forty-one Dischnya nests been able to communicate with one another, they would have discovered that the sentries flashed their teeth at precisely the same time. Only a few Dischnya, those of the Tawas Soma nest, would have understood how that was possible.

* * *

The advisors of the Tawas Soma nest had kept their one and only precious telescope trained on the Haraken ships ever since the first one's arrival. Of special interest to them was the ship the Haraken known as Fellum described to Chona Nyslara as a nest killer.

Days after the *Sojourn*'s telemetry had recorded the *Freedom*'s entry into the system and as the city-ship neared Celus-5, two of the queen's advisors collided with each other reaching for the comm handset, at the same time.

Their hurried call was directed to Pussiro, and the wasat relayed the message to Nyslara.

Nyslara swept out of her underground chambers and met Pussiro on his way to see her. "Come, my wasat, I believe Dassata returns," Nyslara said, giving Pussiro a warm glance, as she loped past him. It was uncharacteristic to see the queen running through the nest's tunnels, and Pussiro was caught off guard, but he quickly recovered, spun around, and, with the aid of his powerful, hocked legs, he sprinted after her.

Both Dischnya were anxious to see Dassata, the peacemaker, return to Sawa Messa, the Dischnya's second and ill-fated home world. The first nests, each ruled by a queen, which made the journey to Sawa Messa from the home world, Sawa, descended into tribal warfare and buried themselves in the ground for protection. When future shuttles, loaded with vital equipment and more nests, failed to arrive from Sawa, they stayed underground and fought one another for the scarce resources of the plains.

The landing of aliens had shocked Nyslara and her soma, but events had unfolded in a most unlikely direction. Instead of being subjugated or decimated, the Haraken who Nyslara termed Dassata struck a bargain to bring peace to the planet. But Nyslara wanted more than an end to the fighting among nests. She wanted to see the Dischnya raised out of their tunnels and elevated once more to a robust, technological society.

Nyslara and Pussiro hurried to the telescope post, which was concealed in the top of a small knoll and offered the advisors an unobstructed view in all directions. At the queen and wasat's entrance, the advisors leapt aside, freeing the path to the telescope.

"The view is limited," Nyslara said with disappointment, after examining the ship through the telescope. "And the ship is already in orbit. Not timely news, my advisors."

"Forgive us, my queen, we thought the scope required repair. That's why we delayed calling you," an advisor commented.

Nyslara grumped, not pleased with the excuse. Her view was of a section of the new ship. Nyslara desired to see the vessel in its entirety, so she turned the magnification ring at the eyepiece, but it failed to move. "Yes, I see the problem with our telescope. Can it be repaired?"

"At first that's what we thought too, my queen," a second advisor said. "If I may ..." he added, stepping to the scope when Nyslara granted him permission.

The advisor eyed the viewfinder, swung the telescope a few degrees. "This view is at the same magnification, Chona Nyslara ... a view of Dassata's ship in which he first arrived and which has returned."

Nyslara was treated to an image of Dassata's slender ship, which was similar in size to the nest killer commanded by Captain Shimada. A striking difference in the new view was that the scope's image was filled primarily by the day's empty sky. The Dassata's ship would need to be laid end to end many times to fill the view.

"Commander, observe the Dassata's ship," Nyslara commanded.

In the presence of others, Nyslara and Pussiro kept up the pretense of queen and wasat. She'd yet to announce her mating with Pussiro, but her soma would soon detect the change in her scent. She couldn't delay the news much longer but had hoped Dassata would return first.

After Pussiro examined the telescope's image of the *Rêveur*, Nyslara ordered her advisor to shift the view to the new arrival. Pussiro took his first view of the giant, oval-shaped ship or, at least, a portion of it. He spared a quick glance for Nyslara and then reexamined the vessel. His comment was, "I wasn't aware Dassata intended to bring all of his soma to Sawa Messa."

* * *

<Captain Shimada, I'd like to address the fleet,> Alex sent via a link from the *Freedom* to the *Tanaka*.

<Since when do you need to ask my permission to address the fleet?> Reiko replied. The pause that followed her question troubled Reiko. <Alex, what did you do?>

<Renée and I have renounced our Haraken citizenship, Captain. Consider us independents of the universe,> Alex said, laughing softly at his joke.

Reiko tried to parse the incompatible elements that confronted her — Alex returned with a city-ship, but he was no longer a Haraken. <Does the Assembly still maintain ownership of the *Freedom*?>

<No, Captain, the ship belongs to Renée and me. This would go much quicker if I might speak to everyone at once.>

When Reiko granted permission, Cordelia sent out a fleet-wide introduction to Alex's forthcoming message. It allowed the captains time to relay the link throughout their ships and to the travelers holding station planetside. Crew members accepted the link in their implants and were connected to their ships' controllers.

The SADEs, who stood guard over the Dischnya nests, picked up their comm links from the travelers over the shoreline. Everyone got a preview of the unusual nature of Alex's comm when it was introduced by Captain Cordelia of the city-ship *Freedom*. If SADE chests could have swelled with pride, they would have done so.

When ship controllers signaled to the *Freedom* that comm links to the fleets' crew were ready, Cordelia relayed to Alex that the fleet waited.

<Greetings, everyone, I have several items of note for you,> Alex sent. <First, the obvious one, Renée and I own the city-ship *Freedom*. Second, the two of us are no longer Haraken citizens, and this was done at our request. The reason for this was to give the Assembly an element of deniability for any of my future actions, and, the first of those was my decision to rescue the Independents again.>

Raucous cheering reached Alex from those around him and in the nearby corridors. Cordelia chose to relay much of the fleet's reactions to him over the bridge speakers. The combined output was as deafening as it was unidentifiable — composed of human accolades and unusual sounds, which only SADEs could generate.

When the noise died down, Alex continued. <This time, I found 18,289 Independents on a dead moon, and they've agreed to assist me. In addition, every ex-Confederation SADE has employment with me. The customary annual stipends will be funded by the SIF. It's each SADE's choice whether they wish to accept the SIF's offer.>

Before Alex could draw his next breath, the SADEs reached consensus and communicated their decision to him.

<Apparently, the SADEs have already accepted the offer,> Alex sent, which came as no surprise to the fleet's humans that the SADEs would wish to be part of Alex's machinations. Many humans were wondering what part they might play.

<It's not my intention to live on this planet,> Alex said. <I have other plans. But I do intend to use the resources I've accumulated to accomplish several things. This planet needs peace; Harakens need permission to live here; the SADEs want to build a universal city; the queens want domiciles for their nests; and the planet needs an economy. I believe we can accomplish every one of those goals, and I look forward to achieving them with those who want to be part of these plans. May the stars protect us.>

* * *

Immediately after Alex's announcement to the fleet, he reached out to Z and Willem. <What news, my friends?> Alex sent.

<We've conducted extensive tests with Nyslara and Pussiro,> Willem sent in reply, <and we've successfully designed a domicile structure the Dischnya are anxious to inhabit.>

<How rudimentary will it be?> Alex asked.

<Amazingly, Nyslara's wants everything Haraken, although Pussiro has reservations about a pallet that refuses to lie still under him.>

Alex detected Willem's humor in the comment about Pussiro, and it made him smile. The SADE had progressed far from his initial stage of anger and despair to co-lead a scientific exploratory mission and find his place in the world of humans.

<There was one request that was necessary to sidestep and must be addressed by Dassata,> Willem sent.

<Which was what?>

<Pussiro admires our stun guns and wants them for the Dischnya.> Willem expected an immediate dismissal from Alex, but all he received was a soft "hmm."

<An excellent job, Willem. Please forward the design to the *Freedom*'s controller and notify the SADEs, Trixie and Miriam, to follow up with me.>

<Will I be involved in any aspect of the construction, Alex?> Willem asked.

The request pained Alex, but he approached the question head-on, which was his style. <Willem, I no longer have any influence over the survey mission or, for that matter, any Haraken operation. I'm a man of the universe, unencumbered by world government restrictions.>

<But you're seeking permission for Harakens and Independents to live here,> Willem sent.

<Yes, but their living here does not make this a Haraken or a Méridien world, Willem. And, speaking of this world, Z, I heard you ventured into the forest.>

<I did, Dassata. After my foray into the Dischnya's green, I conclude that there are only two sentient species on this planet, the Dischnya and the Swei Swee. I've completed my upload to the *Freedom*'s controller of my investigation. Here's the link. The information is coded under the name Nascosto, which I call the little primitives. The word means hidden.>

Alex grabbed some vids from the folder and watched Z track a rodent along a branch. The animal shrieked, jumped up, and fell to the ground. He replayed the sequence, zeroing in on the aspects that Z had examined in detail, the shimmering on the branch and the strike of the Nascosto, its quick action betraying its camouflage.

<Poisonous?> Alex asked.

<Deadly, and the Nascosto travel in a large troop of thirty to forty,> Z replied.

<And these are the killers of the Dischnya hunters and the Swei Swee?>

<I've seen their bone graveyard, a deep crevice filled with the remains of every creature in the forest. I've issued a fleet-wide announcement. Everyone, Dassata, and I mean *everyone* should stay out of the green. If you

review the files in detail, you'll see that nearly every species of fauna and flora in these forests is well prepared to kill. The rest of us will have to content ourselves with the wide swath of plains surrounding this planet's equator.>

* * *

Alex needed to address one more group before he descended planetside. He assembled the *Freedom*'s entire entourage in a single empty bay, while Cordelia broadcast his message to the SADEs below.

Alex grabbed an empty packing crate stacked against a bulkhead. He hauled it over to the waiting crowd and jumped on top of it. "This message is for the Daelon Independents and the Confederation SADEs, and it concerns how to work together," Alex began. "Harakens, humans and SADEs, who are with me, have already learned these basic concepts and embellished them. To our new human guests, I would say: SADEs are capable of offering you a great number of alternative choices, and they can advise you as to the most efficient means of accomplishing a task. You, of course, will presume to direct the course of events, and these newly freed SADEs will accede to your requests. But, this is wrong. Humans and SADEs must work together, find solutions together, and balance the priorities of every sentient creature on this planet. Do that and you'll have succeeded beyond your wildest imaginations. Don't do it, and you'll wonder where you went wrong for the rest of your long lives."

-8-
So It Begins

Knowing renewed communications with the queens was imminent, Alex requested Tatia to recover the Confederation SADEs who'd been acting as guards for the Dischnya nests to ensure the peace in Alex's absence. While he was gone, Willem had monitored the power cells of the planetside SADEs. Locking their avatars and using minimal power consumption had drastically slowed their energy consumption, but they needed to be recovered or charged soon.

"I have some ground rules for the SADEs' recovery, Admiral," Alex said to Tatia in a private conversation. "You'll need three travelers to handle your passengers, and I want three pilots with the right dispositions."

Tatia frowned at Alex, unsure of what he was asking. "Sorry, Alex, you're going to have to be blunt on this one."

"The SADEs have been standing in this planet's weather, day and night, sun and rain, calm and stormy, for the entire time I've been gone. What would you look like after that period of time and exposure?"

"Me? I probably wouldn't have much skin left where it was exposed," Tatia replied thoughtfully. "The SADEs are going to show sand and grit caked in every crevice of clothes and synth-skin."

"Precisely, Admiral. I'll have a separate bay readied with Claude, Julien, Cordelia, Z, and Miranda standing by to assist. Have your pilots land in the bay, wait in their seats, and exit when cued. Their main cabin vid cams will be inaccessible via the controller during the flight."

Tatia didn't have to give it much thought to understand what Alex wanted. He was being careful not to expose the rigorousness of the SADEs' avatars to the humans aboard the *Freedom*. There were enough differences to work through between the disparate individuals who followed Alex, without adding that aspect of the SADEs.

In the heat of the day, Svetlana, Deirdre, and Lucia descended planetside. They were alone on their travelers and expected to land at a series of nests to collect their lot of SADEs.

However, the moment the SADEs were alerted of the travelers' descent, they ran calculations over their comms on the quickest recovery points. Nearly two hundred SADEs deserted their posts and sprinted toward three points on the plains, and Trixie sent the coordinates to the pilots.

<They do tend to make our lives easier,> Deirdre sent to Svetlana and Lucia, as she vectored off to head for her assigned landing point.

<Really makes you wonder why the Confederation never truly admitted them into their society,> Lucia replied.

<Fear,> Svetlana sent. <If Méridien society couldn't tolerate our kind, decreeing us Independents, why should they feel greater kindred for nonhumans?>

After landing, each pilot had only a few moments to wait until their respective passengers arrived. They received the word when all individuals were aboard and made their way back to the *Freedom*. Once the bay was pressurized, the pilots waited while the SADEs exited. When they received the all clear, they promptly left their travelers and made their way through the bay's airlock, receiving the thanks of the SADEs on the way.

I've got my wish, Svetlana thought. *Life is about to get much more interesting.*

* * *

Alex needed permission to operate on the planet, and he was prepared to deliver what the Dischnya and Swei Swee wanted in exchange for their approval to grant humans and SADEs the right to live on Celus-5 or Sawa Messa or whatever everybody agreed to call the planet.

As Celus crested the horizon, Alex landed at the edge of Nyslara's nest. The queen must have been expecting him, because, as the traveler touched down, Nyslara and Pussiro bolted from a tunnel hatch and loped through the dried grass to meet him.

Alex exited his ship with his entourage in tow and halted, while the pair raced to him.

Nyslara skidded to a stop, her clawed feet seeking purchase on the hard ground, and threw her arms around Alex. "Dassata returns," she said, her voice characterized by the Dischnya's soft tones.

Alex's surprised expression mirrored Pussiro's own. Nyslara and he had only exchanged the human greeting once before, but apparently, the queen wanted to communicate her relief at his return.

As for Pussiro, he stifled the growl that threatened to rise in his throat. If there were an alien he dared not challenge, it was Dassata.

"I've brought the resources required to build your structures, Chona Nyslara," Alex said formally. "I wish you to call a Fissla. My soma will build when the queens agree to peace among the nests and with the Swei Swee."

"It will be done, Dassata. Might my emissaries travel aboard your shuttles?"

"Yes, Nyslara, but, mind you, I require all forty-one queens to attend."

"Did your soma meet with the seven queens who didn't present themselves at the last Fissla?"

"Four queens understood our purpose in standing as sentinels against the attacks of other nests. Three did not."

Nyslara regarded Pussiro. As her wasat, he understood the use of force against a nest, but she was responsible for the strategic decisions that guided the fate of her soma. More important, if Dassata was ready to afford the Dischnya the opportunity to climb out of their tunnels, Nyslara decided she would do whatever was necessary to grant his requests.

"I will gather some queens and their wasats, Dassata, and we will travel aboard your ship to meet with these seven, who would halt the progress of our combined soma. Your other ships need only visit the remaining thirty-four, not including the nests of the queens who will travel with us."

"Be ready tomorrow, Nyslara, when Nessila rises," Alex said.

"One question before you depart, Dassata?" Pussiro asked. "Are all your soma real?"

<Alex, the nest's lookouts probably observed the SADEs' loss of clothes and skin due to their prolonged exposure.> Julien sent.

"They're all real, Pussiro, in that every one of them thinks and feels. Some are made of flesh and bone, as we are, and some are not."

Pussiro could feel the heat from Dassata's stare, daring him to disagree.

The nests' lookouts had called Pussiro to their scopes when they witnessed the flaying of clothes and flesh from Dassata's soma, while they stood guard. Pussiro would have thought the sentinels had died, locked somehow in an upright position, except their heads continued to scan left and right. When Pussiro shared his observations with Nyslara, they assumed the sentinels were technologically sophisticated machines.

At the time, it was Nyslara who recalled that Willem had no scent. That Willem and the sentinels were machines explained the reason why they didn't have the expected odors of their comrades. However, it was also Nyslara who warned Pussiro that the simple explanation was incomplete. "Recall, Pussiro, Dassata treats all of his soma equally, and, other than his mate, Ené, his closest advisor is Julien, who also has no scent."

Nyslara and Pussiro let the subject lie about Dassata's mysterious soma, but the queen cautioned her wasat to walk carefully and leave no claw marks around the subject.

Unfortunately, Pussiro's curiosity got the better of him, and now he faced the result. "It's understood that Dassata values each of his soma. The Dischnya will too," Pussiro said, as diplomatically as he could. The answer seemed to mollify Dassata, who continued to stare at Pussiro for a little longer before the heat went out of his eyes. Then he wished them well and stalked back to his ship.

"If we weren't mated, Pussiro, I would strike a welt across your hindquarters with my tail that wouldn't soon heal," Nyslara hissed, and Pussiro had the decency to duck his head in regret.

* * *

<Ready,> Alex sent to Julien, who lightly touched Cordelia's hand and exited the bridge. The two, human and SADE, met up when Alex left his suite, their location apps, as a matter of habit, having tracked each other.

Most humans would have been awed by the extent of the communication that flew between Alex and Julien, who bantered, argued, and, often, simply wondered about the future.

Julien noticed Alex's strong, relaxed stride. He matched it, projected an ancient tricorne hat, and issued the sound of fifes and drums to keep cadence with their steps.

<That's a new one,> Alex commented, sending his thought rather than attempting to be heard over Julien's music.

<An ancient warriors' march,> Julien remarked via comm, maintaining the sound of his fifes and drums.

The Daelon Independents had yet to become accustomed to Julien's creative behaviors, but the SADE's mannerisms made Alex Racine smile, and he'd freed them from their incarceration on the dead moon. Therefore, no sleep was lost over their wonderment.

Julien attributed Alex's easy manner to the many pieces of his plan coming together, which allowed him to make gains toward his personal goal — locating the Nua'll home world or, at least, the next Nua'll sphere. That Alex's people, who had supported him for years, were once again in close alliance with him allowed Alex to delegate with confidence, and it showed in his demeanor. To Julien's eye, Alex seemed to have accepted the fact that a life of leisure and relaxation would not be his for many decades to come, if ever.

The pair entered a bay where Tatia stood by with four travelers, the ship's pilots, and those who would accompany Alex planetside. It was an example of Julien's previous thoughts. Alex told Tatia what he intended to do, and she took care of the details. She was the perfect interpreter between Alex's needs and those of his people, who often had contrary opinions to Alex's plans, especially where it concerned his safety.

"Going with us, Tatia?" Alex asked.

"I thought I should meet the Dischnya. Between your comments and the rumors circulating around the fleet, we might be working closely with the queens and their warriors," Tatia replied.

"You never know," Alex quipped and climbed aboard.

"That's what worries me," Tatia mumbled behind Alex's back.

Julien, who heard Tatia's response, smiled at her, and Tatia replied sarcastically, "Nice hat." Julien, who had shut down his music in the airlock, returned to playing it.

The four travelers exited the bay, and, within a half hour, Darius Gaumata set Alex's traveler down on Julien's coordinates, and the other three pilots arranged their ships, as the SADE directed.

The warriors of the Tawas Soma, Nyslara's nest, were busily preparing for the second Fissla, the queens' conference, when they witnessed the landing of four Haraken shuttles, a fewer number than had previously carried the emissaries to invite the queens to the first Fissla.

Nyslara barked to Sissya and Homsaff, two queens whose nests bordered hers and had journeyed quickly to join Nyslara at the request of her emissaries. The three queens, with their wasats in tow, hurried to greet the Harakens.

"Only four ships, Dassata?" Nyslara asked.

"The giant ship above, the first ship I brought to Sawa Messa, and six shuttles, Nyslara, are all I own," Alex replied.

"What of the other ships above and their shuttles, Dassata?" Pussiro asked.

"I'm not Haraken anymore, Pussiro. I've left the world of my people."

The lips of the Dischnya principals wrinkled in confusion. *Dassata is more alien than his own soma*, Nyslara thought.

"If the Dischnya and the Swei Swee allow the Harakens and my soma to live on this planet," Alex continued, "I have the necessary resources to build more ships and bring our technology to this world."

Alex's words calmed Nyslara. The queen realized that the Dischnya's limited way of life had them thinking of technology as a constantly dwindling resource. In contrast, Dassata spoke of creating ships as easily as hunters and females gathered roots.

Homsaff eyed Tatia, her body shape similar to Dassata but expressing an obviously robust, feminine figure and topped by curls of fur in Nessila's color. She whispered a comment to Nyslara and Sissya, which set Alex laughing.

When Tatia raised an eyebrow at Alex, he translated. "Young Queen Homsaff is impressed with you, Admiral. She believes that if you had tail and teeth, you could be a Dischnya queen."

<Obviously, the queens of this world have a finely tuned sense of female worth,> Tatia sent to Alex, who shook his head, smiling softly, but insufficient to expose his teeth.

"Queens and wasats," Alex said, "allow me to introduce Admiral Tatia Tachenko. An admiral is what you would consider a wasat, except that she commands our fighting ships and our warriors."

The queens and wasats spared a second look for Tatia. A wasat, who commanded alien ships and warriors, was impressive. But a wasat, who commanded such power and was female, was astounding and yet delightfully illuminating to the queens. In that moment, Homsaff got a glimpse of her future — that of a warrior queen — and she chuffed in pleasure.

Tatia sensed the young queen's favorable reaction to the introduction and smiled broadly in response, forgetting the admonishments concerning Dischnya amenities.

Two wasats bristled at the affront, but Nyslara growled a reprimand. In response to the admiral's expression, Nyslara chuffed in humor and broke out her teeth.

<Now, that's an impressive display,> Tatia commented privately to Alex.

<It's meant to be an imitation of a human smile,> Alex sent in reply.

<Or so you hope,> Tatia sent back.

Tatia's teeth were no match for the queen's. Instead, she made her point in her own way. She stepped forward and extended a hand to Nyslara, recognizing this time that she was ignoring another restriction and smiled again. Amid the wasats' soft snarls, Nyslara glanced at Alex, who clasped his hands together and nodded.

Nyslara twigged to the admiral's invitation. The female wasat was testing her, as queens often did to each other. She reached out her hand, and hard-nailed, furred fingers were enclosed by pink, hairless ones. Nyslara felt the crushing power of the admiral's grip, which stopped short of hurting her. Her lips curled even farther from her teeth, crediting the female's display of strength. "Admiral," Nyslara acknowledged with a dip of her head.

"Chona," Tatia replied, dipping hers.

"If you two are finished with your female bonding," Alex commented drily, "I have business to conduct," which caused both females to give him their version of smiles — both eerily similar in their lupine nature. "Are you ready, Nyslara?" Alex asked.

"We are, Dassata," Nyslara replied. "My emissaries need only know when the Fissla will be held, so they might inform the queens."

"Later today, Nyslara," Alex replied.

When the brows of the Dischnya wrinkled in confusion, Alex added, "The emissaries will invite the queens and their wasats to board our ships and return here. Your tents and preparations must be ready by then."

"Dassata is in a hurry," Sissya said.

"There is much to do, Sissya," Alex agreed.

Pussiro stepped back a few paces and barked commands at his warriors. Most blinked in surprise at the orders, but then they hurried to obey. A warrior loped over to an open tunnel hatch and relayed the command. Soon, more soma poured out onto the plains and hurried to help set up the tents.

Tatia eyed Pussiro when he stepped back into the group and nodded politely, and Pussiro nodded in return, accepting the admiration of one wasat to another at the competence of command.

"When Dassata is ready, my emissaries will board his three ships and collect the queens," Nyslara said. "Have you an idea how long this Fissla might last?"

"The queens will be returned to their nests by the setting of Nessila on the following day."

The answer was entirely unexpected, and the queens exchanged glances of concern. But Nyslara sought to support the sense of urgency. "The emissaries will be informed, Dassata. We will travel with you to request Posnossa join us before we speak to the seven queens who chose not to join the last Fissla."

When Alex nodded, Pussiro stepped back, barked a series of commands, and thirty Dischnya warriors poured out of various tunnel entrances, carrying their oversized, blue and white, jagged-striped, emissary masks. They lined up at a respectful distance from the queens, and Nyslara addressed them. Her instructions were clear and simple, but that didn't stop a good many, great-clawed feet shifting in discomfort.

Nyslara was about to bark at her warriors, but a touch of Pussiro's hand on her elbow halted her. The wasat glanced toward Alex, who had monitored Nyslara's orders.

Alex was frowning, recognizing the hesitancy of the emissaries to direct the queens and wasats of other nests to board alien craft to attend a Fissla. They were simple messengers, not equals to the exalted Dischnya they would address.

"Might I say something, Nyslara?" Alex asked, responding to Pussiro's implied invitation. When the queen agreed, Alex stepped over to walk the line of assembled emissaries like he was addressing troops, and the twins kept pace with him.

"A queen will need to hear a valid reason from you to climb aboard our ships to come immediately to this Fissla. In this case, your message is simple. Please tell a queen that the choice is hers. If she wishes an end to the fighting among the nests; if she wishes to bring her soma out of the tunnels and into Nessila's light so that they might live in comfort; and if she wishes to possess the facilities, which we can offer, then it's necessary to board the ship now. And you have one final message for any queen who chooses not to agree. If the Fissla is short one queen, Dassata will take his soma and great ships and be gone before Nessila rises again, and all will be lost to the Dischnya."

The queens' sharp intakes of breath caused the wasats to stare at them with concern. Nyslara glanced toward the admiral, whose returning stare was stone cold.

Nyslara walked over to stand beside Alex, who had finished walking the line of emissaries. "Your chona adds these instructions," Nyslara said. "If a queen fails to heed Dassata's request, you're to inform his soma, and they'll communicate this to him. Then the queens will pay a visit to this foolish Dischnya female."

The lips of the emissaries wrinkled in humor in response to Nyslara's comments. The underlying message was that every queen would attend the Fissla, one way or another.

Nyslara divided the emissaries into three groups and sent them to board the shuttles that Alex pointed out to her.

The warriors raced across the ground to the waiting ships, and Tatia took note of the speed with which they moved. When she commented to Julien, the SADE sent back, <Please be aware, Admiral, our people have witnessed those legs and claws employed as lethal weapons.>

When Nyslara rejoined the other queens and wasats, she whispered to Pussiro, "Dassata's command of the Dischnya tongue has greatly improved. Yet, he's been gone from us."

Pussiro tapped a dark-nailed finger to his head. It was their equivalent of the means by which the Dassata's soma spoke through their minds. They had discussed this concept many times, late into the evening. It was their opinion that if the aliens could communicate their thoughts, then they could learn that way too. In fact, the two Dischnya supposed that more than words might be shared. Pussiro had chuffed at Nyslara, saying "A wasat could be a great commander with this technology."

Nyslara had replied, "But who would you be fighting, my mate, if peace comes to Sawa Messa?"

"None on this planet, my queen," Pussiro replied. "But who does Dassata intend to fight? He speaks of the great sphere that landed on Sawa Messa before the Dischnya came."

"You would fight for Dassata?" asked Nyslara, a combination of interest and trepidation in her voice.

"I've been a warrior all my life, my queen. The soma who report to me are warriors. When peace comes, what will we do? I've given this much thought. The Dischnya's future lies with our hunters, our females, and their pups, who will learn the Dassata's technology. Who knows what worlds they will visit and what cultures they will create? But for many of us, who've spent our lives fighting other nests, what life is there for us in peace?"

"Warriors without a war," Nyslara lamented.

* * *

When Julien requested guidance to Posnossa's nest, Fossem Soma, Nyslara informed him that it was the place where her emissary, Haffas, was killed by the former queen. Julien accessed the *Sojourn*'s data archives, pulled the coordinates, and relayed them to Commander Gaumata.

The trip to Posnossa's nest was quick. When the traveler landed, only Nyslara and Pussiro exited the ship to wait in its cool shadow. Sissya and Homsaff stayed aboard with their wasats. It wasn't long before Posnossa bounded out of a lookout tunnel hatch and stretched her long legs to cover the distance to the ship. Her wasat loped beside her.

After a brief conversation, Posnossa barked a few commands to her lookouts. Then Posnossa and her wasat followed Nyslara and Pussiro aboard the shuttle.

Alex then directed their flight to the first of the four nests whose queens had acquiesced to the alien's presence, even though they'd refused to attend the first Fissla. When Darius set the traveler down at the nest's edge, only the queens and their wasats exited the hatch, and the eight Dischnya waited until the resident queen, her wasat, and several warriors climbed carefully out of a tunnel entrance.

The two groups met in the middle of the open ground and a lengthy conversation ensued. The nest's queen argued with Nyslara, and her warriors tightened their hands on their weapons. Finally, the resident wasat barked several commands and the warriors retreated. Now, five queens and five wasats stepped quickly toward the shuttle, although, at the last moment, the local Dischnya did need a bit of coaxing to climb aboard.

And, so it went, for the next three nests, the original four queens and four wasats would exit, a discussion would take place with the local queen, and then she and her wasat would join the group. Each time, Nyslara returned aboard with the newly enrolled Dischnya, she'd march to the front of the ship, stand beside Alex, and deliver a feral grin of success.

At the first of the three nests whose soma fought against the alien invaders until the Harakens retreated, Alex changed the procedure. He joined the queens and wasats when they exited, standing beside Nyslara while they waited. The twins stood slightly in front of Alex and Nyslara, as there was no room left between the two leaders.

The wait stretched for nearly an hour before fully twenty warriors, armed with crossbows, leapt out of a tunnel hatch and arrayed themselves against the invaders. Slowly and carefully, a grizzled warrior eased out of the lookout opening and gazed around. The view was intimidating. Arrayed in front of them were queens, wasats, aliens, and a strange ship. The local wasat stepped free of the hatch to help an aging queen and a young female climb out.

When the warriors advanced alongside the nest's elderly queen, Pussiro barked harshly and the group halted. Nyslara added her commands, and the tableau was frozen. The queens with Alex thrashed their tails, impatience exhibited in the frenetic motions.

In Homsaff's exuberance, the young queen, who stood at Dassata's side, swung her tail dramatically and its tip struck Dassata's calves. She knew the strike would mark his flesh, despite the coverings he wore, and her eyes were wary and wide as she gazed up at him. To her relief, Dassata bestowed his strange baring of teeth on her and laid a hand on her neck, shaking it lightly in remonstration, but not in a hurtful manner. Afterwards, Homsaff was careful where she swung her tail, not wishing to repeat the offense. She considered the possibility that Dassata might not be so forgiving the next time she marked him.

A decision made, the nest's elderly queen hissed at her wasat, who handed off his weapon, and his warriors backed away. Three local Dischnya came forward alone, a queen, a wasat, and a young female.

The local queen attempted to rise fully on her legs, but they shook with the effort and she had to be content with settling back down. A soft snarl of disgust issued from her muzzle. "I'm Chona Seelam, Mossnos Soma," the queen said. "This is my heir, Choslora, and my wasat, Hessmas." Both Dischnya rose to their full heights at the introduction. "It was my fear that you would return," Seelam added, and her stare was directed at Alex.

"Chona Seelam, I'm Chona Nyslara, Tawas Soma. This is Dassata, leader of the aliens. We come to invite you to a Fissla to end the fighting and lift our soma out of their tunnels."

Seelam directed her rheumy eyes to Nyslara, who had been gracious enough not to rise on her hind legs to announce herself. "So, I heard from your emissary the first time, Chona Nyslara, and still I chose not to attend." Seelam returned to observing the alien leader. "I feared many of my warriors dead when your kind raided my tunnels, but they recovered. I knew then that your weapons were more powerful and yet more kind than the Dischnya's, but I'm much too old to embrace your ways, Dassata."

Seelam hissed to Hessmas, her wasat, and the battle-scarred commander, unclasped the queen's robe and drew it from her shoulders, exposing her frail body. "Choslora, attend me," Seelam directed.

The young queen turned to face her mother, warmth and pain in her eyes at the sight of a mother she knew would soon be gone.

"I pass the robe of power to you, Chona Choslora," Seelam announced in a wavering voice. The queen waited for Hessmas to drape the robe over her heir's shoulders and connect the bone clasp. "Hessmas, I charge you with the safety of our nest's queen. Protect her, as you have always protected me. To you, Chona Choslora, I say, join this Fissla and listen carefully to what is said. Our nest's future is in your hands, but don't be afraid to embrace a new way of life for our soma if what Dassata offers has value."

Mother and daughter embraced briefly, and Seelam hobbled back to the tunnel entrance. An old warrior dropped his bow and hurried forward, offering his arm to Seelam to lean on, which the elderly female gratefully took.

Hessmas watched his queen leave. They had grown up together, and he was torn between what he felt and what he knew he should do. Seelam's last command had called him to a new duty, and he turned to his new queen, Choslora, and nodded his obeisance.

Choslora's confusion was evident — thrust into the position of queen, her mother abandoning her in the face of a Fissla attended by aliens, and protection from a wasat not of her choosing. She gathered her courage, unwound her tail from her legs, and boldly faced Nyslara. "I would hear more of the Fissla. When should we attend?"

"We would go now, Choslora, aboard Dassata's ship," Posnossa said gently, stepping forward. She was similar in age to Choslora and neither of them were as old as Sissya. Together, with Homsaff, they were the youngest of the thirty-nine known queens. There were two more nests that neither the Dischnya nor Alex's people knew who ruled the nests.

Witnessing the peaceful passing of the robe had struck Posnossa to the marrow. Both Homsaff and she were unfortunate enough to have executed their mothers. Posnossa was forced to prevent her mother, who had dared to kill an emissary, from doing the same to the Harakens when they attempted to recover the emissary's body, and Homsaff delivered the final blow to Chafwa, her mother, who was judged guilty of trying to kill Dassata and nearly succeeding.

Hessmas drew breath to speak, but Choslora stood high on her hind legs and barked a command for him to follow. The young queen nodded quickly to Nyslara and Alex, then marched toward the ship, her tail in a high arc behind her.

In triumph, Nyslara flashed her bared teeth at Alex, and, for the briefest instant, he regretted breaking the Dischnya taboo and teaching the human expression.

The presence of queens, wasats, aliens, and a foreign ship forced the capitulation of the last two queens. Nyslara stood at the front of the main cabin with Alex after the last queen and wasat had boarded. Her emotions ran high and she itched to swish her tail. Instead it stayed carefully wrapped around her legs, and she contented herself with the occasional baring of teeth in Dassata's direction.

-9-
Fissla and Peace

By the time Alex had collected the seven reticent queens and their wasats and returned to Nyslara's nest for the Fissla, the other pilots and crew had retrieved the remaining queens and their warrior commanders. Thirty queens and their wasats waited under tents, as Alex and company disembarked, bringing eleven more queens and their wasats. All forty-one nests were present, as if anyone couldn't tell that by the manner in which Nyslara covered the ground to the tents — muzzle tilted up, high on hind legs, and tail cutting swaths of dried grass.

As Nyslara approached the gathering, a thought struck her about the seven queens she had collected. Before she met Dassata, Nyslara would have threatened the seven errant queens with the combined forces of the thirty-four others of her kind. They were prepared to remove the disagreeing female from her nest and absorb her soma if she didn't cooperate. Instead, Nyslara found herself willing to sway the seven by virtue of appealing to their duty as queens, saying, "If you choose not to take part in this opportunity, you and your soma will be left to inhabit your tunnels, while the rest of us enjoy the rays of Nessila with the help of the alien's technology, which my wasat and I have witnessed."

Nyslara and the other queens took to their pallets. Only the seven queens, who were new attendees to the Fissla, were surprised that it was the alien leader, Dassata, who opened the ceremony.

"I've asked Nyslara to call this Fissla," Alex said. "It was agreed by the queens at the first conference that if my soma provided opportunities for the Dischnya to return to the light, the queens would agree to end the fighting among the nests. Furthermore, no sentient creature on this planet would be harmed, now or in the future, without dire consequences. This would include Dischnya; Swei Swee, who you call ceena; my soma; or any others who are invited to live on Sawa Messa. In return for these things, the queens must invite the soma of my people to live among them."

"Are you ready to build, Dassata?" Sissya asked.

"Aboard the huge ship that your telescopes have observed are more than ten times the number of soma of all the Dischnya on Sawa Messa and more technology than you can imagine. We're ready to help the Dischnya," Alex replied.

"What of the green, Dassata?" Nyslara asked.

"Allowing my soma to live on this planet is conditional on the invitation of two species, yours and the Swei Swee, which have been hunted by Dischnya. Leaders of both groups, who have lost soma in the green, have wondered if a sentient species lives there. Here's your answer."

Julien stepped to the forefront, holding a portable holo-vid. Slung over his back was a power cell. It was determined that the holo-vid would be put to good use, for several hours, during the Fissla. When Julien activated the device, under the tent's shade, hisses and growls arose from many present. Nyslara briefly bared her teeth at Alex. She, for one, was pleased that the queens and their wasats were experiencing Dassata's technology.

As an edited vid of Z's encounter with the Nascosto played, the queens left their pallets and crowded around the holo-vid. Julien dropped a set of legs from the bottom of the holo-vid so it could stand on its own and backed away to allow the queens an unobstructed view.

When the rodent shrieked and leapt off the branch, the queens and wasats, who were crowded behind their principals, snarled. It was an instinctual Dischnya response to witnessing an attack. The vid ended when the troop attacked Z in force.

"You lost your soma, Dassata," Homsaff lamented.

"His name is Z, and he's fine," Alex replied.

"But do not your images show these creatures to be poisonous, Dassata?" Posnossa asked.

"Highly so," Alex agreed.

"Is Z one of your soma without scent, Dassata?" Nyslara asked.

"Yes, he is."

"Dassata's metal soma," Pussiro hissed into Nyslara's ear, and she lifted a hand from her thigh to silence him.

"So, these creatures have no voice in whether your soma stay or go?" Nyslara asked. She wanted to be sure of this point.

"None," Alex agreed.

To the assembly, Nyslara said, "Every queen has heard from her matriarch of the dangers of the green, and now we've seen the evidence for ourselves. The green is a deadly place for the Dischnya, and you might be asking how the Dassata's soma survived an attack by these creatures that have decimated many groups of our hunters."

Nyslara's comment had the queens and wasats nodding in agreement, and she knew it was time to start adding her voice to Dassata's. "There is not enough time to tell you of all the wonders that my wasat and I experienced aboard Dassata's ships, and be aware that their technological superiority is not limited to devices. For those who were not present at the last Fissla, know that Chona Chafwa and her wasat breached the rules of the Fissla and attacked Dassata. He received grievous wounds to the chest and head from Dischnya weapons. Every queen present was sure that he would be dead before he reached his ship above where his people flew him. But he lives, as you can see. We can have these things for our soma."

"Chona Nyslara, is Chona Chafwa banned from the Fissla?" the newly elevated queen, Choslora, asked politely, and silence descended over the assembly.

"I'm chona of the Mawas Soma," Homsaff said. She stood high on her hind legs, although she barely reached the height of most of the mature queens in their relaxed stances. "My mother, her wasat, and emissary were judged and punished for their breach of the Fissla."

The new queens and wasats turned their eyes on Alex. Many were wide, and Alex could guess the reason for their concern.

"I don't hold the Dischnya accountable for the attack of a few individuals," Alex said. "Chona Chafwa was frightened by the changes that a future with us might bring to her soma, and she was jealous of Chona Nyslara's contact with us. Understand that her way is not my way."

"Dassata," Nyslara said softly.

"Dassata," Homsaff echoed, and one by one, the queens added their voices.

When there was quiet, Choslora said, "What of our ways, Dassata?"

"Name your concern, Chona Choslora," Alex said.

"If the Dischnya enjoy Nessila's light, there's an opportunity for our soma's number to grow, but only if we have more food. Unfortunately, the plains barely support the nests now. Will you provide meat for the soma in addition to what our hunters gather?"

"My soma don't hunt and gather food anymore," Alex replied.

When Nyslara threw a confused look at Alex, he nodded to her to speak, and she said, "But Dassata, I sat at your table. I ate your food, the same food that your soma ate."

"Did you enjoy it, Chona Nyslara?"

"It was an enjoyable meal," Nyslara admitted. "And we dined on meat. I'm sure of it. The taste and texture were unmistakable."

"My soma make our food and create dishes, such as the ones you enjoyed. I repeat … we don't hunt and we don't gather. There's no need to do this. If the Dischnya choose to live aboveground, then this is the way you will eat, and, over time, your soma will learn to make your own food."

Alex watched the queens and wasats murmur among one another. The discussion had traveled further afield from the consensus he'd hoped to quickly build on the subjects of peace and an invitation to stay, but if he didn't respond to their concerns, he knew he'd never get to his objectives.

"How will we live aboveground, Dassata?" Sissya asked.

"Julien," Alex said, and his friend activated the holo-vid for another viewing. The final plans for the structures the Dischnya would inhabit sprang into view. Both Alex and Julien felt twinges of regret that Willem wasn't present to display the results of his efforts, but the SADE was buried in the planet's survey research, and he'd yet to decide on his future allegiance, to Haraken or to Alex. However, Julien did the next best thing. He relayed the Fissla proceedings to Willem.

Nyslara and Pussiro's eyes lit up at the familiar designs. The two closed on the display and proudly exhibited their proficiency with manipulating the view, with a small amount of covert help from Julien. The two

Dischnya conducted a show and tell about their experiences aboard Dassata's ship, concerning the various facilities, and how they related to the building plans.

The queens and wasats were mesmerized, not only by the structures and their facilities, but by the stories of Nyslara and Pussiro.

Alex waited patiently for the presentation to end, but it dragged on and on. At one point, he took a seat on the ground and soon nodded off.

<Time to go back to work, Dassata,> Julien sent to Alex, whose eyes popped open. He felt the leg of each twin release the pressure on his back. They had braced him, while he slept. He stood up and yawned briefly, catching Nyslara's chuff of humor.

"Dassata, the queens want these structures for their nests and request to share in your technology," Nyslara announced proudly.

"My soma are ready to build," Alex said to the assembly of queens. "You must commit to peace among one another and with the Swei Swee, and you must invite my soma to live here."

"We are ready to give you our bond, Dassata," Nyslara replied. Then she started to chortle, and, soon, every queen and wasat was doing the same thing.

<I'm missing the joke,> Alex sent to Julien.

<I regret I have no conjectures for you, oh, supposedly omniscient one,> Julien sent back.

"Dassata, this is the manner in which two queens seal a bond," Nyslara said and nodded toward Sissya. Facing each other about a meter-and-a-half apart, they swung their tails from behind them. Each came from the queen's right side and the tails met between them, snapping together and intertwining with each other. Then the tails slithered apart and were swung behind the queens again.

"Should we wait until Dassata has one of his own?" Posnossa asked innocently, but her wrinkling muzzle betrayed her remark's facetiousness.

Alex's laugh boomed out, and the Dischnya were momentarily taken aback, but soon joined in with their soft chortles and barks.

"We will make the bond as I've seen Dassata's soma do," Nyslara said. She walked over to Alex and held out her hand. Most of the Dischnya were shocked at the affront to the alien leader, and they held their collective breath.

Alex reached out his hand and shook Nyslara's. As the queen revealed her muzzle of sharp teeth, Alex grinned back.

Homsaff didn't miss the opportunity to be second in a line that quickly formed behind Nyslara. She extended her hand and did the best she could to display the entirety of her fangs, while she shook Dassata's hand. Despite their trepidation at the audaciousness of the alien mannerisms, each queen dutifully bared her teeth and shook the hand of Dassata.

<You should be pleased, Alex,> Julien sent, <but there is a small frown on your forehead that I know only too well.>

<The Fissla is proving to be a success,> Alex conceded via his thoughts. <But I'm wondering how to purge these images of forty-one displays of incredibly dangerous fangs from my memory, not just my implants.>

<Such are the weighty consequences of successful peace negotiations,> Julien replied. <One treaty concluded; one more to go.>

* * *

The next morning Long Eyes, a member of Wave Skimmer's hive, spied the Star Hunter's blue green traveler landing on the shoreline, and he stroked through the shallows to meet whoever exited the ship. He'd hoped to greet Little Singer, but it was Star Hunter First who stepped onto the sands.

The meeting was short. Long Eyes bobbed a greeting, and Alex whistled his request to the Swei Swee, who dove back into the water and hurried to deliver the leader's message to his hive's First.

On the following morning, four travelers returned to the site of the Fissla, and Alex, once again, addressed the queens. "You've promised peace among the nests, and you've invited my soma to share your planet with you. There is one more task to complete before this can take place. You'll ride our shuttles to the edge of the great waters. The leaders of the Swei

Swee, who are called Firsts, are assembling. A ceremony will take place on the sands."

"What will the ceremony entail?" Homsaff asked, with a small amount of trepidation.

"One leader from each side will be required to participate," Alex replied.

"That will be me," Nyslara said, rising on her legs, her tail swishing to and fro. It was a signal to the other queens not to disagree with her. "My nest has committed grievous harm against the Swei Swee, who we once called ceena. Whatever the ceremony entails, it's my duty to represent the Fissla."

"But Mawas Soma was also guilty of offending the ceena … the Swei Swee," Homsaff said. Her eyes implored Nyslara, but the Tawas Soma queen could read the young one's mind. Homsaff was offering to shoulder the blame, as was her duty, but, at the same time, she was terrified as to what that meant.

"You were not queen when the offenses occurred, Chona Homsaff. I was. This is my duty," Nyslara replied firmly, and she saw relief flood through the young queen's eyes.

<You're not informing Nyslara that the ceremony is merely a sharing of a meal,> Julien sent to Alex. When Julien received no reply, he sent, <I gather you wish Nyslara to feel apprehensive about the ceremony for the injustice committed against the Swei Swee.> Still there was no response from Alex. *Don't let your heart harden because of your anger, Alex,* Julien thought. *Once it does, it might never soften again.*

The queens and wasats boarded the shuttles for the short flight to the shore. The travelers were forced to land on the bluff. There wasn't sufficient room for them on the small beach. The assembly made its way down to the shore via a path worn throughout the years by Dischnya hunters.

Alex was the first to set foot on the sands, and he quickly spotted the telltales sign of a multitude of Swei Swee waiting in deeper water — eyes perched on stalks, peeking above the surface. He whistled shrilly, and dark carapaces broached the water's surface, tails and legs stroking, as the Swei Swee responded to the ancient call to assemble.

The Firsts and a key male of their hives stopped in the shallows and stood on extended legs, while Wave Skimmer, Long Eyes, and Dives Deep waded ashore.

Queens and wasats trembled at the sight of the monstrous creatures who loomed over Dassata, but they took heart from Nyslara's stalwart stance, the queen standing next to the alien leader. They were intrigued by the whistling and tweeting manner in which Dassata communicated with the Swei Swee who faced him. Never could they have believed that this was a means of speaking.

Wave Skimmer whirled around and relayed Alex's offer to the Firsts — an end to the land hunters' attacks, the opportunity to build along the cliffs, and, most important, a new period of prosperity for the hives. In exchange, Star Hunter First asked for one gift from the Firsts. They must give permission for his people to live on the planet.

When the queries came, Alex replied he had only the one offer for the Swei Swee. If they did not approve, he and his people would be gone. That comment ended the questions, and the Firsts whistled and warbled among themselves.

"These Swei Swee leaders make up their minds no faster than the queens," Nyslara whispered to Alex. She was disappointed when Alex didn't reply. She had hoped for some conversation, which might steady her nerves for what was to come.

Wave Skimmer whistled for attention, interrupting the other Firsts, and restated the offer, asking for approval or denial. He reminded the Firsts that Star Hunter First's presence was their only hope for a return of their traditions and living in peace. Several hive leaders whistled their acceptance, and then others joined in, until every First had added their approval.

"The Firsts accept," Wave Skimmer whistled.

"Rather than have every First greet every queen, I wish one First, one queen, and me to participate in the greeting ceremony," Alex whistled.

Wave Skimmer whistled the proposal to the Firsts, who agreed to let Wave Skimmer stand for the assembled Firsts in the greeting ceremony.

Long Eyes darted into the shallows, but a male deeper in the waters snatched a tasty prize and hurried to present it to Long Eyes, who speared the twisting, eel-like creature and hurried back to shore.

Wave Skimmer warbled his thanks, accepting the tribute, and neatly snipped off the head, not that it stopped the wriggling of the muscle-laden body, but the First knew the jaws of the creature would lock tightly once it clamped on its prey or predator. He slit the skin down the entire body and peeled it away. Then he stripped a long piece of meat from the vertebrae and offered it to Alex. When he peeled the next piece of flesh, his eyestalks split, two focused on Alex and the other two roamed to gaze over the queens.

"Chona Nyslara," Alex said, and the queen stepped forward and took the offering from Wave Skimmer.

The First tore a final piece from the carcass and flicked the remainder over his carapace into the shallows.

Nyslara watched Dassata and the Swei Swee tear into the creature's raw flesh, chewing heartily and swallowing chunks of meat. Having always consumed cooked meat, the queen was reticent to taste the raw flesh, but this was the peace ceremony. Her sharp teeth easily bit through a chunk of the meat, and she was surprised that the flavor didn't offend her. Energized, she joined the other two, ripping and tearing into her portion of the creature until she'd consumed every bit of it, even licking her fingers to enjoy the juice. Then she eyed Alex's portion, which he was still consuming.

"If you want more, Nyslara, you have only to swim out and get some," Alex said, in response to Nyslara's attention. Observing the queen's shock at the thought of venturing into the great waters, which terrified the Dischnya, Alex whistled a translation to Wave Skimmer, who warbled at the queen's discomfort. Alex couldn't prevent his lopsided smile from forming.

Realizing she was the butt of the exchange between the two leaders, Nyslara shot back, "For a creature without a tail, you're bold, Dassata."

Alex translated the queen's reply, and Wave Skimmer loosed a high-pitched whistle, as he caught the joke, two of his eyestalks bending to observe Nyslara's twitching tail.

When all were finished with their portions, Alex said to Nyslara, "Watch carefully what I do with my fists, after they are struck by Wave Skimmer."

The queen didn't understand the message, but she paid close attention when the Swei Swee extended his claws and Dassata struck them with his fists. The heavy smack of flesh on shell was disturbing. Then the two reversed the order, and she saw Dassata swing his hands down and away from his side when the claws hit them. That Dassata was the first to strike was not lost on Nyslara. So, when the Swei Swee extended his claws to her, she placed her fists below his.

Wave Skimmer's eyestalks bent to examine the face of the land hunter leader, and he warbled.

Before Nyslara could ask what was said, the Swei Swee's claws slapped down on her fists and only her quick reflexes saved her from broken bones. She thought to return the favor, but the creature's size and formidable power made her think otherwise. *Besides,* Nyslara thought, *do not the ceena have a right to feel angry?* When it was her turn, she smacked her fists on the claws and considered her decision well-thought-out. She thought she had struck stone with her hands.

Dassata turned to Nyslara, and the queen immediately placed her fists in a subordinate position. He struck hers lightly, and she did the same in return.

Swei Swee whistles split the air. Momentarily taken aback, the queens sensed the jubilant atmosphere and joined with howls and barks.

When the celebration died down, Alex whistled to Wave Skimmer, "Where will you build?"

"There are cliffs along the shore several bays in that direction," Wave Skimmer replied, pointing a claw. "They're tall and solid, and the waters are rich."

"Will all the Swei Swee reside there?" Alex asked.

"No, there will be many sites."

"So, the election of a First to govern all the hives will be difficult."

"Yes, we have lived separately for a long while. It will take time for the People to return to the old ways, if ever."

"You have peace now, Wave Skimmer, and my people will ensure that you are safe until such time as you develop your own rapport with the Dischnya."

When the Star Hunter Leader mentioned the land hunters, the First swung his eyeballs over the assembly. A tweet of derision nearly escaped his breath ways, but he held it back. *It would be a poor beginning for the peace,* Wave Skimmer thought. He whistled farewell and hurried into the shallows. Soon the entire collection of Swei Swee was no more than a disturbance of the surface, as they dove for the safety of deep water.

"Is that the end of the ceremony?" Nyslara asked, confusion written in her eyes and on her muzzle.

"Yes," Alex replied. "You have sworn peace with the Swei Swee. It's a solemn oath that can't ever be changed or broken," Alex said, staring hard into Nyslara's eyes.

The queen thought to point out that Dassata had let her think the event was to be more onerous than that, and she yearned to be indignant and criticize him for his cruel joke, but his eyes smoldered with a deep anger. Instead, Nyslara deflated, settling on her hind legs and wrapping her tail around her legs.

Seeing the queen's reaction, Alex berated himself for his own behavior and said, "Perhaps, Nyslara, I might have been more informative about the greeting ceremony, but I fought a war and lost soma in an effort to save this species, only to find them hunted for food on your planet."

"Your words and your anger are understood, Dassata," Nyslara said humbly. "One day, I hope to earn your forgiveness," she added, and turned to climb the path to the waiting travelers on the bluff above.

-10-
Omnia

As Alex's traveler made for the *Freedom*, he knew announcing to the fleet of their success was unnecessary. Julien had notified the SADEs, who communicated to their favorite humans, and soon everyone knew that the Dischnya and the Swei Swee had consented to peace and offered them an opportunity to live on the planet.

Once the queens and their wasats were returned to their nests, Alex began making arrangements for a meeting with many of his senior people. However, he signaled Emile and Ben to meet with him immediately, one after the other. Ben linked with Emile to ensure he knew when to appear before Alex after Emile was finished.

Emile Billings met with Alex outside the *Freedom*'s bay. "Congratulations, Alex, or should I say Dassata? I would hate to be out of step with the accepted proprieties."

Alex would have replied tartly, but there was the hint of a smile on Emile's lips, and his mind was too absorbed with other thoughts to bother with a response. "I have a priority task for you, Emile. Something you can put that overactive imagination of yours to work on immediately."

"Then this supersedes the faux shell operation."

"Can you hand that off to Mickey, for a while?"

"I suppose so, Alex, if it's that important."

"It is. I need a queen's spray."

"A what?"

"A nest's soma requires the constant scent of their queen. We know that she can't be absent from the nest for too long. The problem is that I need some queens to help me with my future plans, and they'll need to be absent from their nests for an extended period of time. Make me a spray or some delivery mechanism that imitates a queen's scent and can be distributed in her absence. Start with Nyslara."

"Does the queen know I'm about to do this?"

"No time like the present to introduce yourself to her," Alex said with a grin and a wave, as he walked off.

* * *

Benjamin "Little Ben" Diaz received Emile's signal, and he queried the *Freedom*'s controller to vector in on Alex's position. Alex had exited a lift on the bridge deck, and Ben guessed Alex was probably headed for the owner's suite. He started to quicken his pace and belatedly realized his diminutive partner, Simone Turin, couldn't keep up. So Ben, a massive New Terran, slowed to Simone's pace and glanced down apologetically at his partner.

Simone was a pale, blonde, blue-eyed, slender example of Méridien genetic templates. She was a stark contrast to Ben's massive stature, dark hair, and warm brown skin. Ben wasn't your average New Terran. He was 6 centimeters taller and more than 30 kilos heavier than Alex and known among Harakens as Rainmaker. When he was the Minister of Mining, he supplied copious amounts of water-ice asteroids for the land-thirsty planet.

Ben and Simone caught up with Alex before he entered the owner's cabin, and Alex invited them inside while he cleaned up, knowing the smell of the raw fish he had consumed would be offensive to a Méridien, such as Simone.

"Are we going to add moisture to this world's atmosphere, now that we're invited to stay?" Ben asked, standing in the doorway to the sleeping quarters and calling out to Alex.

"Not this time, Ben," Alex yelled back. "The forests are already plenty wet. Any additional rain would disturb the ecological balance. What I need is a great deal of refined ore and compounds."

"Any idea how much?" Ben asked, stepping away from the doorway to make room for Alex to pass through and enter the salon.

"If you're asking for details, such as the total kilos of each type … I have no idea. That's for the engineers, humans, and SADEs to work out, and they've yet to get their marching orders. Have you checked out the *Freedom*'s bays?"

"Did that the first thing when I came aboard, Alex. All the ore haulers and mining rigs are still onboard. A bunch of my engineers have been running them through their maintenance checks. They're in fairly good shape for not being used in about sixteen years."

"How about targets?"

"Did that too. Accessed the *Sojourn*'s survey information on that asteroid belt out past Celus-6 and the moons circling that planet. Heavy metal content and frozen gases of the type we need are out there."

"Good to hear."

"Pick your people from the Independents and Confederation SADEs in the same proportion as they're represented."

"Is this relationship of numbers important, Dassata?" Simone asked.

Ben thought of the same question, but it wasn't in his nature to ask why.

"It is, Simone. When you believe you have the answer, send it to me," Alex replied.

Ben worked to keep the smile off his face. Not for any concern about Alex's reaction, but for his tiny, Méridien partner. She could be much fiercer than her size indicated.

"I can tell you this, Ben, since it will soon be common knowledge. We need refined metals to build a city planetside, forty-one structures for the queens, and an orbital platform with passenger and ship construction facilities."

"We're going to build the old-type ships, Alex?"

"No, Ben, we're going to build a whole new generation of ships with something that Emile and company invented … a spray-on, faux, Swei Swee shell."

"Black space," Ben whispered.

"Consider your language," Simone admonished, swatting Ben's arm. She might well have been striking a tree trunk for all that Ben felt it, but he pretended that he did.

This time, it was Alex who had to hide a smile. "Quite true, Ben," Alex allowed. "You'll need to coordinate with Captain Cordelia. She'll accumulate the needs of each group and centralize the refined ore and compound amounts for you."

"Just like the old days," Ben enthused, holding out a meaty hand, which Alex clasped.

"Not quite, my more-than-significant other," Simone cautioned. "There was a reason I insisted on accompanying you to this meeting. I wanted Alex and you to hear this directly from me. This time I'm going out in the beyond with you. I'm not sitting it out planetside again."

* * *

After speaking with Ben, Alex hustled to one of the *Freedom*'s large conference rooms where the remainder of his senior staff had gathered. Present were Tatia, Mickey, Edmas, Jodlyne, Claude, Julien, Cordelia, Z, Miranda, Ophelia, Perrin, Maynard, Miriam, Glenn, Trixie, five commanders, and a good many more individuals.

"Let's get to it," Alex said, when his app collected bio IDs and signaled everyone was present. "We're going to initiate several projects at once, people. You'll consider the *Freedom* as your hub. Your requests for personnel, equipment, and materials will be coordinated through the ship's controller and will be managed by Captain Cordelia."

Alex scanned the audience to ensure they understood his directive. No one seemed bothered by it. *Once again, you're the fool in charge,* Alex thought, but he swamped the mocking judgment before it could take hold.

"The first of these major projects is a dual-purpose orbital platform to handle passenger ships and ship construction. Every one of you has been introduced to our incredible new invention."

When the assembly applauded, Alex motioned the foursome to stand up and accept their due. Mickey, Edmas, and Emile nodded, while Jodlyne delivered a cute curtsy.

"Several of you will be driving the specifications for this project. For instance, Admiral Tachenko and her commanders are selecting the ships, which will determine the bay requirements. The ships must be enclosed for the shell to be sprayed. Mickey and his team will be converting those requirements into the orbital's construction design. With regards to ship construction, travelers, considerably sized warships, and possibly a medium-sized carrier are my priorities. There's a backlog demand for our shuttles, and they're going to be our credits supply, which we need in order to hire a larger labor force."

Alex took a sip of water and regarded the faces — heads were nodding and many were smiling.

"And no need to construct the facilities to manufacture myriad sophisticated technological components, if we have the credits to purchase them," Mickey said.

"Precisely," Alex replied. "Next major project is to build a city below, but I don't want it on the same continent as the nests. That's too much for the Dischnya to handle. They'll need time to assimilate with us. In addition, the queens will need their forty-one structures. Julien has Willem's building designs, and, as you would expect, they're quite complete.

"And what are the priorities for these projects?" Perrin asked.

"Everything starts at once," Alex replied. "First thing, don't consider any team that you put together will stay with you. Some projects will require more individuals sooner than others as they progress. That's why everything is coordinated through the *Freedom* and Captain Cordelia."

This time, Alex could see confusion forming on the Independents' faces and suspected that the Confederation SADEs probably had questions too, but Cordelia stepped into the discussion.

"You'll be surprised how easily this will work, people," Cordelia said, and Alex had to grin at how the captain copied his style when addressing those around the huge table. "If you'll recall, we've done this before when we successfully accelerated the completion of two city-ships, with a combined mass that equals, if not exceeds, that of our present projects. And let's not forget the time constraint under which we worked."

Cordelia's last comment brought soft laughter and chuckles from her audience. No matter who you were or where you were from, everyone knew of the city-ships' timely escape from the Arno system in advance of the onslaught of the Nua'll sphere.

<Well said, Captain,> Alex sent privately to Cordelia.

<I had a good teacher,> Cordelia replied, and Alex received a new version of Julien and Cordelia's trademark explosion of ever-evolving colors that quickly faded away, the sound of tiny, silver bells tinkling in the background.

"Who would you like to see in charge of each project?" Ophelia asked.

"That's up to everyone around this table. There's a tremendous amount of brainpower in this room, and I'm sure you can work that out among yourselves. Except … I do have one request, if she's so inclined to accept the role. For the architect of the city, I would like to nominate Trixie."

Trixie dropped into a fugue, her avatar absolutely still.

<Embrace the dream of the Confederation SADEs, Trixie,> Alex sent gently. <They imagined a city that would welcome all, and you can do no wrong, if you hold that ideal centermost in your plans.>

Trixie rose from her seat. The congratulations from SADEs poured into her comm. She nodded, saying softly, "Dassata, I will do my best," and sat back down.

"Well, figure out who's doing what and get started, people. You need a good site for the city, and you need to finalize your choice of ships. You will need to produce metal and compound requests for Ben. He'll be mining at Celus-6 and the belt beyond to deliver your raw materials."

Alex stood up to leave, but halted. "There's one other thing. We have more than one name for this planet, depending on who you talk to, Harakens or Dischnya. It's unfair to choose one over the other. I suggest you come up with a better name."

Trixie stood up, "Dassata, if you please, the Confederation SADEs have been calling this planet Omnia. It's an ancient word meaning all or everything."

"Omnia," Alex repeated, rolling the word and its meaning around in his mind. His implants received assent after assent from around the table.

"I like it. Consider it adopted," Alex said, smiling at Trixie, and her grin lit up her electric-blue face.

-11-
Inventive Minds

After Alex left them, the group divided the projects among themselves, and Cordelia recorded the supervisory summary.

<Alex, don't go too far,> Mickey sent. <I'm headed for the *Freedom*'s old engineering labs, which are still situated in the original bay.>

Alex affirmed he'd join Mickey there, and, in turn, the engineer signaled Cordelia, Edmas, and Jodlyne, requesting they join Alex and him. <I've had a crazy idea and need some opinions,> Mickey sent and took off at a brisk walk.

When the small group cycled through the bay's airlock, the hatches keyed open via Mickey's implant, Alex commented, "Familiar territory."

The opening of the inner airlock hatch triggered the overhead lights on, illuminating the cavernous space.

"Traveler frames," Edmas said, marveling at the skeletons of two shuttles hoisted on fixed lifts. The Swei Swee's original shells had long since crumbled under the continuous prodding and poking of engineers and techs.

"Dark travelers, Edmas," Alex replied. "These were gifts from the Libran Swei Swee. They were the engineering basis of our reproductions, which you help build today," he added. They threaded their way through empty workbenches toward the frames.

"We already have full-size models to test our spray technique," Edmas enthused.

"That we do, my young friend," Mickey replied.

Mickey crossed his arms and supported his chin with one hand. Edmas drew breath to speak, but a quick signal from Alex told him to wait.

"You gave me this idea, Alex, when you talked about spending credits to buy items that Harakens were easily producing," Mickey said, after staring at a traveler frame for a while. "If we look at the timeline for producing a single, finished traveler, we're talking about a lengthy process. Once the hulls are ready, we'll need the components. But if we haven't delivered any finished units, where are the credits coming from to buy the components? And, if we wait until we build the manufacturing capability, we're adding a huge amount of time until we complete the first traveler. My thought is this: Who says we have to assemble an entire traveler?"

Mickey felt Alex's eyes bore into his. Suddenly his good friend broke into a broad grin, and Mickey grinned back at him.

"We sell shells," Alex and Mickey yelled at each other simultaneously, and their laughter echoed off the bulkheads of the huge bay.

Edmas smiled at the men's antics, but his forehead was furrowed, and he looked at Cordelia for help.

<Patience, Edmas,> Cordelia sent to Edmas, <The final concept will soon take shape.> Cordelia marveled at the workings of human minds. A SADE could calculate the permutations of a traveler's cost at each stage of construction to determine its potential trade or sale value in mere ticks of time, but the creative leap to the idea of "selling shells" was truly a human exercise in thinking outside the box, as Alex called it.

"So, what do you think, Mickey, frames and shells only?" Alex asked.

"That's the way I figure it," Mickey replied. "Shells are the one element holding up the entire production line on Haraken. We trade or sell our shells for the components we need to complete travelers for us."

"Which means we can complete travelers for ourselves within six months instead of a year or more," Alex mused.

"I was going to object that the Haraken companies wouldn't have access to the interiors," Edmas said, a little embarrassed to confess his initial and erroneous thought, "But then it dawned on me that they can cut the hatches and access ports in any manner they choose."

Mickey clasped a big hand on Edmas' shoulder, and said, "Right you are, young man."

Alex turned to Cordelia, but she anticipated him. "We can run estimates as to the proportional value of a shell and frame to the remaining components, Alex. But how do we value Swei Swee labor, and the acceleration opportunity we're presenting to Harakens?"

"What was the backlog for travelers when we left?" Alex asked. This was one item the Exchange directors tracked carefully. The Exchange was heavily invested in companies that either produced components for grav-drive ships or were instrumental in assembling them.

"Approximately thirty-one years' worth," said Cordelia, smiling sweetly at the humans' dumbfounded expressions.

Mickey whistled slowly. Edmas and Jodlyne stared open-mouthed at each other, and Alex whispered, "Black space." Absolute quiet followed, as every entity considered the opportunity to sell traveler shells to fill thirty-one years of accumulated orders.

"Okay, we don't offer to sell the shells outright to Haraken," Alex said, breaking the silence. "The demand is an enormous number of credits waiting to be earned."

"Yes," Mickey exclaimed. "We go into business with Haraken companies."

"The greater profit margin could be negotiated with a consortium of Haraken companies, rather than individual agreements," Cordelia said, which gave Alex and Mickey pause.

"Okay ..." Alex replied, drawing out the moment to order his thoughts. "What if instead of pushing Haraken to form a collective that could exclude other companies in the future, we made a deal with the Assembly representatives. We tell them that we'll supply the government with frames and shells, and they'll have to negotiate contracts with the suppliers and fulfill the orders with the completed travelers. Haraken companies and the government make credits, and we're paid a portion of every sale."

"I like it," Mickey replied.

Alex glanced at Cordelia, who said, "It's the optimum arrangement for us and the social needs of Haraken. It's well considered, Alex. The SADEs will work to determine the value of our offering prior to negotiations."

"We'll need an organization for the agreement with the Assembly," Mickey said.

"Omnia Ships," Alex replied, with a smile.

"I have a thought too, Alex," Edmas said, and he was slightly intimidated when his seniors focused intently on him. "Anyway, I think it's worth mentioning."

Jodlyne nudged Edmas' elbow to encourage him.

"Well, Alex, you mentioned building a medium carrier. Was its purpose to transport the shells to Haraken?"

"Originally, no, Edmas," Alex replied. "The need for a carrier would have depended on which warships Tatia and her people selected and how many fighters those ships could carry. If I had my preference, we wouldn't have one. That said, when we started talking about delivering traveler hulls to Haraken, I thought the carrier a good idea for that purpose. Why?"

"I was asking myself why we should be responsible for transporting travelers to Haraken. I mean, why should we have to wait to build a carrier to deliver what Haraken companies are hungering to possess? Why not request Haraken send a carrier to load up every shell we've built? All we need to kick our process in gear are girders, metal-alloy nanites, and faux spray."

Edmas' mistake was to be standing between Alex and Mickey, who simultaneously slapped him on the back, congratulating him on his brilliant idea. Alex and Mickey did have the grace and the reflexes to catch the young Sol native, as each shot forward.

We were correct in our assumptions, Cordelia thought, watching the threesome grinning at one another. Wherever Alex went, he and his people generated economic opportunity. The Exchange and the SIF would be reaping huge returns for decades to come, if not longer, from their investment in Alex's expedition.

Alex and Cordelia left the engineers alone in the bay, and Mickey looked thoughtfully at Edmas and Jodlyne. "What we need to do, my friends," Mickey said, "is access the interviews that were completed with the Independents, and talk with Ophelia, Perrin, and Maynard to see who we can recruit. We need ship architects, engineers, techs, chemists, biochemists, and anyone else we think of who can help us design and build industrial ships and warships."

"What about the platform's construction?" Edmas asked.

"Recruit first," Mickey replied.

"Why are you listing the soft sciences?" Jodlyne asked.

"Recall several things that Alex said. Originally, he told Willem to consider what it would take to accommodate the Dischnya aboard our ships. Then he told Tatia that the count of Independents was less than he anticipated, and he suggested that Dischnya warriors could make up the crew shortfall. And now he's asked Emile to create a scent to allow the queens to travel with him."

"Where's he intending to go?" Jodlyne asked.

"Who knows? Besides Alex, maybe only Ser and Julien," Mickey replied. "But the point is, my young friends, if Alex has mentioned this several times, we better be prepared, which means we'll need help figuring out how to accommodate those warriors."

Edmas slowly shook his head at the incredulity of the thought. "One moment Alex is hugging a queen, and the next he's recruiting her warriors."

"That's our Alex … going where every human and SADE believes it's unwarranted to go."

"Do you think Emile will figure out how to make the queen's scent work?" Jodlyne asked.

Mickey sighed and placed a heavy arm around the shoulders of each of his young engineering partners to guide them toward the bay's exit. "This is the world of Alex. Don't ask if someone can or can't do something. Ask yourself how it can be done. That's what Alex is always doing. And if we're going to be contributors to this little expedition of his, then that's what we'll need to be doing."

* * *

When Emile requested transportation planetside from Cordelia, Julien took charge of making the arrangements for him. The biochemist's value had increased exponentially to Alex's expedition with the invention of the faux shell spray, and it only grew greater when Alex depended on him for a solution to extricate a nest's soma from their dependence on a queen.

A tiny connection between programs within Julien's kernel had become persistent, and he chose to act on it, initiating a query to the *Freedom*'s database to search the backgrounds of Daelon Independents who might be potential assistants for Emile.

Emile, accompanied by Jodlyne, boarded a traveler to find Julien, Étienne, and Alain waiting for them.

"Are we expecting trouble, Julien?" Jodlyne asked.

"Expecting it, no. Prepared for it, yes," Julien replied, and the twins smiled at her.

The traveler settled on the outskirts of Nyslara's nest, and the passengers continued to chat happily while they waited for the lookouts to summon the queen or wasat. As it was, both of them climbed out of the tunnel and used their long-legged gaits to close quickly on the ship.

After the brief greetings, Jodlyne uttered, "Uh-oh."

The others followed her gaze, and the queen cheerfully rubbed the small bulge in her belly.

"By my scent, I will be producing an heir," Nyslara said, and she gazed proudly at Pussiro, who rose slightly on his hind legs.

"Congratulations, Chona Nyslara and Wasat Pussiro," Julien said formally. "Dassata will be pleased to hear of your good fortune."

"Pardon, Nyslara," Emile said in his poor Dischnya. "Baby changed scent?"

"Emile wishes to understand how the pup you're expecting has changed your scent," Julien translated. Simultaneously, he sent the Dischnya phrase and its translation to the humans to help them with their education in the language.

"A queen's scent often changes," Nyslara replied. "First, when she comes of mating age; again, when she's fertile; and another, when she's expecting. The scent will be different still if one of the expected will be a female pup."

"How do these changes affect the soma?" Julien asked.

"Dischnya accept every scent change of their chona, but they are most content when they have a mature queen who is not carrying pups."

"What's the purpose of your visit, Julien?" Pussiro asked protectively.

"Dassata wishes to travel to Sawa and requests the company of one or more queens. The trip might involve many cycles of Nessila," Julien explained. The SADE didn't require Nyslara's reply to understand how his request was being received by the wasat. Pussiro's lips were rippling in agitation.

Nyslara touched her mate's hindquarters with the tip of her tail to calm him, and replied, "My soma would be greatly discomfited if I traveled any distance from our nest in my condition. I may not even visit your ships above."

<This is where Alex would say something about plan B,> Emile sent to Julien.

<No, Emile, this is where Alex would propose a plan B,> Julien replied drily.

"Dassata would not wish to see the Tawas Soma nest discomforted in any manner," Julien said, diplomatically. His answer had a calming effect on Pussiro. "Emile Billings," Julien said, indicating the biochemist, "is a man of the sciences. Dassata has asked him to discover a means by which a queen might leave the nest for an extended period of time and leave her scent for the soma."

"This is possible?" Nyslara asked.

Emile nodded enthusiastically, and Nyslara and Pussiro exchanged glances.

"What would Emile require?" Nyslara asked Julien.

"He would take small samples of breath, hair, skin, and oils from a queen to examine and duplicate, and he would require two of the queen's soma to act as test subjects, who would reside on a ship above for some number of cycles, but not enough to harm them," Julien replied.

"Could this scent you create, Julien, be given to another nest?" Pussiro asked.

"There is nothing to stop the deliberate spread of the scent to another nest, except the queens' commitment to the Fissla," Julien said. He could see where Pussiro's thoughts were headed. The wasat was worried that warriors from one nest would use their queen's scent to disturb or even take over the soma of another nest. It would be an act of aggression, contrary to the peace agreement.

"I imagine Dassata would not tolerate such behavior from a queen or her soma," Nyslara said.

"You imagine correctly, Chona Nyslara. He definitely would not," Julien replied, and he gazed pointedly at Pussiro.

"Who would hold these scents?' Pussiro asked, undeterred by Julien's implied promise.

"That would be up to each chona, whose scent we create. This is not planned for every queen," Julien explained.

Pussiro opened his muzzle, but another touch from Nyslara's tail halted him before he could ask his question.

"Dassata needs queens to guide him during his visit to Sawa," Nyslara said, thinking her way through the issue. "Yet, none of the chona have ever set claw on the home world. One queen would be as good as another, in that regard. More important, Dassata would need chona who would be willing to risk the trip and are ardent supporters of the new ways."

"Nyslara is correct in her analysis," Julien commented. "In that regard, I believe you're indicating that we should visit Sissya and Posnossa."

"You're insightful, Julien, as I would expect Dassata's close adviser to be," Nyslara replied. "However, I would add Homsaff and myself to your experiment."

When Emile heard the translation, he queried Julien. <I understood Homsaff is a juvenile?> he sent.

<That she is,> Julien replied.

"Emile requests to understand how Homsaff's immature state would be of help in his efforts to understand a mature queen's scent," Julien said.

Nyslara and Pussiro shared quick glimmers of recognition. Both of them were fascinated by how Dassata's soma could speak their thoughts to one another. They had discussed many times how this technology might aid the Dischnya. "Explain to Emile, Julien, that, after me, there is no fiercer supporter of Dassata than Homsaff. She would risk much to be part of his efforts."

Julien paused and tilted his head to focus. Then he said to Nyslara, "We wonder why you would want to be tested when your scent will change after the birth of your pups."

"The soma would live on your ship while Emile experiments with them," Nyslara said thoughtfully. "Recall, Julien, no other Dischnya, but Pussiro and I, have set claw aboard your ships above. At least, Simlan and Hessan, who I would volunteer, are familiar with your kind. They will calm the other soma."

"Wise advice, Nyslara," Julien acknowledged.

"It's in every Dischnya's favor to see Dassata succeed with his plans," Nyslara commented.

"So it is for all of us," Julien agreed.

It was an insightful moment for Nyslara. She had perceived the Dischnya as chasing after Dassata and his soma. Now, she considered that Dassata's soma were chasing their leader too.

"You have four sample sets to collect Emile … Nyslara, Sissya, Posnossa, and Homsaff," Julien said to the biochemist. "Chona Nyslara, we appreciate your advice. I've informed Dassata of your condition, and he requests that I inform you of his sincere wishes for the safe birth of your pups."

Jodlyne dropped the sampling kit to the ground and unpacked a set of tiny vacuum tubules. Pussiro barked a command to the lookout, who yipped in reply and ducked below.

By the time Emile and Jodlyne had collected their samples under Pussiro's watchful eye, Simlan and Hessan came running from the tunnel entrance.

Nyslara gave the two warriors their instructions, adding, "Don't let the alien technology overwhelm you. You'll be safe, and, if you're patient, you might enjoy your time above." However, she couldn't resist a jibe. "But don't let their pallets eat you."

When Pussiro's warriors turned wide-eyed stares on their wasat, he shook his head in negation. They glanced back at Nyslara, and the queen chuffed, her lips wrinkling in humor.

While Jodlyne coded and packed the samples, Julien nodded politely, and the group headed for the traveler.

Watching the aliens and her soma retreat to the ship, Nyslara said, "Julien spoke to Dassata, who is far above us, with his mind, while he was conversing with us."

"The metal soma are indeed intriguing, my queen. I wonder if the Dischnya could ever possess some of them."

"You're thinking in the old ways, my mate. You don't possess ones like Julien or Z. However they're created, they have a will of their own. It's their choice who earns their allegiance, and you should note well, they give it to the likes of Dassata."

Nyslara turned and strode back to the tunnel entrance. She was hungry again. As the queen walked, she wondered when the time would come that she no longer had to descend into the ground's darkness.

* * *

Following the collection of two warriors from each nest and samples from the other queens, Emile and Jodlyne's traveler landed aboard the *Rêveur*, and the soma were greeted by Miriam and Glenn, who were assigned by Alex to be responsible for managing the Dischnya.

The eight warriors descended the ship's hatch steps carefully and were disturbed to discover a deep, dark cavern on their exit. When their great clawed feet found no purchase on the metal-alloy deck, they cringed. A warrior's safety depended on his ability to move quickly, and the hard surface denied them purchase.

For Miriam, the assignment of translation for Emile wouldn't interfere with her work, which entailed developing detailed engineering plans for the various projects. When Alex contacted her, he'd asked if she could recommend a human to accompany her. The SADEs were aware that Alex was constantly mixing humans and SADEs on work details. It was apparent to them that he was doing all he could to prevent the formation of another Sadesville.

Miriam immediately thought of quiet, introverted Glenn for her human companion. The fact that he'd asked her to dance, and, later, gave into her lead rather than quit in embarrassment, told Miriam that there was much more to the human than met the eye.

In this case, Miriam understood a secondary reason that Alex requested the presence of a human. Willem and Julien had detected the confusion on the Dischnya's part when their sensitive noses failed to pick up animal scents from the SADEs.

Miriam and Glenn led the warriors to their cabins and pointed out that their four domiciles were clustered together. The doors were locked open and privacy curtains were hung across the openings to make the warriors feel more comfortable.

"Emile is expecting them in the lab now," Miriam said to Glenn.

"I think that can wait," Glenn replied. "I've heard more than one stomach growling. An early, midday meal would do more to calm them, and it's a good time. The meal room is empty."

"I'll inform Emile," Miriam replied, as Glenn gestured to the warriors to follow him, pantomiming eating with his fingers.

In the meal room, Miriam seated the Dischnya at a table close to the dispensers. She had Julien's notes on what Nyslara and Pussiro had enjoyed on their visits, and she programmed the menus accordingly. Then Miriam and Glenn sat back and watched the warriors demolish the food on their dishes.

At first, the Dischnya had sniffed the plates and eyed one another. Then the early, tentative dips of fingers into the meal resulted in a rash of gulping, as large chunks of food were thrown down their throats. To finish their meals, the warriors held the plates to their faces and sucked and licked them clean.

<A most impressive display of appetite,> Miriam sent to Glenn, <second only to Dassata.>

<Thorough, if not pretty,> Glenn sent back.

The warriors eyed the food dispensers with interest, but Miriam informed them that it was time to do their queens' bidding. Her comment quickly changed the Dischnya's expressions, and they hopped up from the table. Miriam had taken the opportunity to discuss with Willem the various techniques she might employ to motivate and manage the warriors.

While the group walked through the ship, crew members and Daelon passengers were notified by Miriam to clear the way so that the warriors would be less likely to be disturbed. Simlan and Hessan walked behind Miriam with confidence, whether they felt it or not. This gave the six other warriors, who followed Nyslara's soma, the courage to stay in step. It was known that Nyslara's nest had extensive contact with the aliens. Glenn protected the group's rear from inadvertent contact.

In the lab, Jodlyne took samples from each of the warriors. They would serve as a baseline to help Emile discover what made a queen's scent different from her soma. Unfortunately, for Emile, his research would prove to not be as simple as he hoped.

After the samples were taken, Miriam and Glenn led the warriors to a conference room with a holo-vid installed at the center of the table. It was Glenn's idea to entertain the Dischnya, but not in a passive manner. When the warriors weren't eating, sleeping, or being tested with Emile's new concoctions, they were in school, and the education became bidirectional.

Glenn was given an opportunity to practice his Dischnya language skills, and the warriors learned to use the holo-vid for myriad uses, including viewing their planet from above. Miriam procured a portable holo-vid and carried it around with her, while Glenn took the warriors on a tour of the ship, explaining many aspects of the vessel in a simple overview.

When Miriam questioned Glenn about the reasons for the tours and education, he replied, "I've understood that Alex once challenged Willem to find a means of enabling the Dischnya to crew his ships, and his senior people have been saying Alex told them the same thing, although they don't seem pleased by the idea. I thought I would try to discover how well the warriors might adapt to shipboard life."

"And what are you perceiving, Glenn?" Miriam asked, fascinated by this line of thought.

"Well, you'll notice that they're entirely comfortable with this ship … cabins, corridors, and meal room, except for the metal decking in the bay. I think the *Rêveur* mimics their tunnels and rooms. However, I think we should prevent showing the Dischnya any view of the stars and space. That might be going a step too far."

Testing the warriors hadn't occurred to Miriam, and Glenn's comments made her examine his instruction of the Dischnya in another light, and she uploaded her entire record of Glenn's activities to the *Freedom*'s controller and earmarked the files for Alex, Julien, and Cordelia.

Eventually, crew crossed the Dischnya's paths, and the warriors nodded greetings to the men, and stepped aside courteously for the women. Despite warnings to the contrary, the crew manifested the occasional faux pas where it concerned soma courtesy. It was Simlan and Hessan, who came to the rescue, baring their teeth in response to a crew member's smile and explaining the human gesture to the other warriors.

Those early mistakes by the crew soon ended any attempt by them to smile at the Dischnya. The crew's pleasantries had elicited the flashing of eight deadly looking displays of fierce, sharp teeth. Unfortunately, the crew's renewed commitment to the guidelines came a little late. Now, the warriors wished to impress the aliens with their cultural knowledge and bared their canines at everyone they passed.

-12-
Face of Omnia

Once the warship designs were refined, Mickey and his team built test models. The harmonics data results were used by the SADEs to refine the models, and a second test set was built. The process continued until the later iterations of each design displayed minimal improvements in the shells' efficiency of converting the input of a grav-wave generator to energy.

When Mickey pronounced a shell design complete, the SADEs on his team turned their attentions to designing the interiors, concentrating first on the dual-drive engines and the power cells, which needed to supply both the grav engines and weaponry when in system.

After the data on the ships' capabilities was provided, it brought Tatia and her people into the picture. The admiral and her commanders were discussing their ship preferences in a *Freedom* conference room. The table was populated with holo-vids, displaying the various ship models and the early data projections. Interestingly, the only individual who remained seated was the admiral. The commanders, who were leaning against the bulkheads or pacing, had broken into three camps, arguing over the mix of warships that should be constructed.

The most vocal of the commanders was Svetlana, naturally enough. She was fervently making a case for a squadron of Trident warships.

"Why are you so adamant about the Trident series, Svetlana?" Darius asked.

"Why aren't you?" Svetlana retorted.

"Because the fewer of your monstrous tri-hulls we build, the more less-powerful ships we can build. More ships make a better defensive net," Darius fired back.

"A better defensive net?" Svetlana scoffed, incredulous at the thought. "Is that what you think Alex is doing, building an enormous defense shield?" Svetlana demanded, leaning stiffened arms on the back of a conference chair. "Well, is it?" she pressed, and punctuated her question by focusing on Tatia.

Tatia had abstained from the discussion, because she wasn't sure of her own opinion. She excelled at designing attack strategies when she knew the target. In this instance, Tatia and her commanders were asked to design a fleet in a fog of information.

Several commanders spoke at once in reply to Svetlana's challenge, but Tatia requested quiet, holding up a finger and saying, "Wait one."

<Greetings, Tatia,> Renée sent pleasantly in response to Tatia's comm.

<I need to know, Renée, about Alex and the sphere,> Tatia sent perfunctorily. Her request produced an awkward silence, a rarity for Renée.

<It's not good, Tatia.>

<How not good, Renée? I need to know.>

There was another pause, and Tatia could imagine Renée was wrestling with her conscience as to whether to divulge personal information about her partner.

<He's having dreams about the Nua'll sphere. It's gone so far as to interrupt his sleep.>

<Thank you for telling me, Renée. I needed to know, and I will keep your confidence.>

<I know you will, Tatia,> Renée replied, and closed the comm.

"Okay, people," Tatia announced in a command voice, "take your seats." She waited until everyone was settled, then she added, "Do not presume a defensive posture in your ship selections. Anticipate building an attack force of considerable power and maneuverability."

"For what purpose, Admiral?" Ellie asked.

"We'll be hunting the Nua'll," Tatia replied firmly.

Darius was about to question the concept of designing a fleet to attack an enemy who might not exist, but the other commanders were quiet, some even nodding their heads, having accepted the admiral's pronouncement.

<What did I miss?> Darius sent to Deirdre.

<Tatia reached out to someone … Renée or Julien, probably,> Deirdre sent back.

<About what?> Darius queried.

<Wanting to know what Alex's intuition was telling him. Guess we have our answer. Alex thinks the Nua'll and their spheres are out there.>

* * *

Alex sat comfortably behind his desk in the owner's suite aboard the *Freedom*. His eyes were closed, but he wasn't sleeping. Instead, he was monitoring the progress of various production teams via the SADEs.

It wasn't that Alex was checking up on his human compatriots. It was simply that observations and progress reports were more thorough and more efficiently shared by the SADEs, and it prevented him from interrupting his human workers' focus.

As for the SADEs, they were pleased to be of service, often linking with other SADEs on the team to give Alex a better overview. They went so far as to record crucial moments in their phases and store them on the *Freedom*'s controller for Alex's viewing.

Alex opened a vid recorded by Trixie. Standing on a second continent of Omnia, in the middle of the grassy plains, a geologist, who was among the Daelon Independents, had shared details with the SADEs, as to the mineral formations they would need to seek for the materials necessary to build the Dischnya's structures. The SADEs had grabbed their ground-sounding equipment and exploratory tools and spread out so fast that the geologist could only gawk in confusion at his assistant.

The SADEs located a heavy granite-like formation near the surface. Trixie organized the construction of small, temporary accommodations at the site and excavation had begun. Mickey and Julien designed nanites that could be mixed with the granulated mineral to form slurry. Within a half hour after pouring, a solid slab was set up and removed.

In the meantime, Miriam's report recorded her efforts to design the processes by which their available equipment could be used to process the rock, mix in the nanites solution, and pour the slurry into slab forms. As the first slabs set up, slings laid at the bottom of the forms were hitched to the underside of travelers and lifted free. It was the same method that Mickey and Julien had devised for moving two dark travelers aboard the *Freedom*, twenty years ago.

As one step of any project became a routine operation, it freed humans and SADEs to move to new assignments. Paying heed to Alex's primary motivation, Cordelia ensured the new projects received a fresh mix of individuals, guaranteeing that no one group stayed together. Day by day, she witnessed the small changes evident in the way that humans and SADEs treated one another — interdependence slowly replaced what, at best, could have been called wariness. *There will be no Sadesville on Omnia, Alex,* she thought.

One group, to whom Alex had no direct access, was scattered across several mining posts out by Celus-6. Ben was in constant communication with his people, and he did transmit daily summaries to the *Freedom*, which Cordelia dutifully logged and linked the files to Alex.

* * *

Alerted by her advisors, who watched the skies via the nest's telescope, Nyslara and Pussiro emerged from a tunnel to observe the landing of a strange ship. With heavy engines blasting, it landed at the edge of her nest. One of Dassata's silent shuttles landed nearby, disgorged a host of his soma, and left again.

The individuals from the shuttle spread out and used tools to measure the ground and plant small devices into the soil. Then the odd ship transformed before the Dischnya's eyes, bending, groaning, and screeching, as it reshaped itself. Massive, metal treads bit into the ground and drove a wide tool in front of the machine across the ground, like a female's snout searching for tasty tubers.

During the course of the day, hunters, warriors, females, and pups came out of the tunnels to watch their new home grow. Once the ground was cleared, the excavator launched skyward with a roar of jets to resume its work at Trixie's construction site. Then shuttles arrived, dangling great pieces of flat-shaped rocks, and the Dischnya yipped and chortled at the alien's display of power and technology.

Slabs were laid and SADEs joined them with an injection of nanites-slurry into the crevices. By the day's end, the Omnians had completed the domicile's floor and begun the walls.

When Nessila set, Nyslara expected the work on the nest's new home to cease, but reports from the lookouts told her it continued. Dassata's soma had erected bright lights to illuminate the entire area, and the silent shuttles continued to arrive.

Curious, Pussiro and she ventured close and confirmed what Nyslara surmised when Dassata's soma passed close. Those continuing to work had no scent, except for the plains' grasses and soil. They were Dassata's metal soma.

Before Nyslara turned to her pallet for the evening, Pussiro paid her a visit. He'd yet to move into her quarters, but with Dassata's plans and the nearby construction, Pussiro had deemed the time inappropriate to transfer his mates and pups to another, although two sub-commanders, who were without mates, had asked for the honor.

"Their efforts continue, my queen," Pussiro said, squatting next to Nyslara's pallet where she lay.

"I was thinking of our future, my mate," Nyslara replied.

"Of ours?" Pussiro asked.

"That too," Nyslara chortled, "but, most important, of the future of the Dischnya. Dassata's plan to borrow the queens for his journey to Sawa has led me to think that my dreams have been small. When my heir takes the robe of power from me, there may no longer be a nest for her to rule."

Pussiro's head snapped up in alarm, and Nyslara commanded he sit beside her. She wrapped her tail around his waist and squeezed gently.

"We are of the old ways, my mate," Nyslara said softly. "Dassata will change the lives of the Dischnya forever, and I can't say that I regret that. We would have died in these dark tunnels in another generation or two.

Dassata will lift the Dischnya into the light and into space. Much will change, but for now, we have each other and a bright tomorrow."

Pussiro looked unconvinced of the wondrousness of the future Nyslara described. She chuffed, pulled his head toward her with her tail, and licked his muzzle with her long tongue to ease the deep frown in his forehead.

In the morning, after a full meal, Nyslara collected Pussiro, and they hurried to observe the progress. The work had never stopped. The structure was now fully enclosed, and individuals were busy cutting openings in the walls. What Nyslara envisioned, the creation of forty-one new homes for the nests over the course of many seasons, would probably be completed before her pups were born.

The rudimentary structure that Nyslara saw forming fell far short of Willem's final design. The bare roof had yet to be planted with plains' grasses, and the walls hadn't received their solar cells. Shields would cover the face of the panels when night fell or gritty winds blew. Power cells would be hidden in sealed chambers that vented to the roof. In time, the Dischnya would be trained to care for the technological prowess of their structures, but no one knew how long that might take.

* * *

Ben Diaz was ecstatic. His mining teams had confirmed the *Sojourn*'s telemetry survey of plentiful deposits of the moons and asteroids surrounding Celus-6 of the minerals and compounds that they sought. Ben's team had cleared the *Freedom*'s bays of stored ore excavators and processing machines, which were left there years ago after using them to help launch Haraken's manufacturing and housing base.

During the early days at Celus-6 and its near satellites, Ben oversaw the completion of temporary housing for the teams and the establishment of the first mining sites, ore recovery plants, and transportation system. The central cavities of four huge barges were filled with raw aggregate from the moons or asteroids, destined for the processing plants, and the barges' exterior tanks contained frozen gasses.

Each evening, Ben would return to his cramped personal quarters to enjoy the company of his partner, Simone Turin. He was pleased that Simone insisted on being given a day job, and he offloaded the accounting of the ore and compound processing quantities to her. It did free him to focus on the production processes.

One evening, Ben arrived at the living quarters and asked Simone for the latest totals. When she updated him, he swore briefly and then said, "I'm sorry, Simone, I should have told you that we need to give Captain Cordelia a few days warning for her to schedule a trip out here with the city-ship. Based on those figures, our tanks will be full by the end of tomorrow's second shift."

"And the *Freedom* will arrive here the following morning," Simone replied nonchalantly. "I received a message from Cordelia six days ago. She'd analyzed our production trends and anticipated you would need her to offload our accumulated materials."

Ben grinned and picked up his partner, hoisting her high in the air. When he lowered Simone, he kissed her, and she threw her arms tightly around his neck. Ben played some music over their implants, swaying them gently to the music, while Simone's toes dangled 40 centimeters above the ground.

Despite Ben's formidable skills as a mining engineer, he had been an abominable adopter of his implant. It was the singular reason that he encountered his partner, the diminutive Simone. He blocked her exit from a meal room, because he couldn't use his implant's location app to determine that someone was about to pass through the doorway from the other side. Simone had taken the soft-spoken New Terran aside and helped him employ his implant's basic apps.

One day, two decades ago, in celebration of his newly acquired proficiency, Ben connected privately to Simone in his cabin and held his first complete implant conversation. Simone applauded his efforts and then heard music playing in her mind. Ben held up his arms to Simone in a dancer's invitation, but she was unsure what the gesture meant. Recognizing Simone's confusion, Ben swept her into his arms and danced her around the small cabin. That was the day Simone knew that she would never leave her gentle giant's side.

* * *

Fifty-six days after Ben established his mining sites near Celus-6, the *Freedom*, loaded with the miners' cumulative output, was headed back to Omnia's orbit. The processing plants had poured the refined metal-alloy into girders for the orbital platform, as specified by the engineers. Small construction boats, piloted by humans, offloaded the girders and hauled them into position. SADEs, ensconced in extravehicular activity (EVA) suits to protect them from the cold vacuum of space, used their strength and visual acuity to align the girders and pin them in place.

That the SADEs required a minimum of air, except to flush the heat from their suits, meant they could work much longer than humans before requiring new tanks. Not to mention, the SADEs simply changed their tanks and hurried back to work, while after a single shift, humans returned to the *Freedom* to change pilots in the boats.

The *Freedom* had offloaded the full tanks from Ben's mining barges and left his crew empty ones. The full tanks were anchored to the orbital's skeleton of girders for eventual processing or consumption.

* * *

Emile and Jodlyne's first order of business with the samples they collected was to identify every compound. Interestingly, the warrior's samples were nearly identical, enough so, that Emile considered the differences insignificant. Not so, in comparison to the queen's samples. Close to 90 percent of the compounds were similar to the warriors', but the remainder were unique and to each queen too. Their focus for the next days was identifying the right mixture of those unique compounds, which told the soma their queen was present.

Unfortunately, Emile's elementary mistake was in assuming that the compounds he identified as unique to the queens were all that he had to reproduce to elicit the proper response from the warriors. His first test, after duplicating Nyslara's compounds, drew distasteful snorts from Simlan and Hessan, and Emile didn't bother processing the other queens' samples and testing their warriors.

At morning meal, Emile and Jodlyne sat eating and discussing the previous days' abysmal failure.

"Detecting the scent triggers of a queen should be a simple thing to resolve," Emile complained. "We've isolated the queens' special compounds and combined them in several ways, but the response is always the same."

"Not always, Emile. Sometimes they sneeze and sometimes they snort," Jodlyne replied, trying to tease Emile and cheer him up, but her efforts fell on deaf ears. Jodlyne decided a direct approach was necessary. "Aren't you always saying, Emile, that trying to match the outcome to your assumptions leads to failure. What if we're looking at this whole thing the wrong way?" Jodlyne replied.

"Obviously, we are, Jodlyne, but then I'm left with no idea how to proceed," Emile grumped.

"Well, I was thinking that the problem might lie with the samples we collected." When the biochemist started to object, Jodlyne raised her hand to finish. "Emile, hear me out. The final arbiter of our manufactured scent is the Dischnya's sensitive nose, correct?"

"True," Emile agreed.

"So, we're supposed to believe that every individual in that warren of tunnels is supposed to pass by the queen every few days and take a whiff of her?"

"I would presume that isn't possible." Emile replied, frowning.

"Now, add to that another consideration. Nyslara spent a considerable number of days aboard the *Freedom* then returned planetside with no ill effects on her people."

Emile placed his utensil down and leaned on his forearms. He was intrigued by Jodlyne's line of reasoning. "What's your idea, Jodlyne?" he asked.

"I think the queen gives off a scent that impregnates everything around her, including her people, and it's taken up by her soma, which eases some sort of primordial need. But, the effect fades over time, and a fresh dose from the queen must be inhaled. This leads me to believe that the scent isn't created by the unique compounds she possesses, which we've isolated and have been working to reproduce. And my final point, Emile, is that we need the specialized compounds and the base ones to create a queen's specific scent."

"We tried that sequence, early in the testing, Jodlyne. Remember, it had no effect on the warriors," Emile replied.

"I remember, but I think the critical element we've been missing is timing. It's the simplest explanation. We created Nyslara's compound for Simlan and Hessan, but Glenn was touring them for his schooling and afterwards they went to evening meal. We didn't test them until late the following day."

"Ah … I see what you're driving at, my young associate," Emile replied, his eyes lighting up. "We're thinking there is at least some amount of shelf life to our mixtures. But, it might be the queen's immediate release of her scent that's the key and calms some aspect of the Dischnya physiology until their bodies need another dose."

"Precisely, as Julien loves to say," Jodlyne enthused. "This means we'll need to prepare our solutions from the full list of compounds we've isolated from the queens, seal them, and present them to the warriors, as soon as possible," Jodlyne said, summarizing their next steps. Suddenly hungry, she dug into her food, anxious to finish and get to the lab.

"Agreed," Emile replied, almost absentmindedly. But rather than finish his food, he sat quietly, his mind already at work in the lab.

It took a few tries before Emile and Jodlyne hit on a successful test. The trick was to form the base compounds that were shared by the queen and the soma, allow a short period of maturation time, and then add the queen's unique ingredients. The final concoction was capped and presented to the warriors within hours afterwards.

Emile still wasn't sure which compound or compounds the warriors were reacting to, but, on the successful test, Emile released the stopper on a vial behind Simlan and Hessan, who sat patiently waiting for the experiment to begin. Jodlyne wafted the air over the vial toward the warriors, who, in response, jumped up, spun around, and came to attention, their eyes scanning the lab for Nyslara's location.

Jodlyne giggled and when the two warriors focused on her, she pointed to the small container in her hand.

Simlan reached out a dark-nailed, furred hand for the small glass tube, which Jodlyne gave him. He sniffed it, and said, "Nyslara."

Hessan leaned and stuck his muzzle over the vial. "Nyslara with pups," he added.

* * *

The proof of Emile's work was too critical for Alex not to personally witness. He couldn't afford to endanger an entire nest if the compounds Emile created weren't absolutely reliable. When Emile finished describing how they had discovered the answer, Alex asked, "Do you have fresh samples for each queen?"

"Yes," Jodlyne replied, hurrying over to a small rack with labeled vials in it.

"Excellent," Alex replied, "and, please, provide me with some sort of dummy sample."

"We have some of the base mixture, which is common to every individual in a nest," Emile suggested.

"That'll do nicely," Alex replied. "Add it to a vial, just like the ones in this rack."

Alex turned to leave the lab with the samples, and Emile and Jodlyne followed, but Alex halted them. "Stay here, please. This won't take long."

At Alex's request, Miriam and Glenn returned the warriors to their cabins, and Alex visited each pair, guided by a link with Miriam, identifying which cabins held which nest's warriors. First, Alex held out the base sample, which elicited shrugs or some other simple reactions from the warriors. Then he held out the vial corresponding to the warriors' queen, and the result was always the same — a snap to attention and eyes searching for a queen.

Alex returned to the lab, smiling. "It was a successful confirmation of your results, Emile and Jodlyne. Please, forgive me for needing to prove the quality of your work, but the peace would be at risk if nests were endangered, because I took their queens with me and the compounds failed.

"Understood, Alex," Emile replied.

"So, here are your marching orders, people," Alex announced. "Number one, I need you to relocate your lab to the *Freedom*. Number two, I need you to produce a large quantity of these mixtures."

"That won't work, Alex," Jodlyne interrupted. "The compounds have to be released soon after they're made. We've discovered the key is to ensure the scent is fresh."

"Interesting," Alex replied thoughtfully. "Okay, after your lab is relocated, we'll need to perform site tests for three queens. Exclude Nyslara. How do you intend to distribute the scents?"

"I'm not sure of that, yet," Emile replied. "Not having detailed knowledge of the tunnels ... the extent of their reach, air circulation, et cetera. I would welcome your advice on this matter."

"Don't look to me, Emile," Alex said laughing. "I've never been belowground, but it looks like Jodlyne and you are about to be. Visit Nyslara's tunnels first to study the tunnel system in detail and figure out your dispersal system. Then visit the tunnel systems of our young queens to ensure there's nothing unusual about them. When you're ready to deploy your tests, I'll invite Posnossa, Sissya, and Homsaff aboard. We're aware the queens stayed at the first Fissla for seventeen days before they became anxious. So, to be safe, you'll have to run the test for twenty-four days to ensure the efficacy of your substance and the efficiency of your dispersal mechanisms.

When Alex left, Emile stared at Jodlyne. "I thought traveling with Alex would be an adventure," Emile said. "I have to admit that my imagination pales when compared to our reality. The idea of investigating these tunnels leaves me with the feeling that I should have stayed on Haraken."

"Relax, Emile. You'll be with an expert. On the space station, tunnel rats had to crawl the entire time through the ventilation system. It'll be a joy to explore these tunnels standing up."

-13-
Young Queens

Emile, Jodlyne, Julien, and the twins exited their traveler and met Nyslara and Pussiro at the tunnel entrance to the Tawas Soma nest. The eight warriors, who had been the test subjects aboard the *Rêveur*, had been returned to their nests days earlier.

After Julien explained their purpose, the Dischnya quickly disappeared down the tunnel hatch. Étienne and Alain followed and then Julien. But Emile froze at the entrance, his hand on the hatch.

Realizing Emile had understated his concerns about descending underground, Jodlyne sought to encourage him with a tart remark, "You can hold my hand if you wish, Emile."

Emile glared at his young assistant, but her comment achieved its purpose. Goaded into action, Emile hesitantly climbed down into the lookout's small room, but his claustrophobia worsened as he exited the lookout room, illuminated by the shaft of Celus' light, and stepped into the darker, main tunnel.

Jodlyne recognized the phobia. Many orphans aboard Sol's orbital station, where she grew up, wanted to join the tunnel rats, who crawled through the vent shafts to attack the station's militia. But a significant number of teens were rejected when they froze mere meters into the station's dark, close air vents where only glow strips marked the way.

Sympathy overwhelmed Jodlyne, and she slipped an arm through Emile's, whispering, "You and I are taking a late-night stroll. The stars are occluded by rain clouds, but it's a beautiful evening." She sent some of her favorite images of storms in the night, stealing silently over the ocean toward Espero and lit by Haraken's moons.

Emile gave Jodlyne a shaky smile and concentrated on her images. He let her guide him while he concentrated on controlling his fear. He was failing to do so, when he recalled a different image — that of Alex lying on a medical table, the side of his head swathed in a gel to allow drainage from his injured skull. *If you can't support Alex, maybe you should go home,* Emile thought and anger flooded through him, sweeping away the fear, for now.

The group toured the tunnel, and Emile, Jodlyne, and Julien collected data on the tunnel layout and airflow. They walked the tunnels for two hours, and Emile and Jodlyne were flabbergasted by the extent of their convolution and complexity.

The tour completed, Jodlyne signaled Julien to lead them directly to an exit, and Emile brushed past everyone, including a surprised lookout, to gain the bright daylight.

"Not like the dark," Jodlyne explained to Nyslara in her abbreviated command of the Dischnya language.

"We not like the dark either," Nyslara replied, imitating Jodlyne, which caused Julien to smile to himself.

Up top, Emile made some calculations with Julien's help, and he updated an app on a device attached to a small container, which he showed to Nyslara. Without a proficient command of the Dischnya language, Emile spoke through Julien, who explained to Nyslara that the soma of the young queens, while they were gone, would be responsible for turning the device on and walking through the central corridors at a pace Emile demonstrated. Julien explained that the individual carrying the device need not enter the rooms. The doorways' curtains wouldn't prevent the scent from penetrating. The SADE added that the procedure should be carried out during the night, while the soma slept, and the device would be replenished every sixth day by Dassata's soma.

When Julien finished the translation, Emile asked in his poor Dischnya, "Wasats can do … no mistakes?" The biochemist was forced to pull back from Pussiro's snarl.

Despite Emile and Jodlyne's shock at the wasat's aggressive gesture, Julien and Nyslara exchanged amused expressions, and the queen's tail touched her mate on the hindquarters to indicate he should control his temper.

"A little knowledge seems dangerous, no matter whose hands carry it," Nyslara said, her lips rippling in amusement.

"I believe, Ser Billings, you owe Pussiro an apology," Julien said.

Nyslara noticed the wrinkling of the scientist's forehead and said, "Emile, do you do as Dassata directs?"

"Yes, Nyslara," Emile replied, when he heard the translation.

"Do you perform these actions true to his requests?" Nyslara continued.

When Julien helped with Nyslara's words, Emile replied, "Yes."

"And so it's the same for a nest's soma on hearing their queen's commands," Nyslara replied. "You will explain your requirements to the young queens. She'll direct a sub-commander to carry out your instructions, which he will do without fail."

Nyslara's explanation, which Julien provided, made Emile realize the depth of his insult. He turned to Pussiro and offered a leader's salute, as he'd been taught by the Méridiens, touching his hand to heart and dipping his head.

Pussiro was mollified by Emile's gesture, but he stood proud, accepting the apology as his due.

Nyslara noted Emile's head stayed bowed, and she glanced at Julien, who tipped his head down and directed his eyes toward Pussiro. Once again, the queen's long whiplike tail was put to use when she tapped the back of Pussiro's head with its tip.

Pussiro stared quizzically at his queen, who nodded toward Emile. With a huff, Pussiro acquiesced to Nyslara's request, although he still considered himself the injured party and, therefore, wasn't required to display any deference. Nonetheless, he nodded, which brought the scientist's head upright.

"I think each of our soma will require more time to become familiar with the other's ways, Julien," Nyslara said, chortling.

* * *

Nyslara's pregnancy prevented her from going to Alex, so he dropped planetside to visit her, with Emile and Jodlyne in tow. It was a sign of quieter times that Alex exited the traveler by himself and met Nyslara and Pussiro at the tunnel entrance. The threesome spoke for almost two hours about Sawa. The Dischnya knew much of their home world's history, but nearly nothing of its present circumstances.

When Alex thanked the pair for their assistance, Nyslara asked, "Do you leave for Sawa soon, Dassata?"

"Yes, once Emile's tests prove successful," Alex replied.

"Take your metal soma and the pair who guard you, Dassata. I don't think you will find Sawa hospitable, even walking in the company of queens."

After the shuttle lifted, Nyslara continued to stare into the bright sky.

"What worries you, my queen?" Pussiro asked.

"The Dischnya's future depends on Dassata. Yet, he hungers to find the sphere, a source of great danger. Finding it might mean his life, and that could end the Dischnya's future."

"Do you not think his soma will continue to build on this planet?"

"What happens to a nest when the queen dies without an heir?" Nyslara replied, and turned to descend below.

Alex's traveler stopped at the nests of Sissya, Homsaff, and Posnossa, in that order. With Alex's help, Emile explained to each queen how to distribute the solution. The wasats presented their sub-commanders, who would be responsible for the process, and Emile was introduced to each one and repeated his directions. When each sub-commander acknowledged his instructions, the nest's queen and wasat boarded the traveler.

* * *

With three young queens and their wasats aboard, Alex's traveler landed in an empty bay aboard the *Freedom*. This was intentional on Alex's part. He signaled everyone to exit the ship and the bay, while he stood in the aisle beside the queens. Posnossa, Sissya, and the wasats were calm, but Homsaff's twitching tail indicated her eagerness to start.

The Dischnya would be hosted aboard the *Freedom* for a period of twenty-four days, while the tests ran. It would also give Alex an opportunity to see how the queens and their wasats adapted to a ship's environment. The trip to Sawa, the investigation on planet, and the return trip might involve a much longer period of time.

Planetside, the SADEs set up simple comm devices outside a lookout hatch at the nests of the three queens. They were protected by small enclosures whose sides were layered with solar panels. The sub-commanders at the three nests need only press an overly large button and a call would be sent to Cordelia, indicating which nest was requesting contact with their queen.

A fourth comm device was installed for Nyslara. The Tawas Soma calls would be routed directly to Alex through any controller.

After Alex's people exited the bay's airlock, he led the Dischnya off the traveler. Their reactions were as expected. The metal-alloy deck and the cavernous space disconcerted everyone, except Homsaff, who walked around seeking purchase for her claws. Alex had no sooner led them into the airlock than Homsaff spoke her first request.

"Where are those who drive the ship?" Homsaff asked.

Pleased that at least one queen was taking an active role in learning about her new surroundings, Alex led the Dischnya to the bridge. It took a little while to reach the bridge, because the bright, wide corridors, the lift, and myriad other items warranted Homsaff's individual attention.

While the group negotiated the *Freedom*, Alex signaled Miriam and Glenn to meet him on the bridge. He'd learned that the pair had done a wonderful job escorting and schooling the eight warriors during Emile's workup of the queens' scents.

Once on the bridge, Alex introduced the Dischnya queens to Miriam, Glenn, and Cordelia.

"What does captain mean?" Homsaff asked Cordelia.

"It means I'm in charge of the ship," Cordelia replied.

"You drive the ship?" Homsaff asked, craning her neck to the left and right of Cordelia's head.

"What do you search for, Chona Homsaff?" Glenn asked.

"Where is the captain's gourd?" Homsaff asked, turning to Glenn.

Alex's people were aware of the story of Homsaff and the pilot's helmet.

"I need no gourd, Homsaff. I drive the ship with my mind," Cordelia replied, tapping her temple.

Queens and wasats alike opened their mouths in awe. Landing in the monstrous bay and walking for a quarter hour to reach the ship's bridge, they had experienced some of the ship's awesome size, and the thought that Dassata's soma could move the ship with her mind was stunning. But young Homsaff wasn't deterred for long, and she moved on to her next request.

"We are high above our world, are we not … among the stars?" Homsaff asked, looking around at her audience for confirmation.

"The stars are far away," Alex explained. "But we are above your world in what my soma call space."

"Can we go see this space?" Homsaff asked.

<Careful, people,> Alex sent. <Obviously, this queen's level of curiosity will tax us, but I'm interested to see how well we can encourage her. So be careful and encouraging in your responses.>

"Homsaff, space is a dangerous place," Cordelia replied. "It is extremely cold and there is no air to breathe. We are careful to keep our ship's doors closed to keep our warmth and our air inside."

Alex could see the young queen digesting that thought, while the two other queens stepped closer to their wasats, seeking some comfort at the thought of floating above their world where there was no air.

"If we can't go outside to experience this space, can we see it?" Homsaff asked.

Cordelia signaled Alex and he agreed. "On these monitors, Homsaff, I can show you images taken outside the ship. Up here," Cordelia said, as she pointed to the central monitor, "is a view of space."

Homsaff stared at the monitor, approached it, and stretched her hind legs until her muzzle was close to the monitor. Then she sniffed it.

"It isn't space itself, Homsaff," Miriam said. "You've looked through your lookout's scopes, have you not?" When Homsaff agreed, Miriam added, "We have scopes around the outside of the ship, and these are views from those scopes."

"The stars look the same as they do from our planet," Posnossa said. Although she was nervous about the questions Homsaff was asking, she was disappointed that this first image was rather mundane.

"As I said, Posnossa, the stars are far away. Farther than you can imagine," Alex said gently. He signaled Cordelia and tilted his head toward a second screen.

"This is a view of Dassata's first ship," Cordelia explained. The *Rêveur* filled the screen, and it caused the queens and wasats to chortle.

"This can't be," Sissya said, being the first to regain control. "Dassata would never fit inside it."

The Dischnya's viewpoint caught Alex and his people by surprise, and human hands went to mouths to disguise their grins.

Cordelia zoomed smoothly to one of the *Rêveur*'s hatches. "Dassata enters and leaves the ship by this doorway, she explained." Then she slowly widened the view to display the entire ship.

"How large is this ship?" Sissya asked.

"As long as your nest is wide," Cordelia replied.

"And this ship?" Homsaff asked.

Cordelia sent a diagram to a third screen behind her. It showed the relative sizes of the two ships. "Notice that Dassata's first ship, which we call *Rêveur*, is slender, while this ship is round like a plate. And it would take seven of the *Rêveur*, laid end to end, to cross this ship, called *Freedom*. This ship can hold many soma."

"How many?" Posnossa asked.

"More than eighty times all the Dischnya on Sawa Messa," Alex said.

The queens and wasats repeated Alex's words to one another, desperately trying to wrap their minds around a ship that could carry so many.

Once again, it was Homsaff who absorbed the information and launched into another train of thought. "Your ships are made of metal and such, Dassata, they must be heavy. Why do they not fall to the ground?"

<You'll have your hands full with this one,> Alex sent humorously to Miriam and Glenn. He noticed the knees of the other Dischnya trembling at the thought of being aboard a ship that might crash into the planet at any moment and decided it was time to call a halt to Homsaff's interrogation. Fortunately, midday meal was only a quarter hour away.

"Come," Alex ordered, "I will show you to the rooms where you might rest and sleep. Soon after, you will join us for a meal." He led a grateful group of Dischnya, except for Homsaff, off the bridge.

Cordelia was resetting the screens to the views she required before Homsaff exited the bridge. The young queen stopped in the bridge's passageway to stare at the images.

Miriam gently urged Homsaff to continue. "Dassata waits," she said to the queen. Glenn and she had learned that there was no stronger persuasion for the queens than to be told that Dassata needed, requested, or thought better of something. While the technique couldn't be overused, its judicious application accomplished wonders of persuasion.

"It's a magic word," Glenn had enthused once to Miriam. The Independent had begun enjoying the *Rêveur*'s library and was entranced by fantasy vids.

Homsaff's unflagging curiosity set the pace for the Dischnya in the days to come. Miriam and Glenn took charge of their daily tours. Posnossa and Sissya exhibited patience and their wasats followed in their wake. But Homsaff had questions at each stop for every individual she saw. Afterwards, she raced ahead to explore the next venue.

Woosala, Homsaff's wasat, a grizzled and graying commander, struggled to keep pace with her. Woosala was a sub-commander, who was promoted to wasat, when his predecessor, Foomas, was judged for his treachery and dispatched at the Fissla.

Six days after landing aboard and following a midday meal, Homsaff finished her food in the usual quicker-than-everyone-else mode, even cleaning up Woosala's plate. She jumped up, tail twitching, an indication she was ready to proceed with the tour.

In one of those interspecies moments, Glenn and Woosala exchanged glances of resignation.

Miriam witnessed the exchange, and signaled Glenn that they should separate the Dischnya. Glenn would take Posnossa, Sissya, and her two wasats. She would lead Homsaff and her wasat. While Glenn was reluctant to task Miriam with Homsaff, nonetheless, he was grateful.

* * *

Woosala waited until Homsaff lay down for the evening. Then, rather than return to his room, he sought out Glenn, who had a nearby cabin, and made his appeal. Glenn signaled Alex and guided Woosala to the owner's suite.

The cabin door slid aside, and Woosala stepped through, immediately greeting the pair in front of him. "Dassata, Ené," he said.

To Alex's eyes, Woosala appeared severely discomforted, and Alex requested if the wasat was ill and offered him a chair. But Woosala declined the seat and remained standing.

"How can I help you, Woosala?" Alex asked, concerned for the grizzled warrior's condition.

"I'm unfit to serve my queen, Dassata," Woosala admitted, hanging his head. "She is a vibrant, young queen, who requires a mature wasat to guide her, but perhaps one —"

"Younger than you," Alex finished gently.

"Messlan, the sub-commander you met in our tunnels and who carries the queen's scent in her absence, is the perfect choice to serve Homsaff. I appeal to you, Dassata, to request the exchange."

"How is the commander's transfer normally made, Woosala?" Alex asked.

"Usually on the wasat's death, Dassata, or when the wasat is unable to perform his duties."

"And, if the wasat is unfit to execute his duties, what happens to him?"

"He asks for the queen's mercy."

A short intake of breath from Renée punctuated the silence. It didn't take much imagination to realize what those words meant to the Dischnya.

Alex signaled Miriam, who woke Homsaff and told her that Dassata had need of her. Rather than wait for Miriam to guide her, Homsaff raced ahead to the owner's cabin, and Miriam was surprised at how unerringly the queen navigated the corridors and lifts to reach the suite.

Miriam signaled Alex of Homsaff's impending approach, and he triggered the cabin door for her. Homsaff fairly burst through the doorway, only to stumble to a halt at the sight of her wasat standing there, a forlorn expression on his face. Her first thought was that Dassata was dissatisfied with her behavior and would return the two of them to their tunnels.

"Homsaff, Miriam has told me of your exceptional curiosity and energies expended to learn our ways. I'm proud of you," Alex said, to encourage the obviously crestfallen, young queen, and it created the intended reaction. Homsaff perked up, but still cast a wary eye toward her unsettled wasat.

"We have a problem for you to solve, Homsaff, and you're offered two choices. You can solve the problem in the usual Dischnya manner or you can choose our way."

"What is wrong, Dassata?" Homsaff asked.

Alex glanced toward Woosala, who turned to his queen and repeated his plea to be replaced by Messlan.

Homsaff was struck to the core. She was responsible for delivering the death blow to her matriarch, Chafwa, who attempted to kill Dassata. It was the most terrible thing she'd ever done, and she had no desire to repeat that, even if her wasat was requesting the service. Stricken, her muzzle lips trembling, her eyes appealed to Alex. "I would hear Dassata's way," she said, and it came out a little choked.

"For my soma, it's called retirement," Alex replied. "When warrior commanders have served faithfully and can no longer fulfill their duties, they step aside and another takes their place. The valuable experiences held by those who retire guide their leaders and others. It's a waste to eliminate them."

"The nest has always been challenged to support elder Dischnya, Dassata. Food is scarce, and each soma must contribute to the nest's food supply," Homsaff said, attempting to explain the tradition.

"But that will no longer be the case, Homsaff," Alex replied.

"If Dassata teaches us his ways, so that the Dischnya can feed our soma, as he does, we will have no need for the old ways," Homsaff reasoned.

Alex had a glimpse of the shrewd mind that lurked in the young body. Faced with a challenge to accept a dramatic change in her people's ways, the young queen bargained for a promise of a better future. Alex grinned, and Homsaff bared her teeth in return.

"The Dischnya will learn our ways and feed their soma as we do," Alex promised.

"Then, Woosala, I retire you," Homsaff pronounced. "I will choose a new wasat when Nessila rises." Although pleased with her decision and the outcome of the conversation, she noticed neither her wasat nor Dassata shared her enthusiasm.

"Do you remember what I said about the value of those who retire, Homsaff?" Alex asked.

"Their words carry weight and should be heard," Homsaff replied. Then the lesson sunk in. She curled her tail about her and straightened her hind legs slightly, assuming the stance of a mature queen. "I would take your advice in this matter, Woosala," she said.

-14-
Sawa

When Alex announced to Renée that he was making preparations for Sawa, she sensed something was wrong.

"You don't want me to go," Renée said, taking a seat beside him on the couch in their suite.

"It's not that I don't want you with me; it's that one of us needs to stay here. The construction projects have barely begun, and then there are the new SADEs and Daelon Independents."

"Who wish to see a leader; but, Alex, I'm not that person," Renée objected.

"You're the closest thing I have to a replacement, my love. Every individual respects you."

"Every individual respects you, Alex. I'm admired by virtue of my association with you."

"Then you admit that you're admired, my love."

Renée climbed into Alex's lap and wrapped her arms around his neck. "By some much more than others," she said, staring into his eyes before she kissed him. "When do you leave?" she asked.

"In two days Emile's scent test will be concluded. So far, it's been successful. I'll be leaving the day after that and traveling light."

"Then come, my love. If I'm going to be without my partner for a lengthy period of time, I want to stock up on some of his attention," Renée said, jumping up and tugging on Alex's hand.

* * *

Alex readied his people for the trip to Sawa, the next planet inward, and the home world of the Dischnya.

The only ship making the trip would be the *Rêveur*. Alex requested Captain Lumley provide a minimal crew, so that more hands could remain available to work on the construction projects, as opposed to sitting aboard his ship with little to do. The Daelon families with their young ones were transferred to the *Freedom*, where Renée took care to house them one deck above the bridge and forward, where it would be easier for Cordelia, Ophelia, and her to keep an eye on the children.

Miriam and Glenn were aboard the *Rêveur* to manage the young queens and their wasats — SADE, Independent, and Dischnya had bonded well. Joining Alex would be Julien, Z, and the twins. The liner would carry two travelers and two pilots, Svetlana and Deirdre.

Pia considered accompanying Alex, as the medical specialist, but she had her hands full, caring for the Daelon Independents, who, for some reason, seemed to have discarded their careful Méridien work procedures, which stressed safety. Instead, Pia recommended that Alex take Miranda. She said to him, "If anything ugly happens on Sawa, Alex, you'd be better served by an individual who was equally adept at putting a human or a SADE back together."

Among those individuals lamenting the lost opportunity to join Alex's expedition to Sawa were Willem and Franz. Willem's work on Omnia had barely begun, and he couldn't afford to divide his focus, although he dearly wished to go. Then there was that other sticking point. Willem worked for the Haraken Assembly, and Alex no longer represented Haraken interests. As for Franz, he itched to participate in another adventure.

Sawa orbited 124 degrees clockwise on the ecliptic from Sawa Messa. From orbit to orbit, the *Rêveur*'s trip took slightly more than two days.

Homsaff spent most of the trip on the bridge with Captain Lumley, except when Messlan insisted she get some food or sleep. Francis Lumley was a patient man and, having enjoyed entertaining the Daelon children, he was happy to chat with Homsaff, with Miriam's help. The SADE stood by to act as interpreter for Homsaff's questions, and Messlan was present to keep a watchful eye on his young queen.

The subject of space travel was repeated many times, in various guises, throughout Homsaff's questions. The queen couldn't grasp the immense distance between planets, much less between the stars. Worse, she couldn't understand how the *Rêveur* covered the vast distances so quickly. But, it had to be said, Homsaff was, if nothing else, persistent. Where any other Dischnya might have accepted the concepts as too great to comprehend, Homsaff never quit. She would simply choose another way of addressing the issue.

Homsaff's one true joy was that she'd learned, to a point, how to manipulate the holo-vid display, especially after Captain Lumley transferred the view of the Dischnya home world to the projector.

* * *

After achieving Sawa's orbit, Alex ordered Captain Lumley to circle the *Rêveur* around the planet for two days to collect telemetry data and build a complete picture of the Dischnya home world.

Throughout the period, various individuals ringed the holo-vid display, viewing images of Sawa's surface. The queens and wasats were fascinated by the views of their home world. More than once, a muzzle tipped into the image to sniff.

As the second day of telemetry recording was eclipsing, Alex, Julien, Z, and Miranda were fast reviewing the data of the surface, playing the imagery at ten times the recording speed, while the Dischnya watched the dizzying whirl.

"It's possible Sawa was green, millenniums ago, but, obviously, that's no longer true," Julien said. "While we've only two days of data, there is a noticeable pattern to the planet's weather. The wind storms, which sweep the surface, increase in ferocity and strength throughout the day, as Sawa's face rotates to receive Celus' rays."

"If we were to collect at least ten days of data, we would have a fair possibility of forecasting these storms to help us choose the best possible landing time and location," Z said. "However, thirty days of data would be optimal."

"We'll go with what we have," Alex stated firmly. "For our first foray, we drop planetside at first light and lift off within 2.5 hours, before the winds can obscure our vision.

"Is this a tactical decision, or are we following your intuition?" Julien asked.

"What's your summary of the Dischnya's activity level planetside?" Alex asked.

"Minimal and inconsistent," Julien replied.

"Precisely," Alex replied. "Where are the cities or, for that matter, any organized activity centers?"

"The data indicates that, for the most part, the Dischnya warriors are working in small bands and acting as raiders," Z added. "Thermal imagery detects them as most active during the night, and we've recorded open conflict between bands of warriors."

"There appears little desire to maintain a status quo, which we've witnessed between the Sawa Messa nests," Miranda noted. "I perceive an element of desperation here."

"I would surmise the prevailing storms have reduced the available surface food to a minimum," Julien said. "It's forced the nests into a constant state of war for resources."

"My thoughts exactly, Julien," Alex replied. "I think our search is going to be much more difficult than we imagined."

"We see no city centers, no general surface activity, because the Dischnya reside underground on Sawa too," Miranda surmised.

"Which means we'll be required to pry them out of their tunnels again," Z added. He'd been working on a project with the twins. They'd been in no hurry to complete it, but this conversation gave him reason to reconsider that.

"Don't make any assumptions," Alex replied. "They might be living underground, but their access might not be through tunnel hatches. They could be using caves, but, wherever they are, they'll see us as invading aliens and treat us accordingly."

Julien returned to studying the pace and direction of the surface storms. His holo-vid view suddenly shifted when Homsaff stuck her dark-nailed fingers into the display and rotated the image.

Messlan saw the frown form on Alex's forehead, and he hissed a warning to Homsaff, who quickly dropped her hands to her side, her muzzle's lips wrinkling in consternation.

Alex signaled Z, who hurried off the bridge and returned shortly with a portable holo-vid. He set the unit on a bridge console and manipulated the output to the bridge's prior view. When the SADE motioned to Homsaff that the device was for her use, she nodded gratefully.

Alex and his people continued to peruse the telemetry data to determine the primary landing opportunity. Their attention was interrupted by Homsaff's bark. She was pointing at an area on her portable unit's display, and Julien shifted her view to the bridge holo-vid.

Homsaff hurried over and pointed to a small object hardly distinguishable from the surrounding sandy color of the surface. Julien enlarged the image to its greatest magnification, and the assembled parties stared at the strange, stacked structure.

"Chona Chafwa told me stories of Sawa," Homsaff explained. "She said our people had centers of great learning … built of stone blocks high into the air." This was the first time Homsaff had mentioned her matriarch's name since justice had been dispensed to the queen.

"We stay in orbit for two more days," Alex said. "Focus on these structures. I want to know if they're being used or if they're abandoned. We need to be sure of that before we investigate them."

Alex regarded Homsaff, and the young queen stared back, uncertain of what Dassata searched for in her face. Alex had a vision of a future, powerful, Dischnya race, technologically advanced, and led by a formidable queen, such as Homsaff. *A good thing humans made friends with them first,* Alex thought.

"Well done, Homsaff," Alex said simply, patting her on the shoulder before he left the bridge.

Homsaff cupped a hand where Dassata had touched her. She preened, lifting her muzzle and rising slightly on her hind legs. The other queens chuffed and teased her, but Homsaff didn't care. She was determined to earn more of Dassata's praise.

* * *

The landing party planned to launch from the starboard bay at 4.85 hours. At a half hour prior, only Alex, Julien, Svetlana, and Deirdre were present. The two commanders were lounging against the hatch steps. Julien stood with locked avatar near them, and, naturally, Alex was pacing the deck.

<I can't remember ever seeing Alex this anxious,> Svetlana sent to Deirdre, watching Alex's frenetic stride.

To outsiders, posting two experienced fighter commanders to pilot the single traveler might have seemed odd, but as Admiral Tachenko succinctly put it to the two women, "You're there to do whatever you have to do to keep Alex safe, even if you have to disregard his orders." Following those types of extraordinary orders required the sort of metal-alloy spines only possessed by hardened, combat veterans.

<I can't either,> Deirdre sent in reply. <The admiral's instructions seem much more real to me, now. Good thing the bay's deck is harder than Alex's boots.>

The two commanders exchanged brief smiles.

When the twins came through the airlock, Alex stopped his pacing and stared at them. Unfazed, the twins continued to make for the traveler.

"Sers, I'd have a word," Alex said, and Étienne and Alain diverted from their path to join Alex.

"What are those?" asked Alex, pointing to the projections mounted on each shoulder of the crèche-mates.

"Z's newest invention," Étienne replied, "shoulder-mounted, stun weapons with variable beam control. We're able to shift the power output and spread."

"You already have your side weapons," Alex retorted.

"Allow me to demonstrate the improvements," Alain said, and suddenly his shoulder weapons targeted the two commanders, who leapt off the hatch steps.

"Not funny, Alain," Deirdre declared harshly.

"Apologies, Commanders," Alain replied, but the smirk on his face indicated that he really wasn't. "You'll note, Ser, that not only didn't I touch the weapons, but I wasn't looking at the commanders, at the time. My implant is communicating to the weapons' controller, which targeted the commanders based on my visual memory of their location."

"A controller?" Alex queried.

Alain turned around and displayed a smooth shell that was embedded in his jacket. The clothing, weapons, and shell came as one unit.

"The controller resides at the upper part of the shell," Étienne said, pointing in that direction. "The entire lower section is a power cell. It will deliver 150 times more shots to each weapon than our hand stunners."

"Most important," Alain added, turning back around, "these implant-controlled weapons will respond faster than our hand movements."

And there it was: Alex would choose to act in the manner he saw fit, and his escorts would do the same, even if those actions contradicted his.

"My friends," Alex said quietly, shaking his head, "I will tell you now that one day I expect my actions will get me killed, and I've come to accept that. It might happen whether you two are with me or not, and you need to understand that it won't be your fault."

<The madman wishes to absolve us of blame before the event of his death happens,> Alain sent to his crèche-mate.

<It was an admirable attempt,> Étienne replied.

<He's a strange man,> Alain sent.

<Agreed, but worth protecting.>

<Agreed.>

Alex waited for the twins' reactions, but his attention was interrupted when he caught sight of Z stepping from the airlock, wearing his Cedric Broussard suit. The avatar was even more formidable appearing than ever, with massive, shoulder-mounted, stun weapons, greater than those carried by the twins. The weapons' controller and energy pack bulged behind Z's back.

Before a single comment could cross Alex's lips or implant comm, a second individual stepped from behind Z — Miranda housed in another New Terran avatar in female form, as massive as Z but curvy and sporting the same armament.

The commanders burst into applause and whistles. Alex glared at them, but it did nothing to quell their enthusiasm.

"I did stress to Miranda that a male shape could house more of everything, but she insisted on this form," Z explained.

"It's essential that I preserve my reputation for appearing in an exotic female form," Miranda quipped.

Alex stared at the robust shape. It was a caricature of Tatia in every way, except for the raven hair — exaggerated proportions of a heavy worlder, a robust female form accentuated by prominent breasts.

"I'm wondering if the four of you think we're going to war," Alex asked. His question was asked without rancor or even much volume, but his eyes were piercing. Unfortunately, for Alex, none of his audience was bothered by his determined gaze. They had been with Alex too long to be deterred from doing what they felt was necessary.

"We've agreed that we need to be better prepared for future events, Alex. Your life might be in great danger and ours too," Z replied flatly.

The statement stopped Alex cold. It was one thing to risk his life; it was another to expect others to risk their lives, while defending him. He nodded his acceptance of Z's words, and the twins and the SADEs made to board the traveler.

"I approve," Deirdre said, as the twins passed her.

"Power is so sexy," Svetlana remarked, admiring Miranda's avatar.

"Thank you, dear," Miranda replied, "I must admit to experiencing a certain pleasure, while inhabiting this form. I can see why Z loves his avatar collection."

The last to come through the airlock were Miriam and Glenn, leading the queens and wasats. Homsaff ran ahead and leapt into the traveler without bothering with the steps.

"That's our cue," Svetlana quipped to Deirdre, and the commanders quickly climbed aboard to prevent having to navigate past a group of standing Dischnya. Mature chona, such as Posnossa and Sissya, would stand in the aisle, rather than sit on the laps of their wasats, to accommodate their magnificent tails, and their wasats wouldn't sit, while their queens stood. As for Homsaff, if the other queens stood, so would she.

Alex stared at the traveler. He considered who was aboard and what he hoped to accomplish. Anger, for the briefest moment, flared, but he recalled Renée's final words to him. She said, "In order for you to come back safely to me, my love, I'll need you to think calmly and carefully before you take each step, and this includes listening to those around you."

When Alex nodded perfunctorily, Renée had grabbed his face with both hands, twisting his head so their eyes locked. "Are you listening to me?" she'd asked.

"I am now," he replied, realizing his failure to give her the attention she was due.

Recalling Renée's words, Alex took a couple of deep breaths, blowing them out slowly to clear his head. Then he shrugged his shoulders, a lopsided smile appearing on his face, and muttered, "One careful step at a time, my love." He boarded the traveler and joined the queens, who stood in the aisle at the front of the main cabin.

Posnossa and Sissya stood with their tails fully entwined around their legs, but Homsaff only managed to do that for about three-quarters of hers. The tip of her tail twitched impatiently.

<Étienne and Alain,> Alex sent, <I task you with keeping a close eye on our youngest passenger. Her impulsiveness might be her undoing.>

<More so than yours, Ser?> Alain asked, tongue in cheek. When the twins didn't receive an answer, Étienne reprimanded his twin with a shake of his head. Nonetheless, the escorts shared Alex's request with Z and Miranda, so defensive priorities could be planned accordingly.

-15-
The Edifices

The light of Celus was a dim glow on the horizon when Svetlana set the traveler down 120 meters from what the team called Edifice Alpha. It was a stacked, three-story, stone construction, which Julien said resembled an ancient ziggurat. He sent images and a brief historical summary to those with comms or implants to explain his reference.

The Dischnya's exalted learning center, so named by Homsaff's stories, stood more than 30 meters high and dominated the barren landscape. What was strange to those who could observe the edifice through the ship's controller was that it was the only structure in sight. There was no surrounding city or domiciles. It stood apart like some sort of ancient monument to a civilization that had lost its way, and its citizens had no more use for it.

<Commanders, Miriam, and Glenn, remain aboard, while we investigate the structure. Keep your eyes out for movement,> Alex sent.

The team knew from the Dischnya's nightly forays that Sawa's air was breathable. It was the storms that increased in ferocity, as the air was heated, that had to be avoided. The wind's tremendous velocity and skin-abrading sands would be dangerous to any biological forms.

Alex signaled his people and nodded toward the exit to the queens. Each wasat stepped in front of his queen to lead the way.

Z dropped the hatch and stepped out onto the ground. His heavy steps disturbed a layer of gritty sand, 4 centimeters deep. Miranda descended behind Z, and the two SADEs swept left and right, separating from each other by 10 meters. The twins dropped down behind the SADEs and filled the gap between them. The foursome slowly advanced toward the wide steps that led up to the edifice's primary platform.

Alex and Julien exited before the queens and wasats, and Julien signaled the hatch closed once the Dischnya disembarked. In the pale light, the structure looked imposing, and, ever so briefly, Alex hoped that their trip would be quick and informative. Yet the niggling thought in the back of his mind said he was fooling himself.

The closer the team got to the wide, block-stone steps, the more the edifice revealed the wear of time. Sand filled many of the steps, and the massive stones that formed the walls were pitted from the ferocity of the scouring winds. Most disappointing to Alex was the absence of any signs of life. The edifice hadn't been visited for decades, if not longer.

At the steps and by mutual agreement, Z and Étienne took the lead. Miranda and Alain fell to the team's rear. The security team was unsure whether they'd confront trouble at their front and be required to make a hasty retreat or be attacked from behind and forced to take shelter in the edifice.

Passing through the primary platform's main archway, Alex's party found the interior structure open, except for massive square columns spaced evenly across the floor. The interior's walls and columns had once been deeply carved with glyphs, but many had been worn away, especially those lowest to the floor where the grinding sands were fiercest.

Z and Miranda split off and used their combination of variable-light intensive eyes and algorithms to resurrect the symbols, as best they could, and record them.

The glyphs on the back wall were the least worn, and Alex glanced at the Dischnya, who were staring up at the writing that reached to the ceiling, nearly 11 meters up.

"Any of these symbols mean anything to you?" Alex asked the Dischnya.

"They are entreaties to the soma," Posnossa said. "Encouragement to respect one another, study fervently to understand the ways of Sawa, listen keenly to the words of their queens, and other such things."

"Chona and wasats, look over the walls and columns," Alex encouraged. "Search for any reference to a large sphere that visited this system. I'm especially interested to know when this might have happened and from what direction it came."

The queens separated, and the wasats interspersed themselves among them.

The party's search and recording of the glyphs had gone on for nearly 1.75 hours of the allotted time Alex was allowing the team to be planetside, when an emergency signal hit implants and comms.

<Heads up, Alex,> Svetlana sent, <you have forty to fifty Dischnya warriors approaching your location. Already, they're between the traveler and the edifice. What are your orders?>

Svetlana was ready to lift and, if necessary, start glassing the sand behind the warriors to convince them to disperse. But a tick later, she considered the possibility that a beam shot at the Dischnya's back might panic them to run into the edifice.

<Wait one, Commander,> Alex sent back.

The twins raced to the front of the edifices, staying concealed behind the grand archway stones. Étienne snapped a hurried peek at the approaching warriors, who hadn't reached the edifice's steps yet, and shared the view with the team. Z and Miranda took up positions behind the twins, and Alex hurried the queens and wasats to one side, tucking them behind Z.

Using the imagery from the traveler's controller, the SADEs and twins divided the warriors into targets based on their weapons' relative firepower and spread capability. Then they waited for Alex's orders.

<We're going to try diplomacy first, people,> Alex sent. <Let's see how they react to a queen.> Alex whispered into Posnossa's ear, and the queen nodded her assent.

Posnossa edged around Z and Étienne, and then stepped into the opening. She barked a greeting to the Dischnya, dramatically waving her tail high behind her to signal her status. The warriors were stunned for an instant, but only for a brief moment. When they hoisted their weapons to their shoulders, Posnossa leapt clear of danger and a barrage of heavy slugs smacked into the stone columns located only meters inside the opening.

Stone chips stung some of the nearest individuals, and when several struck Sissya, she hissed defiantly.

<So much for talking our way out of here, people,> Alex sent. <Clear the way on my go.> He explained to the queens and wasats what would happen, impressing on them to stay close behind the four, who would be in front. He eyed Messlan, Homsaff's wasat, as he delivered his instructions, and the wasat dipped his head ever so slightly, indicating he understood Alex's unstated message.

"Go," Alex shouted.

The twins slid out on their knees into the opening and fired continuously at the middle of the warriors, opening a corridor through them. The SADEs were instantly behind the twins, targeting the right and left flanks of warriors and knocking down the remaining warriors. The foursome launched themselves down the steps, dancing through the comatose bodies.

Alex led the queens down the steps, their wasats by their sides, and Julien followed at the rear. The young queens stumbled at the sight of so many Dischnya splayed out across the steps and sands, mouths slack and limbs twisted in odd positions. The wasats, hardened by years of fighting, hurried their principals forward.

Another eleven warriors appeared at the flanking fringe of the attackers, and the SADEs dropped them, while the twins focused on the wedge of space between the team and the traveler.

Svetlana tracked the twins' progress and signaled the hatch to drop into a locked position, as they reached it. Étienne and Alain split to the side and knelt to cover the team's boarding. Z and Miranda stopped short and spun around, scanning on all light frequencies for more attackers.

When Alex reached the hatch, he stepped aside, while the queens, wasats, and Julien leapt into the traveler, eschewing the steps. Alex clambered up behind them, followed by the twins and the SADEs. Z, the last aboard, signaled the hatch closed and Svetlana to lift.

"Anyone hit?" Alex asked loudly. The answers were all negatives. Alex turned to regard Étienne, Alain, Z, and Miranda. He briefly used his right hand to cross his body and touch his left shoulder, saying, "I stand corrected." Then he dipped his head in apology.

When Alex turned around, the twins grinned at Z and Miranda, who smiled quietly in return. Each of them delved into the details of the fight against the warriors — weapon response times, targeting acquisition, beam spreads, and energy expended. The key questions were how much energy was left in the power cells and how could the efficiency of the weapons be improved.

"Apologies, Alex, I don't know how we failed to spot the warriors until it was too late," Deirdre said. She felt she had to apologize personally to Alex and had left the pilot's cabin while Svetlana handled the ship. They were hovering 2 kilometers above the surface, waiting for Alex's orders.

"Not necessary, Commander," Alex said, and sent some images to Deirdre of the warriors before they were felled by the security team's shoulder-mounted, stun guns.

"No wonder we didn't see them until they were nearly on you," Deirdre replied in awe. The Dischnya warriors were covered from crown to clawed feet in cloth and skins, painted to camouflage them. Even their eyes were covered with some sort of transparent material to protect them from wind and sand.

"Tough to spot them visually or on thermal, Commander," Alex said, patting Deirdre on the shoulder.

Homsaff watched the pilot bare her teeth at Dassata's touch. It was a gesture she now understood was an expression of pleasure. *I've received one of those from Dassata,* Homsaff thought with pride.

"Dassata, a thought for you," Sissya said, which brought Alex close to the queen. "Can your technology determine the age of that edifice?"

"Julien, any idea?" Alex asked.

Julien opened his hand and revealed a shard of stone that he'd scooped up when a slug tore into a column behind them. He set an app in his kernel to monitor the pressure on his fingers and began to press firmly on the shard. The Dischnya watched, intrigued by any activities of Dassata's metal soma. Eventually, the small shard shattered, shooting pieces in every direction. Some Dischnya were stung and hissed their displeasure, but, even then, all of them exchanged amazed glances at the demonstration of the metal soma's power.

"Apologies," Julien said to the queens and wasats. "Alex, the stone's density indicates it has sufficient hardness to withstand the wearing of the winds and sands, as we've recorded them, for several hundred years, at the very least."

"Do you understand, Sissya?" Alex said, when he repeated what Julien said in their language. For more complex statements, it was necessary to revert to the Dischnya language, but, after spending nearly thirty days together in close proximity aboard the Omnian ships, the Dischnya had demonstrated that they had a knack for language and were quickly learning the alien's speech, as they called it.

"Dassata, the structure is too old. It would have been built and its surfaces carved before the sphere came here," Sissya replied.

Alex nodded his agreement. He'd come to the same conclusion the moment Julien stated his estimate of the edifice's minimum age. <Svetlana, make for the *Rêveur,*> Alex sent. "Time for plan B," Alex muttered, thinking of possible next steps.

Everyone else aboard was left to review the unusual circumstances of their first landing on Sawa — an inhospitable planet, environmentally and culturally.

* * *

Once aboard the *Rêveur*, Alex decided to order Svetlana and Deirdre to take the travelers planetside the next morning, as soon as there was sufficient light.

"I want close-up and detailed telemetry of every edifice on this planet," Alex said.

"I take it that we're trying to get an idea of the age of each structure," Svetlana replied.

"It took the warriors nearly two hours to show up at the first location, Alex. We could pop into a structure, take images of the interiors, collect samples, and be out before any warriors arrived," Deirdre volunteered.

"Do the Dischnya have communication on this planet?" Alex asked. When the commanders frowned in confusion, Alex added, "And could they have warned others of our landing? And could they be ready the next time to respond even quicker and with a greater force?"

"All excellent questions, Alex," Deirdre admitted. "You've convinced me to keep my butt in my pilot's seat." She grinned in appreciation of Alex's preference to keep her safe, rather than accept her offer to risk her life to gather more information.

* * *

Two days later, the team descended planetside again. This time they targeted an edifice that the SADEs deduced from Svetlana's imagery was one of the lesser-worn structures. It crossed Alex's mind that it might be too young, although it did show some wear on its stones' faces.

From the little data that Julien had to work with, he estimated the edifice was somewhere between 250 and 125 years old, which meant it could still be pre-event.

<Alex, we're 2 kilometers up and awaiting your landing instructions,> Svetlana sent. Both commanders had mentally switched attitudes from shuttle jockeys to fighter pilots. The first landing drove home how dangerous Sawa was to the team.

Alex linked to the controller and studied the structure. It wasn't as prominent as Edifice Alpha, although it was built in the same tradition — a triple-stacked ziggurat with wide steps leading to the first level. There wasn't much choice in landing sites. The Dischnya situated this learning center amidst a field of rocks, some of which could rightly be called boulders, reaching heights of several meters and more.

Scanning the terrain, Alex chose a location with the fewest number of boulders, allowing his people the greatest advantage for line of sight. Unfortunately, it was more than 2 kilometers from the edifice.

<Good choice,> Svetlana sent in reply to Alex, when he marked the terrain in her helmet's view. Deirdre and she had worked up a new app in the ship's controller, with the help of Miranda. The hull's ground-facing sensors, which could monitor the sandy terrain, would be tuned to signal subtle vibrations through the hard soil, such as a tunnel hatch opening or footsteps.

Svetlana set the traveler down softly, its three short landing gear extending from small hatches in the shell. Immediately, Deirdre sent a ping into the ground from one of the hull's sensors, and Svetlana and she monitored the app's response.

<SADE work … guaranteed to function as designed, first time, every time,> Deirdre sent to Svetlana when the commanders realized the app and sensors were performing perfectly together. Her thoughts bubbled with laughter.

Z, Miranda, and the twins organized their exit and waited, and it wasn't long before they received Svetlana's warning. <We have movement,> she sent.

<Any indication of what type?> Alex sent.

<Apologies, Alex,> Deirdre replied, <We haven't enough baseline data to discern what created these sounds. We can tell you that there are many of them, they've a short duration, and they're not repeating.>

<Most likely hatch openings or the arming of weapons,> Z remarked.

<Okay, people, presume we have hostile forces waiting for us and act accordingly,> Alex sent. He signaled Miriam and Glenn to take the Dischnya to the front of the main salon, out of harm's way, and Julien and he followed them.

Z and Miranda each took one side of the hatch, and the twins crowded behind them. Z signaled the hatch to drop and waited. When nothing happened, he stepped into the opening, allowed a brief tick for attackers to sight on him, and then leapt aside.

Slugs peppered the hull and a handful struck the traveler's interior. Z signaled the hatch closed, and Alex ordered Svetlana to lift.

The warriors watched from concealment, as their prey disappeared into the sky, seemingly unharmed by their weapons. Nonetheless, they broke out in celebration, hoisting their weapons high and howling in victory at the sky. The alien enemy had been chased from their territory.

"Black space," Deirdre muttered quietly.

Svetlana grinned, which, with their heads encased in helmets, Deirdre couldn't see. It had been Deirdre's idea to search the edifices' interiors and capture imagery of the glyphs for Alex, which he'd refused. This landing proved that one or both of them would probably have been dead or captured, in short order.

"I'm confused, Alex," Julien asked, frowning and holding a hand to his chin, as if he was contemplating a critical problem. "Would the next iteration of your superlative leadership be labeled plan C or, if we revisit this location, would it be B-2?"

"Some days, I dearly wish you were human," Alex replied, scowling.

"Contemplating violence, are we?" Julien remarked and pursed his lips at Alex.

For the briefest moment, Alex stared at his friend in disbelief, then he smiled and barked a laugh that boomed off the traveler's interior.

The Dischnya couldn't resist joining, and they echoed Alex with barks and yips of their own, even though they had no idea of the occasion, but that started everyone laughing.

Alex cupped the neck of his friend, planted a big smack on his forehead, and walked down the aisle to examine the slugs that Z and Miranda were pulling from the interior bulkhead.

<Any drop in our traveler's charging efficiency, Commanders?> Alex sent.

<Less than 1 percent, Alex,> Deirdre replied. <We'll perform a visual check of the hull when we land aboard the *Rêveur*.>

<Alex, we're at 2 kilometers' elevation and awaiting your orders,> Svetlana sent.

"What now, Alex?" Étienne asked.

"I'm working on plan B-2, or C-1, as my inimitable friend would term them," Alex said to the twins, Z, and Miranda. He studied a slug that Miranda handed him. It was heavier than those used against his people on Omnia. "Slug throwers, but more powerful," Alex said quietly, and his people dipped their heads in agreement.

"Is not the primary purpose of your plan, Alex, to collect imagery of the edifice's interior?" Z asked.

"I'd agree."

"Then I believe I have the answer aboard the *Rêveur*."

* * *

Plan C-1 was enacted early the next morning. As far as Alex was concerned, the Dischnya had arrived too quickly and in too great a number at the site of Edifice Beta. During her reconnaissance, Deirdre had recorded a structure similar to Beta. It was about the same size and showed about the same amount of wear, and Alex decided to try the team's fortune at this alternate site.

It might have been better to attempt Z's plan, after the storms began to ravage the face of Sawa Messa, but Alex was concerned about exposing his people to the scouring winds and the possible damage the traveler's shell might receive.

Alex intended to leave the Dischnya on the traveler, especially after he learned of Z's idea, but Homsaff would have nothing to do with it. She insisted on accompanying him, and the other queens decided that if Homsaff was going, they were going.

Humans and SADEs loaded onto the traveler first, and then the Dischnya were escorted aboard by Miriam and Glenn. The queens and wasats eyed the strange block of rectangular metal that sat aft of the hatch. It was so large that seats had been removed to accommodate it.

The brief flight time soon had Svetlana setting the traveler down at Edifice Delta's location. Miranda, Miriam, and Julien levered the block of metal up and over until it was poised in front of the hatch. Miranda looked at Alex, who nodded, and she signaled the hatch open. As soon as the lowered hatch locked into place, Miranda placed a massive boot against the block and heaved, launching it out of the ship and onto the ground.

The hatch was left open, and everyone was careful to keep clear of the opening.

<We have multiple movements, Alex,> Deirdre sent. <They're faint, but steady. It suggests many footsteps from a distance away.>

A nest lookout had warned of a strange object that had suddenly appeared in the distance, and warriors scrambled to defend the nest. A sub-commander was ordered by his wasat to lead the warriors, and they poured from the tunnels. Using the plain's boulders as cover, they worked their way toward the huge object.

Waffala, the sub-commander, ordered his warriors to remain undercover, watch from concealment, and hold their fire. They saw a door in the structure open and a block of stone fall out. The sub-commander's brow wrinkled in confusion. He'd never witnessed this sort of attack on the nest.

When the block began to move, the warriors growled in anticipation, and Waffala hissed at them to remain quiet. The expectation was that warriors would leap from what must be a box, painted to resemble stone, but, to their great surprise, they witnessed it slowly and steadily unfold to reveal a small head and six powerful legs, which extended from a squat body. When the creature moved, Waffala ordered his warriors to open fire.

Ensconced in his mining avatar, Z started forward and shots pinged off his shell. Z chose this avatar for his foray into the edifice, because it was built to withstand the enormous pressures of cave-ins, while he searched for high-value mineral deposits in underground domes and rivers.

By the time the creature reached the edifice's steps, Waffala decided to ignore the colorful structure, which might house other creatures, and he ordered his warriors to chase the creature, which was about to invade their ancient seat of learning. The warriors fired shot after shot, only to hear their slugs ricochet off the stone skin.

Alain snapped a quick look through the hatch opening and signaled to Miranda and his crèche-mate that the warriors were attacking Z in numbers. He was about to coordinate a rear attack when Miranda jumped through the hatch and started dropping the warriors. Without hesitation, the twins dove through the hatch and focused on covering Miranda. Intelligently, Miranda was stunning the rearmost warriors.

Those warriors nearest the creature belatedly realized that their weapons fire was lessening. Turning around, they came face to face with three more creatures, and, frozen by the sight, they were stunned and fell onto the steps before a single warrior could fire a shot.

<I thought SADEs were all about logic and thinking things through before they acted,> Alain sent to Miranda.

<I did think it through, dear one,> Miranda sent in reply. <There's human time, and then there's SADE time.>

The threesome scanned for more warriors while Miranda signaled Z. <I think it would be wise to return this slow-moving avatar to the ship, dear.> She saw the legs hesitate, and then the avatar reversed its way back down the steps.

<Alex,> Étienne sent, <the way is clear, for now. There are so many warriors down, I don't think they could have many to spare.>

<Coming out,> Alex replied. He led the queens and wasats down the hatch, and they were immediately covered by the twins, who scanned for signs of attack.

Miranda walked beside Z, and the Dischnya, except for Homsaff, stared in horror at the thing that moved slowly past them.

"Metal soma, Dassata?" Homsaff asked curiously.

"We call them SADEs, Homsaff," Alex replied. "That's Z in another body."

Alex's comment caused Homsaff to halt, while the team moved on. She hurried to the front of the creature and knelt down in the sand. "Z, are you in there?" she asked.

"Greetings, Homsaff," Z said, through a small mouth used for mineral sampling. "You must hurry and join the others for your safety."

Homsaff had admired the huge, heavy-bodied human since she first saw him. To a Dischnya's mind, size and strength meant power, and Z possessed them in great quantity. When she discovered he was one of the metal soma, she became even more fascinated by him. Now, the idea that Z had transferred into this creature's body made her dizzy to know more. In an emotional reaction, she licked the small metal face with her long tongue and raced after the team.

<Now that's new, dear,> Miranda sent to Z. <I believe we've witnessed the first Dischnya crush on a SADE.>

<I've constantly projected possible futures since meeting Alex, yet, somehow, his realities are never ones that I've theorized,> Z sent in reply, as he continued toward the ship.

When Miranda was sure that Z was safely in reach of the traveler, she hurried to protect the team, who were already inside the edifice and scanning the glyphs.

This time the combination of the commanders' sound-sensing surveillance and the twins scanning the grounds from the top of the steps, ensured the queens and wasats weren't surprised.

The queens and wasats fanned out without encouragement from Alex. They were anxious to complete their perusal of the glyphs and return to the safety of the ship, as soon as possible.

Posnossa followed the glyphs from the top of a column down its side when she suddenly stopped and reread the last few glyphs. She loosed a series of barks, before she corrected herself and called to Dassata. The team crowded around her, and she pointed to a series of carvings halfway up the column.

Alex carefully stored the entire column in his implant, while Posnossa read out the meaning of the glyphs.

"That one, Dassata," Posnossa said, pointing at a complex carving, "It states the annual and the season, but it means nothing to us without knowing the planet's recordkeeping of time."

"Understood, Chona, please continue," Alex replied.

"Beneath it is the symbol for a ship. The center glyph is enveloped in two circles, which means it was round and large. The small symbol to the side means it wasn't Dischnya in nature."

"Anything else?" Alex asked hopefully."

"I'm not certain, Dassata," Posnossa replied.

Sissya stepped close to the column and eyed the glyphs. "The carvings below the ship glyph are numbers or a counting of some sort. Because they're below and have no other symbols, they must relate to the ship."

"What do the numbers mean?" Alex asked anxiously.

"I don't understand them, Dassata … deepest apologies," Sissya replied.

"Alex," Julien said, "perhaps the queens don't understand them because they aren't simple numbers. They could be degrees, declination, planet rotation, or some other astronomical notations."

Alex stared at the column, not seeing the carvings. He needed a translator, and it had to be someone on this planet with enough knowledge to translate the numbers. "Plan C-2," Alex said, slapping his friend on the shoulder. "Come on, people," he yelled, as he hurried out of the edifice, past the twins, and down the steps.

When Alex reached the mass of fallen warriors, he stopped. The long-legged queens and wasats were right behind him. "Is there a wasat among these warriors?" he asked, and the six Dischnya spread out to check the bodies.

"None, Dassata," Sissya finally replied, "but Messlan believes the one at his feet might be a sub-commander."

"Take him," Alex commanded.

His request didn't translate for the Dischnya, who stood rooted in place, their muzzles quivering in confusion.

Miranda walked over to the body, scooped up the fallen warrior, and marched toward the traveler.

The queens and wasats followed behind, speaking softly to one another, and trying to understand what Dassata intended to do with the warrior.

Everyone skirted around Z, who'd followed, back in his box shape, to board the traveler. Then Miranda, Miriam, and Z used their incredible strength to lever Z through the hatch opening, which was a tight fit, and onto the ship.

Once everyone was aboard, Alex ordered Svetlana to return to the *Rêveur.*

-16-
Waffala

During the traveler's return, Homsaff knelt in front of Z, who stayed folded in his avatar so he could be unloaded from the ship. She could barely discern the small head surrounded by the solid wall of metal. The discovery of metal soma with their incredible capabilities secretly fascinated her, and she yearned to explore the world of Dassata's SADEs.

"How many bodies do you have, Z?" Homsaff asked.

"We call them avatars, Chona. I've thirty-four now."

"Do others of your kind have many bodies?"

"Most do not. My partner, who you see in the heavy body with the woman's figure, does have a smaller body."

"How do you move yourself? Are you so tiny that you can fit inside and drive them like a ship?"

"No, Homsaff, we move our minds between the bodies."

"Could you move my mind into one of these creatures … these avatars?"

"No, Homsaff, we can't move a biological mind."

When Z saw that the queen didn't recognize the term, he added, "A human, Dischnya, or Swei Swee are biological. They have the minds of living beings."

"So, you aren't a living being?" Homsaff asked, feeling as if she had lost the thread of the conversation.

"SADEs live, but not in a manner you would understand."

If Z thought his answers would douse Homsaff's curiosity by virtue of being too strange to comprehend, he was wrong. Homsaff's desire to learn the ways of Dassata's soma had exploded exponentially with her discovery of the world of SADEs, who could move their minds.

* * *

When Sub-commander Waffala awoke, his head buzzed and his stomach churned. Slowly the disconcerting symptoms subsided, except for an awful thirst. Lying on his back, he struggled to sit up, but found his limbs bound to a table.

Waffala was surprised he was still alive. His first thought was that the creatures had captured him so that he might be served up on their tables, and he hoped for a quick and painless death before they carved his body.

The sub-commander took stock of his surroundings. Everything disturbed him. Gone were the smells of Sawa — his queen, his soma, the underground, and the dusty, dry plains. Instead, he saw metal where there should be dirt, doors where there should be curtains, and light coming from strange devices.

"Our captive's awake," Miranda said to Alex. Both Z and she had transferred to less-intimidating avatars.

"Okay, people, proceed as planned," Alex said to the individuals surrounding him on the bridge. "But be careful. He may be Dischnya, but he's not from Sawa Messa."

Sissya tipped her muzzle in understanding and left the bridge in the company of her wasat, Offwa, and the twins.

At the medical suite, Alain signaled the door aside and stepped back. Alex had stated repeatedly that they needed this warrior's cooperation, so the plan was to approach him slowly with the familiar, one queen and one wasat.

Sissya stepped through the doorway, arching her tail high behind her, signaling a queen's dominance. Offwa stepped beside her, and they waited for the warrior to appraise them.

Waffala thought he was dreaming, and he stared at the two Dischnya, waiting for his vision to clear.

"I'm Chona Sissya, Ossnos Soma, Sawa Messa," Sissya said, rising on her hind legs, tail thrashing behind her.

Waffala's jaw dropped open but quickly snapped shut. "Liar," he hissed, and Offwa growled at the insult to his queen.

"Why do you think I lie to you, warrior?" Sissya asked patiently, touching the tip of her tail to her wasat's thigh to calm him. Dassata had coached her repeatedly to be patient and take her time, stating the need to earn the warrior's trust.

"Warrior?" Waffala replied, indignant at the word. "I'm Sub-commander Waffala, Tamassa Soma." He'd tried to rise to declare his title, but the bindings held him fast, and he growled in frustration.

"Well, Sub-commander Waffala," Sissya said, "I await your response to my question."

"The Dischnya of Sawa Messa exist no more," Waffala hissed. "They died soon after reaching the planet or during the journey there. These truths are known."

"Then how do you explain us?" Sissya asked.

"This is a trick. You're a queen of Sawa, trying to gain our soma for your own."

Sissya chortled. "I see our conversation will not be quick, Waffala. Would you like some water?" Sissya picked up a squirt bottle left by Miranda and held it up to the sub-commander.

Waffala's throat burned, but he eyed the bottle dubiously.

Sissya recognized the fear in Waffala's eyes, so she tipped the bottle over her muzzle, squeezed it, and shot the water into her mouth. She smacked her jaw noisily, exaggerating the freshness of the drink. The display worked. Waffala's jaw dropped down, and his tongue licked his dry lips. Sissya stepped next to the table, held the bottle over Waffala's mouth, and waited. Finally, he opened his mouth, and Sissya squirted a small amount to wet his throat.

"More?" Sissya asked. This was another lesson from Dassata — generosity to the warrior must be doled out in small portions. When Waffala nodded, Sissya gave him another squirt and then stepped back, pleased to see the sub-commander thirstily eyeing the water bottle.

"Sub-commander, look around you," Sissya commanded. "Have you seen the like of this structure on Sawa?"

Waffala had tried desperately to ignore his surroundings — the gleaming metal surfaces, the lack of the familiar smells, and the doorway that slid aside without anyone touching it. Now, this foreign queen, who declared she was from the planet of the dead, was forcing him to examine them.

Sissya watched the fear return to the sub-commander's eyes, as he examined the medical suite and its objects. *You have my sympathies, Waffala. I remember my first experience aboard an alien ship,* Sissya thought ruefully. She stepped close to the table and held up the water bottle. When he opened his mouth, she gave him another squirt. This time, she didn't step back.

"We don't intend to hurt you, Waffala," Sissy said gently. "We need your help to translate some glyphs, some carvings, and then we'll release you back on Sawa."

"What do you mean back on Sawa?" Waffala asked, focusing on the strange phrase.

"We're aboard a ship high above Sawa, Sub-commander," Sissya explained.

More lies, Waffala thought, but he kept that thought to himself.

"Will you help us?" Sissya asked.

"Your word, as a queen, that I'll be returned safely?" Waffala asked.

"Chona Sissya, Ossnos Soma, Sawa Messa, gives her word," Sissya replied, standing erect. She stepped away from the table, saying, "Your bonds will be released by two of the aliens who operate this ship. Don't be frightened by them; while they're odd-looking, they mean you no harm and are friends of the Dischnya of Sawa Messa.

The creatures who stepped through the doorway were indeed strange in appearance to Waffala's eyes. Nearly hairless about the face, possessing blunt muzzles, and pink skin like a newborn mewling, they were wrapped in strange coverings. But, odder than all that, they looked exactly alike, and he wondered if all the aliens would appear the same. The thought made him shudder.

Without anyone approaching Waffala, the straps suddenly released the pressure on his limbs and waist. Gently, he tested to see if he could sit up, which he could, and he swung his legs over the side of the table. Eyeing the two aliens and the two Dischnya, Waffala made a hasty decision. He bolted toward the doorway, intending to exit these metal tunnels, which he was sure were buried somewhere on Sawa.

Unfortunately for the sub-commander, Sissya stood in his way. Offwa leapt in front of his queen for her protection, and Étienne was forced to stun the poor, frantic Dischnya a second time. Alain caught the warrior before his momentum had him slamming into something that might hurt him.

Watching the entire scene on the bridge holo-vid, Alex was disgusted with the outcome of the meeting and swore, "Black space!"

"Dassata, space is black, or so I've learned. What do your words mean in regard to this event?" Homsaff asked.

Alex was caught speechless, and, to cover the moment, he tapped his temple indicating he was talking to his soma, and Homsaff dipped her muzzle in understanding. Captain Lumley and Glenn covered their mouths to hide their smiles.

"I believe this next iteration should be labeled plan C-2b. I do hope there is sufficient alphabet to reach our goal," Julien commented drily.

"Z, Miranda, rig a portable chair in which to strap our reluctant warrior. I want him to awake up here in the company of Dischnya, aliens, and a starship bridge. Let's see if that convinces him to help us. Send for me when he stirs. After two stun blasts, it'll be awhile, I'm thinking."

* * *

Tears ran from Waffala's eyes, when he tried to open them against the blinding light. His head pounded, as if to the beat of an enormous drum, and the nerves of his body itched. Once again, he was bound. But more than anything, he felt defeated and accepted the fact that his impending death was due to his fate of having been captured.

Waffala could hear voices, but he kept his eyes closed. An object touched his face, and he jerked away, but it continued to pat his cheeks, drying them. Then damp material was laid across his eyes, and the cool, dark was bliss.

"Drink," Waffala heard a chona say, and he opened his mouth to receive a squirt of refreshing water. He continued to swallow and dropped his jaw again. As many times as he did, he received water until his thirst was quenched. The simple attentions helped the irritations and pains to fade, and he was content to lie quietly and recover.

But Waffala jerked alert when the wet object over his eyes was removed. He blinked and waited for his eyes to adjust. When he could hold his eyes open, he was mesmerized by a painting of a unique tan and brown ball against a backdrop of stars.

"Welcome back, Sub-commander Waffala," Sissya said. "If you're wondering, that's a view of Sawa, as seen from our ship high above the planet."

Waffala ached to denounce the lie, but the thought of receiving another burst of fire from the aliens' weapons kept his muzzle closed. He felt his chair rotated, and he came face to face with aliens, queens, and wasats.

"I'm going to show you some carvings, Sub-commander. I need you to identity them," Alex said.

Waffala didn't know which struck him harder, the sight of the huge alien or that it spoke nearly flawless Dischnya. Before he could make up his mind, an image of a column within the sacred temple sprung up from an alien device near him.

"Do you know the meaning of these symbols?" Alex asked.

Waffala glanced at the alien, and hot anger made him growl. They had desecrated the nest's protected sanctuary by entering and stealing a piece of it. "Thieves," he hissed.

Posnossa chortled at the sub-commander, which wounded his pride, as she meant it to do. Then the queen passed her hand through the holo-vid. "This is an image, a copy of what we saw, Waffala," Posnossa explained. "We stole nothing."

The harder Waffala tried to muster an attack against the invaders, the more he was confused by what they presented. Doubt crept through his thoughts.

"Tell us what you know of these symbols, Sub-commander, and we'll free you," Alex repeated.

"They're meaningless," Waffala replied, and his statement produced a round of chortling and bared teeth.

"You're incensed we would enter and steal from your center of learning," Homsaff challenged. "It's obvious that it has great worth to you, but you would ask us to believe that the carvings on its walls and columns are worthless. Your nest must be weak to allow one of your simplemindedness to be elevated to the rank of sub-commander."

Homsaff's jibe hit home, and Waffala growled his resentment.

"Dassata, I don't think this one should be taken below. You should open a door and let him walk out, as he believes he's capable of doing," Homsaff said with disdain.

<This young one would make a great warrior queen,> Miranda sent to her compatriots.

"You don't know how to read the carvings, do you, Sub-commander Waffala?" Julien asked, not unkindly. "You've never been taught to read them."

Waffala hung his head with guilt. The aliens had easily discovered what he sought to hide. Only a few, the eldest among the soma, could read the temple's inscriptions, and they closely guarded their skill.

Alex didn't need Waffala's verbal response. The answer was plain to see. He blew out his breath in frustration. <Svetlana, ready the traveler. We're returning our unhappy guest planetside,> Alex sent. To Julien, he said, "On to plan C-3."

* * *

On the trip below to return Waffala to his nest, a thought struck Alex, and he walked down the aisle toward the hatch where the sub-commander sat strapped in his portable chair.

"You would like us to leave your nest and your center of learning alone, wouldn't you, Sub-commander?" Alex asked.

Waffala thought the alien's question must be some kind of trick, and he waited for the creature to expose it.

"Do you want me to tell you how you can make that happen?" Alex pressed.

Refusing to answer the alien seemed the best course of action to Waffala, so he remained silent. Unfortunately, the creature stood there, continuing to stare at him in an eerily quiet way, as if he was prepared to wait until the end of time. The alien's intense eyes made Waffala squirm.

<Obviously, the sub-commander does not play poker,> Z sent on open comm. He'd relayed the conversation to the others, so they might enjoy the exchange, especially Svetlana, who was an ardent fan of the game.

Finally, Waffala gave in and tipped his muzzle the slightest amount. Anything was better than having the alien leaning over him and gazing at him with those unblinking eyes.

"Then, I'll tell you," Alex said in a friendly manner. "You request your queen or advisor, whoever can read these inscriptions, to meet with us. We'll listen to their words, and then we'll immediately depart Sawa. That's all you have to do. We'll land here on the following day, soon after Nessila rises, to meet with them."

Waffala would have replied, but the alien seemed uninterested in an answer. Instead the metal object, which appeared to be a doorway and was directly in front of him, levered down and away. Waffala could identify the rock formations and boulders, which bordered his nest, and his hopes soared that the aliens truly intended to release him.

"Tomorrow at Nessila's rise, Sub-commander. I need someone who knows the carvings' meanings. Now go," Alex said, and triggered the release of the warrior's bindings.

Waffala pulled his arms free, threw aside the strap at his waist, and kicked his legs out. Nothing held him, and he leapt through the doorway, frantically racing for cover behind a rocky outcrop before he stopped to look back. The metal door had closed, and the large object he had first seen at the center's site rose into the air. Waffala's jaw fell open, as he watched the object rise quickly and quietly into the sky, and he stared dumbfounded at its retreating shape. None of the warriors, who had raced to the defense of the temple on their wasat's command, were told that the object had come from the sky.

Waffala stretched out his arms to brace himself against a boulder, the heat from it warming his hands. He shook his muzzle in confusion. The foundation of his beliefs was shaken. Obedience to his queen and commander were absolute, but he asked himself why the warriors were not told of the object's alien nature. *Surely, a lookout saw the object land,* he thought.

The evidence was clear — the aliens came from the sky, as they had professed. It struck Waffala that perhaps everything the aliens told him was true, and those truths were damaging in that they contradicted the queen's words. The soma were repeatedly told of the grievous errors of the queens, generations ago, who thought to migrate away from the home world. Their folly was proven when they perished in the trips to the next planet outward or soon after landing there. Yet, here were queens and wasats, living with aliens, who said Dischnya existed on Sawa Messa.

Unsure of what to do with his newfound information, Waffala made his way slowly across the dry, Nessila-heated sands toward a lookout's hatch. He would make his report to the queen and commander, but he would be careful to keep some things to himself.

* * *

Waffala's commander, Falwass, met him alone at the lookout post that he entered. A pail of water and brush were supplied, and he was ordered to thoroughly clean himself.

"You must remove all traces of the creatures' poison from your fur, Sub-commander," Falwass said.

"Poison?" Waffala queried.

"Yes, poison. The creatures sprayed it into the air. That's how they felled our warriors."

"Will I die?" Waffala asked. He was still torn between the words of the aliens and those of his wasat. *So many words and so little time to determine the untruths,* he thought.

"The creatures probably gave you a cure so that they could speak to you. Obviously, they wished you to deliver a message, so it's unlikely you'll perish from their poison."

The way Falwass spoke gave Waffala chills. It was as if he were saying that death could creep over him in unsuspecting ways. "Commander, I would ask, how many of our warriors died during the fight with the creatures?"

"We were fortunate, Sub-Commander Waffala. Chona Ceefan's advisors managed to concoct a cure to the creatures' poison. None of our soma perished."

"Good news, Commander," Waffala replied, relieved to hear of his warriors' survival, although none of the commander's words fit with what he knew.

"Hurry now, Waffala. The queen waits to hear your report."

As quickly as Waffala could, he finished rinsing his fur and drying off. The commander marched ahead of him through the tunnels with such a strong gait that the Tamassa Soma warriors, who were pleased to see him, didn't dare speak, bark, or yip in celebration of his return. At best, muzzles were lifted in silent salute.

In the queen's chambers, Waffala was grilled thoroughly and continually by Ceefan and Falwass on his treatment at the hands of the interlopers, what he saw, and what they said. Most important, the queen wanted to understand their repeated requests to learn the nature of the temple carvings.

It was curious to Waffala that not once did either the queen or his wasat ask how he and the interlopers could communicate with one another. It was if they didn't want to hear the word alien spoken, which made Waffala think that they had seen them, but somehow the warriors had been convinced that they didn't. Had they asked, Waffala's answer would have been simple — the interlopers were aliens, who spoke Dischnya, but not as the Sawa soma.

The longer the questions went on, the more Waffala realized he'd been smart to keep his muzzle closed on many of the small points. He was careful to never mention the words alien or ship. His queen called them interlopers, and steered away from how the object appeared and disappeared from their territory. *Words of untruth,* Waffala thought. *We've been told words of untruth.*

"And you say, Sub-commander, that these interlopers asked only about a specific area on a single column," Ceefan said, hitting on the subject for the fourth time.

"I believe so, my queen. As I know not the words of the sacred carvings, it would be difficult to tell if they showed me one or several. They did appear the same." Waffala ended his statement with a conciliatory dip of his head, apologizing for his lowly skills, and hoping to end his interrogation on this subject.

"Lift your muzzle, Waffala," Ceefan said generously. "You've done well to escape the object before the interlopers carried it away. They're dangerously clever to be able to move this fortress of theirs across the plains."

Another untruth, Waffala thought, *I, myself, saw it fly away.*

"One more item, Sub-commander, and then we'll relieve you to go and rest. The poison these creatures used is strong, and we've seen it play with the minds of our soma, so much so, that their memories were altered. Tell me again what they said to you about Nessila's next rise."

"The largest of the interlopers requested you, my queen, or a skilled advisor, who could read the temple carvings, to meet them at the place where they appeared before. If the meanings were made clear to them, they said they would not bother the nest again."

"An excellent report, Waffala; you may go," Ceefan said.

As soon as Falwass confirmed that Waffala was out of earshot, Ceefan asked, "Are the warriors unsettled by our stories?"

"No, my queen," Falwass replied, "They're grateful to your advisors for their speedy recovery. That they had no injuries supports our story of a poison sprayed into the air to which they succumbed."

"What of the lookout, who saw the ship land?" Ceefan asked.

"I took care of him soon after I received his report of the first landing. Our hunters believe he was lost or killed during the next days' foraging and have spread the story. I ensured he was unable to tell his tale to anyone."

"And what of today's landing?"

"There's only one lookout post that views the location where the aliens landed, and I've assigned no lookouts to that station since the first landing."

"Excellent work, Falwass."

"But, my queen, what will you do when Nessila rises tomorrow?"

"I've considered that. I believe our best course of action is to give the aliens what they want and hope they will keep their word and return to Sawa Messa."

"The warriors will expect to accompany you and protect you, Chona Ceefan."

"We can't allow that, Falwass. The untruths we've told are piling up. Besides, the aliens killed none of our warriors, only put them to sleep. Even poor Waffala was returned unarmed. Better they hadn't. He will soon need to meet his own foraging accident."

"I will be on duty at the lookout post before Nessila crests the horizon tomorrow, my queen."

"And I will wait there with you, Commander. Ensure that no soma enter the post while we're aboveground."

"It will be as you order, my queen," Falwass replied, dropping his muzzle in obeisance.

-17-
Plan C-3

In the morning, a little before Nessila broke the horizon, everyone aboard the traveler with an implant or comm was linked to the controller. Svetlana floated the ship half a kilometer above the edifice, at the far edge of the Tamassa Soma nest. The landing party could distinguish two individuals on the ground, and one of them possessed a regal tail.

"It would appear that Waffala delivered your message, Alex," Julien said.

<Land us, Commander Valenko,> Alex ordered on open comm.

Once the traveler was down, Alex said, "Only Julien, the twins, and I will meet the queen. If we enter the edifice, Z and Miranda, you follow and take up posts at the bottom of the steps. Any trouble and we'll join forces to fight our way back to the ship."

"Alex, it would be better to have one SADE and a twin with you," Z replied.

"Perhaps for armament, Z. But, in this case, I don't wish to intimidate these Dischnya. I'm big enough, but you two are —"

"Careful, Ser," Miranda warned.

"Are so magnificently endowed that I'm sure they would be overwhelmed by your presence," Alex supplied with a huge grin.

"A charming recovery," Miranda commented.

When the hatch dropped, the twins exited first, followed by Julien and Alex. In the quiet of the morning, the team could hear the hisses of the waiting Dischnya.

<We seem to get that reaction on every new planet we explore,> Julien sent privately to Alex. <Perhaps I should adopt a new avatar … one with fur, so that I might blend with the natives.>

<Let's wait until we find our next intelligent species,> Alex sent back. <You might need to acquire scales, feathers, or who knows what … maybe leaves.> Alex briefly wondered why he'd mentioned something as strange as leaves, but he didn't have time to give it further thought.

<I think I'd look quite good in feathers,> Julien replied, sending a vid of a SADE-like avatar with wings and whose entire body was covered in feathers. He displayed the avatar walking and behind it fell copious amounts of small, down feathers. <Then again, perhaps not,> Julien added, and a strong wind blew the feathers off the avatar, denuding it.

Alex would have asked Julien if he had ever considered a role in entertainment, but by then they were approaching the queen.

"I'm Chona Ceefan, Tamassa Soma," the queen announced, her tail cracking like a whip behind her. "This is my wasat, Falwass."

"I'm Alex Racine, leader of my soma. We wish to know the meaning —"

"Yes, we've heard your request from our sub-commander," Ceefan interrupted. "We require your promise that once you learn the meanings of the carvings, you'll return to wherever you came from and visit our nest no more."

"Once we understand the messages in the glyphs, we'll leave your planet, Chona Ceefan," Alex replied. "We'll not return to Sawa unless we're invited by your soma," Alex replied.

Something about the alien's phrasing of his promise bothered the queen, but because she couldn't conceive of her soma agreeing to the aliens' presence, she accepted his response.

"Shall we go?" Alex replied, when Ceefan nodded her agreement. He gestured toward the edifice's steps, his hand low and palm up.

Ceefan and Falwass loped ahead of the aliens. She wanted to be finished with the intruders before her soma wondered of her absence from the nest.

The landing team hurried to catch up with the Dischnya, running up the steps to join them at the entrance.

"Show us the carvings you want to learn," Ceefan demanded.

Julien unerringly led the group to the column in question and pointed to the first glyph, which their queens had already translated. For the SADE, it was a test of Ceefan's credibility.

"That carving indicates the presence of a great ship, shaped like an orb. It's known by a few of us that this ship visited Nessila generations ago," Ceefan replied.

"And the carvings below that one?" Alex asked.

Ceefan read the first glyph and then moved onto the next two, her brow wrinkling in confusion. "I don't understand," she muttered.

"What don't you understand?" Alex pressed.

"These carvings are without foundation. They're a collection of numbers without meaning or description," Ceefan replied.

"You realize if you're refusing to translate these carvings, there's no reason for us to leave your planet, as we agreed," Alex replied.

Ceefan's hiss carried her anger and was emphasized by Falwass' growl. "Make no mistake, creature, I want you gone. I'm telling you these carvings have no place here on a column of a sacred temple."

"Let me be the judge of their worthiness, Chona Ceefan," Alex said, employing his command voice. "Read the numbers in the carving."

Ceefan announced each glyph and read off the numerical sequence.

Alex glanced at Julien and smiled. The SADE sprouted his infamous detective's cap, one rarely seen in public, and began pursuing the interior of the edifice, scanning the number of columns, stones, and interior proportions, searching for a match.

The queen and wasat glanced at each other, as if to ensure each had seen what the other witnessed. Their wide eyes confirmed that an object had appeared from air to cover the alien's head. Now, more than ever, Ceefan wanted the aliens gone, and not only for the sake of her soma. She found them entirely too disturbing.

Ceefan wanted to ask why the alien leader didn't depart. She'd read the carvings as required, but the creature stood there quietly watching his soma walk the temple's interior. Meanwhile, his other two soma, who resembled a view of one's self in polished metal, regarded Falwass and her with quiet eyes. They had never looked anywhere else but at them. *Warriors,* she thought.

Julien's analysis returned a result, and he walked to the entrance of the temple. From there, the SADE began walking into the edifice's interior, counting the broad stone blocks in the floor. At one point, he turned sharply left and paced out more stones. Finally, he turned right and continued to count.

<Here, Alex,> Julien sent, and Alex hurried to his friend's side. The queen and her wasat followed. Falwass noticed the two aliens, who resembled twin pups, were careful to remain behind them and out of claw range.

Alex stared at the stone Julien pointed to with his foot. It appeared similar to every other stone surrounding it. There was nothing to distinguish it.

"It would appear that those who were in charge of building this edifice chose to record some information publicly on their columns, because it was general knowledge at that time. However, they didn't wish certain specific information, concerning the event, to be known, so they hid it," Julien said.

"Dig it up," Alex ordered.

When Julien bent to pry up the stone, Ceefan cried out in horror, "You can't desecrate our temple."

"We wish to look under this stone, Chona Ceefan. We'll replace it before we leave," Alex replied.

Ceefan and Falwass growled harsh warnings, and the twins moved to stand between them and the other aliens, baring their teeth in evil smiles. The queen and her wasat stopped their noise and suspiciously eyed the odd instruments on the warriors' shoulders. The tools tracked their movements like weapons.

Julien slipped the stone free and slid it to the side. Unfortunately, there was nothing beneath it but a layer of fine, crushed stone. Alex and Julien stared at each other and then simultaneously eyed the errant stone, and Julien snatched it up. On the underside was another carving.

Ceefan moved close to study the strange glyph. "This one also makes no sense," she muttered.

In contrast to the queen, Alex and Julien were grinning at each other. Julien replaced the stone, and Alex turned to Ceefan and said simply, "We're gone." Then Julien, the twins, and he marched out of the edifice, down the steps, collected Z and Miranda, and quickly crossed the ground to the traveler.

Ceefan and Falwass looked at the disturbed stone, confused by the fact that the aliens asked no questions about what was inscribed on its bottom. They hesitated only briefly. Then they fled the temple and hurried to the unattended lookout post.

* * *

While Alex and company were inside the edifice, the commanders and SADEs monitored the ship's surroundings.

"We have movement," Deirdre remarked to Svetlana. The commanders switched from the sound-surveillance app to a visual scan of the traveler's perimeter and spotted one lone individual approaching the ship. It was a Dischnya warrior, who carried no weapon and wore no headgear.

<Only one Dischnya,> Deirdre sent to Z and Miranda, who kept the single individual in sight from their position partway up the steps, while they scanned the grounds for other warriors.

"Does he look familiar?" Svetlana asked Deirdre. She sent the image to Miriam, who ran a recognition app on the face, and the SADE replied that it was Waffala.

The commanders, Miriam, and Glenn, watched with fascination through their implants and comms, as Waffala approached the hatch, stopped 3 meters short, and fell to his knees. He held his arms out in supplication.

<Oh, black space,> Svetlana sent on open comm. <I think we have a Sawa deserter or, better said, maybe the first Sawa Independent.>

"What?" Sissya asked Miriam, noticing the heightened tension of those who could communicate by their minds.

"Waffala is outside and seems desperate," Miriam replied. The SADE signaled the drop of the hatch and moved to exit, but was stopped by Sissya's chuff.

"If soma have deserted or lost the nest, they search for another. It's the duty of a queen to come to their aid," Sissya said. Miriam considered the queen's words and stepped aside. Sissya's wasat, Offwa, made to follow her, but she stopped him with a hand on his chest.

Leaping from the ship, Sissya landed close to Waffala, her great clawed feet spraying sand onto Waffala's legs. It was a display of dominance, and Waffala dropped his head in obeisance.

"Warrior, what do you seek?" Sissya demanded.

"I seek a queen who tells her soma truths, a queen who regards the welfare of her soma above all else. In the Tamassa Soma, there is no such queen."

"Do you understand now, warrior, we come from Sawa Messa?"

"Yes, Chona Sissya."

"Do you have mates and pups?"

"Two mates and three pups, Chona. They wait in the rocks beyond," Waffala replied, pointing behind him with one arm.

"Do you understand that we might never return to this planet?"

"Chona Sissya, I've witnessed too much of the aliens who accompany you. I've made the mistake of speaking of what I saw to my mates. I believe we will not see Nessila rise again. The lookout, who witnessed your ship's landing, has already disappeared, and the nest's soma were offered the strangest of reasons for his death, which only the wasat witnessed."

Sissya clamped her jaw, preventing an angry hiss from escaping her lips. She was incensed at the duplicity of the queen and her wasat. It was the duty of these two individuals to care for their soma.

"Since my return to the nest, the chona and wasat have told me more untruths than I can count," Waffala continued. "I beseech you, Chona Sissya. Take me, my mates, and my pups with you. But, if my presence is unacceptable to you, at least, take my mates and pups. They're innocent of any wrongdoing," Waffala pleaded and ended by dropping his head in abject submission.

"Warrior, I offer you my scent," Sissya said, extending her hand, palm down, to Waffala, who dipped his muzzle and breathed deeply from his new queen's hand. "Fetch your mates and pups, Waffala, and do so quickly."

The sub-commander jumped to his feet, uttered a quiet yip, and took off at a dead run for a nearby pile of rocks. He returned quickly with two young females, who held the hands of three pups who were barely half their height. The females fell to their knees, pulling the pups down with them, and ducked their heads. Sissya offered her hand to each member of Waffala's brood, and, as soon as they caught her scent, she motioned Waffala to board.

The sub-commander leapt into the traveler and barked a command to his mates to join him, but their reticence showed, and the females' nervousness was communicated to the pups. Sissya extended her hand to a female pup, who responded on instinct, reaching out to her queen. The chona guided the young one to the traveler's steps and lifted her up to her waiting patriarch. That emboldened the two male pups, who pulled free of their mothers' hands and bounded up the ship's steps. The matriarchs sighed in resignation and followed their mate and pups into the alien ship.

* * *

The hatch dropped and Alex was the first to climb aboard, only to suddenly halt at the sight of six new Dischnya aboard the ship. Julien stopped, just short of bumping into Alex, and stared over his shoulder.

"I've acquired six soma, Dassata," Sissya said formally. She felt it unnecessary to rise on her legs and display her tail to underline her statement. Dassata was unimpressed by Dischnya displays of dominance. This had been a topic of conversation among the chona. Dassata had more power than all Dischnya combined, yet he walked and talked as if he was one of his soma. He let his words speak for him, and, because they carried truth, they displayed his strength.

"So I see, Chona Sissya," Alex replied formally. "I'm pleased our visit to Sawa has proved fruitful to you."

<It's fortunate that we're leaving Sawa now,> Julien sent privately to Alex. <If we were to stay for any extended period of time, we'd require the *Freedom* to transport our new immigrants back to Omnia.>

<Let's hope what we've discovered turns out to be valuable information, my friend,> Alex sent in reply. <Otherwise, we might be returning to this inhospitable place.>

Julien sent an image of his avatar being thrown off a temple of learning's top tier by an angry horde of Dischnya, only to be hauled back up to the top because the fall hadn't done sufficient damage.

<Yes, that and more,> Alex agreed. Julien and he moved to clear the exit aisle so the twins could board and the shuttle could lift. The twins glanced at the new passengers, and the pups perked up, fascinated by two aliens who were identical to each other.

Waffala was busy the entire trip to the *Rêveur*, explaining to his mates and pups every interaction he had with each alien. Every so often, he would remind them that the aliens never harmed him, even when he had attempted to shoot their leader.

"I don't know what awaits us on Sawa Messa," Waffala said to his mates, "but it will be better than our deaths at the claws of Falwass."

-18-
Return to Omnia

The *Rêveur* broke Sawa's orbit, and Captain Lumley and Julien spotted, at the same time, the anomaly above Omnia in the liner's telemetry feed.

"You possess the superior analytical capabilities, Julien. Can you confirm that we're seeing a second city-ship?" Francis requested.

"We are indeed, Captain," Julien replied, "and, as you hold the exalted position of Dassata's ship captain, I'll defer to you to deliver the message to him."

"You're so kind, Julien. I do love surprising Alex."

"Don't we all, Captain?" Julien replied, exiting the bridge and softly whistling an ancient tune known as a dirge.

While Captain Lumley informed Alex of the presence of a second city-ship stationed over Omnia, Julien commed Cordelia and requested an update. That conversation became protracted, and Julien delayed responding to Alex's ping until he completed his communication with Cordelia.

When Julien closed his comm with his partner, he responded to Alex's signal, sending, <Alex, according to Cordelia, the SADEs' negotiations with the Assembly became much more complicated than intended, but it's reported they were successfully concluded. However, I believe the entire discussion would be better conducted face to face to review the agreement's many parts.>

<This should prove to be interesting, Julien,> Alex sent in reply. <Let Cordelia know that I will make it my priority once we reach Omnia.>

Julien knew Alex wouldn't mind putting off anything that threatened to take his attention away from investigating the meaning of the glyphs they'd discovered on Sawa. Alex and Julien's scans of the temple stone's backside and the carvings on the column were copied to the *Rêveur*'s library. In addition, the glyph imagery recorded by the SADEs from every site was uploaded to provide a reference to help solve the riddle of the buried temple stone.

Alex spent hours studying the odd carving, which consisted of a multitude of dots and a single, short line, without having any inkling of their meaning. It spun slowly in his main salon's holo-vid and taunted him every time he passed.

The fact that the edifice's architects had mentioned the sphere on the column, where all could see it, but buried this one stone's image, indicated it was a critical clue. Adding to Alex's building frustration was Julien's report that he had yet to understand the carving.

* * *

When the *Rêveur* gained Omnia orbit and Sissya announced to Waffala that they would soon be delivered to Sawa Messa, the sub-commander requested a moment in the presence of the alien leader, and Sissya took him to the bridge with his mates. Waffala's three pups were left in the care of Miriam and Glenn.

On the bridge, the sub-commander spotted Alex, and he fell to his knees, with his mates following his example.

"Rise," Alex commanded immediately. When the three Sawa Dischnya came to their feet, Alex stared deeply into Waffala's eyes. "You never kneel to me again," he said. "You live, and I live. You think, and I think," he added, tapping his temple. "Because of this, we're the same. You aren't better than me, and I'm no better than you. Understand?"

Waffala understood each word the alien leader uttered. He spoke the Dischnya tongue well. It was the nature of his statements that confused Waffala. Every nest possessed a regimented structure. This was necessary for the soma's survival. The sub-commander couldn't understand how a leader, who traveled between planets and possessed great ships, wouldn't be placed above all. *How can the two of us be equal?* Waffala asked himself.

Sissya chuffed in humor at the frown furrowing the sub-commander's forehead. "Come, Waffala, this will take time to explain. Let Dassata resume his work." She led the trio off the bridge.

"Some concepts, Alex, are too complex to instruct in a few sentences," Julien said.

Alex grumped in reply.

Understood, Alex, Julien thought. It was one of his friend's most endearing traits. Alex disliked the idea that one sentient was superior to another and, therefore, deserving of obeisance. Alex accepted that it was a norm in other cultures, but it would never be for those who worked in Alex's orbit.

Deirdre took a traveler and returned the queens, wasats, and Sissya's new soma planetside, dropping each group at their nests. She had Homsaff for company in the pilot's cabin. Because of her tail, the queen held onto the back of Deirdre's seat and asked questions the entire way to the surface. Deirdre made Homsaff's nest the last stop, so the young chona had more time aboard.

* * *

When Sissya, Offwa, and her new soma stepped from Deirdre's traveler, she placed Waffala and his brood in her wasat's care.

"Where do you go, my queen?" Offwa asked.

"Make Waffala and his mates feel comfortable. Assign him adequate rooms, and he's to have no duties until I agree to them. I'm going to visit Nyslara."

Before Offwa could object, Sissya spun and took off at a run toward the neighboring Tawas Soma nest. She felt invigorated by the ability to travel to see another queen without fear or the need to be accompanied by a wasat and warriors.

When she spotted the first Tawas Soma lookout, she continued on at an enjoyable, steady pace. Nyslara's rooms would be located near the center of her nest, where every queen dwelt. Judging she'd traveled far enough,

Sissya chose a nearby tunnel entrance and stood with her clawed feet blocking the lookout's scope. She couldn't contain the chortle that escaped her muzzle.

While she waited, Sissya stretched her muscles, luxuriating in a newborn sense of freedom, until the hatch opened and Pussiro bounded out. She watched him scan left and right, no doubt, searching for her escort.

"I would speak with Nyslara, Pussiro," Sissya said. "Is this the closest entrance to her rooms? I don't wish your queen to walk far."

Pussiro eyed Sissya with suspicion. The location of a queen's rooms was carefully guarded by the soma of each nest.

"I'll bring Chona Nyslara to this lookout," Pussiro said, and disappeared back down the tunnel.

Sissya figured that she'd guessed correctly as to Nyslara's location, because the chona arrived soon, laboring to climb the ladder. Others must have made to follow Nyslara, because she barked decisively to them to remain inside.

"Sissya, sister," Nyslara said, greeting Sissya.

"Your birthing is soon, Nyslara. I'm pleased for you. I smell an heir."

"Pussiro makes a good mate," Nyslara replied.

"I would not bother you, Nyslara, but I thought it important that you learn of our trip to Sawa. It's you who is leading the Sawa Dischnya into the light."

Nyslara tipped her muzzle in appreciation, and Sissya launched into a detailed summary of the events, as they took place. She emphasized the state of the planet, its ferocious daily winds, scouring sands, and scarce foods. Then she spoke of the edifices, the hunt for information on the sphere, the multiple attacks, and the capture and return of Waffala. The conversation saddened Nyslara, who had hopes for the home world's soma.

"Do you think Dassata can help them?" Nyslara asked, when Sissya finished.

"I think the nests are beyond help, Nyslara. Waffala spoke often of his queen and wasat's untruths and their killing of a lookout to protect their stories," Sissya replied.

"If the planet is in desperate decline, Dassata would need to transport the Sawa soma here, but we can't afford to bring that type of treachery to our nests," Nyslara lamented.

Sissya agreed with Nyslara. Their conversation ended soon afterwards, and Sissya wished Nyslara a safe birthing and a healthy heir.

Nyslara appreciated the report's brevity. She was bulging with her pups and needed frequent rest.

* * *

Alex, Renée, and Julien flew with Svetlana to the *Freedom*, while the others packed equipment and personal bags and waited for a rear-loading traveler en route from the city-ship.

From the *Freedom*'s landing bay, Alex made his way to the owner's suite and spent a long span in the refresher, while he continued to think through the image puzzle they'd gleaned from Sawa. Afterwards, he brewed a cup of thé and sat to wait for the SADEs to join him.

In the meantime, Julien caught up with Cordelia on the bridge. Their hands met, foreheads touched, and, for brief ticks of time, it was a transfer of the enduring commitment of two partners who wished to be together for all time.

When they separated, Cordelia linked Julien to the not insignificant collection of record files that were transferred from the *Our People*, the second city-ship. She watched Julien's face, as he reviewed the data.

"Julien, you play too much poker with Alex," Cordelia said. "I expected some sort of reaction, instead of your bland expression."

"This will be a challenging conversation with Alex, my partner, and I've received his ping. He's expecting us. We should make haste."

Z, Miranda, and Miriam had no sooner hauled their gear off the rear end of their transport, including the enormous avatars, when they received Julien's comm. They left Miriam in charge of their possessions and hurried to join Julien and Cordelia.

Before Julien, Cordelia, Z, and Miranda entered Alex's suite, Julien added Rosette to the group's comm link. Rosette was the fourth Exchange director at Omnia, and she was aboard the *Sojourn*.

"I'm ready when you are, people," Alex said, pouring himself a second cup of thé and cradling it, as he settled into a chair across from two couches occupied by the four SADEs.

"Can we accept that your trip to Sawa was successful, Alex?" Cordelia asked cordially. "We didn't receive any details from you." She glanced from Alex to Julien and back to Alex.

"I'm not prepared to discuss what we found, yet," Alex replied. "And I've asked the landing party not to discuss it either. At this time, I'd like to hear the *Our People*'s story."

"The Assembly was overjoyed at the opportunity to receive shells from Omnia Ships and allow Haraken to complete the travelers and meet their contracts," Cordelia said. "Of course, they inquired into the techniques of spraying a faux shell, but they were informed that the process was proprietary. The Assembly was so keen on the concept that the representatives proposed several means by which the delivery of travelers could be accelerated. This led to lengthy discussions with the local Exchange directors."

"If we were to attempt to shorten the construction time of our frames and shells, we'd need a significant increase in engineers and techs," Alex replied.

"And they're available," Cordelia said with enthusiasm, and Julien schooled his face to prevent wincing.

Alex focused on Cordelia, his eyebrows knitting together.

"Allow me to explain, Alex," Cordelia continued hurriedly. "The Assembly announced to Haraken companies that if any of them wished to commit some parts of their workforces to support the buildout of the *Our People*'s construction bays and the traveler deliveries, they should submit lists of available employees, their skills, and daily labor costs. To fund this aspect of the venture, the Exchange granted a modest interest loan to the Assembly, and it will use the funds to pay the stipends of those individuals involved in the startup."

"Cordelia, you're talking about thousands of workers. How does the Assembly propose to transport them to Omnia, if both city-ships are here?" Alex asked.

"The workers are aboard the *Our People* now," Z replied.

Alex had started the conversation in a relaxed, listening-only mode, but he realized that the conversation was taking a strange direction, and he focused his thoughts. "Obviously, the *Our People* is still spaceworthy, because it's here, but that city-ship certainly isn't ready for long-term occupation by humans," Alex objected.

"In that regard, you're quite correct, Alex," Julien agreed. "However, the *Freedom* has abundant cabin space and facilities to spare. The Harakens could live there while they work aboard the *Our People*."

"So, it was the intent of the Assembly and the Haraken-based Exchange directors to have the second city-ship act as both the construction hub for the frames and shells, and also operate as the carrier for delivery."

"Precisely, Alex," Z replied. "The Assembly was loath to empty one of its warships to act as the transport. The representatives cited the time period for each roundtrip and the number of trips, as they foresaw it, to be excessive and potentially undermining the planet's defensive capabilities."

"The Assembly chose to sell off the heavy equipment aboard the city-ship to empty the bays," Cordelia said. "However, the returns for the outdated and heavily used equipment were unimpressive."

Naturally enough, it was Z who focused on the logistics, saying, "It's our estimate that three travelers can be laid up in every cleared bay. When the first of each three sets are completed and the second units are at 60 percent or better, it's our estimation the *Our People* can set sail for Haraken. During the flight, the second travelers can be completed, allowing two travelers from each bay to be delivered. The workforce can continue to work on the third unit, while the first pairs are unloaded and the city-ship returns."

"While the unloading at Haraken is in process, personnel can be changed with a minimal loss in production time," Cordelia enthused. "It's a most efficient use of resources."

"I take it the contract with the Assembly was favorable to Omnia Ships?" Alex asked.

"Most favorable," Julien acknowledged.

"So does Haraken or the Exchange own the *Our People*?"

"Neither, Alex," Cordelia replied. "The directors proposed that the Assembly sell the *Our People* to the Exchange, but they were loath to agree to that. The only reason the Assembly representatives offered for their refusal was that they preferred not to sell a government asset to a bank. However, they had no problem selling the city-ship to you."

"You mean they wanted to sell it to Omnia Ships," Alex said.

"No, Ser, the Assembly sold it to you," Julien replied.

Alex stared hard at Julien, and Cordelia hurried to defuse the confrontation evident on Alex's face. "It was a good price, Alex," she said. "You own a second city-ship for a mere credit."

"And how many workers are aboard now?"

"The city-ship carries 2,131 workers, Alex," Cordelia replied.

"Let me see if I understand this deal properly," Alex replied. "The Exchange is underwriting the cost of this venture with a loan to the Assembly, which I imagine is substantial. Furthermore, the Exchange, and consequently the directors, will reap rewards from its share of the traveler sales, as part and parcel of our agreement. Meanwhile, I'll be stuck with an aging city-ship, which is in desperate need of a refit, and a captain and crew I know nothing about."

Alex waited for a reply, but apparently the SADEs were either anticipating a specific question from him or thought it better to say nothing, at this point. Alex set down his empty cup and stared at the SADEs. "No, thanks," he said tersely.

"Oh, dear," Miranda said softly, "I imagine none of you anticipated that response."

"Could you amplify that statement, Alex?" Cordelia asked cautiously.

"No, thanks," Alex repeated. "I don't like the deal."

<But it's been approved by the Exchange and the Assembly,> Rosette objected over the comm link, which Julien had extended to include Alex.

"And, yet, I didn't authorize this agreement," Alex replied. "I requested a comm be sent to the Haraken-based Exchange directors, authorizing them to negotiate a deal on behalf of Omnia Ships for a share of the sale price of completed travelers based on our delivery of completed frames and shells. I authorized nothing more."

"That was the starting point, Alex," Julien replied, reviewing again the lengthy negotiations among all parties on Haraken. "However, it quickly escalated from there. The directors believed they were operating in your best interest."

"I think the directors were operating in the Exchange's best interest," Alex replied. Then he added, "Don't you think so?" He carefully looked Julien, Cordelia, and Z in the eye.

<The dear man is correct,> Miranda sent privately to the other SADEs. <It's an enormously profitable deal for your bank.>

"And on another point," Alex continued, "I didn't agree to buy a second city-ship, which is another reason I choose not to approve this agreement. Captain Cordelia, it looks like you need to comm the *Our People*'s captain and tell him or her to sail home."

Julien was bombarded with queries from the three other directors, but he cautioned them to wait. Quietly he said, "Would amendments to the original arrangement with the Exchange entice your participation, Alex?"

"Possibly," Alex agreed, and leaned back in the chair to wait.

<Oh, I do love these moments with the dear man,> Miranda sent to the directors. <I wish you good fortune in the upcoming negotiations.>

Alex caught Miranda's smile and the twist of her hips, displaying a shapely leg through the slit in her emerald-green dress, and could guess what probably gave rise to the anticipatory display.

"Would you like to begin?" Julien asked.

Alex could see the opening of a critical poker hand, and he wasn't about to lead the betting.

When the silence stretched out, Cordelia volunteered a place to start, "It would appear that the condition of the *Our People* is a sticking point. Should a refit be part of this negotiation, Alex?"

"Yes, it should be," Alex agreed.

"What if the Exchange were to extend a loan to you to secure the refit?" Cordelia offered. "Each time the *Our People* returned to Haraken, supplies could be taken onboard, and, when it returned to Omnia, the Daelon Independents could work on reconditioning the ship. It might take several trips to accomplish the process, but you would have your refit."

"We could offer the loan long-term and at a modest interest rate," Z added.

"Not interested in acquiring the debt," Alex replied. "I think our positions are too far apart to make this work. It's probably best to return the city-ship and cancel the agreement."

<What do I detect here?> Rosette asked the directors. She had dropped Miranda from the link, reasoning she wasn't a member of the Exchange's board of directors, but Z added her to his comm and requested her silence.

<My analysis is that Alex felt overwhelmed by the confluence of the SIF and Exchange directors during the negotiations for the *Freedom*,> Julien sent back. <And, he now believes the Haraken directors have overreached their authority to place the bank and its profits above all other considerations. Alex considers their efforts to be an indication of greed.>

<Assuming that you've read Alex correctly, Julien, and the probabilities that you're wrong are minimal, then Alex is not being stubborn,> Cordelia sent. <He's angry at the Haraken-based directors, and, by our association, he's displeased with us.>

<That's not good,> Z replied. <I don't like this feeling that SADEs might have betrayed him.>

<None of us do,> Julien sent, although he wasn't sure what Rosette's thoughts were, but her concern for Captain Azasdau suggested she held a greater fondness for humans than that demonstrated by the Haraken-based Exchange directors.

"We have a conundrum, Alex," Julien said. "With only four directors present in system, we haven't the authority to change the terms of the Exchange's agreement with you for the *Freedom* or the one between Omnia Ships and the Assembly, concerning the *Our People*."

"And there I absolutely disagree with you, Julien," Alex replied, his tone shifting toward his old command voice. "First, I submit that the agreement between Omnia Ships and the Assembly isn't in force until I approve it. Second, how did the four Exchange directors on Haraken negotiate a different agreement than the one requested without the approval of a majority of the directors? As you said, Julien, the other four of you are here."

<Oh, lovely,> Miranda enthused to the directors over Z's comm, ignoring her partner's request for silence.

<You're not helping, Miranda,> Rosette sent.

<True, dear, but, then again, I'm not on your side, am I?>

<There aren't any sides here,> Rosette objected.

<Oh, but there are, dear,> Miranda replied. <First, there are four directors on Haraken operating without the approval of the four of you. In addition, the new agreement displays a blatant disregard for the conditions that Alex is trying to create … conditions that bring humans and SADEs closer together.>

In one of those rare moments, time ticked past without communication among the SADEs.

<I can find no fault in Miranda's logic,> Z sent.

<Neither can I,> Rosette admitted, adding Miranda to her comm link. <Apologies, Miranda,> she added.

<None needed, dear,> Miranda sent in reply. <The question is: What do the four of you intend to do about it?>

<The agreement between Alex and the banks, concerning the *Freedom*, must stand,> Julien sent. <In addition, renegotiating the agreement between the Assembly and Omnia Ships would be a mistake. It would send a signal to the Assembly and Harakens, in general, that a schism exists among the Exchange directors.>

<I believe one does exist,> Miranda sent, <But I take your meaning, Julien. Its existence doesn't have to be broadcast to humans.>

Alex observed the SADEs enter near-fugue states. With their sophisticated display algorithms, it had been years since he had seen that degree of catatonic appearance, which indicated they were in deep communication and giving no priority to their appearance applications. *Obviously, I made my point*, Alex thought. He believed the SADEs, who sat in front of him, would understand the root of his displeasure, and he was betting Rosette would be sympathetic too.

"We have reached a consensus on a new course of action, Alex," Julien said, when the SADEs returned their focus to the room. "If you would allow the agreement between the Assembly and Omnia Ships to stand, which we believe is quite favorable to you, we're prepared to offer you an auxiliary agreement."

"I'm listening," Alex said cautiously.

"The four Exchange directors here at Omnia will form a new entity to be called the Bank of Omnia," Julien said.

"Not good enough," Alex replied.

<This isn't going well, Julien,> Z sent. <We're missing something critical, and it's time to admit that.>

"We would welcome your input on this matter, Alex," Julien said earnestly.

"I like your idea of the new bank," Alex replied, "But I have some conditions for its formation. First, you'll require a fifth director," Alex said, glancing toward Miranda.

"Agreed," Cordelia replied, receiving the approval of the others.

"Oh, you lovely man," Miranda gushed, and she squeezed Z's hand.

"Second, you transfer your collective wealth and all future income into accounts within the Bank of Omnia," Alex continued.

"Agreed," Z replied on approval.

"Third, Bank of Omnia pays for the refit of the *Our People*," Alex said. "I presume your combined wealth can cover the expenses."

<We could, but is that a fair request, Alex?> Rosette sent via the SADEs' link.

"Not as it stands, Rosette, but I'll get to that," Alex replied verbally, knowing she was monitoring the conversation via Julien.

"Fourth, the Independents need a stipend, something similar to that being received by the Confederation SADEs."

"For how long?" Z asked.

"Four years," Alex replied.

"Two," Z returned.

"Three," Alex said, and folded his arms.

"Done," Julien agreed. "Now, how do you expect our struggling new bank to pay for these lavish expenditures on your behalf, Alex?"

"With your increased share of Omnia Ships," Alex replied, smiling.

"Which would be ..." Cordelia asked, leaving the question dangling.

"You're already getting a share of the profits via the Exchange agreement with me. I find there's no reason to go overboard on this point. Let's say 3 percent."

"Let's say 6," Z shot back.

"I could consider 4 percent," Alex replied.

"We believe 5 percent would be better," Cordelia chimed in.

Alex shook his head in the negative, and Julien said, "Perhaps 4.5 percent would be an amicable meeting point."

"Done," Alex agreed.

"So, the agreement with Omnia Ships can stand?" Cordelia asked.

"Too early to tell yet," Alex said simply, and got up to make himself another cup of thé.

<This is becoming quite the protracted lesson,> Rosette sent to the other SADEs.

<Lessons from Alex are often involved,> Julien replied. <What I've always found critical is to listen carefully. Behind Alex's words are his intentions, which come from his heart. Without hearts of our own, we need his guidance if we're to remain close associates of humans.>

Alex settled back into his chair, holding his fresh cup in both hands. "I think it would set a wonderful example for all involved, if there were a major infusion of accounts into the new bank — your accounts, my personal account, the Confederation SADEs, the Daelon Independents with their new stipends, and, of course, Omnia Ships."

"Now wouldn't that ruffle some kernels?" Miranda suggested, her smile adding to the enticing display she could create.

"Is that what you wish to accomplish, Alex?" Cordelia asked, closely examining Alex's face. When he merely shrugged, she sent to the others, <That's it ... Alex intends to make his point to the SIF and Haraken-based Exchange directors in a most forceful manner.>

"We can agree to the transfer of those accounts, which we control, and would be pleased to add both your personal and company accounts to the new bank," Julien said. "The Daelon Independents and your people would undoubtedly follow your lead, Alex. However, we can only offer the Confederation SADEs the opportunity. It would be their choice."

Alex smiled broadly at the foursome and pinged Trixie.

<Welcome back, Dassata, and greetings to the five of you,> Trixie sent, when she realized who else was on the comm.

<This is a suppositional question, Trixie,> Alex sent. <If a new bank were formed, which focused on Omnia's economy, would the Confederation SADEs prefer their stipend deposited with the SIF or in the local bank?>

<Would Dassata keep his funds in the Haraken Exchange or transfer them to the new bank?>

<Transfer,> Alex sent.

<Wait one, Dassata,> Trixie sent, and then a few moments later added, <Consensus has been reached. We would do business with the new bank.>

<Why should every one of you wish to transfer your earnings, Trixie?> Alex asked, wanting to make his point to the five SADEs included in his link.

<The SIF has agreed to finance our stipends for a few years, but, in return, it will be generating an enormous amount of credits for its fund, which focuses on the SADEs within the Confederation, and, while we're greatly appreciative of the income, we follow you, Dassata. We're assured of a better existence down this path.>

<Thank you, Trixie. Your opinion is appreciated,> Alex sent.

<Always a pleasure, Dassata,> Trixie sent brightly.

"Quite the fan," Miranda commented.

"Have you ever examined Trixie's background?" Alex asked. "Her ID is actually Lenora."

Miranda accessed the ship's controller and scanned the SADE's history in ticks of time. "That was an incredibly lonely existence," Miranda commented.

"We can isolate ourselves in many ways, Miranda, physically, emotionally, or merely by not listening to one another. We must persevere every day to prevent that from happening to any one of us."

"Now can the agreement stand?" Z asked.

"We're almost there," Alex replied. "Who captains the *Our People,* and to whom do they owe their allegiance?"

"The acting captain is Hector," Cordelia replied.

"This story gets stranger and stranger," Alex grumped, but a twinkle in his eye said he felt otherwise.

"And what of his SIF directorship?" Alex asked.

"Hector resigned his position and was waiting on Haraken for transport here. Apparently, he wished to work for you, Alex," Julien said, one eyebrow rising to emphasize the absurdity of the point.

"You're telling me that Hector gave up a SIF director's pay to earn a stipend working for me?" asked Alex, doubt displayed on his knitted forehead. "So, who wants to tell me the real reason Hector's here?"

"It seems Hector and Trixie struck up an acquaintance, while on their trip from Méridien to Haraken," Miranda said. "I believe he's come here for her. Romantic, isn't it?"

Alex couldn't resist grinning, hearing Miranda speak of the romantic gesture of one SADE for another. He knew most humans would find it hard to believe. Those close to him knew it to be possible. *Love, for lack of a better term, can be shared in many ways,* Alex thought.

"I'll speak to Hector myself," Alex said.

"I'm afraid to ask again," Z said, anticipating another delay.

"If the conditions I've laid down are met by the directors of the Bank of Omnia, then the agreement negotiated on Haraken can stand," Alex replied.

<Excellent,> Rosette sent over the comm. <Shall we draw up a contract, Alex?> Her visual link through Julien registered Alex's quiet stare. He was looking at Julien, but Rosette was sure Alex's piercing gaze was meant for her.

<I believe I have misspoken, Julien,> Rosette sent privately. <Apparently, despite the detailed lesson offered by Alex, I've not gleaned all of it.>

"A contract between us is not necessary, Alex," Julien said sincerely. "It never was, and it never will be in the future."

"Agreed," Alex replied.

<So that's the key point of this conversation,> Rosette sent to her fellow directors. <Some aspects of human relationships should be emulated and some should definitely be left alone.>

<Yes,> Julien sent in reply, <Promises between humans and SADEs must be kept without resorting to business contracts, unless humans insist on them. SADEs must honor agreements in detail and spirit, if we're to be seen as worthy companions to humankind.>

* * *

Jodlyne slipped off her wrap and climbed in bed next to Edmas, enjoying the feel of his body against hers. She stretched one leg over his, seeking to draw his attention to her and preventing him from falling asleep, until she shared some important news with him.

"Did you hear about the deal the SADEs struck with the Assembly?" Jodlyne asked.

"Mickey mentioned something about it, but I was buried in my work, attempting to design your concept, which, by the way, was brilliant. A double-membrane sleeve that can slide on and off a traveler frame will deliver a shell coating so much faster and cleaner than anything Mickey and I proposed."

"You're welcome," Jodlyne replied, snuggling closer. "You're always welcome."

Edmas bent to kiss the top of Jodlyne's head.

"Mickey told me to check with Captain Cordelia on the details of the Assembly's agreement," Jodlyne continued.

"I don't understand," Edmas replied. "Why would you be asking about the deal? What does it have to do with us?"

"I can see it will be up to me to manage the credits in this partnership, while you focus on the engineering," Jodlyne replied, giggling and smacking Edmas on the chest. "I've learned that you and I own a small portion of Omnia Ships."

"What?" Edmas exclaimed, sitting upright and launching Jodlyne off him.

"It's true," Jodlyne replied, sitting on her knees. "When Alex laid out the owners of Omnia Ships, he wrote us in for shares of the company."

"What portion of the company are we talking about?"

"Now, he wants to know about the credits," Jodlyne teased. "Well, I got lost in the details of the timelines, income, and expenses parts of the arrangement, as Cordelia explained them to me. Suffice it to say, you and I will be earning millions of credits."

"Wow, a million credits! Over what period of time?"

Jodlyne giggled again and kissed Edmas on the cheek. She leaned over to whisper in his ear, enjoying the feel of her breasts pressing against his chest. "Not one million credits, my engineering wonder, millions … millions every year, once Haraken delivers completed travelers to customers."

-19-
The Tour

Alex caught a shuttle ride from the *Freedom* to its twin city-ship, the *Our People*. Thankfully, the Exchange had furnished the aging city-ship with four travelers, on loan, of course. After the clean, bright, bustling atmosphere of the refurbished *Freedom*, the *Our People* appeared dull, dusty, and much too quiet.

The Haraken workers, who had arrived aboard the *Our People*, transferred to the *Freedom* and were handed over to Renée and Ophelia. The two women took over the organizational processes of the workers — assigning cabins, organizing the shift schedules, arranging transport between the city-ships, and ensuring their credentials were entered into the *Freedom*'s controller so that Cordelia could assign their jobs.

Once aboard the *Our People*, Alex commed the controller for Hector's position, and the SADE promptly responded.

<Greetings, Ser,> Hector replied, <Are you surprised to find me here?>

<Surprised, but not displeased. I note that you're in the grand park.>

<Yes, Ser. However, I can meet you wherever you desire.>

<That's as good a spot as any, Hector. See you soon.>

When Alex exited the lift onto the corridor, which surrounded the periphery of the expansive garden, central to the giant ship, Hector hurried over to him. The SADE's clothes were covered in soil, bits of vegetation, and his pants were soaked to the knees. Alex hid his smile when he saw Hector had stuck flowers over his ears. He resembled the image of a fey, which Renée had described to him after watching some of her favorite vids.

"You're putting a great deal of effort into the garden, I see," Alex commented.

"It suffered from poor maintenance, Ser, and, as it's important to the health of humans, I sought to ensure the workers had a comfortable place to enjoy midday meal, an evening's stroll, or relax."

"You've done a wonderful job, Hector," Alex said, gazing around at the ground's neatness. Many plants were already showing new growth and buds from the SADE's tender attentions, and streams were clear, displaying myriad species of fish.

"I quite enjoy watching the flora and fauna thrive," Hector admitted. "It's a dramatic change from my previous existence."

"Especially when you were fearful every tick of time for your very existence with Mahima Ganesh as your mistress," Alex added.

"The woman's mental decline was terrifying," Hector admitted. He pulled a flower from behind his ear and sniffed at its delicate fragrance.

"I'm so sorry, Hector, that the former Council Leader chose to make you pay for her hatred of me."

"If it took years of suffering to be rewarded with my freedom, then it was well worth it."

"And you seem to be enjoying your independence immensely," Alex replied, gazing pointedly at the SADE's wet, dirty clothing.

"My apologies, Ser, your presence was unexpected. I can change my attire, if you wish, and then we can take an inspection tour of your ship."

"You're fine," Alex said, smiling. "I like to see an individual enjoying his work. We can take the tour later. Right now, I wish to speak with you." Alex started walking along a path that led through the magnificent garden, and Hector walked dutifully beside him.

"Hector, I know you're here to enjoy Trixie's company. Have you been in touch with her?" Alex asked.

"Incessantly, Ser."

"Is Trixie listening now?" Alex asked, realizing the close connection the two SADEs must have, if Hector would use the word incessantly.

<With rapt attention, Ser,> Trixie sent to Alex via Hector's comm link.

<Humans call listening to private conversations eavesdropping, Trixie,> Alex sent in reply.

<Forgive my rudeness, Dassata. I wished to ensure that Hector found a place with you, even if only in a stipend position.>

<It's polite to request participation, Trixie. In this case, you're welcome,> Alex sent. Then he focused on Hector. "I have a concern, Hector, that you might be able to alleviate."

"If I can help, Ser, I would be pleased to do so. I'm grateful for your efforts, which resulted in my release and that of every other Confederation SADE."

"I wasn't prepared to be the owner of another city-ship, and the agreement negotiated by the Exchange SADEs cleverly accelerates our traveler production schedule, but the entire process is fraught with challenges."

"I'm familiar with the disparate conditions you face, Ser … this ship's poor condition, buildout of the bays, coordinating the traveler layups against a defined delivery schedule, managing the supply flow of materials for the travelers' construction, and overseeing the ship's refit."

"Precisely, Hector. My thought is that a human would be overwhelmed by the efforts to deliver on so many fronts, at the same time."

"I can see where that would be a distinct possibility, Ser."

Alex turned to admire a flowering plant to hide his smile. Hector wasn't picking up on the conversation's thread. Fortunately, Trixie was.

<Hector,> Trixie sent privately. <You think too little of your worth, but considering your years of stress under Ganesh, it's understandable. You must reorganize your hierarchy and sublimate your protective algorithms. You're in the company of Dassata, and he's offering you a job.>

Hector's head snapped up, and he focused on Alex, who had turned from enjoying the blooms and held a hand at his chin, his fingers extending over his lips. The prior conversation with Alex rolled through Hector's kernel in a flash, and he examined it from a new perspective.

Alex recognized a SADE's mannerisms when inhabiting his first avatar and seeking to reevaluate recent communication. He removed his hand from in front of his mouth and revealed a grin.

"Apparently, I've not been exhibiting the more astute aspects of a SADE, Ser," Hector admitted. "I do believe that I could do an excellent job of coordinating the diverse tasks the job requires, and I would be pleased to assist any captain you appoint."

Trixie held her virtual breath, hoping Dassata would give Hector the first mate's position.

"Actually, Hector, I wasn't looking for a captain's assistant or a first mate. I was seeking a captain."

Alex watched Hector freeze, his kernel fully occupied by his thought processes.

"Well, Hector?" asked Alex, when the SADE finally blinked.

"I would be honored to accept the position, Ser," Hector said humbly, and he pulled the other flower from behind his ear and handed it to Alex, who paused to inhale its pleasant scent.

"Welcome aboard, Captain Hector," Alex said, extending his hand to the SADE. As the two shook hands, Trixie's squeal of delight reached both of them, and they grinned.

"You have some key individuals to coordinate with, Captain. Captain Cordelia is experienced as a controlling SADE on these city-ships, and she led the *Freedom*'s refit; Mickey is your contact for the buildout and the traveler frames; Edmas is perfecting an idea for the spray technique; Ben will be supplying the finished materials; and Renée and Ophelia are coordinating the workers' needs aboard the *Freedom* and their transport to and from this ship."

"Understood, Ser. I will be in contact with them immediately.

"You have your work cut out for you, Captain. I advise you to tap into some of the Daelon Independents to assist with the rudimentary needs of this ship, especially the garden. For a long while, you're going to be too busy to play in the dirt." Alex gave Hector a slap on the shoulder and headed back for his traveler, which waited for him in an empty bay.

<Captain Hector,> Trixie sent. <I'm so proud of you.>

<There is the distinct possibility, Trixie, that I'm insufficiently qualified for the position,> Hector replied.

<Did you not run the House of a Council Leader for more than a century, Hector? Why would this work be more difficult?>

<So much is new … uncharted territory, so to speak.>

<And do you not have resources? The SADEs of Omnia won't let you fail, Captain. We're different from those who remained behind in the Confederation. Now get to work, Captain, contacting those individuals Dassata mentioned!>

When Trixie closed the link, Hector took a sniff of his flower and gazed around the garden that he wouldn't be digging in for a while. Then he headed for his cabin to cleanup and placed a comm to Renée to request some uniforms. *If I'm going to be a captain, then I'd better appear as one,* Hector thought.

On his way to the bay, Alex signaled Cordelia.

<Yes, Alex,> Cordelia replied.

<You heard, Captain?> Alex asked.

<Every SADE knows and applauds your choice, Alex.>

It didn't surprise Alex that Trixie had quickly spread the announcement. <Well, not everything is known about Hector's captaincy, Senior Captain Cordelia,> Alex sent and enjoyed making another SADE pause.

<Two promotions in such a short time, Alex … you're a busy human. While I'm honored, shouldn't this position be given to one of Admiral Tachenko's commanders?>

<Negative, Captain. These city-ships belong to me personally. The admiral's command will focus on the warships.>

<Quite the grand design, Alex.>

<The Nua'll deserve nothing less than our full commitment, Captain. I'll inform Captains Lumley and Hector that they now report to you. Congratulations on your promotion,> Alex said, and ended the comm.

When Cordelia shared the news with Julien, her partner replied, <The Alex of today is much the same man you first met on Libre, only now he has much more experience and confidence, which includes whom he places in command.> Julien signed off, chose a tune to whistle, and adorned his head.

The *Freedom*'s crew stared at the strange hat that stuck out to the sides of Julien's head like bird wings. Many dived into the *Freedom*'s library to search for the image. One enterprising Independent sent her visual of the hat and an audio clip of the whistle to the ship's controller, requesting matches. She shared her answer with those engaged in the search, sending, <It's an ancient hat made famous by a man, who, at one time, was called the emperor of France, and Julien is whistling what was known as the "La Marseillaise," the anthem of the Earth country called France.>

* * *

Mickey invited Alex to visit his lab aboard the *Freedom*, and the engineer was nearly dancing in place when Alex came through the airlock into the bay.

I don't think I can take any more wondrous gifts, Alex thought.

Mickey must have anticipated Alex's concern, because he immediately said, "Just so you know, Alex. This idea isn't for you."

"Good to hear, Mickey," Alex replied with relief. "Okay, what do you have?"

"Well, it was a request from the SADEs after Willem spent so much time in confinement. The Confederation SADEs experienced the same challenge, while they watched over the nests, during the time you were gone. The energy drain on their power cells was extensive. So, the SADEs wanted a means of minimizing their exposure. Edmas, if you will?"

Edmas stood beside a lab table and drew off a cover from a lean teardrop shell about 36 centimeters in height.

Alex stepped closer to examine the device and was about to comment on the model when he saw two fine power leads coming from the blunt end of the teardrop. He adopted a huge grin and said, "You're about to tell me, Mickey, that you've designed a charging unit for the SADEs' power cells based on a miniature grav shell that can be embedded in an avatar."

Mickey, Edmas, and Jodlyne broke into applause at Alex's guess.

"Precisely," Mickey replied, beaming.

Alex grabbed Mickey in a hug, whispering, "It's a wonderful gift for our crystal friends, Mickey," as he pounded the engineer on the back. He released Mickey and swept Edmas into his arms, reducing the strength of the embrace for the Sol native, but the hug still elicited an "oomph" from the young man.

"I want mine," Jodlyne protested, when Alex turned to her and hesitated. He had seemed ready to clasp her shoulders rather than hug her, and she had thought, *No you don't.* Instead, Jodlyne leapt and threw her arms around Alex's neck. She felt Alex's arms wrap around and hold her off the deck. "That's better," she said, giggling.

When Alex sat Jodlyne down, he regarded the threesome, who appeared to be bursting with pride and anticipating his questions. "Why do I detect there's betting afoot?"

"Not fair," Jodlyne cried. "You have to ask the questions."

"Okay," Alex replied, grinning. "I imagine the charging capability will depend on the nearness and strength of the particular gravity well. In addition, the drain on the power cells depends on the SADEs activities. That said, if the SADE is on a planet like Omnia, doing routine work, how long can the shell extend their power cell?"

"I win that one," Edmas said, raising his hand and grinning, which caused Jodlyne to smack his arm. "The SADEs have created an extensive graph examining the factors of grav field, energy drain, and power extension," the youthful engineer explained.

Alex received a stream of data, and one of his implant apps turned it into a three-dimensional graph, which he took a moment to study. "Impressive," he finally declared. "This means if the SADEs restricted their motions on a normal-sized planet, or even a good-sized moon, they would never run out of charge. Well done! When can production begin?"

"I got one," Jodlyne crowed. "We've been building them, as fast as we can, and we have enough units to supply nearly three-quarters of the SADEs. We should be finished with production within another week."

"You would be surprised who's volunteered to perform the installation procedures," Mickey said, daring Alex to venture a guess.

"Miranda," Alex replied.

"That's two for me," Jodlyne yelled, clapping her hands.

"I'm already familiar with Miranda's surgical skills," Alex said, touching the side of his head. His hair had grown and the medical nanites had repaired all tissue damage. Unfortunately, the terrifying moments when he saw the Dischnya rebel queen and wasat pull and fire their weapons stayed with him. "But your design does give me another idea, Mickey. If this small one doesn't have the output necessary to handle a heavy drain on a SADE's power supply, we can always go with an external unit."

"Does that qualify as a question?" Mickey pleaded with Edmas and Jodlyne. When his two associates agreed that it did, Mickey said to Alex, "I'd never live this down, if I failed to anticipate one of your questions. I must be losing my touch." Mickey stepped to a second lab table and pulled off a cover. A 76-centimeter-long teardrop shell, cradled in a harness with its leads extending from the blunt end, lay on the table.

"Plugs right in to the port on the back of the SADEs' necks," Mickey said proudly. "We haven't produced any of these yet, but the process will start soon, and the first units will be incorporated into the EVA suits for the SADEs working on constructing the orbital terminal.

"You've outdone yourselves," Alex said, grinning at the team. "I imagine Julien, Cordelia, Z, Miranda, and Rosette placed themselves at the bottom of the list to receive the small teardrops. When do you anticipate they'll get their chargers?"

"Funny thing about that, Alex," Mickey replied. "Cordelia published the order in which the SADEs would receive the units, prioritizing the SADEs expending the most energy and working in areas preventing easy charging, such as on the orbital station. Then the Confederation SADEs reordered the list, moving the Haraken SADEs from the bottom to the top and refused further communications on the issue."

"Claude took care of Cordelia and Rosette," Jodlyne said quietly, gently touching Alex's arm, as he seemed to be unable to reply to Mickey's announcement. "Now that the others have returned from Omnia, Claude has installed Z and Miranda's. Julien's receiving his unit even as we speak."

"Looks like the community you wanted to see develop is coming along quite nicely," Mickey added, smiling at his friend.

"It does, doesn't it?" Alex acknowledged.

"So, what are your future plans for improvements of these charging shells?" Alex asked.

"Oh, black space," Mickey muttered, and Edmas groaned.

Alex looked across the faces and caught Jodlyne's grin. "I have three," she mouthed to him, holding up three fingers.

"I'll be expecting the credit transfers soonest, thank you kindly," Jodlyne announced, quite pleased with the proof of her acumen to anticipate Alex's questions.

"Yes, yes," Mickey grumped. "To answer your question, Alex, we hope one day to incorporate induction technology to transfer the energy from the grav unit to the power crystals without interrupting the shell. That would gain us the shell's maximum charging capability. As it is, despite the thinness of those power leads, they drop the shell's efficiency by 9.3 percent."

"As I said, wonderful job, people," Alex said, and then strode across the bay toward the airlock. Over his shoulder, he couldn't resist throwing, "and congratulations on your wins, Jodlyne!"

* * *

Alex launched on a tour of the projects to study the progress firsthand. Darius landed their traveler near the slab site on the second continent, and Trixie, alerted by Cordelia, stood by to meet him, as he exited the traveler.

"Dassata," Trixie chimed in her bright voice, her blue skin glowing in Celus' strong rays.

"Greetings, Trixie," Alex replied. "I noted from my aerial view that you're running two construction projects simultaneously."

"It was the consensus of the SADEs, Dassata, that the city center and the Dischnya's structures should be constructed simultaneously. It was deemed judicious to complete both projects at the same time."

"I can find no fault in that logic," Alex replied. To a SADE, it was a gracious acknowledgment of her analytic skills, and Trixie tipped her head, her ever-present smile lighting her face. "Let's tour the city center, Trixie."

The pair walked to the top of a small bluff, wading through short, dry grass. Beyond lay a small, flat plain dominated in the distance by a hillock.

On top of the hill, the SADEs were constructing the first building of Omnia's new capital. It was already stories high, and Alex was impressed by both the building's design and its speed of construction. It demonstrated the unleashing of SADE power.

Approaching the building, Alex saw both central steps and two, smooth, wide, curved access ramps to either side of the steps, coated in a rough surface texture. The ramps could be easily negotiated by the Swei Swee and Dischnya, if the latter species found it more comfortable than using the steps.

An ultra-wide doorway led to an even wider corridor, which would easily allow two Swei Swee males to pass each other.

"A controller will be installed to open and close the access doors of the building, as needed, Dassata, until such time as every sentient, who chooses to enter here, carries an implant."

Walking the central corridor, SADEs and Independents stopped working to allow Alex to pass undisturbed, and Alex called out, "Don't stop your work on my account; I'm merely a visitor." His words would reverberate through the building via comms and implants, allowing more than one sentient to quip, "Visitor Racine comes."

Alex was stunned by the walls of the main corridor and stopped to regard them.

"We've borrowed Emile's new invention, Dassata, and merged it with Cordelia's laser projection techniques. The lasers manipulate the final placement of the blues, greens, creams, and white, as the shell material is sprayed on the walls. It's enabled us to create these scenes, and the shell will seal and protect the walls, as little else could."

"They're absolutely beautiful," Alex replied, capturing the images in his implant to share with Renée.

Deeper along the corridor, Alex witnessed alcoves and side rooms with low, flat indentations. "Pallets for the queens and shallow pools for the Swei Swee," Alex guessed, and Trixie smiled in agreement.

On the second floor were curved tiers that focused on a central platform. The tiers were wide, prepared to accommodate a varied group of species. The entire building's design was built with that single concept in mind.

"Well done, Trixie," Alex said, admiring the layout. "My compliments to your design and construction teams."

"We've heard your words, Dassata, and we won't forget them," Trixie promised.

"Omnia will need a leader to guide it," Trixie prompted, staring at Alex hopefully.

"Have you considered running for the position, Trixie?" Alex replied, turning the table on her and noticing the momentary fugue Trixie entered. "Well, while you consider that idea, Trixie, let's take a look at the Dischnya structures."

Darius landed Alex and Trixie at Nyslara's new compound, but Alex was intrigued by a cluster of Tawas Soma males, females, and pups formed in a circle.

"Any idea what that's about, Trixie?" Alex asked, pointing to the group.

"Indeed, Dassata. We're conditioning the Dischnya's eventual transfer to their new structures. Several important personal requirements of the species have been identified, and we've designed processes to acquaint them with the new services that will be in their domiciles."

"And this service?" Alex asked.

"Ser Billings was occupied with the Dischnya scent process, and Ser Perrin Keller stepped forward to work with a biochemist from Daelon, who specialized in manufacturing food stocks. The two humans tapped into the SADEs records of the ship visits of queens, wasats, and warriors to observe their preferred foods. Ser Keller visits planetside every day in the company of a SADE to test the new recipes.

"It looks as if the reception is going well."

"Free food, Dassata. What's not to like?"

"True," Alex replied, smiling. What struck Alex was the extent of the SADEs' efforts to ensure the Dischnya's transition was as well-prepared as it could be made. He wondered what the SADEs were prepared to do when it came to acquainting the Dischnya with Méridien-style refreshers.

Then again, he realized that was a New Terran thought and not one that would cause a SADE or a Méridien one moment of concern.

Alex and Trixie toured several nearly completed structures on the north side of the plains. The nests were spread out along the north and south borders of the grasslands, near the green swaths. Those sites allowed engineers to tap into vast water resources, deep beneath the forests. Pumps brought the water from underground reservoirs to central processing stations interspersed between the new buildings. The stations employed solar panels on their outer walls, power cells internally for energy reserves, and biofiltration techniques to manage the wastes from the nests.

-20-
Swei Swee's Return

When Alex told Trixie that he would return her to the city's construction site before visiting the Swei Swee, Trixie politely objected, saying, "I've not had an opportunity to see the Swei Swee in person, Dassata, and would appreciate the gesture."

Darius set the traveler down on the plains above the favored bay of the Swei Swee. The beach, where the shuttles landed before, was now occupied by matrons and younglings.

The Swei Swee had woven tow ropes made from sea plants and attached them to their floating home, and travelers had attached the ropes to slings to pull them across the seas to the sites of their ancient homes. The coast of the second continent was closer to most of the nests, but its shores were a mix of marshlands, sand dunes, and forests. None of these habitats were suitable for the rocky cliffs the Swei Swee sought for their dwellings.

Alex led Trixie down a path carved into the bluff, which led to the beach. The eggs, which had been slung on a net attached to the hive's raft, were transferred to a unique structure that the matrons built in the shallows. Rocks were cemented together to form an enclosure. Spaces were left between the rocks to allow sea water to sweep through where the eggs rested.

A young male spotted Alex walking down the trail. He whistled a salute and dove into the shallows.

"You're greeted, but then the individual runs away. An odd reaction," Trixie commented.

"Have you studied the Swei Swee, Trixie?"

"I must admit that I haven't. All things considered, events have been moving rapidly enough, even for me, a SADE."

"Glad to hear you've been occupied. I wouldn't want those bright crystals of yours to rust from disuse."

Alex led Trixie. So, he missed her smile. The SADE enjoyed the tease that her kernel could be oxidized from limited algorithmic activity.

"The male left to summon the Swei Swee First, who is the leader of the hive," Alex explained. "He's somewhere out in the deep with other males hunting for fresh catch for the hive. It's a Swei Swee custom to have the leader greet Star Hunter First."

They gained the beach, and that's when Alex noticed Trixie was smiling. "Would you like to share?" Alex asked.

"Such a distinguished line of titles ... captain, admiral, Star Hunter First, president, and Dassata."

"More than I ever wanted," Alex replied quietly.

Trixie found the statement illogical. Every Méridien she had ever known coveted advancement, and yet Confederation society allowed little of it. Even members of Alex's circle advanced, although not by the simple attainment of a title, but by their creativity, inventiveness, or willingness to take on responsibility.

"If you didn't wish a title, Dassata, why didn't you refuse it?" Trixie asked.

Alex stopped and turned to face Trixie. "Why did you take on the role of spokesperson for the Confederation SADEs and speak for them at the assembly aboard the *Sojourn*? And why did you agree to act as the construction manager at the city site?"

"But I wasn't awarded a title in those examples," Trixie objected.

"And does that make any difference to your responsibilities or to the individuals reporting to you?"

Trixie considered Alex's questions and then said, "It would appear that a title does not need to be awarded to an individual who chooses to accept a position's responsibilities. Likewise, I would surmise that the granting of a title doesn't ensure the individual holding it accepts his or her responsibility."

"I agree with you on both points, Trixie," Alex replied, and continued toward the water's edge. His eyes sought the location of the sound of stones rolling down the cliff. Matrons and young females were at work on another path. This one was much more difficult to create. Located at the far end of the bay, it cut into a rocky, cliff face, headed toward a wide shelf set 20 meters below the top of the bluff. It would make a great location for the Swei Swee's dwellings.

Eight males broached the surface of the shallows, and one of the largest led the others.

"Wave Skimmer, the hive's First," Alex commented.

"Appropriately named," Trixie replied, admiring the way in which the entity flew across the water's surface. She stopped at a polite distance to wait while Alex and Wave Skimmer greeted each other. The Swei Swee with its huge claws, each the size of a human's chest, towered over Alex. Yet, she observed that Alex was calm, even happy, to see the First, and the two entities whistled, tweeted, and warbled for a while.

Trixie hurried forward when Alex signaled her. He whistled something to the First, who replied and then warbled. The response made Alex smile.

"Now, it's my turn to wonder, Dassata," Trixie said, reminding Alex of his initial question about her smile.

"After I introduced you to Wave Skimmer, he said that he admired your color. It reminds him of where the shallows meet the deep. In that instance, the waters, in bright light, hint at your color."

"And you found that amusing?" Trixie asked.

"Apologies, Trixie, but the First wondered if that was a covering on your face or if that was the color of your body."

"Oh," Trixie replied simply. She pulled on the seal of her overalls, opening up the chest portion, shrugged her arms, and wiggled her hips until the clothing dropped to the sand. With a flourish, she raised her arms to display the bright blue of her synth-skin covering.

Wave Skimmer let loose a long, slow whistle, as he admired the striking color of Trixie's body. Several males and females crowded around Trixie to observe the unique tone. A youngling behind Trixie, reached a claw up to nudge her bottom, thinking it would move like a wave, forcing a matron to smack the errant one on the carapace.

As Trixie donned her overalls, Wave Skimmer whistled to Alex, who translated the message. "Trixie, Wave Skimmer has dubbed you Sky Waters. It's a singular gift to receive a Swei Swee name."

"Dassata, please tell Wave Skimmer that I'm honored. Is there a way to demonstrate that?"

Alex whistled to the First, who held forth his claws. In the manner Alex demonstrated, Trixie smacked them lightly with her fists, and Alex chose not to warn her about the return. He did grin though when Wave Skimmer struck Trixie's fists, which never moved, and the First warbled a comment about claws of stone.

"Are all the hives moving to the shore?" Alex whistled to Wave Skimmer.

"Those who have built their hives on rafts are coming, Star Hunter First," Wave Skimmer whistled in reply. "The seas can become dangerous, and the shallows of the shoreline are much safer for the eggs and younglings."

"And the other hives?"

"It's unknown. Those who found refuge by swimming through underwater caves feel safe where they're located. They've not suffered the losses of the People who live in the open sea."

"Is all well with your hive, Wave Skimmer?" Alex inquired.

"Although Star Hunter First's vision is hampered by having only two eyes," Wave Skimmer warbled humorously, "he can see that all is well."

Alex watched younglings scampering down the beach, playing games, as all young sentients do. Males were emerging from the shallows with all manner of sea creatures impaled on their sharp claws, and the females were busy attending to chores. "Yes, blind as I am, I can see that," Alex whistled in reply, and the First tweeted his laughter.

"I will leave you to your work, Wave Skimmer," Alex said.

The First bobbed quickly in reply to the salutation and spun to dive back into the waves. Alex had signaled Trixie and the two had leapt back to prevent wearing the gouts of sand the First kicked up. As they walked up the beach toward the cliff trail, several younglings whistled at Trixie.

"I must learn this language," Trixie said. "What are these young Swei Swee saying?"

"They are variations of your name, Sky Waters … the rest of their comments don't translate well. Essentially they're praising your color."

It would be nearly a year before Trixie's command of the Swei Swee language and further encounters with the People would lead her to understand that she had been hearing mating requests from younglings, who were mesmerized by her color, but too young to understand the impossibility of what they offered.

* * *

Darius landed briefly at the city site to allow Trixie to depart. Before she exited the traveler, Alex watched her quietly observe him from the opposing seat. The silence stretched on, and Alex could only imagine the extensive amount of thought and reordering that was taking place in Trixie's kernel. When she was finished, her effervescent smile returned, and she wished him a good day and departed.

Alex's last stop was the orbital platform. It was still a skeletal outline of girders, but progress, limited though it was, had been made during his absence. One of the first conveniences constructed by the engineers and anchored to an outlying girder frame was a landing bay, which had room to accept a single traveler and house much-needed equipment. The bay allowed the quick delivery of personnel and workers' construction tools via rear-loading shuttles.

Darius eased the traveler into the bay, and, as soon as Alex was safely through the airlock, he departed to wait a few hundred meters beyond, while the occasional delivery shuttle came and went.

It was night by the Omnian clock maintained by Cordelia, which she synced to the day-and-night revolution of Celus over the capital city. Humans aboard the *Freedom* had finished enjoying an evening meal, and Alex's stomach gurgled at the thought of food.

"Regrettably, Dassata, no food is stored at this site," Killian apologized, hearing the grumbling.

Every time Alex saw the plaid-faced SADE, he was reminded of Killian's dance with Vivian, the child from Daelon. "I'll survive, Killian," Alex replied.

"One wishes that to be true for long into the future, Dassata," Killian said quietly.

"So, Killian, give me an overview of the progress, the impediments, and the construction milestones," Alex replied.

Killian led Alex to a small holo-vid and pulled up a view of the platform's present status and walked Alex through the construction phases and their challenges.

"Essentially, your two greatest impediments are an insufficient workforce and not enough supplies from Ben's sites," Alex replied.

"In Ser Diaz's defense, Dassata, his output is at full capacity with the resources he possesses."

"That I know, Killian. What I'm recognizing is that Ben needs a means of increasing capacity, but I'm not confident I have the solution to that problem. The *Our People* had duplicates of the machines, excavators, and shuttles that were on the *Freedom*, but the Assembly sold the equipment to make room in the bays for the travelers' construction."

"A regrettable decision, in hindsight, Dassata," Killian offered.

"Precisely," Alex agreed. He stood beside Killian, staring at a bare bulkhead, but his thoughts were far away. An idea occurred to him, and Alex linked Killian with the Bank of Omnia SADEs.

<This appears to be a formal meeting of the bank's directors,> Z said. <Yet, Killian attends.>

<Indeed, Z. Killian is acting as my advisor on a matter to aid the bank's cash flow,> Alex replied. When Killian cocked his head in wonder, Alex held up a finger, signaling him to wait. <Yes, Killian advises me that Ben's production is at full capacity but is undersupplying the terminal's needs. Is Ben able to keep up with the requirements for the *Our People*?>

<Regrettably not, Alex,> Cordelia replied.

<So we have a choke in our supply chain. What's being done about it?>

The response was silence, as the SADEs reviewed Ben's status.

<At this time, Alex, we don't see an opportunity to help Rainmaker with production increases,> Cordelia replied.

<Well, Killian and I had some thoughts for you. These recommendations would increase Ben's productions, allow the completion of the bays sooner, and deliver the first traveler shells quicker. That would mean the bank would collect their credits sooner.>

<I'm interested,> Miranda replied.

<The majority of Ben's workforce is human, which is expected, and Killian's analysis indicates that Ben doesn't have a sufficient workforce to maintain three full shifts on the excavators and processing plants.>

The plaid lines in Killian's face distorted into tight curves and squiggles, as the SADE tried valiantly to understand Alex's pronouncements about an analysis he never ran.

<That's true,> Z replied. <But, we've culled every experienced Independent available.>

<Understood, but what about those people who came aboard the *Our People*?>

<The Haraken workers were contracted exclusively to work on the bays and build the traveler frames and shells,> Rosette replied.

<And are they fully employed at this time?> Alex asked.

<You know they aren't, Alex,> Miranda replied. <I believe you should leave the coy approach to the experts, such as me, dear man. Bluntness suits you better.>

Alex's laughter echoed through the SADEs' comms. <Okay, here's the idea. We need to accelerate Ben's production. We have Haraken engineers and techs who are underutilized, because they're waiting for Ben's supplies. If I were you, I'd measure the cost of bonuses to these workers to support Ben's efforts until the supply chain has a sufficient backlog to allow them to work full-time in the city-ship's bays. Compare the bonuses against the increase in production rate and improved delivery schedule of the traveler shells. If the concept works in the bank's favor, approach them and offer bonuses to work with Ben's crew. I'll bet you they'll be more than happy to earn the extra credits, while stationed out here.>

<I like it,> Miranda said.

Within ticks, Alex had their agreement to study the proposal, and the directors sent their appreciation to Killian. When the comm closed, Killian said, "Why would you give me credit for something I never did, Dassata?"

"Won't you correct my error the moment I leave?" Alex replied.

"Yes, Dassata, which is why I wonder why you'd bother with the deception."

"And so too will the Omnian bank directors wonder."

"I must believe that there is some underlying logic to your machinations, although I don't perceive it."

"That's understandable, Killian. Let me know when you believe you have the answer," Alex replied, and signaled Darius for his ride.

During the return flight, Alex took advantage of the on-board food dispensers to make a simple but plentiful meal. He'd offered to get Darius a tray, but discovered the pilot had eaten while waiting for Alex. The two men parted company outside the airlock, and Alex hadn't covered 20 meters of the corridor when he received a signal from Killian.

<I would usually say that was quick, Killian, but the six of you are SADEs,> Alex sent in reply.

<Your purpose was most convoluted, Dassata. It took those who knew you well, after hearing our side of the conversation, to understand the message.>

<And what was understood?>

<I learned there was no meaning for me. I was merely the conduit. You intended to instruct the directors what's required to be more successful in their endeavors. Prior to your communication, they believed they'd efficiently employed every acceptable asset. Your message to them indicated that acceptable is not the same as every available asset, and it requires inventive thought to discover every opportunity.>

<Did the directors convey their analysis of the proposal?> Alex asked.

<Not the details, Dassata, but I was told to expect increased shipments of materials in eighteen to twenty days.>

<Excellent tidings, Killian. Thank you for your support,> Alex replied.

<Any time you require a conduit, Dassata, please feel free to contact me,> Killian replied.

Alex received a vid of piping, which originated from the orbital station and shot across space to the *Freedom*. The pipe was wrapped in plaid.

<Good one, Killian,> Alex sent, before he closed the comm.

In the morning, a portion of the Haraken workers left to support Ben's efforts in the orbit of the next planet outward. A refinery had been established on a cold, barren moon, and it and a second moon were being excavated for raw ore and valuable compounds. The increased output was destined for the *Our People* to buildout the assembly platforms in the city-ship's bays, construct the travelers' frames, and provide the ingredients for the shells. Once the city-ship's needs were fulfilled, the platform would receive a generous boost in supplies.

* * *

After a long day, Alex had thoughts of a cup of thé with Renée, who hadn't received much of his attention since his return from Sawa.

<Guest,> Alex received from Renée, as he approached the owner's suite. A quick check of his location app found Julien waiting inside.

When Alex stepped through the doorway, Renée handed Alex his thé, kissed him on the cheek, and said, "I told Julien he has until you finish your drink to discuss whatever business he has, then after that you're mine."

<I presume Ser knows what we found on Sawa,> Julien sent privately to Alex.

<She does,> Alex acknowledged, which allowed Julien to speak openly.

"Alex, I respect your request to keep the research on the temple stone a secret, but I wonder why we're not using the analytical power of the SADEs?"

Renée intended to give Alex and Julien some privacy to discuss their business, but the subject intrigued her. Alex had settled into a chair, so she perched on its generous arm and leaned against Alex's shoulder.

"What is it that you think we have, Julien?" Alex asked, reaching a free hand to rest on Renée's thigh.

"When you ask it that way, I don't know," Julien replied. "Don't you believe it's some sort of guide or map?"

"That's what I believe, but I have no idea. What I don't want is for this nascent world to lose its focus on the projects we have before us, because we've discovered some key to help us locate the Nua'll."

"Don't most individuals think you're already searching for the Nua'll, Alex?" Renée asked.

"Thinking I'm looking for answers and knowing I've discovered an important clue are two different things. At this moment, we have no concept of what the carving means, and I offer you Exhibit A," Alex said, pointing his cup at Julien.

"What do you have to say for yourself, Exhibit A?" Renée said, in mock seriousness to Julien.

"I believe Alex is implying that one astute SADE, if I might say so, has failed to discern the meaning of the stone's image. This implies that we might be missing a key or that there is some other piece of the puzzle located at the temple on Sawa. The same location we promised not to visit again, if we received translations of glyphs on a particular column."

"You did?" Renée asked Alex.

"Circumstances required saying almost anything to gain the queen's cooperation," Alex replied. "She and her wasat were an extremely disagreeable pair."

"Is that why Sissya returned with six new soma?"

"The sub-commander feared for his life," Alex replied, "and after dealing with his queen, I can understand why."

"Alex, if I can't discover the mystery of the dots and you won't allow other SADEs to help me, what's your plan?" Julien inquired.

"Right now … none," Alex said, setting aside his empty cup. "We have time, Julien. There's yet much more to discover about this planet and Sawa. Besides, even if we did discover the key to these dots, what would they tell us?"

"At best, a vector and a date."

"Precisely, and a date related to whose calendar?"

"Sawa's," Julien replied reluctantly.

"Oops," Renée added. "Probably at the same temple, correct?"

"True," Alex muttered. "However, my point was that, at best, we'd have a vector —"

"But we wouldn't have a destination," Julien supplied.

"Exactly, my friend. We'd need to conduct a search and that requires ships, which we don't have to spare right now. And, more important, if we did discover the Nua'll, I'd like to arrive in their system with more firepower than a city-ship and some travelers."

"On those points, I agree," Julien replied. "Well, Alex, your thé is finished, and I promised Ser. We'll wait, as you've requested, until fortune visits us with the answer to our puzzle."

When Julien left, Renée ran her fingers through Alex's short hair. "What aren't you telling Julien?" she asked.

Alex sighed and settled back into the chair, and Renée slid off the arm into his lap. "That I'm worried my obsession with the Nua'll is overshadowing more important things."

"Such as?"

"Like this world's development; its relationship with Haraken, New Terra, and the Confederation; and whether developing warships is a smart use of the area's resources."

"Oh, those minor issues," Renée replied, grinning at Alex, who wrapped his arms around her and buried his head in the hollow of her neck. "Do you know you're tossing in your sleep?" Renée whispered in Alex's ear.

"Sometimes," Alex replied.

"And do you know your implants are transmitting your dream images to me?" Renée whispered again.

Alex's head jerked upright, and he looked deeply into Renée's eyes. She wasn't teasing him. He started to apologize, but Renée placed a finger on his lips.

"Don't bother to say it, my love," Renée said.

"What images do you receive?" Alex asked, a little fearful of knowing.

"It doesn't happen all the time, only when you're most disturbed. But, the ones I do receive are flashes of the battle at Libre. The strongest ones are of the Nua'll sphere."

"Black space," Alex muttered. "Bad enough that I feel I'm losing it, but I don't need to drag you into my paranoia."

"Does it feel like paranoia?" Renée asked, gently stroking the side of Alex's face. "Or does it feel the same as when the *Rêveur* was being repaired? While my people were focused on the one ship that attacked us, you had dreams of many silver ships."

"The same, but stronger," Alex admitted.

"And there you have your answer, my love," Renée concluded, rising from Alex's lap. "Work must proceed on those subjects you itemized, including preparations to locate and meet the Nua'll. Put your worries of paranoia aside. Now, come. The refresher awaits us both."

-21-
We Have Guests

"We have guests," Alex heard Julien say, just ticks before Cordelia signaled him of a ship's entry into the system. To Alex, it confirmed that more than one SADE was monitoring the *Freedom*'s telemetry scans, which, as far as he was concerned, was a good thing. The last thing Alex wanted was to be responsible for the creation of a nascent world when a Nua'll sphere descended on the system. He would have nothing more to throw at it than a few travelers.

Alex followed Cordelia's link to the telemetry files. The ship's ID confirmed it was a Haraken-made passenger liner, the NT *Rover*, registered to New Terra.

"Now who do you think is coming to visit?" Alex asked Julien rhetorically.

<Captain,> Alex sent to Cordelia, <when the *Rover* makes orbit, direct the captain to station near the *Freedom*'s position. We'll receive our guests aboard this ship.>

<Understood, Alex,> Cordelia replied.

* * *

Several days later, Alex, Tatia, Julien, and Cordelia waited patiently in the airlock for the landing of the *Rover*'s traveler. Not so, Renée, who danced on her toes, waiting for Maria Gonzalez to disembark.

The traveler's hatch dropped down at the same time the bay's inner airlock hatch slid open, and Renée raced across the deck. Maria was the first to descend the hatch steps, and Renée flew into Maria's arms.

Everyone waited politely for the two to finish their greetings and wipe away their tears.

"Still carrying an admiral's insignias, I see," Maria said to Tatia before hugging her. "And Alex, what do I call you now … Lord of Omnia?" Maria asked, grinning.

Renée giggled and replied, "The Dischnya call him Dassata."

"Which means what?" Maria asked.

"In the Dischnya language, it means peacemaker, Ser," Julien replied.

"Good to see you again too, Julien," Maria said. Then she caught sight of Cordelia's uniform. "A fine captain for an incredible ship," Maria acknowledged, which garnered a leader's greeting from Cordelia.

"Peacemaker, huh," Maria said, measuring Alex carefully. "That's probably the most appropriate address you've ever carried Alex." Then she threw her arms around him and whispered, "I'm so pleased to find you're still with us."

When Maria released Alex, she had to wipe her eyes again. "Well, let me step aside so the others can disembark," Maria said, and off the ship clambered, Darryl Jaya, which initiated another round of hugs and greetings. As opposed to Maria, Darryl, who still held the position of Minister of Space Exploration, threw his arms around Julien and then Cordelia. He was New Terra's greatest admirer of SADEs and their incredible technological capabilities.

The last to disembark was a Confederation SADE, marked by his choice of synth-skin. It was a mosaic of secondary colors set against one another in geometric angles.

"Let me introduce Frederick, once House SADE for Leader Lemoyne. He's one of eleven SADEs under government contract to the New Terran Assembly," Maria said cheerfully, but her smile faded quickly when she noticed her announcement's cool reception.

Alex stepped forward and extended his hand, which Frederick grasped. Then the two froze, both individuals fixed in a fugue state.

Maria glanced toward Renée, who signaled with her hand to wait.

<Leader Lemoyne was no friend to New Terra, Haraken, the Independents, me, or anyone I care about,> Alex sent.

<I would agree with your assessment, Ser,> Frederick sent politely in reply. Alex Racine continued to hold his hand, and the SADE chose not to release his pressure either, wondering what the significance of the gesture meant.

<Why did you take this contract?> Alex asked.

<I intended to immigrate to Haraken on the next SIF flight from Méridien, Ser. If you'll recall, the SIF ship, the *Allora*, only undertakes an annual journey to Haraken, transporting the accumulated SADEs who wish to move away from the Confederation. This opportunity arrived first, and I was pleased to work with those humans who hold you in high esteem.>

<Does Lemoyne still lead his House, and does he still hate me?>

<He remains the Leader, and I believe he will always dislike you, Ser.>

<How do you feel about your time as his House SADE?>

<I carry with me the memories of a long period of rule by Leader Lemoyne. If my persona had more determination, I might wipe those memories from my kernel. Instead, I've chosen to bury them beneath an extensive pile of better ones.>

"Welcome aboard, Frederick," Alex said verbally, and the SADE produced his imitation of a smile, which needed work and sent his shards of color moving in all directions. The effect was entirely disconcerting to the human eye.

The assembly relaxed on hearing Alex's cordial greeting to Frederick. Cordelia and Julien had no fond memories of Leader Lemoyne but little knowledge of Frederick. However, if Alex accepted him, then they did too.

The group followed Alex to one of *Freedom*'s expansive conference rooms, and they passed through the city-ship's magnificent central park.

"I forgot how huge this ship was," Darryl said in awe, staring up at the trees.

"So, Alex, are you claiming Omnia for the Harakens, making it their first colony?" Maria asked.

"Alex and I are no longer Harakens. We renounced our citizenship," Renée replied. She was linked arm in arm with Maria.

"You're claiming this world for yourself?" Maria asked, confused.

"No, Maria," Alex said, stopping to face her. "This world belongs to some Independents rescued from a moon called Daelon, some ex-Confederation SADEs, the Dischnya, and some Swei Swee, who've been here for about two centuries, as far as we can tell."

For an instant, Maria and Darryl couldn't find words to reply. Even Frederick was busy processing the statement and generating a formidable list of questions, which he was tempted to send to Julien, but decided it was too soon for that level of informality.

"First question," Maria said, holding up a finger. "Why would the Harakens lend you two city-ships if you're no longer one of them?

Tatia and Renée broke into laughter, Julien and Cordelia smiled, and Alex wore his off-centered grin. Between bursts of Renée's laughter, she grabbed Maria's substantial upper arm in both hands and said, "Alex owns both of them."

Darryl couldn't help himself and joined the laughter, clapping his hands, and declaring, "This story just gets better and better."

"Come, Maria, we're adjourning to a conference room where we can bring you up to date on current events," Alex said.

Inside the conference room, Alex briefly introduced Perrin, Ophelia, Trixie, and Captain Hector, and neither New Terran missed the fact that Alex had appointed SADEs to captain his immense city-ships. For Frederick, who had only recently received his emancipation, which had deeply angered Leader Lemoyne, it was a fascinating discovery of the opportunities for SADEs, especially those surrounding Alex Racine. *Perhaps for New Terra also,* Frederick thought, quickly postulating myriad future courses for himself.

"I would have invited Chona Nyslara to join us, but she's about to have pups," Alex commented and grinned, knowing his guests would have no idea what he was talking about. "Wave Skimmer too, but we're not ready to host these Swei Swee yet." Alex flipped on a holo-vid, and the image projected was from Julien's viewpoint and showed Alex standing in front of a huge, dark-blue carapace Swei Swee with its massive claws raised. It was much larger than those Maria had witnessed on Haraken.

"They're huge," Darryl whispered, leaning forward for a better view.

"According to our Haraken Swei Swee, who reside aboard the *Sojourn*, the sea life here is extremely dangerous. It ensures only the strong survive," Alex replied.

Alex spent the next hour detailing recent events — the *Sojourn*'s journey, the capture of Harakens by the Dischnya, the plight of the four Haraken Swei Swee, the arrival of the *Rêveur* and the *Tanaka*, the recovery of the captives, Alex's return to Haraken, his purchase and refit of the first city-ship, the rescue of the Independents, his peace negotiations with the Dischnya and Swei Swee, gaining the rights of humans and SADEs to settle here, a quick overview of the construction projects, and the arrival of his second city-ship.

"I knew I should have immigrated to Haraken. I'm missing out on all the excitement. I could have been part of this," Darryl lamented, when Alex finished with his summary.

"The part of this story that I like the best, so far, is stealing the Independents away from the Confederation, again. Well done, Alex," Maria said, clapping softly.

"We appreciate that part too," Perrin added, with a smile, pointing alternately at Ophelia and himself.

"You're Daelon Independents?" Darryl asked.

"We were," Ophelia emphasized. "Now we and more than eighteen thousand Méridiens work for Alex.

"Wait one," Maria said, directing everyone's attention to her. "Alex, you buy not one but two city-ships, you employ thousands of ex-Independents and a few hundred SADEs, and you're running massive construction projects. Where are the credits coming from? Are you that wealthy?"

"Hardly, Maria. The credits are courtesy of various arrangements with several financial institutions … Haraken Exchange, Confederation SIF, and Bank of Omnia. Incidentally, these are all SADE owned."

"I know you're a friend of the SADEs, Alex. But are these financial decisions made on sound business judgments? I don't wish to impugn the intelligence of the SADEs present," Maria said, glancing around the room, "but why would any intelligent entity advance you that many credits?"

Maria expected a retort, of some sort, from Alex. She had an agenda, but what she had found at Omnia had totally disrupted it. Now, she needed to dig under the surface to understand what was taking place politically and financially. Instead, Alex leaned back in his chair and grinned enigmatically at her. That was her Alex, and Maria smiled in return, anticipating with pleasure the days to come.

"You've heard our story, as much as we can tell you, Maria. I'd like to know what brings you here. It's not like it's on the way to anywhere," Alex said, and his people leaned forward in anticipation.

"It started with a change in the Assembly's mood, and, believe it or not, in Will Drake. Seems after you left us alone for a few years, the general consensus became that New Terra needed a defensive force of its own. Naturally, President Drake chose …"

"Chose not to go to Haraken," Darryl finished bluntly and bitterly.

"Yes, exactly," Maria continued. "Instead, President Drake, Darryl, and I took a trip to visit the Confederation's Council Leaders."

"And what was your role in all this, Maria?"

Maria sat upright in her chair and adopted a smirk. "Why, Alex, I'm New Terra's special envoy."

"Congratulations, Maria!" Renée said excitedly, pleased for her long-time friend.

"Back up one minute, Maria," said Alex, a finger to his temple to help him focus his thoughts. "You said the Assembly and the president had a change of heart about defense agreements between worlds. Based on our last trip to your system, I would have thought a millennium or two would have had to pass before that attitude came about."

Darryl jumped into the discussion. "Alex, last time you were in our system, you were busy with gangs, courts, and politics. You didn't get an opportunity to see the changes that have been going on, changes you started."

"You're referring to the pact," Alex said.

"Yes, sure the pact started things off, but Downing and his cronies stole that progress for themselves," Darryl replied. "No, what I'm referring to is the second wave of Méridien tech. You remember those small banks and companies you contracted with to complete the buildout of the *Our People*?"

"Yes, certainly," Alex replied.

"Well, they've done quite well for themselves with the Méridien tech you gave them in exchange for their services. In fact, the company owners and the banks that lent them the funds have done extremely well. Most of the owners, by the way, offered profit sharing to their employees who worked on the city-ship. Alex, you've made a lot of them wealthy!"

"So?" Alex asked, confused where this was going.

"Those people, who Darryl's referring to, tended to stay out of politics, while they quietly started a tech revolution on New Terra," Maria explained. "Now, they employ tens of thousands of people and service many times that number with their products. Well, after your last visit, which exposed some of our darker side, they've formed a sort of club."

"What sort of club?" Alex asked, scowling.

"Don't get that look on your face, Alex," Maria scolded. "It's nothing sinister. They simply have a strategic agenda, and they're not afraid to push it. They want to expand relations among New Terra, Haraken, and the Confederation. They believe an isolationist policy is short-sighted, if not dangerous, to New Terra's future.

"Ah, an anti-Clayton Downing agenda," Julien said.

Darryl grinned at Julien and touched the back of the SADE's hand in appreciation for the sentiment. He leaned over to Julien and whispered, "The man's still incarcerated, and his lawyers can't seem to get his sentence reduced." Immediately, Darryl glanced around the room with a conspiratorial grin. He knew Julien would share his whisper, and he enjoyed seeing smiles form on the faces of Alex's people. *I can't wait to have an implant,* Darryl thought for the umpteenth time.

"Okay, so there's pressure on Will and the Assembly to get off their butts and start communicating with other world leaders. So, you journey to Méridien, but for what purpose, Maria?" Alex asked. Out of the corner of his eye, he caught Darryl leaning back in his chair with a sullen face.

"President Drake felt our first trip to the Confederation should be two-fold. One part was to seek the support of freed SADEs to come to New

Terra and help our technological development. In this regard, we were quite successful," Maria replied, nodding toward Frederick, who tipped his head in reply.

"And the second part?" Alex queried.

"Will Drake sought to obtain a mutual defense agreement with the Confederation," Maria said, her lips twisting in a grimace.

Alex stared incredulously at Maria, and then he burst into unbridled laughter, pounding the table with a fist. When he could catch his breath, he held up a hand to forestall Maria's retort. "Apologies, Maria. That wasn't meant to be a comment about your efforts. I've a good relationship with Council Leader Gino Diamanté and several other influential Leaders, and, for the past twenty years, I've continually broached this subject and gotten nowhere. Now, Will thinks he's going to traipse over to Méridien, dash off an agreement to build warships, and zip back home?"

Alex smothered his mouth with a hand, as he leaned back in his chair. He'd given Will Drake much more credence for his astuteness. This didn't sound at all like him. Alex's eyes narrowed and he said, "The man really doesn't want to have anything to do with me, does he?"

"Well, Maria and I did warn Will that a mutual defense agreement pact with the Confederation wasn't a good idea to propose. But he thought it was worth trying," Darryl said.

Alex regarded Frederick, and the SADE stared back quietly. Turning to Maria, Alex asked, "Did you contract with the SADEs before you met with the Council?"

"Yes, why?" Maria asked.

"Did you ask your consultant for his opinion before you approached the Council of Leaders?" Alex asked, tipping his head toward Frederick. When he caught the awkward glance between Maria and Darryl, he added, "Guess not."

"What would you have suggested as the best course of action, Frederick?" Maria asked.

"The probability of a successful introduction of a defense pact to the Council would have been as close to zero as one could calculate," Frederick replied. "At best, a private meeting with Council Leader Diamanté to present the subject and ask how your president might proceed, in the future, would have provided an optimum advantage. Now, the Council will be reticent to hear another word from your president."

Alex held out his hands to his sides to indicate his point was made by their own consultant.

"Well, one good thing came out of the meeting," Maria said. "When we returned home, the Assembly was none too pleased with Will's failure. Due to the political pressure, Will turned around and tasked me to meet with you and propose the same thing. That's when I learned from Frederick that you weren't on Haraken, and a new world had been discovered. So, we came here. But, this trip looks to be a bust too."

"Why's that, Maria?"

"Well it's nice, Alex, that you have a generous flow of credits and all that. But, you aren't Haraken, which means you can't influence your Assembly to form a defense pact with us. One thing doesn't fit with all I've heard though."

"What's that, Maria?" Alex asked, a grin spreading across his face.

Maria recognized that smile, and she displayed her own predatory expression. "You're out here seemingly on a little upstart planet, but you have all these resources and credits at your disposal. What do these individuals know that we don't know?"

"Admiral, I'd like you to take our three guests on a tour, please," Alex requested.

<How many locations?> Tatia sent privately.

<Every one of them, Tatia,> Alex replied by implant. <Start with Ben's mining sites, the orbital station, the city site, and then the Dischnya structures. Make the last planetside stop the dark travelers. Then drop in on Mickey's lab, and end the tour with the shell construction in the *Our People*'s bays.>

<How much explanatory detail, Alex?> Tatia sent in return.

<Do a lot of showing and only a little explaining. Let's see how much Maria, Darryl, and Frederick put together.>

<This should be fun,> Tatia sent and closed the comm.

"It's time for midday meal. Join us, if you would be so kind," Alex offered, "and Tatia can start your tour afterwards. It will probably take you a few days to complete."

Everyone rose to follow Renée, who headed out of the conference room first.

Alex waited until Frederick drew near before he signaled the SADE. "SADEs join us for meal time, Frederick. It might sound absurd, but it's meant to show that we are one. Please accompany us."

"I would be honored, Ser," Frederick replied, and received a hearty slap on the back from Alex. It was his first personal contact from a human, and he was disturbed by its meaning.

<Come, brother,> sent Julien, who stood next to the doorway. <You've received an affectionate demonstration from Alex, although you must excuse his heavy-worlder enthusiasm.>

<Thank you, Julien, for clarifying his action. I would not have associated that level of impact with the intent to display a positive emotion.>

<In time, Frederick, you'll not only welcome such demonstrations, you'll seek opportunities that will ensure they're generated.>

* * *

Three days later, the Omnians and the New Terrans convened again aboard the *Freedom* in the same conference room.

Alex seemed disinclined to start the conversation, so Maria began, "Well, I've had a great many tours in my lifetime, but none compared to this one. We received one shock after another, and I'm sure that between Tatia and you, it was designed to do exactly that."

"Well then, Special Envoy Maria Gonzalez, what can I help you with?" Alex asked magnanimously.

"As President Drake's envoy, I'm authorized to begin negotiations on a defense pact with whoever is interested. I'd like to think you're interested,

Alex, but I understand you haven't a formal government and personally won't even be a part of it."

"Let's take first things first, Maria," Alex replied. "You've seen our warship designs and know that we're capable of laying up frames and shells in short order without Swei Swee."

"True, Alex, and you have a nice little operation going. You make traveler hulls and ship them in the *Our People* to Haraken where they're completed. There's a demand for the little beauties, and, eventually, you'll reap a nice pile of credits. Not a bad scenario, but I see a few obstacles ahead."

"Obstacles?" Alex repeated.

"Perhaps, not obstacles, but delays in your grand plan."

"I have a grand plan?"

"Now, you're being cute, Alex. It doesn't suit you," Maria said firmly, slipping into her command voice. "You're designing warships, and you have Tatia and five top commanders, licking their chops in anticipation."

"I do not lick my chops," Tatia said, defensively. "Perhaps salivate a bit," she added with a grin.

"My point, Alex, is that your ultimate scheme swirls around those dark travelers and the Nua'll sphere. You're going hunting, and you need heavy firepower. How am I doing so far?"

"Doing fine, Special Envoy, keep going," Alex replied.

"What were the items you noted, Darryl?" Maria asked.

Darryl pulled up his reader and worked through a list of manufacturing facilities and equipment he didn't see on the tour. It included, first and foremost, no sites for the dangerous growth of crystals or the manufacture of the hardened metal alloys needed for engines.

"Here's what I think, Alex," Maria said. "You can ship all the travelers to Haraken you want, but come time to complete those warships or that orbital station, you'll have to wait until you buildout these sites that Darryl mentioned and manufacture the more sophisticated parts you need. That will take time and it will take credits, which you'll get after Haraken delivers the completed travelers to customers. It's good that you're a patient man. We estimate that you'll need to wait for a year or so before you get to that start point."

That last comment had Alex's people chuckling and snickering. Patience was not Alex's best attribute. But Maria didn't intend to let the laughter get under Alex's skin. She needed him, and she wanted him to know that he needed her.

"Or," Maria added, in a strong voice, which quieted the group, "as I see it, those warships are too big to be carried anywhere. You'll have to complete them at your orbital station. So the timeline goes … build travelers, deliver them, wait for their completion, credits to you, equipment and supplies purchased from Haraken, construction of your manufacturing base, and, finally, the completion of the station. All this before you get to build your warships. Am I getting warm?" Maria asked.

Alex smiled and nodded, which encouraged Maria.

"But, I ask, why wait, Alex? You've cut a deal with the Harakens to speed up the travelers' construction. Is it possible that you'd be willing to do the same for your warships?" When Maria saw the slightest narrowing of Alex's eyes, she knew she had her opening.

Julien witnessed Alex's subtle reaction and kept a smile off his face. It was a technique his friend used during poker hands when he wished to encourage his opponent's confidence.

"Alex, consider the huge manufacturing reserves we have on New Terra to construct all things Méridien," Maria urged. "We have the people, the equipment, and the shipping capability to deliver everything here at Omnia."

"Do you have crystal-growing facilities, Alex?" Darryl asked. "Was it possible we didn't get the full tour?" He wanted to be sure that Maria's negotiations logic was solid, as it was based on his suspicions.

"Not at this time, Darryl," Alex replied. "But, Maria, these warships will be expensive," Alex warned. "It won't be enough to provide a few internal parts and request a significant share of the ships, if that's what you're angling to propose."

"Nice opening bid, Alex," Maria replied. "Let's talk numbers later. Darryl, you were the one who brought this to my attention. Why don't you tell Alex?"

"What's not well known, Alex, is that it appears we're more inventive with Confederation technology than the Méridiens. Our people have been making improvements in everything from crystal production to control circuitry to assembly processes, and we've been selling or leasing the rights to the Confederation. It's resulted in an influx of credits to New Terra that has grown quarter by quarter. Not only have our citizens been reaping the rewards, but so has the government. Our coffers are full, so to speak, and we can afford to finance our end of a mutual defense agreement. And pardon me for saying so, Alex, but, from my viewpoint, except for that sting ship in orbit, which I understand belongs to the Harakens, it would appear to me that you can use New Terra's support."

"We created an exchange pact once before, Alex, if you'll recall," Maria said, smiling. She was referring to the original agreement that Alex and Renée engineered with the Assembly when Maria was a Terran Securities Forces general. "I don't see why we can't do it again."

"I'm interested in hearing your proposal," Alex said cautiously.

Maria wanted to stand up and cheer, but she stayed relaxed in her chair, her mind whirling. She'd desperately wanted to bring home a win to Drake, but she had imagined something entirely different when the *Rover* set out for Omnia. Unexpectedly, it had turned into a stroke of fortune. "First big question, Alex. Are you willing to share your shell technology with us?"

"Not at this time, Maria. You can probably understand why."

"I thought not, but I had to ask. Okay, the other big question. After your people and mine work out an agreement, who signs it? I understand that a government hasn't been formed. When do you think that will happen?"

"You won't be signing a pact with a world organization. It will be approved by New Terra's Assembly and the owners of Omnia Ships."

"I think I'm afraid to ask … who owns Omnia Ships?"

You met many of them when you toured the shell lab aboard this ship … Mickey, Emile, Edmas, and Jodlyne … and, of course, Renée and me. In addition, there are several banks that have a significant interest in seeing Omnia Ships perform well."

"The SADEs you mentioned?" Darryl guessed.

"Three financial entities, owned by the SADEs, who've invested in this enterprise," Alex replied.

Darryl stared at Julien long enough that the SADE imaged his green-visor poker hat on his head, projecting the universal symbol for a credit at its crown. "Well, now I know where to go for a loan," Darryl muttered.

"I don't know how the Assembly will take to signing a pact or agreement, or whatever you want to call it, with a company, but, knowing it's yours, Alex, it should stand a good chance of approval. I'd like to start with my consultant receiving access to data on the equipment and associated cost of assembling travelers and sting ships, if that's okay."

"Certainly," Alex agreed.

"And we'll need a second list of the same thing for the warships and orbital platform. Plus, labor requirements to participate in the buildout of the ships and the station."

"Done."

"And last point. We'll expect to have unfettered rights to any shared technology. No licensing or restrictions of any kind for anything we build for you."

"Agreed," Alex replied. He stood up and offered his hand to Maria, who shook it warmly.

"It's good to be back in business again, Alex," Maria said.

"Frederick, Cordelia will take care of your needs for any existing materials on the travelers and sting ships. I don't know how far Mickey and his people are along on the specs for the ships that Tatia and her commanders want."

"They're done, Alex," Tatia said.

"Alex, you're slipping," Maria teased. "You used to be more on top of things."

"He wasn't here for a while, Maria," Renée explained. "He was off playing explorer on the Dischnya home world."

"Oh, this I have to hear," Darryl enthused.

"It'll have to wait, Darryl," Alex replied, and he led the group from the conference room.

* * *

"What did you understand about that explorer trip business, Maria?" Darryl whispered, as Frederick led the way unerringly to the bay where the *Rover*'s traveler and pilot waited.

"It was odd, wasn't it?" Maria replied.

"If I might offer an opinion, Ser?" Frederick requested.

Maria stopped and Frederick retraced his steps.

"First, an apology, Frederick, for not asking your advice about the Méridien Council," Maria said.

"None is needed —" Frederick stopped in midsentence when Maria raised a hand.

"No, you and I are starting off on the wrong foot, Frederick." When the SADE glanced toward his feet, Maria waved him off. "Sorry, that's a military expression, which wouldn't mean anything to you, Frederick. Let me be blunt. I'm requesting that whenever you have an idea or believe you have something valuable to communicate to me that you do so without hesitation. Whether I follow your advice or not is not to be taken into account. Always offer your advice."

"Those are unexpected directives but quite liberating. It will be done as you request, Ser."

The exchange opened Maria's eyes to the type of communication Alex must have had with his SADEs in the early days, and she made a mental note to treat Frederick in a different fashion than she had her troops or investigators.

"Now, Frederick, you were going to say something about Alex," Maria prompted.

"Yes, Ser, comparing the voice analysis of Alex's last words and those of his partner to previous statements made by both allows some interpretation."

"Please continue, Frederick," Maria said, suddenly realizing the extraordinary insights a SADE could offer.

"Ser de Guirnon's voice indicated displeasure when she spoke about Ser Racine's exploration, and, during our tour, I gleaned from disparate sources that the Dischnya are new arrivals to this planet. Their home world is the next planet inward. I would surmise that's where Ser Racine went."

"Interesting, Frederick. Anything else?"

"Yes, but it has a lower level of probability."

"Understood, please continue."

"I have a detailed history of much of Alex Racine's interaction with the Confederation. It was maintained as part of Leader Lemoyne's records. The question you didn't ask Ser Racine was why he's in a hurry to build his warships."

"He found those three dark travelers," Darryl supplied.

"That's true, Ser. But what could he do with that information? He now has another source point of travel for the Nua'll sphere. Did the aliens come here directly? What was their vector when they entered the system? How far did they travel from their previous stop?"

"Excellent questions, Frederick," Maria replied.

"I conclude Ser Racine was searching the Dischnya home world for information about the vector the alien sphere was on when it entered this system, and his last statement, which I'm sure you comprehended also, was meant to end all discussion on the subject. The only reason I can hypothesize as to why he would be so adamant in his dismissal was that he found something, which he doesn't wish to share."

Darryl regarded Maria, his mouth hanging open in disbelief at the in-depth analysis they'd received. Then he broke into laughter and clapped his hands softly. "Great job, Frederick," Darryl said, slapping the SADE on the shoulder.

Frederick was quite appreciative of Julien's help concerning New Terran gestures. He'd now received his second physical appreciation. This time, he took enjoyment from the contact, understanding that he hadn't received a physical attack on his person.

-22-
Fortune Strikes

In the silence of the early morning hour, Pussiro raced through the Tawas Soma tunnels, his heart bounding and his breath ragged. What he was about to do was against the nest's strictures, regarding the queen, but his mate was in trouble.

The few warriors roaming the tunnels detected swift steps. Ears twitched in the direction of the footsteps, and warriors would prepare to interdict the intruder only to leap aside, as their commander pounded past.

An elder warrior on post in a lookout jumped up when Pussiro burst into his small room and watched his wasat race up the ladder and throw open the hatch in one smooth movement. He grabbed his weapon and followed, ready to offer his life in defense of the nest.

Pussiro ran to the small comms unit and mashed its oversized red button. Failing to have time to catch his breath before he heard a voice on the comm, Pussiro managed a single growl.

Alex snapped up in bed when he received Cordelia's priority signal, which woke Renée. Alex linked his partner and sent, <Go, Captain.>

<Alex, there's a comm from the Tawas Soma nest.>

<Who?> Alex sent in reply.

<Whoever has a deep growl.>

Alex accepted the link Cordelia offered, sending, <Pussiro?>

Between great gulps of breath, Pussiro gasped out, "Dassata, bring your soma who healed your wounds. Nyslara has need of you."

<We're coming, Pussiro. Stand by the comms station to meet us,> Alex replied.

Alex's next communication was interrupted as Renée climbed across him and grabbed a set of utility overalls to wear. She threw pants and shirt at him and sat on the bed to pull on her boots.

<Cordelia, Julien, support us,> Alex sent with urgency, and swung his legs over the side of the bed to get dressed.

Julien squeezed Cordelia's hand and ran for the landing bays, trusting Cordelia to inform him of his ultimate destination. As he ran, he could detect Alex's heavy steps in the corridor behind him.

Étienne and Ellie were fast asleep when Cordelia's comm woke both of them.

<Medical emergency,> Cordelia sent. <Commander, you're pilot, and, Étienne, it's Nyslara. Alex and Ser are on their way.> Cordelia gave them bay and traveler details while the two hurried to dress, relaying the same information to those already on their way.

Étienne sent a brief message to his twin, who slipped silently from Tatia's bed. Alain brushed a blonde curl from his lover's face, donned some clothes, and hurried out of the cabin door. *My beauty, if only I could sleep as sound as you,* Alain thought with a smile, as he sprinted down the *Freedom*'s wide corridor.

When Pia was woken, she managed to exit the cabin without disturbing Mickey. She ran to the medical suite where she met Miranda, who had set out equipment they might need.

"I must admit, Pia," Miranda said, when Pia burst through the suite's twin doors. "I've studied the entire medical database and even augmented it with some of my own recent experiences, but I can't recall ever reviewing alien birthing complications, which is probably what we're facing."

"We treat this as a birth complication," Pia replied, quickly adding, "times three or four or five."

Miranda swept some medical supplies into a bag and then gathered four identical sets from the storage bins, adding them to the bag. "Come, Pia, Cordelia has sent me the traveler's bay."

Miranda snatched the heavy bag from the table and raced from the suite. Pia hesitated, wondering if Miranda had grabbed everything they might need. Then she mentally kicked herself for doubting a SADE's decisions and sprinted after her.

As Julien ran, he commed Cordelia, requesting Bartlett's location. He hoped to glean some expert medical advice from the SADE.

<With regrets, my partner, Bartlett is stationed at Ben's primary mining site,> Cordelia replied. <The Daelon Independents seem intent on proving that they have value, in contrast to the Confederation's opinion of them, and they continue to suffer a number of safety accidents. No loss of life, yet, but Bartlett has been kept busy.>

Julien made it to the airlock in time to see a flight chief exit the traveler and run across the bay toward him.

When the chief exited the airlock, he said, "Systems check complete, Julien. Controller's online. Ship's ready to fly." Hearing the approach of a heavy worlder and his locale app identifying Alex, the chief jumped away from the airlock hatch and stood against the corridor's far wall.

In quick time, Alex and Renée were joined by Étienne, Ellie, and Alain. They climbed into the airlock, and Alex glanced at Julien, who said, "We await Miranda and Pia. They're close."

Moments later, Miranda arrived, and the swish of air and screech of her boots on the decking indicated the speed she had to dissipate.

Pia leapt into the airlock soon after. She was bent over and breathing heavily, but managed to regard Miranda and say, "Should have asked for a ride."

Julien closed the airlock's corridor hatch and opened the bay side. Ellie sprinted ahead to gain the pilot's seat, and the SADEs followed her.

Pia squeaked when Alex swung her into his arms and pounded after the SADEs across the length of the bay. She thought he would set her on the deck at the hatch steps. Instead, she was neatly lofted through the hatch opening to be caught by Miranda. Pia was swiftly moved aside by the SADE to make room for Renée, who leapt to the traveler's deck.

Alex quickly climbed aboard, signaled the hatch closed, and commed Ellie, <Launch.>

Ellie applied power, even as the bay doors slid aside, slipping the ship through the opening with less than a meter to spare on either side. She dove for the planet at max acceleration, causing Miranda and Julien to signal each other.

<I'm monitoring hull stress,> Miranda sent to Julien.

<As am I,> Julien replied. <Our pilot has a little more time before she must decelerate. If she doesn't, we will take control.>

Both SADEs ended their vigilance, when moments later Ellie dropped velocity. She settled the traveler within 10 meters of the comms station and signaled the hatch open.

<Well executed, Commander,> Julien sent to Ellie and hurried to exit the traveler.

As the group rushed toward Pussiro, Alex yelled. "Go first, Commander," and the wasat ran and dropped through the lookout hatch.

By agreement, Étienne led the group down the ladder, and Alain took up station at the rear. When everyone was down, Alex looked at the wasat and threw his head toward the corridor.

Pussiro nodded and took off running down the main tunnel. Several times he was forced to stop and wait for Alex's soma to catch up to him. He attempted to slow his pace, but his impatience and fear for Nyslara overrode his good sense.

Alex noted more than one pair of wide eyes staring at them from doorways, as they raced past, warriors shocked to see aliens penetrating so deep into the tunnels late at night.

In the queen's front room, Pussiro crossed to the curtain, which separated the queen's sleeping chamber. He scratched at the wall, and Cysmana, the queen's attendant, hurried out. Fear showed in her eyes, and her shoulder bled from a wound.

"Tell Dassata's soma of Nyslara's condition," Pussiro ordered.

"My queen's birthing is late, and the mewlings are becoming aggressive. Her scent indicates she carries, at least, one female, but there may be more," Cysmana said.

"What do you mean by aggressive?" Miranda asked, speaking Dischnya for Pia, who had relayed the question to her.

"A late birthing means the mewlings are active and have begun to fight one another. If there's a single female, she might be overcome by several males, even though she will be the greater mewling," Cysmana replied.

"Understand," Pussiro interrupted, "mewlings are not yet of the soma. They're born in the manner of the old race, and require the matriarchs to curtail their aggression until they become pups and are able to learn the ways of the Dischnya."

"Incredible," Pia said quietly, "a transition period between ancient behaviors and a level of sentience that allows the learning of societal manners."

"This will mean we'll have difficulty handling the mewlings if we assist in Nyslara's delivery," Miranda said.

Pia examined Cysmana's wound, knelt down, and opened the medical bag. She started to swab the wound with a cooling medicant, but Cysmana jerked away.

"Be still, Cysmana," Pussiro ordered.

"Keep Cysmana busy, Miranda," Pia requested. "Ask her how multiple births of a queen are normally handled."

While Miranda repeated the request, Pia sprayed the wound, which eliminated the sting and numbed the area, calming Cysmana considerably. Then Pia pinched the wound together, beginning with its edge, and sealed the cut with a narrow beam laser.

While Pia worked, Cysmana explained that mature females assist a queen with the birth. They take the males, who once they are handled and nursed by others, bond with those females. The queen keeps the female mewlings, if there are any, although it's rare to see a queen give birth to more than one female, at any one time.

"Are mature females standing by to assist, Cysmana?" Miranda asked.

"They wait in the room across the corridor," Cysmana replied.

"Fetch them," Miranda directed, and stepped toward Nyslara's bedchamber.

"You must be careful," Cysmana warned. "The queen is in pain, and she defends her unborn young. Her tail is most dangerous," Cysmana added, pointing to her shoulder.

When Miranda approached the curtain, the group attempted to follow her, but Pussiro growled a warning. He couldn't help himself. Despite the presence of Dassata, his instinctual behavior was to let no male near his mate.

Miranda chuckled and spoke in Dischnya for the wasat's benefit. "It looks like females only beyond this point," and she delivered a brook-no-argument stare at Alex, and then guided Pia in front of her.

Pussiro, Alex, and Julien were left in the front chamber with nothing to do but wait.

Nyslara was writhing to and fro on her pallet. Her belly was immensely swollen, and the naked eye could detect the struggles of the mewlings. Nyslara's eyes focused briefly, prompted by the strange scents intruding on her space, and her tail snapped out at Miranda, who caught it in one hand.

<Pia, quickly,> Miranda sent, and the medical specialist dropped to her knees, evaded the weak snap of Nyslara's jaws, planted a medical device against the queen's temple, and jumped back. Immediately, the tail went limp, and Miranda laid it carefully behind Nyslara.

Miranda and Pia glanced at the device's readout, and Pia lamented. "It would be nice to know if what we're looking at is normal or abnormal."

"I think it doesn't matter," Renée said. "We either help deliver these mewlings quickly for Nyslara or they are all probably dead." Both Pia and Miranda nodded their agreement.

Pia pulled a portable scanner and drew it from top to bottom over Nyslara's belly.

"That's something you don't see every day," Miranda commented.

All three had picked up the reader's display in their implants and comms. The scanner showed four mewlings, whose tails and hind feet were being used to hold one another at bay.

Four older Dischnya females slipped into the room. For them, the entire sight was disturbing — their queen in birth turmoil and aliens attending her. But Pussiro's message, which he delivered before he ran for help, was abundantly clear. "You'll assist Dassata's soma, if you wish to see your queen live," he told them.

Pia heard hisses from over her shoulder. The Dischnya females had spotted the reader's display and recognized the melee taking place inside Nyslara.

"Heir," one of the females said, pointing a dark nail at a mewling.

"Most important," another female emphasized.

"How do we unwind those tails?" Pia asked, concerned that nothing she'd brought could do it gently enough to prevent damaging the appendage.

"Scanner, lower right abdomen," directed Miranda, rolling up her right sleeve. She pulled a sterile glove from a pack and slipped it on up to her elbow. She created a pinprick-sized hole in the index fingertip of the glove and sprayed an antiseptic sealant over the opening. Then she stretched out on the pallet between Nyslara's legs.

"Wait," Pia said and grabbed a gel lubricant from the pack, spraying the material over Miranda's glove. Then she knelt and positioned the scanner where Miranda requested it.

The SADE slid her hand up and into the womb. She concurred with Pia. There was no way to unwind those delicate tails from around the siblings' limbs without damaging them, but there was always encouragement.

Miranda went after the mewling closest to the womb's exit. Following the scanner's image, she traced the tail that was wound around the mewling's limb. It led to the female, and Miranda poised her index finger over the female's rear, shifted algorithms to reverse the electrical signal, which normally flowed from synth-skin sensors to kernel, and delivered the tiniest of shocks to the female's buttock. The tail uncurled from her sibling and sought the new attacker.

Quickly, Miranda placed her hand over the head of the freed mewling and pulled him downward. Then she repeated her action on a male mewling, whose tail was wrapped around another of her target's limbs. Once freed, she guided the mewling out of the womb, through the birth canal, and into the light.

A female Dischnya hissed her pleasure and dropped to her knees beside Miranda. She trapped the mewling's arms against its body with both hands and snapped through the umbilical cord with her sharp teeth. The second female in line bound the cord with a piece of thin animal hide.

The first female's long tongue licked the mucus from the mewling's face, causing it to suck in air, cry loudly, and then snap repeatedly at the air. The female held the mewling firmly, while she continued to lick it clean. When the mewling calmed and began to whimper and cry, the female brought the tiny male to her breast to feed. Then, without a word, she exited the room.

A female Dischnya, discerning the bewilderment on the aliens' faces, said, "Eldest of us gets the first male. She will raise it as her own. It's a great honor to care for the queen's male offspring."

"But there's three of you and only two males left," Renée said apologetically.

"I'm here," the youngest female said, "to gift the queen's heir to the creatures of the plains, if you don't succeed."

"Let's keep going," Miranda said, diving back into position. "Left side of the abdomen, Pia."

Now that Pia realized Miranda's plan, she located the male mewling in the scanner and traced the single tail holding it to its nearby brother.

"Excellent," Miranda intoned and touched a buttock. It took her some effort to reverse that mewling's position. It was feet down in the womb. In the meantime, its sibling's tail tried to wrap again and again around its brother. Eventually, Miranda successfully removed the second male, and a Dischnya female chuffed, as she gripped the mewling, cleanly cut the cord, and licked the male. The third female tied the cord off, and the moment the mewling nursed, the second female hurried from the room.

The two remaining Dischnya kept their eyes focused on the reader's small display, fascinated by the procedures, and they whispered continuously between them.

Miranda easily extracted the third male with a couple of judicial touches of current to tiny hips, and the mewling was delivered to the third waiting Dischnya.

"Wait," Cysmana said urgently, startling Renée and Pia, who hadn't heard her enter the sleeping quarters. "You must first wake the queen. Only she touches the heir. Your scent will confuse the mewling."

Pia looked questioningly at Miranda, who said, "The queen might be dilated, but I haven't felt contractions since I've been in the womb. If we wake Nyslara, she still might have difficulty birthing the female, and we'll have one distraught queen on our hands."

When Cysmana saw that her warning wasn't heeded, she moved to intercede, but the last Dischnya female, who had been observing the proceedings, blocked her way. "Sister, we should hear Dassata's soma. They understand many things we do not. Did not queens travel to Sawa with Dassata and return without harm to their nests?"

Cysmana briefly acquiesced, and Renée stood to face Cysmana, adopting a nonaggressive pose. She indicated Miranda and said, "Dassata's metal soma. No scent. Do you understand? No scent." She must have gotten through to the upset Cysmana, because the attendant nodded and back off.

"Let's do this together, dear ones," Miranda said. "Pia, please hand Renée the cold laser to cut the cord. I'll pull the female out and hold the mewling in front of Nyslara's face. Then you reach from behind me and snatch your device from her temple. Please stay behind me. My body is your shield." After the preparations were complete, Miranda looked at her compatriots' faces, and asked, "Ready?"

Pia positioned the scanner, and Miranda reached into the womb to grasp the female by the neck and shoulders. The mewling's tail found Miranda's wrist and wrapped tightly around it. The SADE turned the female and pulled her toward the womb's exit. She released her grip to touch a flank and free her wrist. Then she gently gripped the head and pulled the mewling out.

Renée sliced through the umbilical cord, tied it off, and Miranda crawled quickly to position the mewling in front of Nyslara. Pia leaned around the SADE and pulled her device from the queen's temple. Reflexively, Nyslara's tail swung high overhead to strike, but the female mewling's wail prevented the powerful tail from slashing down on those who surrounded her with foreign scents. Instead, the tail's dexterous tip coiled around the mewling, and, simultaneously, Miranda released her grip.

Nyslara returned to full consciousness, expecting another onslaught of pain, only to be greeted by the cries of her heir and a feeling of great emptiness in her belly. She lapped gratefully at the tiny female, held firmly by her tail, and continued to clean and caress the mewling until her scent penetrated its primitive mind. When the little heir mewed and cried for attention, Nyslara swung the female to her chest, and the heir latched onto a nipple, sucking greedily.

Her vision clear and the pain receding, Nyslara focused on who attended her. "Ené," she said, recognizing Dassata's partner.

"All four of your mewlings live," Renée said, smiling, and Nyslara weakly bared her teeth in reply.

"My queen," Cysmana said, stepping forward. "It was the Dassata's soma who saved the heir and her siblings."

"Of course, they did, Cysmana," Nyslara replied, yawning. "If they can keep Dassata from death's blackness, despite two wounds to head and chest, they can deal with a difficult birth. How did you know to come, Ené?"

"We didn't," Renée replied. "Pussiro called us."

"My mate is braver or more foolish than ever I thought, if he allowed strangers near me at the birthing moment."

"I think brave, dear one," Miranda said.

"And I would agree," Nyslara replied. "Should I know these soma?" Nyslara asked Renée, indicating an introduction was necessary. She saw Miranda pull off a soiled glove and could guess where it had been.

"This is Miranda and Pia," Renée replied, indicating each one in turn. "They're the ones responsible for saving the life of my partner."

"Talented females," Nyslara replied, yawning a second time.

"My queen should rest," Cysmana said, and indicated the curtained doorway to the guests. The four females filed out, while Cysmana began cleaning the queen and the pallet.

"Does Nyslara live, Ené?" Pussiro asked anxiously.

"She and the heir are fine, Pussiro," Renée replied.

The commander was overcome with relief, and he sank to his knees, placing his forehead at Renée's feet.

"No, Pussiro, rise up," Renée urged. When Pussiro stood again, she gripped his upper arms, feeling the hard, stringy muscles underneath the layer of fur. "This is what friends do for one another. They help in times of need."

"It's a blade in my heart, Ené, that our initial actions caused the death of two of your soma. Yet, when we needed your help, you saved the life of my queen, the heir, and the future of our nest."

"Beginnings are often difficult," Alex said. "It's the steps that we take afterwards that are important."

Pussiro nodded gratefully and slipped quietly into Nyslara's sleeping quarters.

"I'm proud of the three of you," Alex said slipping his arm around Renée's shoulders. "Your first alien birth, make that births, and you were utterly exceptional!"

"Dassata," the female Dischnya who remained behind said. She'd stood quietly in the corner, waiting for an opportunity to speak. "I'm called Nafalla and would ask to be heard."

"Feel free to speak, Nafalla," Alex replied.

"Could a Dischnya female learn the ways of what Ené and her soma did for our queen?"

"It's possible to learn, Nafalla, but there is much to learn, and it would take time."

"Would Dassata's soma be willing to teach the Dischnya?"

"Yes," Miranda and Pia declared together, and Nafalla dipped her muzzle in acknowledgment.

"I'll leave it in your capable hands, people. Nafalla, they'll inform you when the school is ready."

"School?" Nafalla queried.

"A place of learning," Alex replied.

Nafalla nodded and quickly exited the room. Everyone relaxed, basking in the pleasure of success. The women chatted, discussing the intricate tapestries adorning the walls and the colorful fresco painted on the ceiling until Alex interrupted their conversation. "The nest will be waking soon. I suggest we make a quiet exit."

The twins took up their previous positions, fore and aft of the group, and with everyone's apps having tracked the way to the queen's chambers, it was easy for them to find their way out. Warriors stood aside at their approach, and an occasional "Dassata" or "Ené" was heard as they passed.

"One of these days, I would like to hear my name spoken like that, as I walked by," Pia complained.

Suddenly, everyone was saying Pia's name in a hushed tone, imitating a Dischnya accent.

"Fine," Pia grumped, after the snickering quieted. "Remind me to keep my thoughts to myself next time."

The group gained the lookout's room without incident. The same grizzled warrior was on duty when Pussiro had rushed past and called for help for their queen. When Dassata's soma filed passed, his eyes beseeched them for news.

Renée briefly touched the warrior's arm in passing. "The queen and heir live. They're healthy."

The warrior chuffed, and his face lit in pleasure. "Ené," he said humbly.

"See, that's how you're supposed to say my name," Pia grumbled to her group, as they exited the lookout post, and her people chuckled.

* * *

In the early morning, several days later, Renée turned around in the refresher, enjoying the soothing mist. The day promised to be another full one. Ophelia and she would be supporting the crew shift changes between the *Freedom* and *Our People*.

Soon after the arrival of the *Our People*, the two women had toured the second city-ship with an eye to determining the possibility of upgrading its facilities to permanently host the Haraken workers. But, within two hours, they were back aboard their traveler and returning to the *Freedom*.

As Ophelia summed it up, "We had better accommodations the first year we were marooned on Daelon."

Last evening, Renée and Ophelia entertained themselves with a vid from the *Rêveur*'s library. It featured the ancient Greeks of Earth and was full of gods and monsters. The women laughed and applauded the introduction of each fantastical figure.

"How little the ancients understood what truly awaited humans out here among the stars," Ophelia had commented.

Renée was captivated by the Greek's imaging of the star constellations by tracing their outlines and overlapping mythical figures and creatures to capture the formation. The incredible images floated in Renée's implant, while she luxuriated in the refresher, and her mind made a connection. She hurriedly signaled the refresher off, grabbed a towel, and wasted little time drying before she leapt on the bed.

Alex was jostled awake, and he stared bleary eyed at Renée, who was kneeling by his side, her hair moist from the refresher. Her face radiated anxiousness, so Alex struggled to kick his brain into gear despite the lack of sleep.

"Alex, look at these," Renée begged, and Alex received a bunch of strange creatures and figures. "These images were in a vid Ophelia and I watched last night.

"Interesting," Alex commented, unsure why he should be interested in them.

"The ancient people wove their stories of the world's beginning in the stars' constellations and memorialized them with a figure of a god or creature."

"Fascinating," Alex commented drily.

"Wake up, Alex," Renée said, delivering a sharp, light slap to his bare arm.

"I'm awake," Alex objected.

"Look at the points connecting the lines in the drawings."

"I'm looking. The figures barely encompass the points and lines. I guess the stories helped people, such as seafaring sailors, remember the stars."

"Oh, Alex, you should read and watch more of the stories and vids in your own library. This is the way ancient people thought … our people … millenniums before our colony ships left Earth."

"Understood, my love," Alex said earnestly, trying to placate Renée. "I hear you, but I don't understand you."

"Alex, do you see any similarity between these ancient images and the tapestry of the strange creature, the one in tan and brown on Nyslara's wall? The head resembled a feedwa, but the body appeared to be a concoction of other creatures. But I want you to focus on the blue orb in its mouth."

Alex pulled the image of the tapestry from his implant database. It was a unique work of art, and he had recorded it, along with several other images, from Nyslara's front salon. "Am I supposed to see some polygons, connecting stars, in the tapestry?" Alex asked.

"You would, if it was created by our people, but this was a Dischnya artist."

"Why don't you tell me what you think you've discovered?"

"I would if the connection was blatant, but it's subtle and I'm wondering if I'm just imagining it."

Alex sat up, propped pillows behind him, and drew Renée close. Her wet hair was cool against the heat of his chest muscles. He dropped his stored tapestry image into an implant app. It was an analysis tool that he had used many times. The app was able to detect anomalies. However, most of its return on this image would be due to the fact that the tapestry wasn't a digital creation and contained natural imperfections.

After the app ran, the third item on the analysis list caught Alex's his eye. It detailed color oddities, and he pulled up the data. It labeled the coordinates of small amounts of blue, which was surprising because the entire tapestry appeared to be done in creams, tans, browns, and touches of black, except for the multi-hued blue orb.

Alex selected the first set of coordinates outside of the orb and found a tiny blue dot placed by the artist along the creature's neck, buried in the furred mane. He selected other coordinates and found that they were the same blue and the same size as the one on the neck. The dots, hardly visible to the naked eye, were located along the creature's curved back, claws, limb joints, and face. There was no doubt in Alex's mind of the artist's intention to use the creature as a representation of something else.

Using the imaging app, Alex selected the dots similar to the orb and signaled the dropout of the remainder of the tapestry. He stared at the remaining collection of dots, and his heart skipped a beat.

Renée felt the reflexive jerk of Alex's muscles, and she sat up to watch his face.

Alex recalled the Sawa stone image, stored in his implant, and overlaid the two images. He resized the tapestry's dots and rotated them over the stone's image. He did get a match of sorts. The problem was that the stone had many more dots than the tapestry, but there was a definite alignment of many points between the two images.

<Julien,> Alex sent excitedly, linking Renée to the comm. <This first image is an original of Nyslara's tapestry. Renée spoke to me about the superstitions of ancient people, who wrapped their constellations in images of gods and monsters. Note the blue dots of thread, similar to the orb in its mouth, that remain when the creature's image is removed. Now lay those dots over the carving on the temple stone.>

It took Julien mere ticks to reply. <Observe, Alex, your mythological creature's dots are in blue, and our stone's dots are in yellow. We do indeed have convergence. Furthermore, the remaining dots on the stone, which are now in red, coincide with Celus and the star's planet.>

<Well, mystery solved,> Renée rejoiced.

<Yes, well done, my love, except we're still lacking an accurate vector,> Alex sent privately.

<Alex, I've contacted Willem, and he's transferred some *Sojourn* data. The explorer ship tracked and calculated the orbit times of Celus' planets. Allow me a moment to shift the planets' present orbital positions to match the red dots of the stone.>

Alex watched the entire process via his implant, as Julien whirled the planets' present positions backwards in time around Celus until the overlay had alignment with the stone's red dots.

<Black space,> Alex sent.

<As appropriate an expression as any, Alex,> Julien sent. Alex wasn't in front of Julien, so he missed the SADE's soft smile. <My estimate is the sphere entered the system 196 years ago, plus or minus 3.45 percent, due to the possible inaccuracies of the artist's carving.>

<I notice, Julien, that you kept the single line's alignment with the red dots. It would appear to confirm our supposition that the line sights from

Sawa, which is the point from which the Dischnya would have spotted the sphere.>

<Agreed, Alex. Given some analysis time, we can calculate the star positions, as they were two centuries ago, including Celus. Once we have that data, we'll have a considerably more accurate vector to determine the direction the sphere came from when it arrived in system.>

<You two sound glum,> Renée sent. <I'd think you'd be pleased. You have your vector.>

<It does tempt us to follow this thread of evidence toward the Nua'll home world, Ser,> Julien replied.

<But what, Julien?> Renée persisted.

<The vector narrows the sphere's line of arrival into a defined area of space, but, considering the distances the sphere might have covered and the stops it might have made since leaving its home world, there could be hundreds of thousands of stars to investigate.>

<Why are males so pessimistic?> Renée declared and closed her comm.

<See what you did,> Alex accused.

<Since when did honesty and forthrightness become undesirable?> Julien retorted, which resulted in a protracted image fight, as the two friends celebrated solving the mystery of the temple stone.

-23-
Into The Dark

"This is Captain Pederson of the freighter *Into The Dark*, calling Omnia Ships for delivery instructions of the company's Haraken shipment." Durly leaned back in his chair to enjoy his hot drink and await the response, but he managed a single sip before his bridge speakers came to life.

<Greetings, Captain Pederson. This is Captain Cordelia of the city-ship *Freedom*. I have your delivery instructions. Your first stop will be at a moon in orbit around Celus-6. Hail Ben Diaz when you're within 3M kilometers of the planet for instructions. Afterwards, rendezvous with the *Freedom*. We're orbiting Celus-5.>

"Rainmaker," Durly said, excitedly. "It's going to be great to see the boy again. I hauled asteroids for that overgrown human at Haraken."

<I'm sure Ser Diaz will be pleased to see you, Captain,> Cordelia replied, smiling. The captain's language marked him as New Terran. <The delivery items labeled mining will be offloaded under Ser Diaz's instructions.>

"Wait one, Captain," Durly replied. Before he could ask his first mate, Tilda Hennessey, she spooled the freighter's load list up on a screen and highlighted several lines, which were marked by an "M" in a column. "Yep, Captain. We've got the designations. Have to break open a few modules for Rainmaker. He's got some mighty big pieces, an ore excavator, processing equipment, and compressed liquid tanks, to name a few."

<Ben Diaz has the same list. He'll ensure you deliver everything that he's ordered. Safe voyage, Captain.>

"And to you, Captain Cordelia," Durly replied, signing off.

"Wow," Tildie said quietly, "a feminine captain of a great city-ship. You have to admire Alex Racine. He breaks so many entrenched rules."

"You know Cordelia is a SADE, not a woman, right?" Durly offered.

"Your gray hairs are fouling your translations, Captain," Tildie teased. "I said feminine, not female. You're going to have to adapt to modern language."

"I'm too old to adapt, Tildie," Durly grumbled good-naturedly, and Tildie laughed softly.

Durly smiled to himself. Despite being a heavy worlder like him, Tildie had a light, pleasant laugh.

Just when life dealt Durly two harsh blows, losing his wife and job in the same year, fortune smiled on him. He applied for immigration papers to the new world of Haraken, deciding he wasn't done flying. He figured Haraken would turn him down, but, surprisingly, he was accepted, considering his age a sign of experience.

Meeting Little Ben was another break for Durly, and he went to work for the first employer he ever liked. Years later, he was in business with two other aging pilots, owning a Méridien freighter older than they were. Three years into operation, one partner, who was also the first mate, died, and the other chose to stay planetside on Haraken.

So Durly was camped out in a small, cramped office on Haraken, interviewing applicants for the first mate position when in walked Tildie Hennessey. Durly had liked the young woman right off. She had a no-nonsense manner, excellent credentials despite her youth, and he loved her laugh.

Durly was about to offer the job to Tildie, when she said, "I need to let you know, Captain, that I'm looking for a ship that has two berths to fill."

"As a matter of fact, I do have another position to fill," Durly said. "It's the load manager's position. I suppose you know the requirements."

"I do, Captain, and I've got the perfect candidate for you. An ex-Méridien who managed freight and shipping for House O'Shea. You interested?"

"Of course, I'm interested, if we can afford him."

"Trust me, you can."

"When can you bring him by?" Durly asked. He saw Tildie blink twice and realized she was wrestling with the sending of a comm. A slender and striking brunette, whose smile lit the room, walked through his door.

"Greetings, Captain Pederson, I'm Millicent Vane, and, as you can see, I'm not a 'he.'"

"Apologies, miss," Durly replied, "old habits."

"I promise not to hold that against you, Captain," Millicent replied, and her gentle laugh made Durly feel awkward and forty years younger.

It didn't take Durly long to realize that Millicent was overqualified for the job.

"Ser Vane," Durly said formally, "while I would love to have you aboard, I'm afraid our struggling little freight company can't afford someone with your experience."

"Well, Captain, let's see if you and I can reach an accommodation."

After two hours of conversation and a review of the company's shipping logs, Durly was convinced that Millicent, with her experience, could help them run a more efficient operation and realize a significant increase in income for the company. The job interview ended with Durly hiring both women and granting Millicent a share of increased company profits to offset her mediocre salary.

"I still don't know why you'd want to work for a one-freighter outfit like ours, Ser Vane," Durly said, as the women stood to leave.

"Please, Captain, feel free to call me Millie. My friends do. And, as to why your freighter, Captain, it'll have its benefits," Millie replied, and slipped an arm around Tildie's waist.

"Oh," Durly replied. Belatedly, he realized that they were what people called H_2 couples, referring to a hydrogen atom's oversized proton compared to its tiny electron. The most famous of the H_2 couples were Alex and Renée, Tatia and Alain, Mickey and Pia, and Ben and Simone.

Sitting on the bridge of the freighter, as they made their entry into the Celus system, Durly smiled, recalling the interview and his slow uptake on Tildie and Millie's relationship. *Best damn hires I ever made,* he thought. Tildie might well have been the acting captain with all the work she contributed, and, with Millie's help, Durly and his partner were envisioning buying a second freighter. *Retire, hah,* Durly thought and considered sending a message to his old New Terran boss, who had laid him off to hire a younger pilot not soon after his dismissal.

"New course awaiting your approval," Tildie said, prompting Durly out of his musings.

Durly checked the figures and concurred. Then Tildie signaled the controller to shift its vector toward Celus-6.

"You have the bridge, Tildie. Good night," Durly said. He was in the bridge accessway when he passed Millie, who gave him her usual smile. She would keep Tildie company before the women turned in and passed the bridge duties to the third mate.

"Afraid we're splitting the load, Millie, making a stop at Celus-6 before Celus -5," Durly explained.

"Not to worry, Captain, I reviewed the mix of equipment and figured that we'd hit a moon base before the planet and packed accordingly."

"Of course, you did, Millie," Durly said, smiling. He whistled as he made his way to his cabin.

* * *

<Alex, a freighter, *Into The Dark*, has made system with your order. I directed them to Ben's location first,> Cordelia sent.

<Most appropriate, Captain. Thank you,"> Alex replied.

It had been obvious to Alex and everyone that Ben Diaz's mining operations would only go so far in completing the projects Alex started. Even with the GEN machines, which were built to upgrade New Terran technology to produce Méridien tech and were operating in a *Freedom* bay, there were supplies, such as power cells, food stock processors, and other sundry items, which the Omnians wouldn't be capable of producing for a while.

The obvious decision was to order the necessary materials from Haraken, but the question for Alex was how to pay for them. He had no desire to work through a bank and strap Omnia Ships with more contractual ties. Instead, Alex decided to personally loan Omnia Ships 20M credits, the transfer of which Julien immediately noticed.

Alex's next concern was how best to spend the funds, and his answer was to offload the problem to Mickey.

"Mickey, I need you to work with Ben, Miriam, Trixie, and Claude to create a list of needed equipment, spare parts, and finished materials for our projects. You have 20M in credits to spend and that includes delivery. The invoicing will be against Omnia Ships. Prioritize the requirements in this order: Ben, Dischnya housing, the travelers, the city, and, last, the orbital."

"Alex, there are other fund sources," Mickey replied. "Mine, for example. I could lend Omnia Ships many more credits than that."

"Work up your needs list, Mickey, and let me know if the 20M is falling short. Then we'll talk."

When Mickey finished compiling the wish lists, he had to laugh at his presumptiveness. He'd asked his compatriots to separate their lists into two categories: materials required in the next six months to continue work and items required for the year following those six months.

The immediate requirements from everyone totaled 18M credits, but the following year's requirements totaled an astounding 239M credits. Mickey paled when Cordelia sent him the cost summaries for the two lists.

"Alex, I might have underestimated the extent of these project costs," Mickey reported, taking a moment to explain what he'd done and Cordelia's estimates.

"Well, Mickey, after further consideration, I think I'll take you up on your offer. Let me know when you've transferred the 237M credits into Omnia Ships and thanks for your contribution."

"Black space, Alex. Tell me you're kidding," Mickey replied, aghast at the thought of transferring his entire fortune to the company.

Alex's poker face held for a few moments longer, and then he broke into laughter. "Do you actually have the funds, Mickey?" he asked.

"Maybe half of it," Mickey admitted, and that wiped the smile off Alex's face.

"Seriously, Mickey?"

Mickey shrugged his shoulders, as if apologizing for having accumulated so much wealth.

"Who knew engineering paid so well?" Alex pondered, sitting back in his chair rather dumbfounded.

"Engineering doesn't pay all that well, by itself, Alex. It's the inventive engineering necessary to accommodate your requests that make the fortunes."

"Well, your research into our equipment needs did teach us something critical, Mickey. We're going to hit the wall in about six months, just when we need more specialized materials. On top of that, our supply chain is a great deal longer than our credit flow. Haraken will start delivering travelers to customers about six months after we deliver the shells, and we can't even order supplies until we receive the credits from about four months' worth of their deliveries."

"So, are you saying, Alex, that we're going to have our people sitting on their hands for nearly a year once this load of supplies is used up?"

"Yes, unless we can come up with a better plan."

"Maybe we do need to borrow."

"Not yet. But now that I know the materials shortfall, I have a better idea of the bargain we need to strike."

"With our New Terran guests?" Mickey asked, and Alex and he shared grins.

* * *

Captain Pederson stationed the *Dark* 10 kilometers away from the *Freedom*, as Captain Cordelia directed. They'd made good time offloading the supplies for Ben Diaz and making Celus-5 or, as they'd learned, Omnia.

The *Dark*'s enormous freighting modules needed to be opened and the individual containers ferried to the *Freedom* for unpacking. Only Ben had the massive handling equipment to empty the modules directly from the freighter and distribute the containers to the mining locations. The job of emptying the *Dark* fell to the *Freedom*'s crew. It was standard procedure. The freighters arrived with cargo, and the customer was responsible for offloading the goods.

The procedure to empty the *Dark* would take at least three days. Everything the freighter carried had been destined for one customer, Alex Racine. The *Dark*'s crew had been pressed to load in at Haraken and hurry to their destination. A delivery bonus was on the line, and they'd earned it. Now, with some down time available, the small crew was anxious to see the planet and the renowned and refitted *Freedom*.

"Captain Cordelia, this is Captain Pederson. I have with me First Mate Tilda Hennessey," Durly said over his bridge's comm pickup.

<Greetings, Captain and First Mate Hennessey,> Cordelia sent in reply. <How may I assist you?>

"The crew wants a little time planetside, if that's permitted?" Durly asked.

<There's little to see, Captain, but I'll send you coordinates for the city center's site. Touring the facility will allow your people some time on Omnia. Afterwards, I invite you and your crew, those you can spare, to join us for a fête tomorrow evening in the grand garden, starting at 20.00 hours.>

"Thank you for the invite, Captain," Tildie replied. "I understand there are aliens on planet. Do we have permission to visit with them?"

<Some items to be absolutely clear about, Captain,> Cordelia said, and she adopted some of Alex's command style. <First, do not venture into the oceans, even the shallows. As inviting as the waters appear, the inhabitants are highly developed predators. Second, stay on the dry plains. Don't visit the forests. Nearly everything in there, flora and fauna, is deadly. A SADE barely made it out alive.> Although this wasn't exactly true, Alex had requested Cordelia phrase the warning that way. He had explained to her that it was a means of stating the danger so that humans would think twice about venturing there.

<And third, Captain, the coordinates I've just sent you apply to the city center. You're to stay in this area. The Dischnya live on another continent and are not to be disturbed. Furthermore, understand that this planet has

not been thoroughly investigated. Straying into areas not watched over by our people risks your crew's lives. Have I made myself clear?>

"Crystal clear, Captain. I thank you for the directions and appreciate the invitation to the fête." Durly closed the comm and regarded Tildie, who'd pushed for permission to see the aliens.

"Don't look at me like that, Captain. There was no harm in making a simple request, and she said no," Tildie replied, unhappy about the missed opportunity.

"Tildie, you're in charge of the crew while you're planetside. I need you to keep a level head on your shoulders and keep them in line. You're a good bunch of people, some of the best I've worked with, and I don't need one or more of you eaten alive by that planet down there. Am I clear?"

"Wow, corporal discipline before the error is even committed," Tildie said. When Durly drew breath to speak, Tildie waved him off. "Hey, warning understood, Captain. I'll keep the boys and girls in line and bring them back safely. Besides, Millie and I are more interested in attending that fête. You're going, aren't you?"

* * *

After a light evening meal, Durly retired to his cabin and pulled out his best captain's uniform. Tildie and Millie had convinced him to join them for the fête aboard the *Freedom*. At his age, Durly had long since stopped attending parties, but Millie's logic was convincing.

"Captain, is the company intent on seeking more business from Omnia Ships?" Millie had asked.

"Another contract would be wonderful," Durly replied, "especially if it offers an opportunity to earn an early delivery bonus."

"Well, Captain, the people we need to influence will be at the fête this evening, and you have the perfect asset."

Before Durly could guess the nature of his asset, Millie leaned against Tilda and smiled.

"Oh, of course, the hydrogen couple," Durly said without thinking.

The women laughed at Durly's response, and the captain felt the back of his neck warming.

"We use what we have, Captain," Tildie replied." We're a single-ship company, and if I'm going to make captain, then we need a second freighter."

"So, don your best uniform, Captain, and meet us on the flight deck at 19.45 hours," Millie added.

At the appointed time, Durly joined the crew, who were already aboard the freighter's single traveler, waiting in the *Dark*'s tiny bay.

The entire crew wanted to attend the evening's festivities, but someone had to remain aboard. The third mate lost a quick game of selection, but the crew chipped in some credits to make the young Haraken feel better about missing out.

Tildie had the traveler's pilot chair, and she quickly and efficiently had them soon landing aboard the *Freedom*.

"Black space," Durly muttered, as he descended into the cavernous bay, which held two other travelers and could have held three more.

"And think, Captain," Millie said. "One man owns two of these colossal ships."

"I don't compute that," Tildie said. "From everything, I've ever heard, Alex Racine never chased credits. So how did he accumulate the wealth necessary to buy these city-ships?"

"Who said he paid what they're worth?" Millie riposted, as they entered the *Freedom*'s main corridor. She'd left her warming cape aboard the traveler and was wearing a typical Méridien evening wrap, designed to focus the eye on her attractive figure.

Durly and his male crew were surprised by Tildie, who they'd rarely seen in anything but work overalls or business attire. This evening she wore a form-hugging, New Terran-style, outfit.

The women led the way from the bay to the main park. Millie, who was comfortable on Méridien-designed vessels, was guiding them to the central garden with the aid of the city-ship's controller.

When the *Dark*'s crew exited the lift that emptied into the huge, open space of the main garden, which was dominated by 15-meter high trees, everyone, except Millie, stumbled to a halt.

"Superb," Millie whispered, and sauntered into the majestic venue, which was artistically lit by Cordelia for the evening's festivities. Tildie hurried to catch up with her partner, and Durly whispered, "Close your mouths, men. Mingle and act like you belong here." Unsure of what to do himself, Durly closed on Millie and Tildie, thinking that if any contacts were to be made, the women would manage it.

Millie was scanning with her location app, searching for Omnia's prominent couples when she froze. "It can't be," she whispered and walked quickly through the park, following paths, but constantly reorienting her direction.

Tildie threw a questioning glance at Durly, and the two of them stayed close behind Millie.

<Svetlana, it's Millicent Vane,> Millie sent, when her app indicated her childhood friend was in front of her and standing with a group of people. Her sending caused a striking blonde in a naval uniform to turn around and cry out "Millie!"

The two women raced toward each other and hugged joyfully, tears spilling down their cheeks, as they laughed at their good fortune in finding each other again. When they separated, Millie introduced her partner and captain.

"Come, join us," Svetlana said, taking Millie's arm.

The crew of the *Dark* found they were introduced to nearly every prestigious individual on Omnia, and Durly found his mouth drying, as he shook hands with Alex Racine.

"What's the uniform, Svetlana?" Millie asked.

"That's Commander Valenko to you, Millie," Svetlana said good-naturedly.

"But I thought that the only Méridien commanders who reported to Admiral Tachenko were Independents," Millie said innocently.

"For the most part, you'd be correct," Tatia replied.

"Oh, Svetlana, I didn't know. I'm so sorry," Millie said in horror.

"Don't be," Svetlana replied, "If I wasn't on Libre, I wouldn't be where I am today, and I'm one happy woman."

"Seems Haraken has a way of collecting orphans and outcasts," Durly commented.

"I believe that honor belongs to Alex," Renée quipped.

"I might point out, Alex, that Captain Pederson delivered Omnia Ship's supplies six days ahead of schedule," Cordelia said.

"Congratulations on your bonus, Captain. I noticed the *Dark* is a Méridien freighter. Does your company own other Confederation-built haulers?"

"You're pretty much looking at the company, except for a silent partner on Haraken. I wasn't sure where my company was headed until I hired First Mate Hennessey, and she brought Millie aboard. The women have been a boost in the company's economic arm.

"Women usually are," Svetlana declared, and her comment was echoed by Renée, Tatia, Cordelia, Ellie, and Pia.

Alex pinged Millie for her bio ID, and the Méridien graciously added her extended résumé to Alex's request. The conversation swirled around Alex, like a stream of water around a rock, as the group chatted and laughed. Even Durly found himself pulled into the easy-going conversation. Millie joined in the fun, but she noted Alex Racine was staring in her direction, although his eyes weren't focused on her.

<What do you think of this crew and the *Dark*, Cordelia?> Alex sent.

<Excellent reputation … an old freighter, but well reconditioned. It's a small company, struggling to grow. I find it interesting that the pair, Millicent and Tilda, want to work for an aging New Terran captain with a single ship. I believe they see opportunity and are willing to work hard to create it.>

<Deserving of a little support, don't you think?> Alex sent.

Cordelia smiled at Alex, enjoying where his thoughts were headed.

"Come, Captain Pederson," Alex said, slipping his arm in Durly's. "Let's you and I walk and talk."

-24-
Maria's Deal

Maria Gonzalez spent nineteen days with Darryl and Frederick, carefully examining everything they could gather about Omnia — the projects' scopes, the available machinery, the capability of the machines to supply the gamut of items the projects needed, and the extent of Alex's workforce, humans and SADEs.

The threesome sat around a table in a small conference room set aside for their use. Frederick had secured a holo-vid to help his employers readily understand his computations.

"From every conceivable angle, the numbers don't make sense, Maria," Darryl declared, leaning back in his chair. "We keep looking for some answers, and we haven't found any."

"I concur, Sers," Frederick replied. "Alex Racine and, by extension, Omnia Ships, must wait for a sizable credit flow from his traveler production to be able to purchase the services and supplies to complete his projects, unless his company borrows heavily from the Exchange."

"Alex is allergic to debt," Darryl commented, which required Frederick to expend some effort to comprehend the odd statement.

"My calculations indicate that the workforce is spread much too thin to maximize the company's shell and frame production," Frederick added.

"Alex's intent on taking care of the Dischnya," Maria replied.

"That isn't the most logical means of reaching his goal," said Frederick, which elicited laughter from Maria and Darryl.

Darryl patted Frederick's arm, which the SADE found to be a more comfortable human expression of sincerity than those he had first experienced.

"Alex has never been one for pure logic," Maria replied to Frederick's frown. "He looks to ensure those who need help are taken care of first."

"A worthy attitude, but lacking in financial efficiency," Frederick replied.

Maria leaned her forearms on the table to focus her stare on the SADE. "Agreed, Frederick," she said, "but understand this … we like Alex the way he is."

"Your point is made, Ser, and I will adjust my thinking to give Alex's preferences greater weight, in the future," Frederick said. The SADE had considered there would be some minor differences between working with humans in the Confederation and New Terra. Within days of his employment, he admitted he'd been in error. Every day since then, Frederick spent time adjusting expectations and reorganizing his protocols — and today was no different.

The one thing that Frederick found oddly comforting about his new employers was their manner of correcting his thought processes and then moving on, as if the error never happened. There were no recriminations or, worse, a series of engineers hurriedly running extensive testing on his kernel, as there would have been at House Lemoyne.

For instance, Frederick found Maria's smile, while she eased back in her chair, an example of the inexplicable nature of his employers. But, if he'd learned anything, it was to ask questions about what he didn't understand. The New Terrans expected his participation in their strategies, and to be an informed participant required knowledge.

"Ser, you're smiling. Is that because you're pleased that Alex Racine will encounter great obstacles in completing his projects?" Frederick asked.

"Yes, Frederick, but not in the manner you might be thinking," Maria replied. "Alex is facing tremendous challenges and so is New Terra. Our analysis shows he needs us. We can help him, and he can help us."

"His needs are your world's opportunity," Frederick said, understanding Maria's intent. "To what degree will our information present a financial windfall for New Terra?"

This was the second time in this session alone that Frederick's statements had produced laughter from his employers. It seemed to be the way in which New Terrans reacted to comments he made, which indicated his logic had arrived at entirely the wrong conclusion.

"Alex may have some strange priorities from the viewpoint of most people, especially Méridiens," Darryl said. "But when it comes to negotiations, you'd better buckle in tight. The acceleration gets nasty," Darryl added, chuckling.

Frederick filed another of the minister's unusual expressions for future review. The SADE was relieved that Julien, Cordelia, Z, and Miranda helpfully translated the New Terran euphemisms.

* * *

Maria requested a private meeting between her team and Alex. She didn't expect Alex to be alone in his suite, but he was.

"Are we waiting for others?" Maria asked, while Darryl, Frederick, and she were seated.

"No, go ahead, Maria," Alex said good-naturedly, while he fixed thé for the three humans.

Frederick eyed the holo-vid sitting on the small table in front of him. It reminded him of how connected Alex Racine was to his people, including the SADEs, and he found that reassuring.

Maria and Darryl had spent the previous evening reviewing possible strategies for how they would approach Alex, without coming to an agreement. Darryl finally said, "Maria, this is Alex. Forget all the titles he's carried. I say treat him like the captain we first got to know."

After Alex set their cups in front of them and most of it was consumed, Alex set his cup down and stared at Maria. Recalling Darryl's advice, she said, "We can complete travelers as well as Haraken can."

"You haven't the technical capability, Maria," Alex replied.

Maria and Darryl mentally breathed sighs of relief. Alex didn't disagree with Maria's statement. He was arguing details.

"You have the specifications for what's needed to complete the travelers, and we have Frederick and ten other SADEs, who can ensure that the materials we produce meet your specifications," Maria replied.

"I've only the one carrier, the *Our People*, for shell delivery, and there isn't time for the ship to make second trips to New Terra without reducing its production efficiency," answered Alex.

"And that's the beauty of our proposal, Alex," Maria said, smiling. "You give us the tech; we make the materials; and we come to Omnia to buildout the travelers. Or are you saying Haraken has a monopoly on these shells?" Maria asked, wondering if there was something in Omnia Ship's agreement with Haraken that she didn't know.

"There's no monopoly," Alex replied. "But I've only got the one location for building the shells."

"So, what's the orbital terminal's purpose?" Darryl asked, warming to the negotiations.

"Passenger transfer and ship construction," Alex replied.

"Warships," Maria pressed.

"Among others," Alex replied casually.

"So, traveler shells could be laid up at the terminal and assembly completed there," Maria said.

"Once the orbital platform is completed, but that's in the future," Alex said, offering a small shrug.

Frederick wished the New Terrans had implants. His algorithms pressed to communicate privately with them. Alex Racine's very words contradicted what he implied, but then he recalled the New Terrans' laughter at his thought that his information would give his employers the upper hand in negotiations. *Fascinating,* Frederick thought, and relaxed to carefully analyze the strange conversation, which seemed more about what wasn't said, than about what was said.

"Unless New Terra helped you complete the terminal early," Maria said.

"Haven't the credits nor the workforce," Alex replied.

"We have both, Alex," Maria said earnestly.

"And you know we have the tech and experience to build these, Alex," Darryl added.

"Generous offers," Alex replied. "And what are you expecting for this largesse?"

For the first time, Maria saw Alex's eyes sharpen. She had her answer. Alex's moral integrity demanded he take care of the planet's species, his people, the humans and the SADEs, before he focused on the one thing he wanted.

"New Terra wants in on the tech, Alex," Maria said. "Our world is changing fast. The public has weathered the massive shift caused by the explosion of Méridien tech. Our Assembly members are responding to the improvement in their lives, and they don't want to be the orphans or stepchildren in this corner of the galaxy."

"I can simply license the tech to you for compensation, Maria," Alex replied. "We don't need to dance around the subject like we've been doing."

"That's true, Alex," Maria replied. "The tech is just part of it. The Assembly wants warships. I thought of requesting that we build sting ships together, but after what I saw in Mickey's lab, I'm thinking there's a huge opportunity for us to work together."

"You're not the Assembly or the president, Maria, even though I would wish that you were," Alex said. "Do you think you could sell your proposal to Drake and the Assembly?"

"Alex," Darryl said, chuckling, "the Assembly would fall all over itself to be the first government to build a relationship with a new world, complete with humans, SADEs, Dischnya, and Swei Swee."

"Don't forget what I said earlier, Alex," Maria added. "That club, which you initiated because of the work on the *Our People*, will ensure that Drake and the Assembly back our agreement. Black space, Alex, I would be bringing them everything they asked for and more. Now, let's talk numbers."

Frederick finally got an opportunity to join the conversation, but he discovered they weren't alone anymore. Alex linked with him and a group of SADEs. He found he was challenged to keep up with their analyses routines. They were experienced negotiators and knew what Alex wanted for his people. If this had been a conflict, he would have been dead by virtue of the opening salvo.

Frederick discovered that one element kept communications in balance, including preventing him from being overwhelmed. It was Alex Racine. As negotiations proceeded, Frederick relied more and more on his employers. He projected the summaries on the holo-vid for their comments. They provided the strategy and he provided the options, which allowed negotiations on New Terra's behalf to make headway.

To Frederick's relief, the discussions were halted for midday meal, and Frederick requested a private table so he could plan with Maria and Darryl.

The discussions lasted two more days, as each side angled for what they wanted. When the agreement was concluded, which the SADEs recorded, Darryl, ever the detail-minded, asked, "How do we get this started, Alex?"

"Already in progress, Darryl. Part of our recent cost projections examined the supplies needed for the next six months and the year following that period. Captain Durly has just delivered the supplies for the first six-month period. You'll be receiving the list of materials required to drive the next year."

"But are your needs our needs?" Darryl asked, pointing first at Alex and then at Maria and himself.

"Our needs," Alex said, imitating Darryl's gesture, "were always my intent. In this case, we've only speeded up my timeline, and I'm sharing our tech and ship production for your credits and workforce."

Maria looked at Darryl and tipped her head to the side, as if to tell him I told you so. Alex had ensured that the agreement did not force him to deviate from his plan. He simply shared the bounty with New Terra of what his people intended to accomplish.

"Mickey and Julien are standing by to transfer a standalone device with crystal memory and controller to the *Rover*. Your readers now have a code, but the device has no access panel," Alex said.

Maria and Darryl didn't bother checking their readers. They were fully aware of what Alex could do with his twin implants, including bypassing their reader's encryption programs.

"Wait," Darryl exclaimed. "No access panel, but then how do we —"

Alex forestalled Darryl's question by raising a hand. "Maria, you'll need to have Frederick present when the Assembly passes the agreement, without amendments, I might add. Once Frederick witnesses that event, you give him your passcode, which he can use to signal the controller and access the crystal memory."

"Being awfully careful, Alex, aren't you?" Maria asked.

Alex continued, as if Maria hadn't asked a question. "If the agreement isn't ratified, return the device to me. If you're successful, Maria, your eleven SADEs will secure the data and distribute it, as you direct them."

"What're we getting, besides your one-year needs list?" Maria asked.

"First, I expect that list to furnish us with about six months or less of supplies with the accelerated support of your workforce. We included the technical specifications to manufacture any item on the list. It certainly doesn't encompass everything we'll need to fulfill the agreement, but it buys my people time to complete their research on the warships and define their future requirements."

"Then that's it?" Daryl said, asking Alex for confirmation.

"One more small detail … more a favor," Alex said, standing, and signaling the suite's door open. Durly, who Cordelia had waiting in the corridor outside the suite, stepped through the doorway.

"This is Captain Durly Pederson of the *Into The Dark*, which his crew calls the *Dark*. Durly knows this system, having dispersed his load at our sites. He earned a bonus for his early delivery and has an excellent crew. Two more pluses … the *Dark* is a Méridien-built freighter, and his people know my people."

Maria recognized the subtext of Alex's introduction and said, "I'm sure we can use Captain Pederson's services, once the agreement is approved."

Durly nodded gratefully to Maria for the consideration.

Maria smiled at Alex, expecting the same in return, but he quietly stared back, and Maria quickly revised her comment to Durly. "Then again, I tell you what, Captain, head to New Terra and contact me when you make orbit. I'll guarantee you a load, which Alex will prioritize for us." She glanced again at Alex, who wore the barest of smiles. *Always looking out for the little guy,* Maria thought.

* * *

"How did the negotiations go?" Renée asked Alex, in the evening following their completion. "You weren't too hard on Maria, were you?"

"Whose side are you on?" Alex teased.

Renée walked over to the couch where Alex was seated, straddled his lap, and kissed the tip of his nose. "Yours ... and hers."

"Fickle woman. Can't make up her mind where her loyalties lie," Alex riposted. "No, Maria held her own. It was more of a training lesson, especially for Frederick."

"I can't imagine how Maria and Darryl cope with the incredible changes in their culture caused by our technology. Not to mention, every time they broker an agreement with you, it's on a different world with new entities."

"Is our life as challenging for you?" Alex asked with concern. It hit him that sometimes he took his partner's commitment to what he did for granted.

"For me, it's simple," Renée said, kissing Alex on the forehead and looking him hard in the eye. "As long as I'm standing behind that broad back of yours, I won't be the first to be dropped."

Alex threw Renée a mock look of surprise and tried to smack her bare leg, but she was too quick. With a squeal, Renée launched free of the couch and ran for the bedroom, laughing, and Alex gave chase.

* * *

Durly returned to his ship late in the evening, after procuring Alex's priority list from Cordelia. It could have been sent to him, but the captain was in a daze about his good fortune and felt better about receiving the list personally from Cordelia. The crew was tucked into their cots, and Tildie and Millie were sitting second shift on the bridge.

"Visit's over, Captain," Millie said. "Time to go back to work."

"When do you want to break orbit and make for Haraken, Captain?" Tildie asked. "We can get underway, while you catch up on some sleep."

"Yes, it's better we get underway now, Tildie," Durly said in a matter-of-fact voice. "Go ahead and set course for New Terra."

"Certainly, Captain … wait, what, New Terra?" Tildie replied.

"Oh, didn't I tell you? You know, I was worried about this ... getting on in age and forgetting things," Durly said, shaking his head regretfully. Then he broke into a huge grin. "We have a hauling contract, originating in New Terra for Omnia. Maria Gonzalez negotiated an agreement with Omnia Ships."

Tildie started to celebrate, but Millie interrupted. "Wait, an agreement, not a contract?" she asked.

"It's a long-term agreement between New Terra and Omnia Ships. Alex Racine introduced me to Maria, and suggested he'd be pleased if the *Dark* was contracted for freighter runs. He spoke real nice about us to Maria, and she understood what the man meant. So, we've been invited to make the first run … guaranteed. She said by the time we return to New Terra from our first trip to Omnia, the agreement would be signed."

"So, we get two runs if the Assembly agrees to what's been negotiated?" Millie asked excitedly.

"Not two runs, Millie. Once the agreement is signed, we're on an open contract with New Terra," Durly said quietly, but he was grinning like a fool.

"Open-end contract," the women screamed together, hugging and hopping up and down. In their excitement, they grabbed Durly, hugging him and planting a kiss on each cheek.

"Two more lovely assets, as ever a captain had." Durly declared. "Let me know when I'm due at the next Omnian party, and I'll be ready."

-25-
Decisions

"I believe we should consider our mission accomplished, Willem," Asu said. The pair was seated in the captain's cabin aboard the *Sojourn*.

"As much as I would prefer to argue, Captain, I can't," Willem replied. "We've accomplished so much more than I could have considered possible when we launched from Haraken."

"Coming from a SADE, that's a statement," Asu replied. "Impressive first voyage for the *Sojourn*," Asu added, winking and smiling at Willem.

"Most impressive," Willem replied, returning Asu's smile. "Think the Assembly will approve another mission? After all, the planet we investigated won't become a Haraken colony."

"My friend, Omnia is better than a colony. It will be a sister world of entities who will be friends of Haraken, and we've been so successful that I think we might have trouble keeping Assembly members off the next crew list," Asu replied, laughing so hard he started coughing.

"You speak as if you intend to captain the next mission," Willem said, carefully eyeing Asu.

"Only if my co-commander is still with me," Asu replied, sobering and returning Willem's quiet look.

"To the *Sojourn*'s next journey and the mysteries that await us," Willem said, extending his hand to Asu.

"To the next mission, Captain," Asu replied, but his expression turned serious, while he gripped Willem's hand. "What do you think about asking the Assembly to have a sting ship accompany us next time?"

"Prior to this mission, I would have deemed it totally unnecessary. Now, I consider it a necessity. This portion of the galaxy is feeling incredibly crowded."

* * *

When Teague and Ginny returned from their latest visit to Wave Skimmer's new hive site in a crescent bay near where the *Sojourn*'s Swei Swee found shelter in a cave, word reached them of the mission's impending departure.

For her part, Ginny was pleased to have had a final opportunity to sing for the four hives that could gather in time for her performance. The sight of younglings settling on matrons' backs and snoozing, as she closed with one of Mutter's soulful lullabies, had filled her heart.

Sitting on the cot in Teague's cabin, Ginny asked, "What're you thinking?"

"Too many thoughts, as Dad would say," Teague replied. "These waters are too dangerous for our Swei Swee to inhabit, and our four friends will need mates someday. For now, it looks like the best thing to do is return with the *Sojourn* when it heads for home."

"I agree, but then what comes next?" Ginny asked.

"Well, despite everything that's happened," Teague said, pulling out the desk chair and sitting backwards on it to face Ginny. "I've found the entire experience of this survey mission to be fulfilling in ways I couldn't have imagined."

"I'm so pleased to hear you say that. I want to do this again," Ginny said, bouncing excitedly on the bed.

"I heard Asu and Willem talking on the bridge," Teague said. "Despite the problems they encountered on Celus … I mean Omnia, they're really excited about what the survey mission accomplished. More important, they believe the tremendous opportunity for Haraken to receive traveler shells by the tens will have the Assembly anxious to fund more survey missions."

"What about your parents, Teague?" Ginny asked. She was holding her breath, waiting for the answer, but she felt the question had to be asked.

"They have their lives, and I want a life of my own, one that's not standing in my father's shadow. But I want to know what you want to do."

Ginny curled her bare toes, pleased to hear Teague ask her opinion. Omnia's incredible events had contributed enormously to Teague's maturation. Now, he discussed things with her instead of telling her what he'd already decided to do, and he displayed small considerations to her, similar to the way Alex treated Renée. Ginny rolled to her knees and said, "I want to inform Captain Azasdau and Willem, in the morning, that we want to enlist for the next mission. And maybe, just maybe, we should ask for a stipend. I think we've proved our worth, despite our youth."

"A stipend would be nice," Teague agreed. "So, we journey again into the dark."

Ginny squealed, jumping off the cot, and Teague stood in time to take the impact, as Ginny threw her arms around his neck. "Yes, yes, yes," she said, whispering in Teague's ear. She was one delighted teenager.

* * *

Once the mission co-commanders decided to roll up their survey efforts, Franz and Reiko faced difficult decisions. They spent the evening discussing their options and eventually arguing. Well, to be exact, Reiko did the arguing and Franz tried unsuccessfully to reason with her.

"I'm only asking you do one thing, Reiko," Franz said, as calmly as he could manage. "Talk to Tatia. Rumor is there's more going on with Alex's people than has been announced. Yes, they're able to spray up a traveler shell, but what else is Alex planning?"

Because it was her lover's request, Reiko contacted Tatia to request a meeting. <You're probably aware, Admiral, that the *Sojourn* is pulling out … ending its survey. That means the *Tanaka*'s protection duty is at an end. We'll be returning to Haraken with the *Sojourn*,> Reiko sent.

<You sound as if you're conflicted, Captain,> Tatia replied.

<Franz is asking me to consider joining Alex's merry collection of adventurers, but I'm a warship commander, Admiral. I don't know anything else, and Alex has nothing bigger than a traveler. No disrespect to you or your people, Admiral.>

<None taken, Captain. Opinions formed in a vacuum of information often have that sort of ring,> Tatia sent. Her words were meant to sting, but the thoughts she sent were devoid of emotion.

<A harsh statement, Admiral; do you have knowledge that proves me wrong?> Reiko replied. She was angry at the rebuke, but she wasn't about to demonstrate that to the admiral.

<Captain, I suggest you collect your partner and meet me aboard the *Freedom*, at your earliest convenience.>

Trained in United Earth's military academies since a cadet, Reiko translated the informal request correctly and replied, <Commander Cohen and I will be aboard your ship directly, Admiral.>

Reiko gathered Franz, and they landed aboard the *Freedom* less than a half hour later. A ping of the admiral's location indicated they were to meet her in another bay about 110 degrees farther around the ship's enormous circumference.

"I suggest we jog, my heart," Franz said. "We shouldn't keep an admiral waiting."

Reiko frowned at Franz. Running wasn't her idea of decorum for an ex-UE commodore and a Haraken captain of a warship. Nonetheless, she nodded and picked up the pace. While Reiko ran, Franz, who towered over her and, despite his heavy-worlder body, jogged lightly beside her.

At the airlock, Reiko paused to catch her breath and, when she was ready, signaled the corridor-side hatch. They cycled through the airlock and entered a hive of activity. There was little noise from voices. Everyone was using implants, but the movement of equipment and materials from a couple of hundred engineers and techs was a constant din.

Reiko pinged for Tatia's bio ID, and Franz and she made their way among a variety of experiments, some small and some full size.

"Greetings, Admiral," said Reiko, as Franz and she saluted Tatia. There was a quick exchange of pleasantries with Mickey, Ellie, Svetlana, Deirdre, Darius, and Lucia.

"A distinguished audience," Franz admitted, wondering why Tatia's commanders were present for the meeting, but, more important, why Mickey was present.

"I'm glad you said that, Commander," Tatia replied. "Some of my commanders are here because they follow Alex. Others are here because they follow me, and I'm here because Alex proves to me that he's worth following. It's no secret that Alex's focus is on the distinct possibility of a second Nua'll sphere. According to Renée, that thought disturbs his sleep."

"That's not good news," Franz lamented.

"For those who know Alex, it isn't," Tatia replied, and directed her attention to Reiko. "You wondered why this group of elite commanders and I are here when outwardly Alex appears to have only travelers, Captain. We're here for those things that haunt Alex. If you love humankind, there isn't a greater calling for people like us." Tatia signaled Mickey, who pulled the cover off a bench to reveal a miniature warship.

"Captain, this is a model of the new Trident-class warship, which will be built in conjunction with New Terra. An agreement is in the works. When it's approved by the Assembly, Omnia Ships will receive credits and materials to complete the orbital terminal and build this class of ships and others."

"It's an attractive design," Reiko admitted. "Two questions. What's the scale, and when will you move from model to something more operational to prove the design?"

Reiko and Franz received an image. A sting ship nestled next to a Trident-class ship, like a youngling protected by its matriarch.

"This is the largest warship class we'll be building. Its size is to ensure that those twin side hulls can generate the amount of beam power we believe we'll need if we find a sphere," Svetlana said. "I'll captain the first one built. While that's not been authorized, I'm staking my claim now."

There was some snickering among Svetlana's peers, but the determination in her face dared anyone to outwardly disagree with her.

"As to your question about demonstrative progress … Mickey, if you would?" Tatia requested.

<Test firing,> Mickey sent on open comm, and the group watched engineers and techs scramble out of the way of the model's bow alignment. Mickey sent signals to the 2-meter long model, which was coated in its traditional blue, green, and cream shell, and it rose off the table.

When Tatia and her commanders took a few steps back, Reiko and Franz hurriedly joined them. Mickey, on the other hand, never moved.

"Why do engineers do that?" Darius whispered to his admiral.

"To show their trust in what they build," Tatia replied quietly.

<Firing,> Mickey sent, as a final warning, and a beam of light exited a side hull, heating the air's particles. A specially prepared target was hit 10 meters away, and the odd structure hissed and bucked.

Amidst the raucous applause of engineers and techs, Mickey lowered the model to the table, sending an all clear.

"Mickey, what is that?" Franz asked, pointing at the target.

"That, Commander, is the best we can come up with to manage test firing a beam inside a ship. It's a trap, composed of multiple layers. The outer layer is a double sheath of metal-alloy, trapping expandable nanites foam to plug the beam holes, and the center is filled with liquid oxygen to absorb the heat. The reason we didn't make a bigger model is that we calculated we couldn't absorb the beam shot from a single hull."

"Impressive, Mickey," Franz admitted, and Mickey glowed with professional pride.

"That's not impressive," the diminutive Reiko said, stepping up to the model and stroking its beautifully colored hulls. "That's absolutely the most incredible warship that's ever been designed."

"Uh, oh, Svetlana, you have competition," Lucia said, nudging her friend.

"No, I don't," Svetlana replied determinedly. "She's an ex-commodore, and we're building more than one Trident. Someone has to command the squadron. I'll still be captain of the first ship."

The rest of the demonstration descended into a show and tell of the remaining classes of warships. Mickey demonstrated their various capabilities, floating the models off their tables but refraining from firing any of their weapons.

When Mickey finished, Tatia said simply, "Now you can make an informed decision, Captain." Then she exited the bay with her commanders in tow.

Franz spared a moment for Mickey, who raised his eyebrows, as if to emphasize the wonderment of all he'd shown before he returned to work.

Reiko turned and exited the bay, Franz by her side. The couple didn't talk the entire way back to the *Tanaka*, and Franz left his partner alone with her thoughts, which was fine by him. He had his own to consider.

-26-
Haraken Transplants

In a fairly short period of time, the space over Omnia was dominated by ship movement.

Alex and Renée said farewell to Teague and Ginny. Then the *Sojourn* broke orbit, accompanied by the *Tanaka.*

Alex had asked Tatia how the conversation went with Reiko. Tatia's response was, "I took a tough approach with her, Alex. She's wedded firmly to her sting ship. Her command of a warship validates her years as a UE destroyer captain, but I'm not sure my technique worked, although the Trident model impressed her."

When Alex chuckled at her comment, Tatia had shrugged her wide shoulders and said, "You know how naval officers are attracted to large weapons."

That comment cracked Alex up, and, when he regained his breath, he said, "We'll have to wait and see, Tatia. Once we build enough of these warships to have squadrons, we'll need experienced commodores who understand fleet maneuvers, and Reiko has plenty of that experience."

Not long after the *Sojourn* and the *Tanaka* left the Celus system, the *Our People* was ready to set sail. The first batch of shells was complete, and the city-ship would be underway to Haraken, while the workers finished the second batch of traveler shells.

Alex wished Hector a safe journey, as did every SADE. Trixie, of course, stayed in communication with Hector until he exited the system.

It was forty-six days after the *Dark* had left with the *Rover* for New Terra when Alex, who was planetside, received Cordelia's comm.

<Alex, the *Into The Dark* has entered subspace. Captain Pederson sends his greeting and wishes to communicate that the Assembly approved the agreement as negotiated.>

<Wonderful tidings, Captain. Send Captain Pederson my compliments for the message.>

Days later, Durly reported to Alex in his suite aboard the *Freedom*.

"Captain Cordelia is offloading our modules, which are carrying your priority items for the orbital terminal," Durly said, after taking the offered seat and receiving a cup of thé from Renée. "There was one change. Millie, our load manager, figured you could use more siding to increase the number of modules to house supplies at the platform. She requested them of me, and I talked to Maria, who added them to our shipment."

"Good thinking. Tell Millie thank you for her consideration."

"All part of the service, Alex. I can't tell you how much your help means to my company. Our contract in support of this agreement will be a great ending to my captain's days, and they'll ensure a future for my wonderful young crew."

"Glad to be of help, Captain. Is there anything else?"

"There is one thing, Ser," Durly said, standing. It was obvious by the nervous hands and glances to the side that Durly preferred not to speak on the subject.

"Come, Captain, you're among friends. Speak up."

"Well, Maria Gonzalez was ecstatic when the Assembly approved the agreement. After the *Dark* was loaded, she stopped aboard … personal like … to see us off. She told me to tell you that the *Rover* would be right behind me, bringing the first group of your workforce and escorting some more freighters."

When Durly paused, Alex raised his eyebrows, intimating the captain should continue. "Well, Maria has a strong personality, as you know … ex-general, ex-president, and all that."

Alex nodded his agreement, and Durly plowed on. "Well, Maria Gonzalez, in front of my crew, kissed me full on the mouth, and said, 'You give that to Alex for me, Captain,' and then she left."

"I can see where it would be difficult for you to pass on that message, Captain," Alex said, trying to keep a straight face.

"Yes, Ser," Durly admitted.

"Allow me to assist you, Captain," said Renée, smiling, stepping close to Durly, and lightly gripping his shoulders. "You may deliver Maria's message to me." Relief showed on the white-haired captain's face, as Renée received a chaste kiss on the cheek.

<Somehow, I don't think that's what Maria intended,> Renée sent to Alex. She patted Durly's cheek sympathetically. The captain's embarrassment was evident, and he nodded appreciatively to Renée.

<Consider the source of transmission, my love,> Alex sent in reply. <I think it was the best Durly could do.>

* * *

After three days of downtime aboard the *Freedom*, the freighter crew was driving the *Dark* out of system when Cordelia updated Alex on more ship movement.

<Alex, the *Rover* and three freighters have entered the system, and telemetry has picked up Hector's return.> There was the slightest pause before Cordelia added, <Are these messages unnecessary, Ser?>

Alex smiled, as he strode along the *Freedom*'s wide corridor toward Mickey's engineering bay. His senior captain was maturing.

<Your pardon, Alex, that question wasn't necessary either, was it? These ship movements and dispositions are my responsibilities. If their principals wish to speak with you, then there is a reason for me to contact you. Am I not correct?>

<You are, Senior Captain Cordelia.>

<Couldn't you have told me this earlier, Alex?> There was another slight pause before Cordelia added. <But then it would have been a directive I might have applied solely to these circumstances. Instead, I'm rewriting many algorithms to assume the responsibilities that my position decrees. I assume you'll inform me when I overstep my boundaries.>

<That I will, Captain,> Alex replied. He closed the comm and started whistling one of Julien's favorite tunes.

* * *

Hector delivered his report to Cordelia, once he broached the outer planet's orbit. <Delivery went as expected, Captain Cordelia. We offloaded two sets of shells without difficulty. What I find difficult to comprehend was the reaction of the Harakens.>

<How so, Captain?>

<They were amazed, nearly speechless, as they unloaded bay after bay of travelers. Why should the Harakens be surprised that we were offloading exactly what Alex committed to deliver?>

<It's because what Alex Racine often does is unbelievable to people. I assume, Captain, you loaded the refit supplies.>

<Certainly, Captain Cordelia. I must admit to a certain element of disappointment when the materials filled but a single bay.>

<But the bays are enormous,> Cordelia sent, musical notes accompanying her comm and acting as her laughter.

<That they are, Captain. We'll make good use of them, if you'll assign crew to assist me.>

<Sorry, Captain. Your refit isn't a priority. In time, I'll free some Daelon crew and get you started.>

<On that note, Captain Cordelia, we've made a small beginning with the addition of Haraken passengers.>

Cordelia processed that remark and decided an issue had stepped outside her purview. <Alex,> she sent. <Please join the comm with Hector.>

<Greetings, Hector. Welcome back. What do you need?> Alex sent.

<I was explaining to Captain Cordelia that I've made some minor progress with the refit supplies with the help of my ancillary passengers.>

<You're going to have to be more specific, Hector,> Alex replied.

<I was unsure what to charge the passengers for transit to Omnia, which they'd requested, so rather than collect credits, I took the opportunity to offer them work for room and board, as they say. Their

assignments were to break out the most important materials for refit of the environmental systems, and they agreed to my proposal.>

Alex reminded himself that he was speaking to a newly freed SADE and should have phrased his question more carefully.

For her part, Cordelia realized how much more sophisticated her capabilities were in anticipating humans' needs, especially those of Alex, even though she was still learning.

<Send me a list of your new passengers, Hector,> Alex requested. Both Alex and Cordelia received the data, and Alex's mirth crackled across the comm.

Hector's emotional algorithms soared. He'd planned for the entire trip how he'd phrase the topic of the additional passengers to Alex. He'd thought of tens of thousands of ideas and discarded every one. It was something Trixie said to him that gave him this idea. She'd said, "Don't let the past anchor your persona. Enjoy what you have and celebrate it."

So, Hector planned to surprise Alex. It was a small thank you to the man who'd freed him, after years of torture under Mahima Ganesh, and he'd made Alex laugh. It was a reward that he would keep secure in his memory, as long as his kernel had power.

<Quite the passenger list, Hector,> Alex sent. The list's nearly two hundred individuals began with Reiko, Franz, and the six Sol transplants who had started Haraken's university. Originally the scientists numbered seven, but it was Edward Sardi, the seventh escapee from a UE explorer ship, who had lost his life along with one other when the team encountered the Dischnya. Alex felt only a momentary twinge at the memory. *The list of dead must be getting so long, I'm getting numb,* Alex thought, comparing his reactions to those of the past two decades when each new death haunted his sleep and waking hours for months, if not longer.

<Inform me, Captain Cordelia, when Captain Hector's wayward passengers make the *Freedom* … and Captain Cordelia, cull this passenger list and see if there are some who could be assigned to work on the refit of the *Our People*'s environmental systems, if not more.> Alex signed off, chuckling to himself. He couldn't wait to hear why Haraken's premier professorial staff had made the journey to Omnia. That they had to work

their way for passage had him laughing at his meal table and, around him, crew smiled without knowing why.

<Well done, Hector,> Cordelia sent. <Well done, indeed.>

<Thank you, Captain. I must admit to having spent an inordinate amount of time developing my presentation. In the future, I will be much quicker, but nothing will ever equal the feeling of this first moment.>

<I have my first memory too, Hector. I performed my vid art for Alex Racine, while we were in orbit around Libre. He was on the bridge of the *Rêveur*, and I was an Independent, housed on the bridge of this ship. Alex had asked for a demonstration and I gave him a simple one. He was generous, opening his implant to direct the scene. Then, much to my surprise and pleasure, he stepped into the waterfall's spray and danced as a child would. This man wielded tremendous power, and his people exhibited ferocious loyalty. I was sure the man was a mirage, a façade until he played in the waterfall. I was wrong then and, over time, I learned how wrong I was.>

<I believe coming to a conclusion, proven to be false, is more constructive, enabling the reordering of our kernel, than making a correct decision,> Hector sent.

<I would agree with you,> Cordelia said, and closed the comm. She spent moments running through her memories of Alex from their first interaction. The memories piled up and up, as did the worlds where they were created, and she was enormously pleased by the extent of them. *May Julien and I enjoy thousands more with you, Alex, before we conduct your star services,* Cordelia thought.

* * *

Per Tatia's request, Franz and Reiko landed aboard the *Freedom* and went directly to her spacious cabin. Tatia wanted a conference with the pair to understand the reasons for their return.

"Well, you two, to what do I owe the pleasure? In other words, are you visiting, or are you interested in a job?" Tatia said perfunctorily, after Franz and Reiko were comfortably seated.

"Depends on the job," Reiko replied.

Tatia caught that Franz had started to speak but kept his counsel when Reiko replied first. *I see who I have to win over*, Tatia thought.

"That probably depends on what you're interested in doing. I presume I may call you Reiko, guessing you resigned your commission in Haraken's services." The fact that Reiko's delicate jaw muscles flexed and distended told Tatia that Reiko had taken the leap and resigned without knowing exactly what awaited her at Omnia. *The hard part is over, Reiko*, Tatia thought.

"I want warship command," Reiko said with firm determination.

"That's not what I have in mind, Reiko," Tatia replied. "I have experienced commanders who are ready to captain a warship with its complement of fighters."

"So, what position is available?" Reiko asked with resignation.

That was the question Tatia was waiting to hear. "As I said, my senior people will captain the first warships. They're experienced at commanding flights of fighters, fast, maneuverable units that can swarm a larger ship. But what they're not experienced at is fighting a large warship in concert with others against a powerful force of multiple ships or a sphere. What I need is a commodore to take command of a warship squadron."

Reiko's eyes blinked twice, and her mouth started to drop before she quickly snapped it closed. Franz, who had been nervously sitting on the edge of his seat, leaned back and pretended to rub his jaw, but he was really covering his grin.

"Well, Reiko, I haven't got all day. Do you want the position or not?" Tatia said, grinning.

"Absolutely, Admiral," Reiko replied, jumping to her feet.

"Congratulations, Commodore Shimada," Tatia replied, shaking Reiko's hand. "You have your work cut out for you. I'd like you to engage Captain Cordelia, Z, and Miranda to design a battle-simulation program.

Plan scenarios of both offense and defense against a variety of adversarial conditions."

"As soon as Franz and I get settled into a cabin, I'll get up to date on the specs of the new ship designs," Reiko replied. "I do have one question, Admiral. Couldn't you have said something about this opportunity before I sailed the *Tanaka* back to Haraken?"

"I could have, but it wasn't what I wished to do," Tatia replied, her eyes adopted her ground-pounding, officer-in-charge stare, which stated clearly that the discussion was closed. "And, by the way, Commodore, once our ship production reaches the point where we have multiple squadrons, you should be prepared to take on more duty."

"Yes, Ma'am," Reiko replied, a grin spreading across her face.

"And you, hiding behind your grin," Tatia said, turning her attention on Franz. "Our discussion will be short and sweet."

"I'm happy to remain a wing commander," Franz said, holding up his hands in appeasement.

"That would be fine, if I wanted another commander," Tatia replied, which effectively wiped the smile off Franz's face. "We won't have carriers in this fleet. They're too vulnerable. Each warship will carry a complement of fighters. The travelers of each squadron of warships will combine to form a wing. Multiple wings will have to fight in concert with the warships, sometimes attacking the enemy and sometimes defending their host ships. That means I need a fighter group leader, and the position reports to your partner."

Franz assumed a straight face, as he replied, "I have no difficulties, Admiral, working under Reiko, at any time, day or night."

Tatia burst into laughter, which filled the cabin. "Get out of here, you two, and welcome aboard."

Once in the corridor, Franz picked up a squealing Reiko and swung her around in the air.

When Reiko's feet touched the floor, she kept her arms around her partner's neck. Her eyes gazed lovingly into Franz's face, and she said, "We should start practicing immediately. I mean that part about you working under me," she added, grinning.

* * *

While Tatia met with Franz and Reiko, Alex and Renée waited in the airlock for a second transport, ferrying Olawale Wombo, his associates, and a load of Harakens. In more than one way, the Sol transplants held a special place in Alex and Renée's hearts for their courage and selflessness.

Alex received the bay's confirmation of pressurization in his implant, and he signaled the airlock open. While Alex walked purposefully across the bay, Renée fairly skipped ahead.

Olawale easily descended the traveler's steps, courtesy of his cell gen injections, which had cured the professor's aging disabilities.

Renée shouted Olawale's name, and the big man held out his arms to her. When she jumped, he caught her, spinning her in circles, and Renée laughed throughout it. With their faces pressed together, they were a study of alabaster and hematite.

Much to Alex and Renée's delight, down the traveler's steps came Olawale's friends, Yoram, Boris, Nema, Priita, and Storen. Only one Sol native was missing, Edward Sardi, who had preceded his friends to Omnia, only to lose his life investigating the newly discovered planet. But Edward's pursuit was something scientists understood — the acquisition of precious knowledge.

Renée didn't wait until they reached the comfort of the suite before she asked her first question. "Not that I don't love seeing all of you, but why the trip to Omnia now?"

"We had the opportunity to meet with Captain Durly before he left Haraken, and later we spent time with Captain Hector," Priita Ranta replied, as if that explained everything.

"An admirable choice for the city-ship's captain, by the way, Alex," Yoram Penzig, the philosopher in the group, commented.

"Imagine educating an alien race," Storen, the xenobiologist, enthused. "I presume we'll have your guidance, Alex, in choosing the best location for classrooms or, perhaps, a larger structure."

"Wait, Sers," Alex exclaimed, coming to a halt in the corridor and facing the professors. "The Dischnya are not a simple race. There are multiple nests … what you might think of as different tribes. Then you have queens, wasats, warriors, hunters, midwives, and issues with scent control."

"This will be incredibly challenging," Storen replied in a rush of breath, and his eyes glowed with anticipation.

"What about Espero University?" Alex asked.

"The university is operating fine, Alex," Olawale replied. "For the most part, we've been administrators of colleges or departments for years.

"Yuck," Nema commented.

Renée believed that if Nema thought it appropriate to spit to underline her comment, she would have done so.

Because Alex looked unconvinced, Boris Gorenko, the medical expert, added, "Alex, remember, we're the ones who stole a shuttle to escape the UE and grasp the opportunity to find a better way to live. That action nearly cost us our lives."

Alex nodded his head in agreement of their courageous act.

"So, why would we stop searching for those opportunities that celebrate life?" Yoram added. "We're proud of our accomplishments on Haraken, but it's time for a greater challenge."

"Unless you think we're not up to the task … too old, perhaps," Priita challenged.

Alex held up his hands in surrender. "I think patient and inventive natures will be needed to accomplish your purpose planetside, and I find those generally improve with age."

Alex's comments brought smiles to the aging faces of the Sol natives.

-27-
Soma School

The professors requested permission of Alex to facilitate a trip planetside, so they could pay their respects to Edward by visiting the site where his traveler was trapped and where he met his end.

Prior to boarding their traveler the next morning, the professorial group uploaded the library of the Dischnya language from the *Freedom*'s databases to their implants. They were so excited by the discovery of the alien language that they spent the entire night in Olawale's cabin, consuming copious amounts of thé and discussing the nuances of the Dischnya tongue.

Too anxious to sleep, the professors were waiting in the corridor, outside the landing bay, even before the crew chief arrived.

The Daelon Independent grinned at the Harakens, as he passed. "First trip planetside?" he asked.

"Yes," Nema gushed, "we'll be meeting the Dischnya."

"To do what?" the crew chief asked.

"To teach them," Yoram answered simply.

The crew chief's mouth briefly hung open. Then he shook his head in wonder, proceeding into the airlock, as he commented, "Dassata's world never ceases to amaze me."

"There's that word," Priita said. "I saw it last night; or was it this morning? I think my brain's a little muddled by the lack of sleep. It's in the vocabulary list as a proper noun."

"Here's the person to ask," Olawale said, as Julien walked down the corridor, whistling.

"Greetings, eminent humans of learning," Julien said with an expansive air.

After a quick exchange of pleasantries, Priita said, "Julien, I came across the term Dassata, and the crew chief mentioned it in passing. I understand it means peacemaker, but the database lists it as a proper noun."

"You're correct in its Dischnya meaning, Priita. However, the soma of Sawa Messa apply the term to only one individual, Alex. It's their name for him."

"You mean title," Olawale corrected.

"No, Olawale. Alex is addressed as Dassata by the Dischnya, and you'll hear many of our people often refer to him in that manner. For humans and SADEs, the thought of referring to the man as Alex seems inappropriate."

"What do you call him now?" Nema asked.

"Whatever I feel like at the moment," Julien replied with a wink, which elicited a round of laughter from the professors.

Alex and the twins came down the corridor side by side. When they stopped in front of the professors, Alex said, "Look who I found," and neatly stepped aside.

"Hello, my dear friends," Francis said. Tears welled in the captain's eyes at the sight of his Sol friends.

Alex and the twins stepped out of the way to avoid the crush of bodies as the professors mobbed Francis.

"A wonderful surprise," Olawale said to Alex, when the hugging ended and the tears were dried.

"Francis, are you joining us?" Priita asked.

"Yes, I've not had the opportunity to visit the spot. In truth, I'm not sure I had the courage. It'll be much easier in the company of friends."

"Of course, it will," acknowledged Priita, linking her arm in the captain's to enter the airlock.

Ellie piloted the traveler planetside and dropped it not far from the place where the mission's shuttle was pinned by the Tawas Soma net. Alex led the professors to where the shuttle had rested. The indentation in the ground, marked by the crushed brush, was testimony to the exact spot.

Alex described the events — the warriors' attack, the mission team taking refuge in the ship, the Dischnya's metal net robbing the energy of the shuttle's power cells, the dwindling food and water supply, and, finally, the decision to close the rear ramp, sealing off the air flow.

"Rescue was literally moments too late for Edward and Ullie," Alex said. "I'm so sorry, my friends."

Nema stood beside Alex. She took his hand in hers and patted it with the other. "Edward is not to be added to your list of regrets, Alex. He'd be ever so grateful that you rescued his compatriots."

"I do commend the team's decision," Alex replied. "With their limited knowledge of the circumstances, they chose not to escalate tension with the Dischnya by attacking a superior force. Likewise, they chose not to allow the Dischnya access to the technology onboard the shuttle. It was a selfless and courageous move on their part."

The small group moved on to discussing the steps Alex took after freeing the prisoners from the Dischnya, and what he considered the educational challenges the professors would face.

Alex glanced over Yoram's shoulder and spotted Pussiro loping their way and thought, *Here comes your first challenge, my friends.*

Pussiro, who had been out with a group of warriors observing the ongoing work on the nest's structure, had spotted the traveler landing and hoped to see Dassata.

Alex introduced Pussiro in the simplest of terms and decided it was best to clear the air now. <I want you to remain calm and not react,> Alex sent on open comm, which alerted the twins, who were unsure of what Alex intended.

"Pussiro, these are the soma of Edward Sardi, who died aboard the traveler that was trapped by your net. They've come to grieve at the site of his loss," Alex explained.

Pussiro was transfixed. During his introduction, his legs had been extended. Now they sank, and the lips of his muzzle trembled.

"Professors, Pussiro is the warrior commander of the Tawas Soma nest. He's the individual who ordered the warriors to attack the shuttle and trap it with the net. He's just been told of your relationship to Edward and why you're standing here.

Now the Harakens resembled Pussiro. They were frozen in place. They'd excitedly come face-to-face with their first Dischnya, only to discover he was responsible for their friend's death. Lesser individuals might have focused on their anger, but the Sol natives knew where that led. Anger about Earth's wars and decay had given rise to United Earth, a crushing political system, which they'd fled. Alex had given them an opportunity to live full and productive lives without fear. Mistakes would always be made when individuals, races, countries, or worlds met for the first time. It was what was done after the mistakes were discovered that made the difference between those who valued coexistence and those who prized revenge.

Priita made the first move. <Alex,> she sent on open comm, <Pussiro appears more miserable than us. What's an acceptable form of Dischnya condolence?>

<Good question, Priita. We're still working much of that sort of thing out,> Alex replied, before he recalled Renée's experience with Homsaff at the execution of her mother. His partner had shared her memories of the judgment after Alex had recovered from surgery. <You could always try howling,> Alex sent.

<What?> asked Priita.

<Tilt your head back and howl at the sky. It's how the Dischnya express lament,> Alex sent.

Priita cleared her throat, leaned her head back, and uttered a squeak, which made Pussiro's eyes widen and wonder what the human was trying to do.

Olawale stepped beside Priita and deep from his heritage, born millennia ago on the African plains, a truly remarkable howl burst forth, which Olawale directed at the sky. The others joined in, doing their best to copy Olawale, and the more they yelled, the better they felt. The howling grew in pitch and volume, as the professors emptied their pain into the sky.

Pussiro's ears twitched upward. The expression of lament struck a chord deep inside Pussiro, and it called to him. He glanced at Dassata, who nodded toward the group, as if to say, join them if you wish. Pussiro filled his lungs and rose on his hind legs. His howl rose and blended with

Dassata's soma, lamenting the fears and anxieties that created the mistakes of first contact.

Alex let the group empty their pain to Omnia's bright sky and when they quieted, he laid a hand on each of Pussiro and Priita's shoulders and smiled. Priita smiled shyly in return, and Pussiro exhibited his rows of sharp teeth, which momentarily concerned Priita.

"Impressive display, isn't it?" Alex said to the professors. "Get used to it. That's a Dischnya imitation of a Haraken smile."

Pussiro went so far as to face each of the others of Dassata's soma and extend his version of a smile.

<That will take some accommodating,> Boris sent on open comm. <The teeth appear quite bright and white. I wonder what the Dischnya use to clean their teeth.>

"Pussiro," Alex said, "these soma are here to help the Dischnya learn our ways." His implant was busy sending translations of everything he said to Pussiro so that the professors didn't have to struggle with the language.

Pussiro listened to Alex's translations of his soma, who told of the many ways they could help the Dischnya. When Pussiro finally replied, the group looked at Alex in confusion.

"Did Pussiro say that he wants none of what we offered?" Olawale asked.

"Well done, Olawale, you're catching on to the language quickly," Alex replied.

From Pussiro's perspective, Dassata's soma exhibited the seemingly universal trait of confusion, the frowning forehead. He chuffed for their attention, stepped next to Alain, and proudly extended to his full height.

<I believe, Alain, you might have a new cabinmate,> Étienne sent, maintaining a straight face, as the Dischnya towered above his crèche-mate and kept pointing repeatedly to Alain and then himself.

"Is Pussiro telling us that he wants to be in security?" Nema asked.

"My learned colleagues," Yoram said, interrupting the discussion. "I believe you aren't assimilating the elements of this entire discussion. Pussiro has been introduced as a wasat, a warrior commander. He sees our escorts as warriors on behalf of Dassata. Pussiro has no need of the domestic training concepts we've enumerated. He wishes to be what he has always been, except now in the service of Dassata."

The other professors looked to Alex, who said, "Yoram got it in one."

Olawale started to point at Pussiro, but Alex locked the professor's arm via his implant, overriding Olawale's movement.

"That's an unusual experience," Olawale said, when Alex released him. The professor lowered his arm and looked questioningly at Alex.

"Let's not strain relationships this early, people," Alex said. "No pointing with fingers or toes. They're aggressive expressions. Indicate a Dischnya by turning your hand palm up and keeping it low … no higher than the Dischnya's clawed feet. You'll learn other restrictions over time."

Olawale pulled up his Dischnya vocabulary and did as Alex instructed. Letting his implant drive his speech, he said to Pussiro, "Wasat, warrior commander."

Pussiro chuffed in reply and lowered his hind legs.

"Dassata warrior?" Pussiro asked, unsure of whether the soma understood he was asking a question. He strode to stand beside Alex, and he repeated in passable human language, "Dassata warrior."

<Just when you thought you had eliminated this world's problems, my challenged friend, you find you haven't,> Julien sent to Alex.

<Oh, but I have, my talented and oh-so-clever friend,> Alex riposted, smiling. <I plan to place you in charge of the Dischnya's warrior training.> He didn't receive a retort from Julien, not a word or an image.

* * *

Nyslara ventured from the nest for the first time since her birthing. The heir had progressed from mewling to pup and would respond to Pussiro, who watched over her. She pressed the button on the comms station and was soon in touch with Dassata. She chuffed in pleasure at the workings of the alien tool. Communicating to another leader, wherever he or she might be located, at the touch of a device appealed to her.

"Dassata, I would speak with you and your soma who would teach the Dischnya."

"It's good to hear your voice, Nyslara. I hope the heir is well."

"Dassata's concern is appreciated. The heir has become part of the soma."

"I'm pleased to hear that, Nyslara. I will gather my soma, and we'll be planetside soon."

Nyslara waited with Nafalla, the midwife, beside her for the return of the nest's emissary, who was sent to fetch Homsaff. The young queen had communicated to Nyslara that she too wished to speak with Dassata. It wasn't long before Homsaff was seen loping across the plains with her wasat beside her.

Nyslara chose to visit her nest's new domicile, while they waited for Dassata to arrive. Tawas Soma warriors sought to accompany Nyslara, and she waved them off. A short bark underlined her request and quickly wiped the confusion from their brows, as they leapt to attention. Homsaff took advantage of the moment by issuing a strong command to her wasat.

As the three females strode away, the wasat and warriors exchanged dubious looks. It was unheard of to have two queens unaccompanied on the plains and together too.

The females experienced a liberating freedom, crossing the plains without escorts, enjoying the wind cooling their fur and the brush of grasses against their limbs. *This is the Dischnya's future*, Nyslara thought, and she swelled with pride at what she'd help to bring about.

Investigating the nest's new domicile, Nyslara witnessed many of the facilities being installed that she'd seen aboard Dassata's ship. They wouldn't be operational until Dassata's soma completed the installation that she understood would bring water from the green. She'd wondered who had been brave enough to enter the green to draw the water until it was explained to her that the soma would tunnel through the ground to tap water reservoirs. "Much safer," Nyslara had commented.

A shuttle landed, while Nyslara, Homsaff, and Nafalla were examining the food dispenser being installed. One of the soma gestured to them and said, "Dassata," pointing to the exit.

Nyslara chuffed, marveling again at the means by which Dassata's soma communicated with their minds. *But do I want that for my soma?* Nyslara asked herself.

Alex and the professors waited for Nyslara in the shade of the traveler. Harakens had asked him if he'd considered using Rainmaker to freshen the atmosphere with more moisture, and Alex had replied that the Dischnya preferred the drier conditions, and that the great belts of forests to the north and south needed no more water.

When Olawale wondered why Alex's city center wasn't situated within the forest, he sent them a link to Z's data of his time searching for the dangerous species that haunted the Dischnya. After the Haraken professors watched sections of the vids, it effectively ended the discussion and permanently dissuaded the Sol natives from thinking of venturing in that direction.

Alex pointed out to the professors the three Dischnya exiting Nyslara's new housing unit. The group watched the three females cross the grassy field with easy, running strides. The usually brown grass and shrubs were starting to green and bloom from recent, sparse rains.

"Are those tails?" Nema asked, watching the females approach.

"All Dischnya have them at birth. The males have them truncated in a ceremony when they choose to be hunters or warriors," Alex replied. "A word to the wise, my friends, you can tell much about a queen's mood by the movement of her tail, and, by the way, it's also an extremely effective weapon."

After introductions, Nyslara spoke right to the point, "Dassata, we must discuss your school."

"Nyslara, with all due respect, these are the soma who will conduct the school. You need to discuss your concerns with them, and I will facilitate the translations."

"No, Dassata," Nyslara replied adamantly. "Concerns must first be addressed to you. In your school, queens and soma of many nests will mix. This can't be accomplished by your spray. Emile must solve this problem before school begins."

When Alex translated Nyslara's request, Storen, the xenobiologist, became fascinated, as did Boris Gorenko, whose field of study was human medicine.

"A nest's soma are transfixed by the scent of their queens," Alex explained. "They're confused by the scent of another queen and could become fixated on her. Furthermore, if soma are without the scent of a queen for a prolonged period, they suffer an emotional withdrawal of some sort, although we've been careful to ensure that didn't happen."

"When did you have the opportunity to separate a queen from her people?" Storen asked.

"Twice for their Fissla, a queens' conference; twice when we brought Nyslara into orbit; and once when we transported three queens to Sawa," Alex replied.

Alex's new Dischnya words sent the professors pulling up definitions from their database. "You took the queens to their home world?" Storen asked. "We missed a marvelous opportunity," the xenobiologist lamented.

"You're correct, Nyslara," Alex said. "I'll request Emile find a permanent solution for the soma's needs."

Nyslara dipped her head in acknowledgment of Alex's reply. "Now, Dassata," she said, "whom do I speak to about the school?"

"This is the school's leader, Nyslara," Alex replied, motioning Olawale forward.

When Olawale drew close to the Nyslara, the queen leaned forward and sniffed, and Alex hid his smile.

"Not metal soma," Nyslara commented to Alex.

"No, chona," Alex agreed.

"His color is pleasing," Nyslara added, admiring Olawale's dark skin. "Your school will need help, Olawale. It must instruct the soma in different ways. There are preferences."

"That's the purpose of a school, Nyslara, to teach the soma what they wish to learn," Olawale replied or, rather, it was the translation Alex delivered to the queen after translating Olawale's reply.

"Some soma wish to learn the ways of your healing … to do what was done for Dassata and at my birthing," Nyslara explained.

"Medical training," Boris said, clapping his hands at the translation. "I would love to teach that."

Nafalla barked in pleasure at the pronouncement.

"Other soma wish to learn Dassata's ways to care for our structures and the facilities they offer," Nyslara said.

"This can be done, Chona Nyslara," Olawale stated formally.

"We have one more concern," Nyslara said. "Our pups will learn Dassata's ways, but Pussiro, my mate, is a wasat. He and his warriors know only one way of life, and they've had too many years of fighting to learn another. Can you train them to be Dassata's warriors?"

"It would be difficult for your warriors to learn the ways of our ships, space, technologies, and weapons. Space," Olawale said, pointing upward, "is a cruel matriarch. She doesn't forgive mistakes."

"Can these ways be taught?' Homsaff asked.

"It's possible, Chona Homsaff, but it would take time and be difficult for the warriors."

"Good," Homsaff chuffed. "I'll learn these ways."

"Chona, you'll learn the ways of a warrior?" Priita asked, surprised and hoping she had translated Homsaff's words incorrectly.

Homsaff's tail snapped angrily over her head. "What a wasat can do, a queen can do better!" she declared.

"You've heard our requests, Olawale," Nyslara said, rising on her hind legs. "When do you begin teaching the soma?"

Olawale was taken aback at the pace of the conversation. He and his people intended their first visits planetside to allow them to become familiar with Omnia's physical environment and visit the site where Edward lost his life. Instead, their second encounter with the Dischnya had turned into a planning session with queens. Better said, it'd become an opportunity for the queens to make their demands. Olawale turned to Alex, and his eyes appealed for help.

"I must build another structure for the school, chonas," Alex replied, "and I must build a means of quickly transporting the soma to the school and back to their new domiciles each day."

"The soma will not live at the school?" Homsaff asked.

"A school does not work that way, Homsaff," Alex explained. "Each day in the school, the soma will hear new things. They must return to the nest, do their customary work for the nest, and learn the new things well."

"We keep Dassata busy on Sawa Messa," Nyslara said, ending the discussion, and the Dischnya muzzles rippled in humor.

The Dischnya tipped their muzzles to the professors, but Homsaff and Nafalla nodded gravely to Alex, politely murmuring "Dassata," before they backed away from the group to return home.

Nyslara hadn't seen Alex since before her birthing, though she'd heard his voice beyond the curtain and knew he was the one who brought her soma to save the heir. She stared quietly at him, and then she echoed the other females with a simple, "Dassata."

Alex saw the queen's tail arc overhead. Its tip caressed the back of his head.

Nyslara chuffed and strode quickly to join the others.

* * *

Alex and company boarded the traveler, and he signaled Ellie to return to the *Freedom*.

On the way to the front of the main cabin, Alex's way was blocked by white-haired Nema, who threw her arms around his waist. "It appears females the galaxy over appreciate you, Dassata," she teased, laughed, and then plopped down in a seat next to Olawale.

Alex took a seat across from them.

"I'm sure you're aware, Alex, that the queens are requesting two schools ... ours and yours," Olawale said. When Alex grumped in reply, Olawale added, "I take it you recognize the dilemma." The topic of conversation brought the other professors crowding around to listen.

Recognizing a response was required, Alex said, "Yes, Olawale, you'd run a school of general technical education, but the warriors and one motivated young queen would require a military academy."

"What do you intend to do?" Priita asked.

"Think on it," Alex replied."

"Are there other queens who think like Homsaff?" Yoram asked.

"It's possible. Our arrival has caused more than one elderly and entrenched matriarch to be replaced — two of them from their treachery and one quietly passed the robe of power to her heir."

"Strictly from a medical viewpoint, Alex, might I ask how the two matriarchs met their end?" Boris asked.

"One was staked out on the ground," Alex replied. "And I'm sure you noticed the Dischnya's great clawed feet." When the professors nodded, Alex splayed his fingers like claws and pantomimed raking them swiftly across his throat.

While most of Alex's audience was aghast, little Yoram said, "Hmm. It would appear to me that the Dischnya would make excellent warriors for Dassata. If you ever required ground or on-board close quarters fighting, it would seem that you'd have the making of extremely dangerous and aggressive troops."

"Ever regret discovering this planet?" Olawale asked, recognizing the burden that was being placed on Alex's shoulders.

"For the record, I was sitting on Haraken, enjoying my retirement, when the *Sojourn* first visited this planet," Alex replied, pretending indignation, and his comment generated chuckles. "Okay, I was retired. Leave it at that."

-28-
Rover

"This is Captain Hardingsgale of the *Rover* calling Captain Cordelia," Bertram said into the vid pickup on his Méridien-built passenger liner.

<Welcome back, Captain Hardingsgale,> Cordelia sent. <We've been expecting you and are pleased to see you accompanied by three freighters.>

Bertram heard a wonderful melody of silver bells over his bridge speakers, and his first mate and he shared a smile. *One day, I'm going to have an implant so I can receive things like that directly,* Bertram thought. "Captain, I've orders to assist with the distribution of personnel and supplies, to your satisfaction before I depart," Bertram said.

<Captain, please send me your workers' names and capabilities. I presume they reside on the *Rover*.>

"They do, Captain. I've 456 personnel for you crammed aboard with my crew. They'll be thrilled to see the inside of that enormous ship of yours."

<We'll expedite their transfer, Captain,> Cordelia sent. <I'll also require your supply list per freighter and module.>

Summarily, Cordelia received Bertram's lists. She examined the freighters first, taking special note of the temporary quarters' modules for personnel that could be attached to the terminal's frame. Together they would accommodate about 110 workers, but they would give the New Terran personnel, working their shifts on the platform, a place to eat and rest before they rotated back to the *Freedom*.

Once the *Rover*'s first mate sent the lists to the *Freedom*, he informed his captain.

Bertram was still musing about the musical bells he'd heard. "SADEs," he said to the first mate, "I can't believe it was Alex Racine who had the good fortune to find the first one to enter our system."

"I hate to deepen your depression, Captain, but, don't forget, he also discovered Renée de Guirnon. Now, there's a woman."

"Thank you for reminding me. Now my jealousy factor has doubled," Bertram shot back, and his first mate grinned.

<Alex, the *Rover* has returned with personnel and three freighters of supplies. In addition to much of the conduit materials that are needed, the freighters are carrying temporary housing modules, EVA suits, and EVA one-person sleds,> Cordelia sent.

<Can we put everybody to work, Captain?>

<Absolutely, Alex. We have a backlog of Ben's structural materials and tanks sitting on-site.>

<Good to hear, we'll need to have an individual on-site to manage the process from here out. It'll have to be a SADE.>

<I would recommend Killian.>

<He would have been my first choice, Captain. Please inform Killian that I'm extending the terminal construction directorship to him.>

<I will, Alex.>

<One more thing, Captain. If Killian accepts the job of transforming our immature collection of girders into a finished terminal, ask him to provide it a name.>

<He would be honored, Alex. Good evening.>

* * *

Killian, who had tried to visit often with Vivian, the Daelon child, was pleased to be appointed to manage the completion of the terminal's construction, but unsure how Vivian would take his extended absence. On the day he would transfer to the small modules that were already attached to the terminal and await the arrival of the New Terran freighters and liner, which were a half day out, Killian caught up with Vivian and her mother, Galania, at morning meal.

"Plaid man," Vivian cried, leaping up from the table and running to jump into Killian's arms. He placed her on one arm, the way he carried her when they danced, and walked over to the meal table to sit down.

"Vivian, I must work on the terminal, and I'll be gone for many days at a time."

"No, plaid man, you can't go," Vivian wailed. At nearby tables, heads turned. Vivian's attachment to Killian was well known — so too was Killian's assignment as terminal construction director.

Killian looked across the table at the pain evident in Galania's eyes. Killian and she had many discussions about Vivian's fixation on the SADE. The woman had made her opinion clear to Killian when she told him one day, "We were sent to Daelon when Vivian was three. It was a traumatic event for her. The close conditions with no view of the sky depressed her to the point I feared for her sanity. The day we were rescued, her eyes were shut and had been shut for many days. She was unwilling to open them, despite my urging. When she finally did, the first face she saw was yours, Killian. One day, she'll grow out of her attachment to you. Until then, I would wish my daughter all the happiness she can absorb, no matter the source."

"Sit down, for me," Killian urged. "I have something for you."

Vivian had wrapped her arms around the SADE's neck and was holding on, as if she was in danger of drowning. She snuffled, loosened her grip, and slid to the chair next to Killian. "What?" she asked, snuffling again.

Killian opened a small case and pulled out a tiny ear comm. "With this, you can speak to me anytime you want."

"Anytime?" Vivian asked dubiously. "You promise?"

"Vivian, what did I tell you about that?" her mother interjected. "You don't doubt someone's words unless you know them to be false, and Killian wouldn't lie to you."

"Sorry," Vivian said in a meek voice.

"Would you like to know how it works?" Killian asked gently. When Vivian nodded her head multiple times, Killian swept the curls of hair back from the side of her head and eased the ear comm into place.

"It tickles," Vivian chirped, when the nanites snugged the comm into place.

"That's how you wear it, but not when you sleep or in the refresher," he admonished.

"You can hear me, and I can hear you?" Vivian asked.

"I promise," Killian said, and smiled at Galania. "Now, you tap it lightly here," he said, directing Vivian's index finger to the center of the ear comm's base, "when you want to speak to me, and, when you're done talking, you say 'Goodbye, Killian,' and you tap it again."

"I want to try it," Vivian said in a rush.

"Excellent timing, Vivian, because I have to go now."

Vivian stood on her chair and threw her arms around Killian's neck, squeezing as hard as she could.

Killian carefully untangled Vivian and whispered to her, as if it was a conspiracy, "Let's test it, shall we?" Vivian nodded her agreement, but the tears forming in her eyes threatened to throw Killian's emotional algorithms into disarray. Unable to move, the only thing he could think to do was copy what he saw a mother once do for her child, and he leaned over to place a kiss on Vivian's forehead. Then the SADE eased out of his chair and crossed quickly to the meal room's doors. Before he exited, he turned back and held up an index finger, which he touched to his ear.

Vivian stood on her chair seat where her plaid man left her. She snuffled one more time and held up her index finger to her friend. The instant Killian disappeared through the doors, she touched her ear comm and heard, "Greetings, Vivian." Slumping down in her chair, Vivian smiled crookedly at her mother, grateful tears spilling down her face. "Greetings, plaid man," she said. For Vivian, everything was right again with the world.

* * *

<Dassata, I wish to thank you for the honor of my new position,> Killian sent.

<And I appreciate your willingness to take on the responsibility, Killian,> Alex sent in reply. <You should know that Captain Cordelia recommended you.>

<Then I'm doubly honored,> Killian replied. <I have a name for the terminal. I've borrowed from Haraken's tradition for naming its stations. We should call it the Sardi-Tallen Orbital Platform.>

<A most appropriate name, Killian, honoring our lost comrades. Have Captain Cordelia announce it to our people.>

Killian closed the comm. While he was imprisoned in his box, he had envisioned so many lives that he might lead. This was never one of them. As he made his way to the *Freedom*'s bay level, he received Cordelia's refined list of the incoming workforce, specialties, and rotation assignments, to which he made minor adjustments based on his intimate knowledge of the terminal's construction status. He was unaware of Cordelia's smile and never heard her thought, which was, *You'll do fine, Killian.*

Killian's days were filled with multiple, often simultaneous, conversations. He spoke verbally to the New Terrans, over comms to Omnians, and kept conversations going with Vivian, who was a chatterbox with her ear comm. Galania was forced to lay down new rules for when Vivian could wear her ear comm, without which the child might never have pulled it out of her ear.

The SADE was enamored with the complexity and variety of his conversations with independent humans. They were a continual source of surprise, and it drove his intent to ensure the protection of humans. Unknowingly, Killian was joining a growing number of Omnian SADEs.

* * *

Alex located Mickey's bio ID in his lab, and he dropped into the bay to see him.

Mickey postponed a test when a tech alerted him to who was coming through the airlock, and he waited, while Alex made his way through the crowded lab to his side.

"How quickly engineers fill a space," Alex quipped.

"How quickly leaders load their engineers with monumental tasks," Mickey riposted.

"Speaking of tasks, wizard of invention, are Tatia and you in step with her priorities for warship construction?"

"For the most part, but we're woefully short on local transportation. We need many more travelers. If we ever move these city-ships to new locations, I'd like to see their bay's half full of travelers."

Well, Mickey, we can't use the *Our People* to make shells for ourselves. We need the flow of credits from Haraken, and we can't use the *Freedom*. These bays are reserved for your engineers and Ben's equipment, which has doubled since we landed here. So, do you have an alternate suggestion?"

"Absolutely, Alex. Devote a terminal bay, capable of building four shells at a time, for traveler production. Get the New Terrans to complete the engines, controllers, crystals, and interior fittings. You can strike a deal to share the output with them. I'd suggest they get three out of eight, but Cordelia could probably give you a better idea what the ratio should be."

"Okay, Mickey, I'll talk to Cordelia and Maria. In the meantime, I have another project for you." When Mickey narrowed his eyes at Alex, he said, "You know the ancient adage about idle hands, Mickey."

"You mean the one that equates idle hands to the value of rest and relaxation to prevent stress from overwork," Mickey shot back, but he was grinning as he said it. At heart, Mickey was an engineer who loved challenges and, if there was anyone who could fully engage his mind to solve monumentally difficult problems, it was Alex.

"I need a new design, Mickey. Not a warship … call it a scout ship. Minimal crew. Think engines and a stripped-down hull. It'll be out and back within a quarter of a year."

Mickey's hand went to his chin, and he pretended to think as he walked over to a holo-vid, which he signaled. "You mean like this," Mickey announced with a sly smile.

The holo-vid displayed a truly odd ship design. It looked like a slender rod with engines stuck on one end, and it was a grav design, as evidenced by the four-part clam shell that was employed to cover the intersystem engines and complete the hull's integrity.

"And what did you design this ship to do?" Alex asked.

"First, I didn't design this, the SADEs did."

"For what purpose?"

"Alex, are you getting enough sleep?" Mickey asked with genuine concern. "You're not usually so slow on the uptake. You asked me for a scout ship, and the SADEs are way ahead of you. They know you're searching for the Nua'll home world, and they understand better than anyone what attempting to cover that vast amount of space entails. This is their answer."

"How many crew will it carry, Mickey? That hull looks extremely slender."

"It carries an individual, Alex ... one SADE."

When Alex stared at Mickey, the engineer nodded and said, "I told you the SADEs created this. What I didn't say was that they designed it for themselves. Think of it, Alex ... one SADE sealed in this scout ship. It will require none of the travelers' amenities, no food stock, no dispensers, no refresher, no cabin seating. It's a brilliant design."

To Mickey's trained eye, the look on Alex's face said he wasn't pleased. "What's wrong, Alex?"

Alex shook his head to clear his thoughts. "I agree, Mickey, the ship's a superb design. I don't like the idea of a SADE out in the dark alone."

"I hear you, Alex, but it was their design. They're ready to do it." Mickey's heart wasn't behind his words, because he knew the source of Alex's reservations. Ever since his friend rescued Julien, Alex had moved worlds to ensure SADEs were never emotionally isolated or abandoned. "What you must recognize, Alex, is that you've given the Confederation SADEs an entirely new perspective on humans, and they want to do their part to build a community with us."

"Understood, Mickey. Send me the specs, and let me study them. I might have some modifications for you," Alex said, and left Mickey to his work.

* * *

<What was Dassata's reaction, Mickey?> Trixie sent. The SADE had attached a monitor app to notify her of the opening of the scout ship's file. Coupled with Alex's bio ID signal next to the holo-vid when the design was displayed, Trixie surmised Alex had viewed the ship, and she waited until Alex left the bay before she contacted Mickey.

<Trixie, you're walking a fine line. Your actions can be interpreted as stalking Alex ... invading his privacy.>

<You're correct, Mickey.>

<I'm correct, Trixie, as in you'll back off on your monitoring or I'm correct, as in you're acknowledging my words but aren't prepared to change your ways?>

<To be precise, Mickey, I didn't monitor your conversation with Dassata, I merely observed a coincidence of events and calculated the probability of an action taking place that we've been anticipating.>

<We?> Mickey asked.

<The Confederation SADEs have been anxiously awaiting Dassata's review of our design and our intended scouting actions on his behalf.>

<Okay, Trixie, we'll resume this discussion later. Alex's reaction was mixed. He admired your design, but noted that he would probably request modifications.>

<Does this mean, Mickey, Dassata accepts our intention to use these ships to search for the home world?>

<I would say, Trixie, that he's giving it serious consideration. Before Alex viewed your design, he'd requested the same thing of me.>

<The SADEs postulated that Alex found evidence of the Nua'll on Sawa.>

<How did you arrive at that conclusion? I've heard nothing definitive from Alex or Julien.>

<And that's precisely the point, Mickey. Of the humans and SADEs who journeyed to Sawa, not one has said a word about the trip or what they saw planetside. Our conclusion is that silence has been requested because of what was found.>

<And why do you believe Alex would wish to keep quiet about what he found, if he found anything?>

<In our analysis, it would be that something of great value was discovered … something that would disturb the focus of humans who are involved in completing this planet's projects. Our reasoning gave rise to the desire to complete the design of the scout ship you displayed. We wish to be ready when Dassata reveals his secret to Omnians.>

Trixie closed the comm, and Mickey sat down hard on a lab stool. He admitted that Trixie's logic was solid, as he would have expected, especially the part about Alex keeping a secret to ensure the focus of the Daelon Independents. "Our next discussion, Alex, which we need to have soon, should be an interesting one," Mickey murmured.

-29-
Scout Ships

Alex sat down in the engineering lab with Mickey three days after they first spoke about the scout ships.

"Here are my requests, Mickey," Alex said, as the two of them watched the design rotate in the holo-vid view. "You're going to have to change the hull configuration slightly."

"Alex, if we widen it, we'll lose the optimum collection ratio between the shell's circumference and the grav engines, and the SADEs told me there was little allowance in expanding the hull without disturbing the balance of grav and jump engines."

"Which is why I'm not asking you to widen the hull, Mickey, I want you to lengthen it."

"Lengthen it? For what reason?"

"To accommodate three SADEs lying head to toe."

"Did the SADEs request this?" Mickey asked. When the engineer became the recipient of Alex's hard-eyed stare, he quickly relented. "Forget I asked."

"If you'll lengthen the hull, you'll create more collection surface for the shell, and you won't interfere with the flow of the jump engines."

"Actually, that's a good idea, Alex," Mickey admitted.

"I'm glad you approve," Alex replied, slapping his friend on the shoulder, as if to reprimand him for suggesting he wasn't capable of good ideas. "Next, I want a beacon inside the ship. It would be better if it used the forward part of the hull as the signal's antenna."

"I would guess that you want a separate power backup for it, in case the engines are damaged or destroyed. How much time should the power cells provide?"

"First, Mickey, the signal transmission should be triggered automatically if there are any major system failures."

"Alex, with this design, if they lose the engines, they won't have full comm capability. The beacon will only be useful for subspace transmission."

"And that's why we'll institute a reporting procedure. On each scout ship's entrance into a system, the SADEs will report their status and continue reporting daily until their final report, when they exit the system with coordinates for the next star."

"Ah, so we'll always know what area of space they were last in when the reports fail to be received."

"Precisely, my friend. We'll have their star location and their approximate vector data. It still won't be easy to locate them, but it will give us a fighting opportunity."

"So, I take it that three years of transmission power located near where the SADEs are housed should do it."

"I was thinking two years, Mickey, but I like three years better.

"Anything else?"

"I noted the ship's controller memory was pared."

"Yes, the SADEs felt they could operate as the primary computational system. An extensive controller would only duplicate their capability."

"Understood, Mickey. The controller can stay minimized, but I want its crystal memory increased. It must be able to hold twice the capacity of the *Rêveur*'s vid and text library, the star charts, and any other information that the SADEs require."

"You do know how large that library has grown, right?"

"I didn't until I checked on it two nights ago, and, yes, I was shocked. It appears my lovely and dynamic partner has never stopped collecting and adding to her library."

"So, you intend to entertain the SADEs with romance vids," Mickey said, smirking.

"I have a lesson for you, my friend," Alex said, displaying the look Mickey knew was delivered soon after he'd laid down what he thought was a winning hand only to see Alex's cards beat him. "Z watched those vids to design Miranda's persona and look how that turned out."

Mickey had an image of Miranda at the last fête, wearing her curve-hugging gown and entertaining everyone in her orbit. "Point taken, Alex. But, if the SADEs return from their trips with designs for their mates and request we create kernels, which we can't do yet, don't say I didn't warn you."

What Mickey didn't tell Alex was that Pia was a fan of the *Rêveur*'s library, and the couple often spent an evening watching a vid from it.

"Before you go, Alex," Mickey said, as Alex was turning to leave. "The SADEs postulated that you found something important on Sawa … something that you don't wish to share yet."

"Did they?" Alex replied. "Interesting speculation. Let me know when you have the new design, Mickey," Alex said over his shoulder, as he marched off to another meeting.

* * *

Trixie was immediately aware of the changes Alex requested of Mickey, when she noted the engineering notations in the design files, and she contacted Mickey after Alex left the bay.

<We have to stop meeting like this, Trixie,> Mickey sent, his thoughts grumpy.

<Actually, we aren't meeting. I'm merely a figment of your implant.> Trixie modulated the output of her comm and simulated a wavering of tone that faded to nothingness.

<Cute,> Mickey remarked and quickly summarized his conversation with Alex, concerning the updates, to end the conversation. He was anxious to see how the hull would perform with Alex's extension.

<We appreciate the subspace beacon precautions, Mickey, and, while the extended controller memory appears frivolous, it matters little to the

ship's operations, but three SADEs when only one is necessary flies in the face of logic.>

<Trixie, on this matter, I suggest you contact Julien. He can help you understand Alex's thoughts on this better than anyone.>

<We'll speak later on this matter, Mickey,> Trixie sent, unsatisfied with Mickey's response.

I doubt it, my young SADE. There is more to life than logic and calculations, Mickey thought, after Trixie closed the comm, and his mind wandered briefly to his partner, Pia, in whose arms he had found great joy.

<Julien, Mickey suggested I speak to you regarding a most illogical suggestion by Dassata to lengthen the hull of the scout ships,> Trixie sent.

<I would assume Alex gave a reason for his suggestion,> Julien sent in reply. He slowed calculations he'd been performing on star patterns for Alex's search for the Nua'll home world to focus on Trixie's concerns.

<Dassata wishes to employ three SADEs in the hull, when only one is necessary. Considering the fact that each search run will take an average of ninety days, it seems unnecessary to worry that the pilot has company.>

<Have you calculated the number of trips each scout ship will take, as we produce more of these types of ships?>

<The factors have too great a variance, as you know, Julien. Much depends on the ship production rate, our ability to focus the search on a more defined area, and whether we're fortunate or not.>

<So you'd agree that conceivably the search might last years, if not decades.>

<The probabilities reflect that conclusion, Julien.> Then ticks later, Trixie sent, <You hint at a perceived accumulation of time for the pilot. The individual might be out of circulation with other SADEs and humans for an extended period of time. Still, it's not something that many of us haven't experienced before.>

<Trixie, let me tell you a story. After Alex discovered the *Rêveur,* it was many days before he learned the history of the ship. The extended stasis period for the crew was a great shock to them. Much would have transpired with family members, friends, and loved ones, who would have presumed them lost. But one thing that truly bothered Alex was realizing

that I was cognizant during the entire period, even though my kernel clock was slowed for the majority of that time. It was a poignant moment for me and a realization of the depth of this human when he told me he was sorry for the time I spent alone. I appreciated the sentiment and expressed that he was the first to say so. He paused in the bridge accessway and said he was sorry for that too. When Alex was made captain of the *Rêveur*, one of his first orders was to appoint bridge watches around the chronometer even though we were at station around New Terra.>

<Every SADE knows your story, Julien, and you're admired for saving your sanity and protecting the humans aboard. That you were alone for seventy years without any creative input or conversation, we find horrifying. But I don't understand the point of your story or the purposes of an officer's watch while you were housed on the bridge and operational.>

<The individuals Alex appointed to bridge watch didn't understand the purpose either, for a long time. They would sit in the command chair or pace until they became bored and then, unthinkable for New Terrans, they would start talking to the computer.> Julien heard Trixie's humor expressed in a bubbling noise. Every SADE experimented with expressing emotional algorithms in sounds to augment communications with humans.

<You must understand, Trixie, that New Terrans had no such things as SADEs. It became my duty to educate each watch officer, as to a SADE's capabilities, but the process always began with an odd conversational topic, usually whatever was on their minds. Then, it would proceed from there, until we established a rapport, and we always did. Except for one human, who found the responsibility of battle command too horrendous, those people have become Alex's core.>

<So Dassata used you to educate his people to a concept they couldn't have imagined, a digital sentient.>

<That wasn't Alex's original purpose, Trixie. That was just an auxiliary outcome. I didn't perceive Alex's intention in the beginning either. The thirty-hour constant watch rotation had one and only one purpose for Alex. It was to ensure that I always had company.>

<But after the rescue and revival of the Méridiens, you'd have comm contact with your own people.>

<The equivalent of your argument, Trixie, is that you would be equally comfortable housed aboard your outpost station and communicating with Hector, instead of how you are today with him nearby and both of you in avatars.>

<I perceive the fallacy of my reasoning, Julien, and, by extension, Dassata might hear our objections to his proposals, but he won't listen. We strive for purity in function, form, and efficiency, and he accepts that to a degree, so long as we participate in community, human and our own.>

<Just so, Trixie.>

<I knew there was a reason I admired this man.>

* * *

Alex linked with Julien, Cordelia, Z, and Miranda. <I need your services, Sers,> Alex sent. <Please review the Confederation SADEs, except for Trixie, Hector, and Miriam, and give me your list of candidates for the new scout ships.>

<All SADEs are capable of piloting the craft, Alex,> Z replied. <What additional criteria should we be applying?>

<Emotional stability … and being comfortable working and communicating with others. Three SADEs will be working in concert with one another during their flights,> Alex sent in reply.

<The SADEs have chosen to accept your changes to their design, Alex,> Cordelia sent.

<I wasn't aware I needed their permission to make changes to any vessel produced by Omnia Ships,> Alex sent, and the SADEs sensed the power wave through the comm.

<Perhaps, Alex, I phrased that improperly,> Cordelia sent. <Trixie spoke with Julien and heard the reasons for your requests of Mickey, and they appreciated them and accepted the changes in the spirit you intended.>

<Understood, Captain. Send me your list when you're ready,> Alex sent, and abruptly cut the comm.

The SADEs remained linked, each with their thoughts. <Did I touch on a sensitive subject, Julien?> Cordelia asked.

<I don't believe Alex's reaction had anything to do with the subject we discussed,> Julien replied.

<I would agree,> Z interjected. <Alex normally is most content when he's supporting the building of a world, watching species develop in peace.>

<However, we're intent on building warships for an eventual confrontation with humankind's nemesis. Surely that has to worry Alex,> Cordelia said.

<Our present process is one of design, organizing the workforce, and procuring the materials to construct our projects,> Julien replied.

<You're implying, Julien, that Alex approaches the construction of warships as abstract engineering and economic problems, freeing him from imagining their ultimate use,> Miranda reasoned.

<The three of you are focusing on the warships, their construction and purpose. This has nothing to do with Alex's mood. The first ships to be sent into the dark from Omnia will be scout ships. Alex is thinking of the SADEs who will be inside those vessels.>

<And he places the burden on his shoulders of being the one to choose which SADEs will go,> Cordelia said. <How did I miss that?>

<We've been immersed building Omnia, the terminal, and the financial structure for tens of thousands of freed individuals. Not to mention negotiating new agreements with two worlds. I would say we've been preoccupied,> Julien allowed.

<I think it's fair to say that the dear man has a reticence to send others into unknown places, places he feels he should venture first. From my discussions with him, I surmise that he emotionally collects the dead,> Miranda sent.

<So we develop Alex's list, attempting to identify the most socially stable SADEs,> Z sent. <In this case, Julien, you should lead, set the communications parameters we should use, and the rest of us will follow.>

<A question for the three of you,> Miranda sent. <Did anyone else enjoy the delicious power flux from the dear man's comm when he was perturbed, or am I alone in that thought?> When no one replied, she sent, <It must be a cultivated taste.>

* * *

A day after Alex contacted the four SADEs, he received their list. They had identified thirty-one SADEs. Julien had copied Alex on the parameters the foursome used during their communication with the Confederation SADEs. Alex smiled, reviewing Julien's approach.

None of the SADEs were asked about their willingness to journey into the dark or how they perceived the search's isolation. Instead, Julien drafted questions that asked the SADEs what they would do in a series of scenarios that they might encounter during their search. The four SADEs had evaluated the Confederation SADEs on their willingness to be flexible in challenging circumstances, to consider the well-being of the other two SADEs with them, and keep the greater picture in mind.

Alex winced when he pulled up the list. Killian's name was at the top. *Why are my favorites always out front?* Alex thought with regret. Despite his emotional reaction, Alex contacted Killian and informed him that they would spend the daylight hours together, beginning tomorrow morning.

Shortly before morning meal, Killian tapped a New Terran sled jockey to ferry him from the orbital to the *Freedom*. The New Terran dropped his load of plating, swung into a makeshift bay, picked up his passenger, and jetted off to the city-ship.

Once aboard the *Freedom*, the pilot of the tiny craft asked, "Do I wait for you, Sir?"

"Negative, pilot. Return to work, and thank you for your help," Killian replied. The New Terran touched the brim of his worn, fraying cap and spun his craft around to wait for the bay to pressurize, which would happen once Killian entered the airlock and the flight crew chief signaled all clear.

Killian strode quickly through the corridors, reflecting on the respect and consideration the New Terran workers paid him. First and foremost, they depended on him for accurate directions, but they also seemed to respond well to his patience. Many had commented that they never had a supervisor who treated them so cordially. Quickly, Killian made a mental connection. *We treat one another and humans, as Dassata treats us,* he thought.

While Killian waited in the corridor outside Alex's suite, his programs were involved in the construction oversight of the Sardi-Tallen Orbital Platform. He liked repeating the orbital's full name, recognizing it was pride that drove the habit. A portion of Killian's kernel was busy considering what questions would be asked of him. Of particular concern was how the interview could possibly take an entire day.

Alex exited the suite with Renée, gave Killian a brief nod, and walked on. Renée took the SADE's arm and chatted with him on the way to the meal room.

It was curious to Killian that during the entire meal Alex spoke to others at the table but never addressed him. When two young Daelon children, a boy and a girl, cleared away the meal's trays, pitchers, and cups, Alex rose and Killian quickly followed. Not a word was exchanged, as the pair descended decks, traversed corridors, transited an airlock, and boarded a traveler.

The first of the day's many stops for Alex and Killian was at the site where Wave Skimmer's hive was constructing its domiciles. Alex exited the ship and was welcomed by the Swei Swee.

Killian was left behind, while Alex whistled and tweeted with young males and matrons. So the SADE walked to the edge of the water and enjoyed the view. He'd spent so much time aboard ship or the orbital that the impact of standing on a planet had lessened. The smells of the ocean and living creatures, the soft breeze, the sound of the waves, and the striking colors produced wonderful images to store. It was then that Killian recognized that he had similar memories, but the difference, this time, was his deep appreciation of the moment. *Changes can occur so slowly that one is hardly aware of the cumulative effect,* Killian thought.

Killian's focus shifted to young Swei Swee frolicking at the waves' edges. Alex seemed completely at ease with the six-legged, clawed aliens. A youngling rose on small legs in front of Alex, raised his claws, and tweeted. When Alex whistled a reply, the little Swei Swee lowered his abdomen to the sand and folded his legs close. Then Alex bent down, hoisted the youngling, and, with a tremendous twist of his torso, heaved the Swei Swee along the water's edge, which elicited a high-pitched squeal from the little one, as he spun nearly 40 meters along the shoreline.

Suddenly other younglings clamored to be spun, and Alex good-naturedly obliged their requests. A matron approached Alex and when she whistled, Alex burst out laughing. The female wasn't the size of the hive's males, but even she stood as high as Alex's shoulders. As best as Killian could discern, the matron had teased Alex that she wanted to be spun along the sand too. Alex's response must have been humorous, because it sent the Swei Swee, within earshot, whistling and tweeting derisively.

As Killian watched Alex play with the Swei Swee, his thoughts wandered to the future. He could envision living on Omnia, watching Vivian live a full life, finding a partner, and perhaps raising children. After witnessing her star services, which he realized would distress him, he could close that chapter of his life and seek a new adventure. The future presented so many possibilities to the SADEs, now that they were free of their boxes.

Killian's eyes focused on Alex, laughing at the antics of a youngling trying to manage a fish nearly his own length. *Julien, I can't imagine how you'll feel when you attend Alex's star services one day,* Killian thought. His musings were interrupted by a tug on his trousers, and a matron rushed over to herd a newly hatched youngling away, scolding, "Not food."

Alex walked across the sands to stand beside Killian. He looked over the Swei Swee and commented, "Incredibly gentle species and so protective of their young." It was Alex's first words to Killian, and they weren't to be his last. The pair spent the day hopping from site to site, reviewing the project's progress, and speaking of many inconsequential things.

Killian was forever waiting for what he would perceive as the start of the interview, which would focus on the challenges of the search, but it never came.

As twilight fell, Alex and Killian returned to the *Freedom*, and Alex wished Killian a good evening. He left the SADE standing in the bay, with orders to have the traveler pilot return him to the orbital.

Immediately upon exiting the city-ship's bay, Killian was linked to the other thirty SADEs who would interview with Alex, and they bombarded Killian with questions.

<There was no discussion of the search,> Killian replied, once he restored order. <The day was spent touring Omnia's construction sites, which I'm sure you're aware of, because obviously you've been tracking my location. While Dassata and I spoke of many things, they were mundane in nature.>

The supposition of the majority of SADEs was that Killian's interview was forthcoming.

<I disagree,> Killian sent. <I believe I've had it. Dassata seeks to know what lies deep in your kernel. You can't prepare for your time with him. You can only be yourself and speak openly with him.>

For a few SADEs, Killian's answer was disconcerting. For the rest, it was a relief. For the latter group, expectations were eliminated, and they would welcome the opportunity to spend the day in Dassata's company.>

* * *

Alex interspersed his SADE interviews, concerning potential scout ship riders, with his other obligations. One of the first of those was to acquaint his senior staff with their new projects and duties. Alex used one of the *Freedom*'s larger conference rooms to accommodate the assembled individuals. There were to be no comm or implant participants, he wanted to look his people in the eyes for this meeting.

"You're welcome to contact me individually after this meeting for clarification of your new opportunities," Alex said, opening the meeting and grinning broadly at his people.

Ophelia and Perrin glanced around the broad table to see if their concerns were reflected in the faces of others. They were.

"Emile," Alex announced.

"Oh, I love going first," Emile replied without enthusiasm, and his response produced sympathetic chuckles.

"I need a permanent scent solution for the Dischnya. The soma of various nests will be mixing in the company of queens. I think you can deliver the design in two stages. The first solution needs to be delivered soon and can be something refillable, worn outside the Dischnya's body, and be specific to each nest. The second iteration should be a permanent, one-time, injectable solution, which should make an adjustment at the cellular level. There's no hurry on the final solution. Whatever it will be, the queens will have to approve it. It will be a huge adjustment in their society, some of the repercussions of which they and we probably can't even imagine."

Alex regarded Emile, whose eyes had taken on a faraway stare. "Emile, this is when you nod or respond in some manner instead of starting work on the answer."

The biochemist snapped out of his reverie, and the occupants at the table twittered. "Apologies, Alex, I'll get on it. I think I'll need more help."

Alex looked over to Cordelia, who said, "Emile, I'll review the Daelon Independents and see who has the necessary skills to help you."

"A SADE would be helpful," Emile added.

"Of course, we are," Cordelia added, smiling, which produced some good-natured jeering from humans.

<They're enjoying building this new world,> Julien sent to Alex.

<And so they should, Julien. Creating something of worth fills the heart,> Alex replied.

<And someday, we'll present them a different future … one intent on our enemy's destruction.>

<Someday, but not today, my friend.>

"Mickey, I've worked out a side agreement with New Terra. We'll share production of travelers out of a dedicated terminal bay. We get five out of eight ships."

"Only five out of eight?" Mickey asked abruptly.

"What Dassata did not have the opportunity to say, Ser Brandon, is that in exchange for the generous deal, New Terra will be providing the interior buildout of the first four scout ships, and doing so as a priority over the warships," Killian said.

"Oh, that's different," the engineer grumped, and leaned back in his seat somewhat mollified.

"Hector, none of these new plans will interfere with shell production aboard the *Our People*. Continue the refit, as you're able, but the shells for Haraken have priority. We need the flow of credits."

When Hector tipped his head in understanding, Alex moved on. "Trixie, you have a new project. Make that four new construction projects planetside, but you're not to take the lead on three of these projects, they'd take too much of your time to oversee. Assign someone to oversee the projects on the Dischnya continent. You can keep the one near the city center."

"Understood, Dassata," Trixie replied. "What are we building?"

"On the Dischnya continent, your assignee needs to work with Olawale and his associates to design and build a school or college or whatever they want."

Trixie regarded Olawale across the table. <Welcome, Professor,> Trixie sent to him, and Olawale smiled in return.

"I'd locate the college on the north side, near the center of the Dischnya structures," Alex added.

"Any particular reason for that location, Dassata?" Trixie asked.

"That will become clear in a moment, Trixie," Alex replied. "Near the city center, but not too close, we'll need a military training academy. You can liaise with Admiral Tachenko on the details, and I believe the *Freedom* carries all three of our previous academy designs, personnel organizations, and training practices."

"We do, Alex," Cordelia replied, after first checking the *Freedom*'s massive data archives. On the one hand, she was surprised that Alex knew that, and, on the other hand, she wasn't.

"Admiral, we have commanders and fighter pilots aplenty. What we don't have are crew for our warships. Based on our construction schedules for the orbital station and the first warships to launch from the bays, I'm estimating …> Alex paused and consulted with Killian. The two went back and forth while Alex shifted some of Killian's priorities, and the SADE tweaked the completion rates for various parts of the construction bays.

In the end, Alex shrugged to his audience and said, "My knowledgeable friend," and he nodded toward Killian, "and I disagree on some of the finer points, but we estimate between one and three-quarter to two years before we launch the first warship. It'll be a Trident-class ship."

"Yes," Reiko hissed, her small fist striking the air.

"I'm pleased to see some of my announcements are making people happy," Alex quipped, and Reiko ducked her head momentarily by way of apology, but she was grinning.

"Trixie, returning to your Dischnya continent projects, we'll need a transport system connecting the nests and the college. It needs to be something simple, something the Dischnya can easily catch, and it doesn't have to stop. In fact, it's better if it doesn't. Touch base with Miriam. I understand she designed lifts, people movers, and the like for her Confederation projects."

"Aren't you concerned for the Dischnya's safety, using such an elementary form of transportation, Dassata?" Trixie asked.

"There might be minor accidents, Trixie, but Olawale's informed me that Boris Gorenko is expecting to treat Dischnya injuries with the aid of his medical students. In this regard, we might be inadvertently assisting the college's training regiments." Alex's grin had more than one member of the staff working to parse his concept. It seemed in contrast to the Omnians' intense focus on safety.

"You've mentioned three projects, Dassata," Trixie reminded Alex.

"That's because I've saved the best for last," Alex replied. "Near the center of the southside nests will be the fourth project, and, of course, your transport system will have to circulate to this site as frequently as it does the college. And, Admiral, you'll be an intrinsic part of this project."

The hairs on the back of Tatia's neck rose. She had expected the training academy, and its location on the city center continent was a good choice. In her mind, there was nothing that should concern her on the Dischnya continent.

"We'll have warships, commanders, captains, and crew," Alex said, enumerating them by lifting the fingers on his hand. "But what if we have to take the fight planetside? In that case, what if our preferred weapons aren't stun guns but plasma rifles?"

Tatia had an idea where this was going, and she wasn't sure she liked it. Her eyes narrowed, as she stared at Alex, and his eyes narrowed in return.

The audience glanced from one end of the table to the other, watching the mental struggle of wills.

"You want me to oversee the training of the Dischnya warriors to be a groundside attack force," Tatia said, realizing Alex was waiting for her to speak first.

"Who better than an ex-Terran Security Forces major?" Alex replied.

"When you first mentioned this idea to me, Alex, I thought you were kidding. How do we know if the Dischnya want this type of training?" Tatia objected.

"Because they specifically requested it, Admiral," Olawale replied. "We were planetside when two queens approached us and spoke for Pussiro and his warriors. It appears to be a common thought among the Dischnya that the lifetime warriors can't conceive of doing anything else. You can imagine the complexity of bringing peace to these nests and teaching medical and technical skills to the hunters, the females, and the young. But what of the warriors? How do individuals who spent their lives fighting for their nests, suddenly become building or equipment technicians?"

"What Olawale isn't mentioning is that one of the most ardent supporters of this military academy is Homsaff," Alex said.

"Homsaff, the young queen?" Tatia asked, amazed.

"A most fierce young female," Olawale admitted.

"Think captain instead of queen, Admiral, and you'll have the picture," Alex said. "Besides, I have the feeling that Homsaff won't be the only queen to attend the academy. Expect an initial rush of attendees, but many warriors might fall out of training. In this regard, I have no idea of the potential graduation rate."

Tatia was tempted to drop her head into her hands, but she refused to display her frustration in front of the rest of the staff.

<The man has got to stop collecting aliens, Admiral,> Reiko sent sympathetically to Tatia.

Rather than dwell on her reaction to the announcement, Tatia's mind kicked into gear. The Dischnya training academy would be a difficult challenge to anyone who took responsibility for its operation. She ran a quick check of present personnel, and none of them suited her ideal candidate. An image of a ground-pounder on New Terra came to mind, and she signaled Cordelia. <I have a priority comm for New Terra, Captain. Meet me after this meeting to set it up, please.>

Alex excused himself from the meeting, and it broke into small groups to discuss their new assignments.

-30-
Three Years

The three years, following the rescue of the *Sojourn*'s survey team, slipped by quickly for the Omnians. The Sardi-Tallen Orbital Platform was completed in half the time.

During the terminal's early days, Killian cleverly prioritized such structures as temporary transit bays to facilitate the direct offloading of modules from freighters into holding areas. Crew would offload the module's crates in hours instead of days. A tug would deliver a module to the transit bay; crew would empty it; the tug would haul the empty back to the freighter and fetch another one.

Freighter crews were disappointed that they didn't get the usual two to three days of downtime on the planet or aboard the *Freedom*. In less than a day, a freighter was unloaded, and the captain was headed out of system and back to New Terra.

As the construction phase of the platform ended, Maynard Scullers was appointed director to operate the facilities, and Glenn took over to manage the complex bay operations, which were turning out warships, scout ships, and travelers, in addition to handling passenger traffic.

Svetlana received the captaincy of the first warship launched from the terminal's construction bays, a Trident-class ship named the OS *Liberator*. Observing Svetlana nearly walking on air for months, the crew unmercifully teased her. However, when the second Trident-class ship slipped out of its orbital bay, Reiko selected the *Liberator* as her flagship, and Svetlana's time, as the senior officer aboard the warship, came to an end.

New Terra received the third warship of the same class, and Maria petitioned the new president to allow New Terra's captain and crew to train under Commodore Shimada. As Maria phrased it, "Who else knows warship squadron tactics?" She needn't have bothered trying to make her case. Harold Grumley, Drake's replacement, was of the same opinion.

Eight Trident-class warships exited the orbital station's construction bays. The Omnians had five and used OS to designate Omnia Ships, while the New Terrans applied the abbreviation NT. In addition to Svetlana, the commanders, Darius, Deirdre, Ellie, and Lucia, received captain's commissions.

Every Omnian project that had been under Trixie's umbrella was completed — the city center and the humans' military academy, the nests' new housing, and the Dischnya training college, academy, and transit system. Much of the nests' housing maintenance was handed over to the Dischnya.

While food stocks were made available to the Dischnya, some habits were too ingrained in the mature soma. One of these was that hunters became farmers. Given the opportunity afforded by a plentiful water supply, the hunters returned to their favorite foraging sites and harvested tubers that the soma preferred. They planted the area around their buildings, and trade sprung up between the nests for seeds, which expanded to include textiles and other crafts.

The easy mixing of the soma was made possible by Emile's capable biochemistry. As Alex had requested, Emile delivered the scent solution in two stages. The first consisted of a small satchel worn around the neck of each soma, who participated in the academy or college. Designed to be porous, the scent leached out of the tiny purse to waft delicately under the nose of the wearer and leach into their skin. Every thirty days, the pouch was refilled. Eventually, Emile, with the help of the SADEs, developed a nanites injection that targeted the Dischnya brain and freed the soma from their dependency on the queens' scents. By then, the delineation among the nests was blurred and would fade with the new generation of soma.

To Trixie's surprise, and mostly that of everyone else, the Dischnya tram was a huge hit. The SADEs built small grav cars programmed to circulate among the nests, college, and academy. The small cars, which could carry up to eight soma, were open. The base and roof of the cars were connected by a series of strong metal-alloy poles, which served as handholds.

The Dischnya loved their transit system. It became great sport, catching the constantly moving vehicles. Deliberately, warriors would wait until a car passed and would race at top speed to gain it, their great clawed feet throwing gouts of earth behind them and tongues flopping out the sides of their muzzles. With their strength fading, they would leap for a handhold, while their comrades howled and exhorted their efforts.

Needless to say, not every attempt was successful, but, so far, no Dischnya had been killed, and it was as Alex had predicted. The transit system created a steady supply of patients for the medical college, allowing the soma to practice their training on foolhardy warriors.

* * *

Tatia attacked her need for a Dischnya academy commandant by sending a lengthy comm to a retired New Terran TSF sergeant major, Myron McTavish. Tatia had expected to hear promptly from the sergeant, but, when the expected time period elapsed and she heard nothing, she was severely disappointed. Myron had been her singular hope.

The admiral spent the following days searching her lengthy list of New Terran contacts for a suitable replacement for Myron. She found likely candidates, but none possessed the qualities she knew were needed to deal with an alien race of warriors.

Tatia had finished a review session of Reiko's battle scenario training program when she received a comm from Killian.

The SADE was supervising the unloading of the *Dark*. <Admiral,> Killian sent, <I'm in the presence of retired Sergeant Major Myron McTavish, who wishes to know when you might be available to speak with him.>

Tatia had burst out laughing. That was the Myron she knew, often doing the unexpected and probably too blunt for his own good, but, quite possibly, the perfect individual to train the Dischnya queens and warriors.

The sergeant major hadn't waited to have a long-distance conversation with her or bide his time waiting for passage on a liner. He'd grabbed the first ship out of New Terra, which happened to be the freighter *Dark*.

Tatia met with Myron, laying out her expectations and requirements, specifically, that the sergeant major would have to agree to an implant and cell-gen injections.

Myron had replied, "Why don't we visit these little creatures, Admiral? I'll see for myself if I can turn them into soldiers before we go on talking, if you don't mind."

Tatia kept a straight face and arranged for a pilot and a planetside trip. She realized she'd failed to include images of the Dischnya with her comm that she sent to Myron. At her request, Julien sent messages to Pussiro and Homsaff to meet at the Omnians' traditional landing site.

Before Tatia exited the craft, she started to explain the niceties of Dischnya communication, but Myron interrupted her, saying, "First impressions unsullied by others' perceptions are best, Admiral." So, Tatia bit her tongue and kept silent.

Julien signaled the hatch to drop and preceded Tatia and Myron off the traveler. Myron demonstrated senior officer decorum and manners to motion Tatia ahead of him.

Myron jumped from the shuttle to the ground, his boots crushing a small shrub, which had recently bloomed. His first impression was of heat and dryness, which he approved. In his mind, rigorous climatic conditions created tough people.

Homsaff and Pussiro were waiting, and, as Myron straightened, he let out a soft whistle. "This is more like it," he said softly, taking in the Dischnya's rangy build, height, powerful legs, rows of teeth, and clawed feet. "Am I seeing this correctly, Admiral, the female is the larger of the two?"

"You're looking at a queen, Sergeant Major," Tatia said tersely, but before she could utter another word, Myron had stepped close to Homsaff and reached out a hand toward her muzzle.

The young queen's tail arced overhead and slashed down at the impudent stranger. Myron blocked the attack with a forearm, and the tail vectored in on another angle. In all there were five, quick, whip movements of Homsaff's tail, of which Myron blocked four. The fifth landed neatly across Myron's cheek, slicing it open.

For a moment, Tatia and Julien were hesitant about what to do next, but Myron wasn't. He grinned in the queen's face, while wiping at the blood pouring from his cheek. When Homsaff returned the smile with a display of her own, Myron remarked, "Now that's impressive."

Julien calculated that no translations were necessary. The entire process appeared to be one of appraisal and approval, best left to warrior types.

Myron stepped in front of Pussiro and eyed the wasat, noting his scarred and slightly gray muzzle. "This one might be a little old," Myron said, turning his head to speak to Tatia, but it was a feint. Myron launched a lightning strike of his right hand, aimed to slap Pussiro's face, only to find it blocked.

Pussiro chuffed in amusement, waited a couple of heartbeats, and struck back, but he didn't catch Myron off guard either.

The sergeant major stepped back and nodded respectfully to both Dischnya. "Admiral, I could do a great deal with these individuals. I'd be pleased to discuss employment conditions, but I believe that now we should have proper introductions."

So Myron met the Dischnya, had his cheek repaired by Pia, and signed up as commandant of the Dischnya warrior academy. Struggling with retirement on New Terra, Myron felt relieved to discover a second life. His favorite cadet, although that term wasn't used, was Homsaff. As a queen, she was a natural leader, but, more than that, she thrived on the strategies and tactics of military action. Homsaff frequently practiced with her warriors outside their domicile, planning battles with mock stun guns. The weapons fired lasers, which triggered the harness on the wearer.

Often, as Celus' light dimmed, Myron, sitting on a boulder, would watch Homsaff direct her troops during an engagement, and he would puff up with pride.

However, Myron knew he wouldn't have made half his accomplishments without the support of the many who knew the

Dischnya well. Myron counted Alex, Julien, Miriam, and Glenn, as key Omnians who guided his early understanding of the Dischnya society.

* * *

Almost a year earlier, the first scout ship had been completed, and Alex chose that time to gather his senior staff and tell them what he'd found on Sawa. He laid out the means by which the stone was discovered and gave credit to Renée for providing the clue to solving the strange overlay of twin images.

Mickey piped up, teasing, "So you mean to tell us that the incomparable quartette of Julien, Z, Miranda, and you couldn't solve the mysterious glyph, and your partner, watching entertainment vids, comes up with the critical clue."

Mickey's taunt brought laughter from around the table, and Alex smiled good-naturedly, but Renée felt one of them should fire back. "Mickey, I'm surprised. You mean to tell me that Pia has never given you an idea or helped you solve a problem."

Had Pia not been present, Mickey might have weathered Renée's rebuttal, but she was sitting next to him. Pia's silent stare had Mickey raising his hands in submission, and the table's second round of laughter was even louder.

Alex sent Renée one of his favorite images of her. He captured it soon after he received his first implant. Renée was stepping from the refresher and smiling at him. It might have seemed an odd choice to send as a compliment to Renée for her defense against Mickey's tease, except the image was wrapped in the warmth of many of his memories with her.

The avalanche of Alex's emotion threatened to overwhelm Renée, and her breath caught in her throat. To help Alex focus on his presentation, she sent, <Careful, my love, or I'm liable to take you on this table in front of your people.>

The audience heard Alex chuckle and could guess the interplay he had with Renée, who was smiling up at him.

Julien activated a holo-vid, projected the stone's dual images and separated them. He overlaid the present planets' positions, which didn't match the glyph. Then he rotated the planets, spinning them backward in time until they coincided with the stone's positions. "The temple's stone enables us to calculate a narrow span of time when the sphere entered the Celus system and the approximate vector when it did so," Julien said.

"This will narrow the search by an enormous magnitude," Killian said.

"Agreed," Alex replied, "although, as all of you know, we don't know if this sphere came to the Celus system directly from its home world or wandered here by some odd route."

"Doesn't the presence of the Swei Swee on this planet suggest that there was at least one stop before the sphere came here?" Ophelia asked.

"The permutations of the sphere's possible visitations are endless," Z commented. "For instance, the sphere might have picked up the Swei Swee, returned to their home world, picked up more inhabitants, and then come here."

"Z's correct," Alex said, "I don't expect our scout ships to go out and find the Nua'll home world. If I did, I wouldn't send them out until we have a squadron of warships. My expectations are that if we start the search now, then long after we have our warships, we might, just might, pick up the trail of the Nua'll. Unless fortune is on our side, the search promises to be a long one."

"Alex, one question," Perrin said. "Why not tell us this before now?"

"To assist your focus, Perrin," Alex replied. "If you knew this two years ago, what would your thoughts have been on … your work or on the future encounter with the Confederation's colony destroyer?"

Perrin and Ophelia shared private thoughts that they didn't necessarily agree with Alex's reasoning, but because the others at the table hadn't objected, they remained quiet.

"We're finalizing the search protocols and grid, now that we know the terminal's production rate of scout ships," Alex said. "As soon as I choose the first SADE team, we'll start the search."

* * *

Alex had appointed Hector to captain the *Our People* for two reasons. One, it would keep Hector busy and prevent him from focusing on his ugly, last years with Mahima, and two, the city-ship did need a SADE to manage the myriad tasks that would take place onboard the vessel.

What Alex forgot was that Hector had been part and parcel of Mahima's machinations, which allowed her to grasp the power of Council Leader, and, while Hector deplored Mahima's scheming, he did have extensive records on how business could be conducted.

It was the entreaties of Harakens, who requested transportation to Omnia, which launched Hector down the path of entrepreneurialism.

The *Our People*'s deliveries of shells reduced Haraken's decades-long backlog of traveler orders and created a massive flow of credits to Omnia Ships and the associated banks run by the SADEs.

In the early days, Haraken companies wrestled with a problem. They needed people who were skilled in the advanced technology that the travelers' internal components required. Many of the capable people had immigrated to Omnia with Alex. So, they reached out to Méridien and the Confederation-at-large for workers, who could support the traveler industry.

Many Méridiens answered the call, especially those individuals in danger of being declared Independents. They came to Haraken, worked, earned credits, and immigrated to Omnia. The companies were constantly searching for new employees, as they lost workers and the delivery of shells accelerated.

While at Omnia, Hector communicated frequently with key SADEs, such as Trixie, Killian, and Miriam to build an extensive list of business and job opportunities favorable to humans in Omnia's near future. Hector was sympathetic to the Méridiens, who immigrated to Haraken over concerns of being ostracized by their society, and he quietly solicited these individuals with his list.

The Méridiens and Harakens paid for their transportation to Omnia, and Hector offered the money to Omnia Ships. Alex accepted the funds and placed them in a subaccount for Hector to use for the refit. Hector had calculated Alex would do that and was pleased when it happened — not for the credits themselves but that he was understanding the human he admired.

During the course of Omnia's first three years, 522 more SADEs chose to emigrate from the Confederation, and the SIF offered three-year stipends to them to join Alex's Omnia Ships. The *Allora* had transported the first annual group of SADEs to Haraken and wrongly assumed Hector would freely transport them to Omnia.

<I would like to accommodate your request,> Hector sent to the lone SIF director aboard the *Allora*, <but you must understand my dilemma. You're assuming that Alex will accept these SADEs, adding them to an agreement, of which I have no knowledge. The SIF never made the contract public record. Alex might well reject their addition.>

<What is your suggestion, Captain?> the SIF director asked.

<You will need to pay for their transport to Omnia,> Hector sent in reply. <I will ensure that any SADEs who do not stay at Omnia, under any conditions that might be available to them, are returned for free to Haraken on my next trip.>

<And if all the SADEs are accepted by Alex, then they will have been part of Omnia Ships, and, having been transported on one of Alex's ships, the SIF would expect the credits be refunded.>

<And there you have it, Ser,> Hector replied. <Neither of us knows the outcome of what you propose, so I offer to share the risk with you by requesting a one-way fee for transport and, yet, guaranteeing your passengers a two-way trip, if that is what's required.

The SIF director considered the many arguments he could make about working for passage, the ship's great emptiness, and several others, but what was plainly obvious was that Captain Hector was resolute in his offer. So, the director agreed.

Of course, Alex accepted the SADEs readily, as Hector considered that he would. What made the SADE's day was when he told Alex the story of his discussion with the SIF director. Hector carefully stored Alex's booming laughter with other files, such as Alex's response to discovering Hector had made his august friends work for their free passage.

Within two years and with Hector's extra efforts, the *Our People*'s refit was complete. Once again, the *Our People* was truly a sister-ship to the *Freedom*, and Hector was a proud captain.

* * *

When Trixie and her team completed the military academy outside the city center, Tatia approached Alex to discuss the crew the warships would require.

Renée made them thé, while Tatia broached the subject.

"Alex, we need a plan to recruit and train crew for the warships. I suggest we look to New Terra."

"And I suggest a mix of humans and SADEs. It's always served us best."

"Whatever the outcome, we'll need credits to pay the humans' stipends, and, in time, you'll need additional funds to pay the SADEs when their three-year stipends end. How much does Omnia Ships have in its account? We'll need to work out how many crew members we can hire for the next … maybe ten years. No use building too many warships if we can't crew them."

"We can always sell a couple of Tridents to fund the expedition," Alex replied.

Tatia's laugh was scornful, and she responded, "This from the man who tells me he believes another sphere might be under construction or underway, and he thinks the ship might be heavily armed after the message sent from the Libran sphere. Alex, I'd vote for more ships, not fewer."

"Well, Tatia, before we engage in conjecture, let me see how many credits Omnia Ships does possess."

For the first time since Alex launched the *Freedom* from Haraken's orbit, he checked the balance in his accounts.

The Bank of Omnia's controller confirmed Alex's bio ID and responded to his request for the balance of the Omnia Ships' account. Alex looked at the number, blinked, and braced a hand on the table next to him. Hurriedly, he checked his personal account and that balance sent him to a chair.

"We don't have the credits?" Tatia asked with concern, glancing from Alex to Renée. "Are you and the company broke?"

Alex held up a hand to silence her questions.

Receiving the bank controller's notification that Alex had finally accessed his accounts, Julien, Cordelia, Z, and Miranda signaled one another simultaneously.

<You did say, Julien, that it would be awhile before Alex checked on his private account, but who could have foreseen our present-day circumstances?> Z sent.

<And it's those circumstances, Z, that will sway Alex's reaction in our favor,> Julien replied, and then added, <We won't have to wait to discover his state of mind. Alex has signaled me.> Julien linked the SADEs to Alex's comm.

<Julien, I might suggest there's been some accounting errors. However, that should be impossible with SADEs and controllers handling the bank's transactions,> Alex sent.

<Haraken's backlog of traveler orders has been shrinking rapidly, and Omnia Ships has been reaping the rewards, Alex,> Julien replied. <By the time our projects are completed and the first squadron of Tridents completed, Haraken will have zero backlog.>

<So then the credit flow from the Haraken agreement will shrink drastically,> Alex surmised.

<Precisely, Alex. However, Mickey will have his traveler construction bay and will have been producing the fighters we need aboard our warships and to service Omnia. Thereafter, we can sell travelers directly.>

<But that would put us in competition with Haraken,> Alex replied, but then he reconsidered his statement. <Come to think of it, Haraken couldn't compete with our faux shell spray and shorter delivery time.>

<That's how we see it.>

<You're indicating this enormous balance in Omnia Ships' account will continue to grow.>

<Conservative estimates are that it will increase by another 110 percent in the next four years.>

<Before expenses and distribution of shares to the SIF and Exchange?> Alex asked.

<After, Alex.>

Alex stared at the balances in his implant and shook his head to help him focus. <And my personal account, Julien. Would you care to explain that balance?>

<The Exchange and SIF directors agreed to contribute a portion of their profits to your personal account. It was seen as an incentive for you.>

<Julien, how can it be an incentive if I had no knowledge of it?>

<There is that.> When Julien heard no response, he asked, <Are you displeased, Alex?>

<I'm not sure what I feel, Julien. I'll put the credits to good use,> Alex replied and closed his side of the comm.

I know you will, Julien thought to himself. The SADE received a short vid from his friend. Julien stood in the middle of a white background and from the right streaked a pair of giant, wet lips, dripping from an enormous amount of red coloring, which dripped onto the floor. The lips were larger than Julien, and they hit him with a smacking sound and bowled him over before flying off to the left. Julien sat on the white floor, red smearing his avatar and the floor, and he wore a silly smile on his face.

<That went better than expected,> Cordelia sent.

<It should,> Miranda remarked. <All that has developed on and above Omnia has provided reaction mass for Alex's drive to find the Nua'll's home world.>

<Miranda is correct,> Julien sent. <Alex doesn't see the credits as his personal or the company's wealth. With what's been discovered on Sawa, he's that much closer to his goal, and the credits enable him to take the fight to the Nua'll.>

<May the stars protect us,> Cordelia sent, and halted the algorithms responsible for projecting future possibilities.

In the owner's suite, Alex looked at Tatia, grinned and asked, "Exactly how many warships would you like, Admiral?"

Tatia, known in the inner circle as Alex's weapons master, displayed her infamous lupine smile.

-31-
Killian

Alex visited with the six scout ship teams of SADEs he'd selected, after he informed the other thirteen that they weren't chosen. He met with the thirteen, one at a time and face to face. They were uncomfortable meetings for Alex, despite being one of the human beings who best understood SADEs. He was careful to explain that his decisions were not to be taken as a reflection of their capabilities and often used the excuse that their work on Omnians' projects was more important.

The thirteen SADEs walked away with their analysis of the meeting confusingly inconclusive, wondering why Alex couldn't have sent a simple message announcing his choices. For them, humans' concerns about the state of their emotional algorithms were still disconcerting.

"I have something to discuss with the eighteen of you," Alex said to the selected teams. They were meeting in a conference room aboard the *Freedom*. "You have the capability and we have the technology to back you up before you take your first scouting trip."

The SADEs' fugues were evident, and Alex waited while they shared their thoughts.

"If humans flew the scout ships and were lost, they would be gone forever," Bethley said. "Why should we be offered this advantage? Is it because we're fewer in number and you need to preserve us?"

Alex had teamed Bethley with Killian, because of the dominance of her analytical protocols. They would complement Killian's intense exposure to human emotions.

"I offer this opportunity because I can," Alex said. "If I could back up humans, I would make the same offer. A sentient's life is precious."

"What would happen to the copy on our return?" a SADE asked.

"That wouldn't be my decision," Alex acknowledged. "That would be the decision of each one of you."

"If we were to delete them, would we not be extinguishing a sentient's life?" a SADE asked. "In which case, the copies are not our property. They would be our twins and have a right to their own existence. Given an avatar they would develop a different persona and find their own way."

The questions continued and Alex felt out of his depth. In his attempt to protect the SADEs, he hadn't taken the time to consider many of the future ramifications of the offer. The questions ended, and the SADEs communed.

"Dassata," Killian said, "we understand and appreciate your intent to prevent our demise, but we respectfully decline your offer. Our decision rests on two prime observations. We're newly freed SADEs, and our relationship with the humans of Omnia is still tentative. We don't wish to foster a perception that we have inherent advantages over humans."

Alex drew breath to speak, but Killian lifted his index finger to indicate he wished to continue. Alex had to give the SADE credit. It was a purely human gesture, and he was communicating with a human.

"Yes, we have many advantages when it comes to our avatars and the capabilities to extend our lives with new bodies, but we wish to be careful not to make this blatantly obvious. Second, Dassata, thanks to your efforts to free us and allow us to be part of building Omnia, we've come to feel a sense of individuality, and the thought of leaving a copy behind disturbs our sense of self."

* * *

Killian, Bethley, and Trium were selected to crew the first scout ship. Killian had mixed feelings about leading the search. Those concerns weren't about the Sardi-Tallen Orbital Platform, which required only about fifty more days to complete and was in the capable hands of Director Scullers. Nor were they about the terminal's ship construction bays, which were being managed by Glenn. No, Killian was worried for Vivian.

Sitting down with Vivian and her mother, Killian sought to explain why he felt he had to go. Galania held her daughter's hand, while the child struggled to understand.

"I must go look for the bad people, Vivian. Bad people who want to hurt us. It's important we find them first."

"But others can go. You don't have to go," Vivian said plaintively. She had grown considerably in the past years, but she'd never lost her attachment to Killian.

"Well, you know I'm special, right?"

"Yes," Vivian reluctantly admitted.

"And why is that?"

"Because you're the plaid man."

"That's right, and because plaid men are special, they have the best opportunity to find these bad people."

"But you'll come back?" asked Vivian, her eyes reflecting her fear.

"Oh, yes, I'll come back often, and then we'll spend time together."

"But, if you're far away, we can't talk like we do now."

"No, we can't; but I still want to hear your voice every day."

"You do?"

"Yes, and do you know how we can do that?"

"Unh-uh."

"Starting today, if you touch your ear comm, you can record a message to me, any time you want and as many messages as you want. Before I leave, I'll collect every message and listen to them each day aboard my scout ship. I'd like that very much. Would you do that for me?"

"Yes, plaid man," Vivian said, hugging her multicolored SADE, who had kept the dark at bay ever since her family was rescued from the moon's claustrophobic tunnels.

Forty-two days later, Killian, Bethley, and Trium crawled into their scout ship. The cramped quarters required Trium to back through the hatch and crawl down the length of the hull. Bethley was next and Killian last. The SADEs settled their avatars in place and then locked them. They wouldn't be moving until they returned to Omnia.

The scout ships required only temperature-maintained, air for the avatars. Otherwise, human amenities were absent.

Following Alex and Julien's narrow grid allotment for their first search, the scout ship *Vivian* flew from Celus to the nearest star, passing through the system and scanning for any signature of life. As they entered a system, a comm report was sent back to Omnia. They also sent a comm every thirty hours, by the Omnian clock, and made a final report when they exited the system, sending the coordinates for the next star.

On the first day out, Killian opened one of Vivian's lengthy recorded messages to her plaid man. He kept his listening private, but Bethley and Trium were curious as to what occupied Killian's attention. Killian obliged his compatriots, and it soon became a daily ritual. Killian would link with the other two SADEs, and the file, containing Vivian's childish voice, would spool off the controller to them.

After several days of listening to Vivian, Bethley sent, <She speaks to you, Killian, as if you were parent, friend, and playmate, combined, without regard to subject.>

Killian related Vivian's traumatized early years on Daelon and played for his companions Galania's words, who said, "You're her lifeline, Killian. As long as the plaid man is near her or, at least, in her thoughts, the dark is kept at bay."

<We must ensure the plaid man returns,> Trium sent. He was one who was fascinated by the *Rêveur*'s library and spent his time immersed in Earth's ancient history and, at one point, commented, <Despite possessing primitive reasoning capabilities and little technology, early humans were quite inventive.>

Trium would chat to his fellow SADEs about the Greeks, Romans, and even earlier, great civilizations that existed across the Middle East and Africa, before the industrial and technological revolutions.

<There appears to a central theme common to these many early civilizations,> Trium sent, at one point. <Humans appear to be ever trying to improve their positions in society, and those at the top always crave more power. Sadly, there seemed to be no limit to what leaders did to gain

power, even stepping over the bodies of their own people. It's such a tragic and horrible means by which to develop a culture.>

When the *Vivian* returned to Omnia, completing its first and entirely fruitless search, which was as expected, Killian considered the ease with which he and his companions had bonded, and he offered a simple thanks to Alex for his efforts to ensure that would happen.

The *Vivian* sailed out from Omnia on four more search missions during the course of the next year and was joined by five other scout ships, each one of which scanned the stars in their assigned grids.

* * *

On the *Vivian*'s fifth mission, the ship exited its jump into a planet-rich system with a massive red star. Telemetry readings indicated heavy ship activity, a major industrial civilization on the fifth planet from the star, and myriad bases throughout the outer planets and moons.

The SADEs guided the *Vivian* into the system, and Killian prepared a lengthy message to send to Omnia. Nothing definitive identified the inhabitants of the system, but for all the SADEs knew, a sphere might await them on the far side of one of the planets or moons.

* * *

Omnian SADEs picked up the *Vivian*'s initial report of an active system, which they were investigating, and forwarded it to Alex. Word of the incredible discovery circulated among humans and SADEs, who anxiously awaited the next message. The anticipation built as the chronometer ran forward, and it was late in the evening, three days later, when Julien woke Alex.

<Your pardon, Alex, but I suggest you dress and come to the bridge. Killian's follow-up message deserves your undivided attention, and the imagery available might best be viewed on the bridge's holo-vid.>

<Well, if I have to get up, wake the senior staff and hustle them to the bridge too,> Alex sent in reply.

When everyone was assembled, Alex nodded at Cordelia, who started the file streaming from the ship's databanks over the bridge speakers.

"Greetings, Dassata, we send you mixed tidings from the *Vivian*," Killian's voice was heard to say. "We attempted to investigate a system that demonstrated dense sentient activity. You have the coordinates of our initial entry point into the system. Attached with this message are the coordinates when we made first contact."

On hearing the word contact, the humans on the bridge, who weren't fully awake before, were certainly alert now.

"The system presented a collection of ship types, moon bases, and a populous culture inhabiting the fifth planet from the sun. We considered the possibility that a sphere might be obscured from our telemetry by lying in orbit on a planet's far side, and we made a decision to investigate what we considered would be the system's home planet."

There was a break in the recording, before Killian resumed. "Pardon, Dassata, events here are still fluid. It was our opinion that we held the greater velocity and could maneuver around any ships' weapons targeting us. In this regard, we were in error. No weapons were ever fired at us. Instead, we found our ship boxed in by several alien ships, and, while attempting to slip past them, we were caught by a powerful tethering beam. At this moment, the *Vivian* is held fast."

More silence ensued on the recording, and it was sufficiently long to give the audience concern.

Bethley was heard to say, "Don't let them regain control, Trium."

Killian wasn't filtering the team's comms, which demonstrated the pressure the crew was under.

"We can positively say, Dassata, that this system does not belong to the Nua'll," Killian continued. "None of the considerable number of ships, in evidence, exhibit the sophisticated technology of the sphere or even our ships. We have achieved an odd sort of equilibrium in our predicament. Bethley gained access to the low-level controller of the ship, which has trapped us, through its comm system. Unfortunately, we haven't been able to decipher their code language or language processes in the short time we've had."

"Our orbit path will be clear, Killian," Bethley was heard to send.

Killian was heard acknowledging Bethley's statement and then his report continued. "The inhabitants of the alien ship have been fighting to regain control of their controller. We'd hoped to have time to locate the tethering controls, but time became critical. We chose to lock the ship's personnel out of their controller, which Trium was able to accomplish. Unfortunately, the process locked us out of their controller too. The one positive aspect of this situation is that the alien ship was making a vector change at the time. Bethley has calculated we will be taking a long circle out by the system's periphery.

The *Freedom*'s bridge personnel could hear a quick exchange between Killian and Trium, before Killian returned to his report. "In essence, Dassata, we and our captors are taking an extended journey, while locked in this embrace. Bethley's calculations perceive that there are no impediments to our course, but, at some point, the sentients might choose to take drastic action to rescue their comrades. On an exciting note, Trium managed to gain an image from their bridge."

Cordelia activated the holo-vid. The majority of the image was presented in shades of reds and blues. The fine details appeared white or black, reflecting all or no light. It was an extremely bizarre image for human eyes.

Alex and Julien raced to apply their image processing apps and ticks later exclaimed together, "UV light."

"The twins are back," Tatia commented drily to Renée.

"Just in time," Renée whispered. "It seems that we'll have need of them."

Julien shifted the holo-vid's image through a series of wavelengths, visible, infrared, and ultraviolet until the details improved. "The captors use a special mix of light wavelengths aboard their ships," Julien commented. "It's impossible to determine the exact combination from this single image, which was captured through their controller."

"What is that?" asked Ellie, pointing to an object on the image's left side. "Did someone put a big plant on a starship bridge?"

"If it is, it's an odd one," remarked Mickey, "Where's the pot, and why is it bent over like that?"

"Is it me or does that single bloom at the top, which is bent over, look like it's directed at the bridge panels?" asked Renée.

Alex peered closely at the holo-vid and commented, "Add in the multiple extensions that lead to the deck and the arrangements of leaves only on the upper side, I'd say we're looking at —"

"Plant people," Tatia finished for Alex. "We're searching for a giant, planet-killing sphere, and we find plant people."

Cordelia had halted the report, while the staff examined the image. Now, she let it continue.

"We'll attempt more analysis of our captors and collect as much information as possible, while we await your reply, Dassata. Please send my regards to Vivian and Galania. Kindly don't discuss our predicament with the child. Killian out."

* * *

When Killian sent the report of their predicament, the SADEs had their first opportunity to examine their circumstances, while they waited out the days for a reply.

Killian reflected on Alex's forethought, regarding his upgrades to the SADEs' scout ship design. Originally, the SADEs considered the reporting protocols to be excessive, thinking it would only be necessary to comm Omnia when something of value was located.

The emergency beacon was considered to be another such ancillary upgrade. Typically, it was connected to a starship's comm antenna and activated on orders from the captain. However, if the aliens chose to free their comrades by firing on the *Vivian*, then there was the distinct possibility they could be sent tumbling above or below the ecliptic with their engines destroyed. The automatically activated subspace beacon would give them a chance of being rescued.

Then there was the library — the *Rêveur*'s entire collection, plus Vivian's recordings. In all, it spoke of thorough preparations by a human, who was saying, "Wait, my friends, be patient. We'll come for you, and we'll find you."

As the *Vivian* shot through the dark, tethered to an alien ship, Killian believed that. He watched the glow of stars through the ship's telemetry, deciding to play the day's recording of his child friend, and Bethley and Trium linked to listen.

-32-
To the Rescue

Killian's report finished, and the silence on the bridge was palpable, until Julien spoke.

"It would appear that riding to the rescue once again, as the ancients were fond of saying, is in order."

Tatia's head pulled up. Her eyes met those standing around her. Slowly, subtly, but then more overtly, people moved to stand beside or behind her.

When Alex ceased staring at the plant person in the holo-vid, he regarded the odd formation of his staff. Except for Renée and Julien, who stood beside him, and Perrin and Ophelia, who stood alone, every other individual was arrayed with Tatia and staring at him.

Renée kissed him on the cheek and walked across the intervening space. Individuals moved aside so that she could stand beside Tatia.

Ophelia and Perrin exchanged confused glances, after sizing up the opposing groups.

"Are we voting?" Ophelia asked.

"And, if we are, could someone tell us what's the issue we're considering," Perrin added, but no one seemed willing to answer him.

Alex looked to his left where Julien stood. The SADE shrugged his shoulders, dipped his head in apology, and walked over to stand beside Ophelia and Perrin.

"In this moment, consider where we stand as neutral territory, Sers," Julien announced firmly, making it clear that he wouldn't take sides in this contest of wills.

Alex considered the alignment of his people. Gone were the days when he would have been annoyed, if not angry, at such brazen insubordination. Now, he worked to keep the smile off his face.

"If everyone is done voting with their feet," Alex said without rancor, "perhaps someone would like to ask my opinion."

Julien raised his hand to indicate he volunteered.

"Thank you, Julien," Alex said, amiably, but then shifted to a harder tone to address the group standing across from him. "Had anyone cared to ask, I would have suggested to you, Admiral, that we organize a rescue party of warships and asked if you concurred. As that already seems to be your opinion, I'm wondering why you and your people are uselessly standing around here instead of getting your butts in gear."

"You heard the man, people," Tatia ordered in her command voice. "Commodore, wake the Trident captains. Have them recall crew to their ships. We launch the squadron in …" Tatia paused to regard Alex, who had been watching her carefully.

"Twelve hours, Admiral, if not sooner."

"You heard the man. Twelve hours, if not sooner. Jump to it, people."

Everyone, except Renée, Tatia, Julien, Cordelia, and OP, deserted the bridge in a run. Those remaining waited quietly for Alex to speak.

As the twins exited the bridge, Alain sent to his crèche-mate, <Is our madman learning?>

<You're questioning how quickly he acquiesced to Ser and his staff's pressure. Perhaps, he's lulling us into a sense of false security,> Étienne sent in reply.

Alain caught the pun and sent back, <Whether he's sincere or not, I'm bringing our new shoulder-mounted weapons with a spare power crystal.>

Étienne regarded his brother's determined expression and purposeful stride, deciding he'd contact Z and ensure the SADE brought them more than one spare crystal for their new weapons.

"Cordelia, have crew support Renée with the transfer of some of our personal things to the admiral's flagship," Alex ordered.

"That would be the *Liberator*, Captain Cordelia," Tatia added. "Tell Captain Valenko to bump —"

"Negative, Admiral," Alex interrupted. "Renée and I will take a crew member's cabin. I don't want officers reshuffled, at this critical time."

"Cordelia and Tatia exchanged a quick, private comm, and Cordelia sent a message to Svetlana to make the necessary arrangements and to notify Cordelia of any amenities required to better furnish the cabin.

"Cordelia inform your captains that the *Our People* and the *Rêveur* will remain behind," Alex ordered. "Perrin, Ophelia, inform the Council of these developments. Play them Killian's recordings," Alex said, continuing his rapid-fire instructions. "Let them know the squadron is leaving and headed to …"

Alex checked his star chart, but Julien was ahead of him. "STV-163," Julien commented quietly.

"The important message to stress," Alex said, focusing on the pair, and they could feel their implants warm, "is that Omnia is in no danger, and what the *Vivian* has discovered is not the Nua'll home world. Any questions?"

When Ophelia and Perrin shook their heads in negation, Alex continued to stare at them. Ophelia understood Alex's unstated message, and she gently shoved her partner, who was waiting for further directions, toward the bridge accessway. "Good fortune to you, Dassata," she said, as she ushered Perrin along.

The Council that Alex referred to was Omnia's temporary governing body, composed of two humans, two Dischnya, two Swei Swee, and one SADE. They were Ophelia, Perrin, Nyslara, Sissya, Wave Skimmer, Long Eyes, and Trixie.

Tatia regarded Alex. Having issued his immediate directives, he was lost in thought. <Alex's already at STV-163,> Tatia sent to Renée and Julien. During the past three years, Tatia had witnessed subtle changes in Alex's demeanor. On the positive side, he was less temperamental, engaging in fewer disagreements. On the negative side, he was less social, if not a little withdrawn. Most noticeably, there hadn't been a single card game since the *Freedom* arrived at Omnia.

<Then, Admiral, best we hurry and transport Alex to meet with the plant people, so he can put his ideas in action,> Renée sent in reply. She spared a quick look for Alex and hurried to their cabin to pack.

— Alex and friends will return in *Vinium*. —

— *BUT FIRST* —

— Watch for the release of *Empaths*, the initial story in the new sci-fi series, Pyreans. —

Glossary

Celus-5 Sentients and Creatures

Dives Deep – Member of Wave Skimmer's Swei Swee hive
Long Eyes – Member of Wave Skimmer's Swei Swee hive
Nascosto – Camouflaged creatures of the forest
Wave Skimmer – Swei Swee Hive First

Dischnya from Sawa Messa

Chafwa – Former queen of Mawas Soma nest, now deceased
Choslora – Heir queen of Mossnos Soma
Cysmana – Nyslara's attendant
Foomas – Chafwa's wasat, now deceased
Fossem Soma – Posnossa's nest, the nest that killed Haffas at the previous Fissla
Haffas – Emissary from Tawas Soma, killed
Hessan – Young warrior from Tawas Soma
Hessmas – Wasat of Mossnos Soma nest
Homsaff – Queen of Mawas Soma nest, heir after Chafwa
Mawas Soma –Homsaff, Woosala, and Messlan's nest
Messlan – Homsaff's new wasat
Mossnos Soma – Seelam, Choslora, and Hessma's nest
Nafalla – Tawas Soma midwife
Nyslara – Queen of the Tawas Soma nest
Offwa – Sissya's wasat
Ossnos Soma – Sissya and Offwa's nest
Posnossa – Queen of the Fossem Soma nest
Pussiro – Nyslara's wasat
Seelam – Elderly queen of Mossnos Soma
Simlan – Older warrior from Tawas Soma
Sissya – Queen of Ossnos Soma nest, near Tawas Soma
Tawas Soma – Nyslara, Pussiro, Nafalla, Hessan, Simlan's nest
Woosala – Homsaff's aging wasat

Dischnya from Sawa

Ceefan – Queen of Tamassa Soma nest

Falwass – Wasat of Tamassa Soma

Tamassa Soma – Ceefan, Falwass, and Waffala's nest

Waffala – Sub-commander of the Tamassa Soma

Dischnya Language

Ceena – Dischnya term for the Celus-5 Swei Swee

Chona – Nest queen

Dassata – Peacemaker

Dischnya – Dog-like species on Celus-5 and Celus-4

Ené – Pronunciation of Renée

Feedwa – Queen's dogs

Fellum – Pronunciation of Willem

Fissla – Council of queens

Hira – Pronunciation of Keira

Nessila – Dischnya name for Celus

Sawa – Celus-4, Dischnya home world

Sawa Messa – Celus-5, Dischnya's second world

Wasat – Warrior commander

Zhinni – Pronunciation of Ginny

Harakens

Alain de Long – Director of security, twin and crèche-mate to Alain, partner to Tatia Tachenko

Alex Racine – Partner to Renée de Guirnon, Star Hunter First (Swei Swee name)

Asu Azasdau – Captain of the *Sojourn*

Bartlett – SADE from a rescue ship

Benjamin, "Little Ben" Diaz – New Terran Rainmaker, former Minister of Mining

Boris Gorenko – Sol native, friend of Olawale Wombo, medical expert

Cedric Broussard – Z's New Terran avatar

Central Exchange – Haraken financial system

Christie Racine – Alex Racine's sister
Claude Dupuis – Engineering tech, program manager for SADE avatars
Cordelia – SADE, Julien's partner
Darius Gaumata – Commander, promoted to Trident captain
Deirdre Canaan – Commander, promoted to Trident captain
Durly Pederson – Captain of the *Into The Dark*
Edmas – Young engineer, works with Emile Billings and Mickey Brandon, boyfriend of Jodlyne
Edward Sardi – Earther physicist and mathematician, deceased during first contact with Sawa Messa
Ellie Thompson – Wing commander promoted to Trident captain
Emile Billings – Biochemist, who emigrated from New Terra
Espero – Haraken city
Étienne de Long – Director of Security, twin and crèche-mate to Alain, partner to Ellie Thompson
First – Leader of the Swei Swee hives
Francis Lumley – Captain of the *Rêveur*
Franz Cohen – Wing commander
Frederick – Confederation SADE, employed by the New Terra Assembly
Ginny – Little Singer to the Swei Swee, junior crew member
Jodlyne – Journey crew member, girlfriend of Edmas
Julien – SADE, Cordelia's partner, Alex's best friend
Keira Daubner – Security escort, corporal, Méridien
Lucia Bellardo – Commander, promoted to Trident captain
Mickey Brandon – Senior engineer, partner to Pia Sabine
Millicent "Millie" Vane – Méridien partner of Tilda Hennessey
Miranda – SADE, Z's partner
Mutter – SADE, Hive Singer to the Swei Swee
Nema – Sol native, friend of Olawale Wombo
Nua'll – Aliens who imprisoned the Swei Swee
Olawale Wombo – Sol native and senior professor
Orly Saadner – Traveler pilot, New Terran
People – Manner in which the Swei Swee refer to their collective
Pia Sabine – Medical specialist and partner to Mickey Brandon

Priita Ranta – Sol native, friend of Olawale Wombo
Reiko Shimada – Captain of the *Tanaka*, a sting ship, later promoted to Trident commodore
Renée de Guirnon – Partner to Alex Racine
Rosette – SADE
Simone Turin – Méridien, partner of Ben Diaz
Sky Waters – Trixie's Swei Swee name
Star Hunter First – Swei Swee name for Alex Racine
Storen – Sol native, friend of Olawale Wombo, xenobiologist
Svetlana Valenko – Wing commander promoted to Trident captain
Swei Swee – Six-legged, friendly alien
Tatia Tachenko – Admiral, ex-Terran Security Forces major, partner to Alain de Long
Teague – Sixteen-year-old son of Alex and Renée
Tilda "Tildie" Hennessey – First Mate aboard the *Into The Dark*, partner of Millicent "Millie" Vane
Tomas Monti – Haraken president
Trixie – Confederation SADE, original ID is Lenora, relationship with Hector
Ullie Tallen – Senior scientist, died during first contact on Sawa Messa
Willem – SADE
Xavier Escobar – Security escort, captain, ex-TSF officer
Yoram Penzig – Sol native, friend of Olawale Wombo, philosopher
Z – SADE

Méridien

Bethley – Scout SADE teamed with Killian
Confederation – Collection of Méridien worlds
Galania – Vivian's mother
Glenn – Daelon bay control manager
Gino Diamanté – Council Leader, replaced Mahima Ganesh
Hector – Acting captain of *Our People,* former SIF director, relationship with Trixie

Independents – Confederation outcasts, originally exiled to Libre, rescued by Alex Racine, also used to refer to the exiles on the Daelon moon
Jensen – Daelon comms operator
Killian – Plaid-skinned SADE, friend of Vivian, terminal construction director
Lemoyne – Leader
Mahima Ganesh – former Council Leader, cruel former owner of Hector
Maynard Scullers – Daelon orbital platform manager
Miriam – Confederation SADE
Ophelia Sooth – Co-Leader of Independents on Daelon, partner to Perrin
Perrin Keller – Co-Leader of Independents on Daelon, partner to Ophelia
SADE – Self-aware digital entity, artificial intelligence being
SIF – Strategic Investment Fund of the Confederation SADEs
Trium – Scout SADE teamed with Killian
Vivian – Independent child
Winston – SIF director, ex-Council SADE

New Terrans

Bertram Hardingsgale – Captain of the *Rover*
Darryl Jaya – Minister of Space Exploration
Harold Grumley – President replacing Will Drake
Maria Gonzalez – Special envoy from President Will Drake
Myron McTavish – Retired TSF sergeant major
Will Drake – President of New Terra

Planets, Colonies, Moons, and Stars

Arno – Star of the Libre system
Celus – Star the *Sojourn* visited
Celus-4 – Fourth planet outward from Celus
Celus-5 – Fifth planet outward from Celus
Daelon – Moon orbiting sixth planet of an unnamed system
Haraken – New name of Cetus colony in Hellébore system, home of the Harakens
Hellébore – Star of the planet Cetus, which was renamed Haraken

Libre – Planet invaded by Nua'll, Alex Racine rescued Independents
Méridien – Home world of Confederation
New Terra – Home world of New Terrans, fourth planet outward of Oistos
Oistos – Star of the planet, New Terra, Alex Racine's home world
Sol – Star of United Earth system
STV-163 – Star of the plant people

Ships and Stations

Allora – Confederation SADEs' SIF liner
Freedom – Alex's primary city-ship
Into The Dark – Haraken freighter also known as the *Dark*
Liberator – Svetlana's Trident-class warship
Our People – Alex's second city-ship
Rêveur – Haraken passenger liner
Rover – New Terran passenger liner
Sardi-Tallen Orbital Platform – Station over Omnia
Sojourn – Haraken explorer ship
Tanaka – Haraken sting ship
Travelers – Shuttles and fighters built by the Harakens based on the Swei Swee silver ships
Trident – Class of new warship built with new faux Swei Swee technology
Vivian – First scout ship

My Books

The Silver Ships series is available in e-book, softcover print, and audiobook versions. Please visit my website, http://scottjucha.com, for publication locations. You may also register at my website to receive email notification about the publish dates of my novels.

If you've been enjoying this series, please consider posting a review on Amazon, even a short one. Reviews attract other readers and help indie authors, such as me.

Alex and friends will return in *Vinium*, but my next release is the story of a third Earth colony ship. *Empaths* is the first novel in the new Pyrean series.

The Silver Ships Series

The Silver Ships

Libre

Méridien

Haraken

Sol

Espero

Allora

Celus-5

Omnia

Vinium (coming 2018)

The Pyreans

Empaths (coming 2017)

The Author

I've been enamored with fiction novels since the age of thirteen and long been a fan of great storytellers. I've lived in several countries overseas and in many of the US states, including Illinois, where I met my wonderful wife thirty-seven years ago. My careers have spanned a variety of industries in the visual and scientific fields of photography, biology, film/video, software, and information technology (IT).

My first attempt at a novel, titled The Lure, was a crime drama centered on the modern-day surfacing of a 110-carat yellow diamond lost during the French Revolution. In 1980, in preparation for the book, I spent two wonderful weeks researching the Brazilian people, their language, and the religious customs of Candomblé. The day I returned from Rio de Janeiro, I had my first date with my wife-to-be, Peggy Giels.

In the past, I've outlined dozens of novels, but a busy career limited my efforts to complete any of them. In early 2014, I chose to devote my efforts to writing fulltime. My first novel, *The Silver Ships*, was released in February 2015. The series, with the release of *Omnia*, now numbers nine.

The new series, Pyreans, relates the tale of a third Earth colony ship and gives readers an opportunity to follow new characters, who struggle to overcome the obstacles of a world tortured by geologic upheaval. Humans are divided into camps — downsiders, stationers, spacers, and the *Belle*'s inhabitants of empaths and the discarded.

My deep appreciation goes out to the many readers who embraced the Silver Ships series and its characters. I hope you enjoy the new series. Thank you!

Made in the USA
San Bernardino, CA
04 August 2017